REPRISAL

Also by Mitchell Smith

Sacrifice

Karma

Due North

Stone City

Daydreams

REPRISAL

Mitchell Smith

A DUTTON BOOK

DUTTON
Published by the Penguin Group
Penguin Putnam Inc., 375 Hudson Street, New York, New York 10014, U.S.A.
Penguin Books Ltd, 27 Wrights Lane, London W8 5TZ, England
Penguin Books Australia Ltd, Ringwood, Victoria, Australia
Penguin Books Canada Ltd, 10 Alcorn Avenue, Toronto, Ontario, Canada M4V 3B2
Penguin Books (N.Z.)Ltd, 182–190 Wairau Road, Auckland 10, New Zealand

Penguin Books Ltd, Registered Offices: Harmondsworth, Middlesex, England

First published by Dutton, a member of Penguin Putnam Inc.

First Printing, May, 1999
10 9 8 7 6 5 4 3 2 1

 REGISTERED TRADEMARK—MARCA REGISTRADA

LIBRARY OF CONGRESS CATALOGING-IN-PUBLICATION DATA
Smith, Mitchell, 1935–
    Reprisal / Mitchell Smith.
    p.   cm.
    ISBN 0-525-93979-2 (alk. paper)
    I. Title.
PS3569.M537834R46   1999   98-51571
813' .54—dc21   CIP

Printed in the United States of America
Set in New Baskerville
Designed by Leonard Telesca

PUBLISHER'S NOTE
This is a work of fiction. Names, characters, places, and incidents either are the products of the author's imagination or are used fictitiously, and any resemblance to actual persons, living or dead, events, or locales is entirely coincidental.

This book is printed on acid-free paper. ∞

To Linda,
beautiful and brave

A wound of the heart need not be made by steel;
Lack and loss make more than ample institution.
Nor must its distance run be metered by a wheel,
To leaf the thorn of pain past any restitution.
A search for what medicines that sore may seal,
Is sure to come at last to healing retribution.

JOANNA REED, *Cut Flowers*
Sansome, Day & Co.
Boston, 1994

REPRISAL

Prologue

She knew the dock watchman's rounds. She'd learned his hours. Charis came down the dark wooden stairways at five forty-five, carrying her duffel and the crutches. At the end of the fourth dock finger, past ghost boats softly bumping, whispering in the last of night, she found *Bo-Peep,* an eighteen-foot half-decked strake-wood sloop with a cramped cockpit—an outboard, cocked and covered, fastened to its transom.

She sat by her duffel a few yards down, her back against a bollard, and laid the aluminum crutches across her lap.

Then she was still, and never moved as the night slid away and the day came on.

Frank Reed left the cottage in veiled dawn light, breakfast still warm in his belly. He started down Slope Street, careful on night-damp cobbles, and conscious—as he rarely bothered to be—of settled near-perfection. Reminded of it, really, by having forgotten his wedding anniversary the day before . . . so stupid because he'd had it on his office calendar, and then they'd come out to the island a couple of weeks ago and he'd forgotten.

Had been reminded pretty briskly, however—by Joanna, then Rebecca calling from the college. Two reminders of their twentieth wedding anniversary. Twentieth. God almighty. . . .

That interesting date, and a good breakfast this morning— ham steak, eggs over easy, wheat toast, and Colombian coffee. A twenty-year marriage and a good breakfast made for some self-congratulation.

Health: very good for forty-three. Work: coaching going well—one of the best college soccer teams in New England. No complaints about work, except your typical small-school budget for athletics. No football.

Cobblestones made for slippery walking. Slope Street looked quaint, but a sidewalk would be a definite plus. However, try to persuade these island people of that, talk about changing anything—and good luck. . . .

At the foot of the hill, Frank turned right and strolled along Strand, the town's main street, its pavement shining damp from the night's sea mist, the stores and shops still closed. It was too early for the morning's small ferry load of summer tourists. —That long ride through the islands, with three tedious intermediate stops, had been Asconsett's salvation from becoming a major tourist trap.

. . . So, twenty years of a good marriage—and the lady still beautiful, even with the breast thing. Twenty years, and a great kid out of it, Rebecca. No other children—which meant no son, meant living in a house of women, which had become a pleasure in itself. But even so, no son, despite trying. If Joanna *had* tried for a second kid, not secretly vetoed that. —Who knows? Who knows what women get up to with that machinery of theirs? It runs the world, and the men plod along behind them wondering what the hell happened.

"Mr. Reed . . ." An older man walking toward him—tall, balding man with a short gray beard. Walking a little dog, some sort of terrier. Man was wearing slacks and a white short-sleeved shirt.

"Morning." Frank recognized him as he went by. Had been fooled for a moment by the slacks and shirt. —Porter. Captain Hollis Porter. Had had that interesting talk last week at the Hatch. . . .

So, here was Anniversary Frank Reed—one of the plodders, no doubt. His mother had spent an afternoon with Joanna when he'd first brought her over to the house. And all Megan Reed had said to him afterward was, "Frank, she's lovely and she's smart as a whip and she loves you—and son, you've got your work cut out the rest of your life, because she's a kitten I doubt will ever make a cat."

Truer words never spoken. And his mother—no fool, a successful businesswoman and a widow who'd raised her son alone—had liked Joanna, liked her very much. But she'd seen the necessary protection and care, even though Joanna was already somebody, an achiever at eighteen. She'd had her stuff published—new young Radcliffe poet and so forth. . . . People at Boston U., that had never met her, already knew her name. He'd gotten congratulations from his friends on Joanna—congratulations on those long legs, too.

Frank stepped off the curb at Ropewalk, crossed the alley to stay on Strand. He walked past the post office—still closed. But the grocery store, Barkley's, down the block at the corner, was opening for business. Mr. Barkley—with a gull's beak, a gull's sharp eye—and probably the tenth Barkley to run the place, was setting out small fruit stands.

Passing him, Frank said, "Good morning."

"—Mornin'."

. . . So, twenty anniversary years ago, the South Boston boy, college student, good athlete—but not quite in the young lady's league, let's face it—had been very happy to accept that responsibility, to take what care of her he could. . . . And no regrets now for having done it.

Joanna'd wakened him last night, at some ungodly hour, whispering, "Hey, What's-your-name—I didn't pick you up in that bar and bring you home, to not get laid." Tough talk from a shy girl. It had taken him only a few months of marriage to confirm what his mother had said, to realize all Joanna's "I can handle it" energy was armor over softness, apprehension. Last night, she'd said, "Does this feel good? Tell me if what I'm doing . . . tell me if this feels good." Her hands on him always harsh, hard hands, callused from rock climbing, cave-scrambling. Stone and ropes. With words, and with rock and ropes and caves, she was absolutely confident. It was life, it was people, that frightened her.

This looked to be becoming a bright morning, fine and clear. South-southwest breeze. A perfect day for sailing, unless you liked a little more sea running, a heavier wind. One advantage of forty-three years' living; you learned not to ask for trouble, weather or otherwise.

Bakery was open. Frank glanced at himself in the store's plate glass as he went by. Short, sturdy-looking man in a green windbreaker, carrying a small blue-and-white beer cooler in one hand. Middle-aged man in good shape. Still had all his hair, graying ginger Irish hair.

. . . Boston people had already known her name, had known her work. And when he'd read Joanna's poems, at first he'd thought, hell, stuff is nothing like her. . . . But turned out that wasn't true. The longer he knew her, the better he understood that poetry and where it came from. It was like verses to a song she was singing to herself through the years. Private song made public.

Sometimes uncomfortable stuff to read—yes, there it was, nice steady breeze coming up the cross streets from the sea. Bringing fish smell with it—from Manning's, down on the dock. Still finding fish. But evidently not enough to keep their boats, live the old fishing-fleet life. . . .

Frank turned left, down Dock Street to the stairs.

The sea wind was stirring back and forth, eddying off the old brick buildings, the much older, smaller, gray clapboard structures stepped down to the piers. Rich, rich odors of fish and tarred wood and the sea. . . . Four Miller beers and two tuna sandwiches in the cooler—two beers and one sandwich too many. Have to watch the pot, be careful he didn't wind up like one of those fat coaches couldn't demonstrate any moves at all. . . .

Frank went down wide wooden steps past four fisher-crewmen coming up out of dawn mist. They had that awkward stomping way of moving . . . didn't have their land legs yet. Older men, middle-aged. The young fishermen must be drifting away, leaving the island.

So, the twentieth anniversary—what was it, silver? bronze? Some metal. The anniversary, a good breakfast, and an island summer to look forward to. Already more than two weeks of good sailing—even with the old man along for a few days there. An interesting stretch of coastal water. *Very* interesting that morning last week, even with old Louis aboard making a mess cleaning his catch, grumbling about having to fish from a sailboat. Used to lake fishing in that canoe, for God's sake. . . .

Frank turned left across the landing, and down the last flight of wooden stairs to the lease dock. Some of the docks along here were doubled, with another pier platform built eight feet beneath them for unloading into the warehouse basements. . . . The shadow of night was moving across Asconsett Bay, drifting west as sunlight heated clouds red-gold over the Atlantic. The island's fishing boats were already out and rigged, two of them tracking white wakes through the bay's dark water.

Frank's sneakers thumped softly on the pier decking. Water moved through the pilings a dozen feet beneath him; between the planks, he could see it flicker and stir. It was a pleasure. Church or no church, it had always seemed a natural, an unarguable thing that man, that all life had come from the sea. —From where else? Dry dirt? Empty air?

He walked down the lease dock, past two Hunter sloops with their fancy preset rigging. Yet to see one of those beauties out. There was a ketch that did go out. . . .

Lease, don't buy had seemed sensible, concerning boats. How many friends they knew who were stuck with boats, some big boats, that they took out only a few times a year. . . . Even so, if you only leased, you never really had a boat.

Bobby Moffit was halfway down the first dock finger, setting out paint and tarps to work on a four-oar dory he'd been sanding for a week. Moffit looked a little drunk, even this early in the morning. Looked old, too. Years, and booze, and fishing in hard weather were wearing Bobby out.

Frank walked along to the fourth finger, turned down it, and saw a boy—no, a girl—sitting out there beside a small blue zipper duffel. Angled metal crutches lay across her lap, aluminum shining red in sunrise light.

Nice-looking girl, tall and slender, dark-blond hair up under a red baseball cap—Cardinals cap. The duffel appeared to be new.

"Hi."

" . . . Hi. Could you tell me if this is C-dock?"

"Yes, it is—it's the lease dock."

"Oh. Well, I thought it was."

"Somebody picking you up?" Frank loosed *Bo-Peep*'s stern line . . . the heavy nylon stiff with night dampness.

"Supposed to, last night—yesterday evening—but I guess they changed their minds." The girl smiled, seemed to think it was pretty funny.

"And you waited down here all night?" Frank loose-coiled the line, tossed it over into *Bo-Peep*'s cockpit.

"I thought maybe they were just late, you know. We were talking, yesterday, and I told them I'd never been out sailing, and they were going to take me out for a while. Moonlight . . . moonlight sailing. I thought it was more definite than it was." She got up with some difficulty, hauled herself up on the crutches.

Don't say it, Frank said to himself, and said, "Listen, then how about a sunrise sail? Couple of hours out—couple of hours back. Would you want to do that? . . . Name's Frank Reed, by the way."

"Charis. Charis Langenberg." She stood leaning on her crutches, looked at Frank and the boat. Her eyes were hazel, and slightly slanted.

"I guarantee we won't sink. An absolute guarantee."

A pause, considering. Then a second smile, better than the one before. "Well . . . if it's an absolute guarantee. And you're sure you don't mind?"

"I'd like the company."

A good two hours out, and the girl hadn't been seasick, thank God.

Also seemed pleased to get wet when *Bo-Peep* swung across the wind on a new tack. She'd sat there in the cockpit, very solemn at first, looking out over the bay—and now didn't appear to mind the open sea. Seemed to enjoy it.

When he'd helped her onto the boat, gotten her into a life jacket and settled her on the small cockpit's cushions clear of the tiller, she'd laid the metal crutches down along the devil, and said, "Accident, when I was in high school."

The wind was fair, the weather mild and clear as glass. *Bo-Peep* was a plain boat, down-east and broad in the beam—a solid little sailer with that deeper seat in the sea that wooden boats seemed to have. You could weight a fiberglass keel very heavy, and still the boat would have a faint vibration to it under way, a little of that milk-jug high-floating feeling.

"Tell me when you want a sandwich. I've got two tunas. And beer."

"I don't need anything, thanks." She'd put on dark glasses.

"You'll get hungry. And it's an extra sandwich I probably shouldn't have, anyway. So you take it whenever you're ready."

" . . . Okay. And thanks, Mr. Reed. Thanks for taking me out."

"No thanks necessary. Sailing's better with company."

The sea had been making up, but only very slightly, a cross fetch that lifted *Bo-Peep*, swung her a little starboard as she ran—wonderful easy sailing. Early summer weather, and a good day to be out. The sea colors showing various jade. . . . A shame the college hadn't been built on the coast instead of midstate, in the hills. They would have the sea year-round then.

"How far are we out?"

"Oh, a few miles."

"Too far to swim back, I guess."

"Too far in these waters. Much too cold. —You want to hold the tiller?"

The girl thought about it. Careful, Frank supposed, with a cripple's caution. " . . . If it's okay."

"It's okay. Piece of cake. Here—scoot over here. . . . That's it. Now put your right arm over the tiller as if it was a friend's shoulder. Good. Charis, that's good. Now, just hold her steady as she goes— you like those nautical terms?"

"Yes, I do." And she hung on, seemed a happy girl now, peering forward from under the baseball cap's brim. There was sea spray on her glasses.

Good deed, Frank thought, and stepped along the *Bo-Peep's* cable-strand rail to the bow, then around and back, checking her rigging. It occurred to him—well, he'd been considering it before—that with field hockey now a solid Olympic sport, it made a natural low-cost adjunct to soccer. Low-cost being the key, of course, as far as college administration was concerned.

A good game, too. An interesting game—about which, of course, he knew damn-all, but he could learn. Fast game, ancient game with some violence to it, but not as rough as lacrosse. . . . Girls' game *and* men's game. East Indians played the hell out of field hockey. Be interesting to coach, and it was definitely coming on, particularly in schools with no football budget. Talk to Perry, see what the board thought about it. . . .

The girl still steering pretty well. Cross swell was throwing her off a little, sagging to leeward just a bit. She didn't know to correct for that.

"Pull left—toward you—just a little bit. You're doing a really good job. Wheel's a lot easier than that tiller."

"This much?"

"That much . . . that's just right. And I think we've earned an early lunch, mate." He ducked under the half-deck, retrieved the small cooler, and opened it.

"Beer okay? I have some Cokes stowed if you want."

"No, beer's fine."

Frank passed her a sandwich and an open can of beer. "You want to sit back where you were, I'll take the helm."

Bo-Peep was riding larboard up, so the girl was awkward getting to her feet to change seating on the slant. The boat bucked a little as Frank slid in to take her place, and he felt quick cold run down his back.

"Oh god*dammit,* I spilled beer all over your life thing—your life jacket."

"No problem; it's been spilled on before."

"Oh, it'll smell. Do you have another one?"

"Two more in the locker—don't worry about it."

"No, please take it off and I'll rinse it in the ocean. It'll smell. So stupid of me. . . ." Sounded almost in tears. Any clumsiness probably a reminder of her handicap.

"Really, it's no big deal. Here, hang on to the tiller." Frank unbuckled the jacket and shrugged out of it. Then, balancing to the boat's motion, he raised the transom's cushioned seat, knelt up beside it, and leaned over to lift another life jacket out of the locker. Boat was pitching; she mustn't have a good grip on the tiller. . . .

There was an instant of sudden hard pressure against the small of his back—that became terrific pressure and he was up in the air without knowing why. Up in the air upside down and going over— and saw the girl from upside down and she was leaning with her shoulders back against the edge of the half-deck, both legs still straight out from the effort of her kick.

And he was going over, and thought he could hold on to the cable rail as he went. Almost did. Almost, but not quite. The leverage snapped it out of his grip and he was over and down into the sea.

Cold came as he sank, and he swam and rose . . . rose up into the air—caught his breath and saw *Bo-Peep* sailing away, already yards past and going.

Frank kicked level and began to swim after, swim better than he ever had, and faster. *What mistake, what mistake?* And reviewed what became more real as he swam, and grew calmer, swimming, and first thought about what clumsiness might have struck the girl— what saving herself from a fall might have ended in kicking him over into the sea. . . . Then decided there couldn't have been such clumsiness.

He raised his head, spit salt water, and shouted, "LET GO ALL LINES! *TILLER HARD OVER!*" Still swimming, still swimming fast, bucking swells. . . . Went under cold salt water and came up—raised his head to shout again, and saw brightness off the boat as the girl tossed her crutches overboard. And still swimming, he saw her take the baseball cap off and shake her long hair free. Dark-blond hair that bannered out in the wind. And she jumped to the sheets and nicely close-hauled *Bo-Peep* due south, so the boat ran fast and free.

The girl looked back once as Frank still swam. She looked back with little interest, then turned and sat to the tiller, steadied, and settled on her course . . . sailing the boat very well. Sailing away.

Frank stopped swimming, lifted his head and shouted, *"Why . . . ?"* Too far, now, for her to have heard him.

Charis, holding a true course south through the day, ate both sandwiches, drank two beers—and was very hungry again by night, when *Bo-Peep* ran through moonlight along the line of breakers to Peck's Cove beach.

She left the tiller then, let the boat sway and slide into the fetch of the waves, turning, broaching beneath their crests. The beach was a moonlit line of white a hundred yards off when she ran her left arm through her small duffel's handles, then stepped up and over the landward cable rail. She balanced to a sudden lurch and drop—then, on the rise, dove sliding into the nighttime sea.

Chapter One

Joanna dreamed the ocean had brought Frank home, delivered him in a rush of breaking waves up the walk, so seawater thumped and foamed against the cottage door . . . ran under and soaked the rag rug there.

She dreamed he stood up laughing on the stoop, dripping salt water, stomping squelching sneakers, and called to be let in.

Joanna dreamed she rose, went out into the hall and down the narrow stairs, trailing her fingers along white-painted pine paneling. Then, in the entranceway, saw the puddle spreading on the floor. Rag rug would be stained for sure with salt, she thought—and with that hesitation, woke, and lost her chance to open the door and let him in.

She lay in bed, rigid as if terrified, and felt an agony of strangling sorrow rising in her chest, so severe, so dire, it frightened her. It rose, stopped her breath, then exploded in a muffled howl. Rage and regret. After a while, she grew less noisy, and only wept into her pillow.

Finished, she sat up into late morning light, blew her nose on a Kleenex from the bedside table, and got up to pee and take her shower. For the past week, Frank's ashes scattered on the hill, she'd slept naked, without her usual T-shirt . . . as if, she supposed, to lure him alive and home to her. Her body—a few years from forty, long, lean, and lightly Indian brown even in deep winters—still seemed sufficient to call a man home to her, even with the right breast gone . . . replaced by a pale fading scar curving across and up to her armpit. Even with this brutal lack, this missing, surely a man must like the rest—a good body, muscled and smooth, matched by an almost Indian face, strong-nosed and high-cheekboned, its eyes the near black her grandmother's had been, darkened by Mohegan blood.

One of her poems—only one, "An Amazon"—had been written in comment on her breast, lost to cancer. Joanna traced the long, curved scar with a finger as she turned, rinsing . . . chanting the poem over the shower's white sound.

> *My right breast, sliced away and gone,*
> *Permitted the bow such a sweeter draw,*
> *That willing I whistled a tit so-long,*
> *Rode out to fight, and in slicing saw*
> *New freedoms for my sword arm's swing,*
> *In raids from our steppe to the ocean.*
> *I found the plus that minus can bring,*
> *With those pleasures of easier motion.*
> *Aren't one-breast women who can fight,*
> *Completer than weak two-titted ladies?*
> *For by war is darkness beaten to light,*
> *And bright heavens hammered from Hades.*

Joanna lifted her long, soaked hair to rinse again, the shower spraying meager and barely warm, as if fresh water here on the island was shy in the presence of the ocean.

" 'The plus that minus can bring . . .' " But nothing had been won in losing Frank.

"Mom, I've registered for my courses, and I'm going to do the summer session. I really don't want to stay out here, and I don't know why you want to." Rebecca's round inelegant face—her father's face, and intended to be merry—still slightly pale with shock, blue eyes milky with pain and confusion. Too sudden and early a loss for her. . . .

A conversation on Sand Hill, the long slopes of the hillside—duneside, really—furred with sea grass, tangles of sea grape. A conversation as they'd walked across and down to the cottage, the small bronze jar held empty in the crook of Joanna's arm. There hadn't been many at Frank's memorial on the mainland, at White River—the college's faculty scattered for the summer. Eric and Donna'd been there. Susan Thom—who, Joanna suspected, had been half in love with Frank for years—weeping in the chapel. Susan had gone out to soccer games innumerable; more of them than Joanna had.

Those, and maybe two dozen others . . . the dean, the McCreedys, Dornmann from Math, and his improbable wife. Jerry Conner, and some summer-session students, graduate students who'd known Frank, played ball for him, sweated to his jokes and whistle.

Coach Reed.

Good-bye to Coach Reed in a fieldstone chapel—fake Norman, like all the old college buildings—but beautiful, cupped in green hills.

The fieldstone—streaked with karst limestone—had been Professor Budwing's clue years before, a geologist's notice of which ridge to search to find a possible cave. And he'd found it six years later, the only major limestone pit and multimile galleries in the state. A labyrinth of passages, pitches—and two duck-unders in the White River, running deep beneath its hills in the dark. A caver's dream—by far the largest, most extensive of the few big caverns discovered in New England.

Merle Budwing had been a notable caver, and his "Concave" a notable find. Budwing had confirmed it only a few months after Joanna joined the Midstate Grotto. Confirmed it past its narrow scrub-grown entrance—then, in only a few yards and not yet anchored, not yet rigged, he'd slid into a chute, thirty steep downslope feet of wet slime-clay.

Chris Leong and Terry Parsons had followed Budwing in, heard the sudden struggle as he slid down . . . then suddenly no sound except a long descending shout, not really a scream. A shout that ran out of breath many silent seconds before a dull and distant sound of impact almost four hundred feet down.

It was a record pit for the state, for all New England—and one of the deepest in the country. A geological surprise, a TAG cave, a Tennessee Alabama Georgia–type limestone cave where none were supposed to be, thanks to Whitestone Ridge—a lone coral reef in a Laurasian sea, forty-two million years before—and the White River, that had sculpted it, hollowed and carved it all the ages afterward.

Joanna's first major caving with Midstate had been the body rescue. They'd anchored at Concave's mouth, and double-roped down the chute. Then the long pit rappel down four hundred feet of 7/16th Blue Water II, a slender spiderweb strand of rope vanishing into descending dark, silence, vastness.

Merle Budwing, cave-cool, damp and undisturbed, lay waiting

for them on slide shale far, far below, alone except for small skeletons of animals who'd fallen his forty-story fall, but years or centuries or millennia before.

. . . Professor Budwing's memorial had also been held in the college chapel. But that had been midterm, and the chapel crowded with faculty and students, and cavers from around the country.

For Frank, last week, only a few—thirty, forty people from summer session—sat in the pine pews, listening to Father Hayes's Episcopal and measured compliments.

Joanna's father, come from upstate, had sat at the back of the chapel, aged, bulky, noncommittal through the service. Louis Bernard hadn't been impressed by Frank. "A pleasant young man," he'd said to Joanna, the first time he'd met him. "—Is there anything more?" The "there" almost a "zere," a touch of Quebec still sounding from his childhood. . . . Her father always superior, a little snotty to Frank, rude even when Frank took the old man out two weeks ago—during a visit from hell—and let him fish off the *Bo-Peep*, mess her up with fish guts.

Only those few attended the memorial at White River—and none except Rebecca's roommate came back across the state and out to Asconsett Island afterward. Only the three of them to watch Frank Reed's ashes, and tiny white chips of his bones, go spilling, drifting on the wind of a breezy, bright summer afternoon. Good sailing weather.

"Rebecca, I have things I need to do." Mother and daughter in hillside—duneside—conversation, starting down a long path eroded in soft sliding sand. Both slipping a little as they stepped. Asconsett Township had been considering setting wooden staircases into Sand Hill, from the town on up to the ridge . . . had been considering it for three hundred years.

"Mom—things to do out here?"

"That's right. Did you bring the albums?" Joanna, stepping down sideways, had had a vision of herself tripping, rolling down the long slope clutching the little bronze jar. Tumbling down the hill with Rebecca crying after her.

"Yes, I brought the albums. I went out to the house and got them, and all those old boxes of photographs from upstairs. We brought them out; they're still in the car."

"Good."

"That's really—I think it's really the worst thing you could do is go through all that, with Daddy . . . Daddy just gone." The slope of sand shifting beneath their feet.

"I want them, Rebecca. I want to be able to look at them."

"Mom, you should be home. We don't know anybody out here. You just rented a summer cottage and that's it, and you need to be home. All our friends are there . . . and somebody has to get the mail sometime. Francie's called."

"Rebecca, you had a chance to stay in the house instead of on campus. You chose the dorm as an independence thing—fine. So now there are two instructors in our house, paying us three months' summer rent. . . . If you were so worried about the house and the mail, you should have stayed there. It was your choice."

"Mom, I'm not worried about the house. . . . You could come back and stay with Lianne."

"Oh, wonderful. What a prospect, having the McCreedys for comfort. —And as far as the mail is concerned, you can pick it up. It's not too much to ask for you to drive out to the house. . . . When can you get your car?" The going had gotten easier, less steep. Tall sea grass grew in runs and bunches.

"It was the fuel pump. Mr. Lubeck said in a couple of days."

"Okay. Have him just charge it to us."

"All right. —And he said he was terribly sorry about Daddy."

"A nice man. —So it's not too much for you to drive out and get the mail from the renters."

"I'll go get it."

"—Because your father and I came out for the summer, and I . . . I want to stay here a little while."

Walking down across the duneside . . . two women having lost a man at sea. By no means the first for this little island's old whaling and fishing port. How many women in dark and heavy dresses had walked this sand and sea grass, had looked out over the paths down to steep streets of white clapboard houses, gray clapboard houses . . . out to the small harbor's bay, and the Atlantic.

And each woman taken by surprise—after no matter how many years of apprehension. Still a sickening surprise, as if they'd never heard of drowning. As if their husband, their father, their son, was the first man ever to go out and drown in the sea.

"Mom, okay. I'd just like to know when you're *planning* on coming home." Rebecca's voice had risen slightly in pitch the past few days, become faintly childish. She'd stepped back a year or two, wounded . . . and three days after the memorial had had to be driven over from college—the old Chevy in collapse—driven to Post Port and accompanied out to the island by her roommate, an older girl, a student picking up summer credits.

This girl—young woman—had waited for them at the bottom of the hill. Very quiet, and seemed to find Joanna interesting. Perhaps checking out widowhood, loss—though apparently already familiar with loss of another sort. "Awful abuse, really disgusting," Rebecca had said, "—when she was a little girl. . . ."

"I'd just like to know how long."

"Rebecca, I don't know. I have some things to do out here."

"Well, do you want me to stay? I can stay."

"No, sweetheart. Go back and do your classes. Summer credits will give you an advantage for your sophomore year."

"I can stay."

"I don't *need* you. —I don't mean I don't need you; I mean not right now."

". . . All right."

Relief in her voice. And it had seemed to Joanna they both wanted to be away from each other for a while. Have Frank to themselves in memory.

Two women, mother and daughter, walking down a summer sandhill through sunshine and blowing sea grass, the little bronze jar sun-warm under Joanna's arm. Below, the small island ferry, fresh-painted white and green, had come in. Tourists had been filing off it, walking down Strand Street. . . . And at the foot of the path, the waiting roommate—tall, pretty, her dark-blond hair coiled up in a French knot—had stood slender in a somber slate-gray long-skirted dress with a white collar. She'd been looking up at them, apparently observing sorrow.

Joanna soaped and rinsed, rinsed again in rusty water. She cupped her single breast, then put her right hand down to cover her vulva, held it, pressed it gently for comfort. . . . Still a woman. But not beautiful enough to call back the dead.

She turned off the water, stepped out of the stall, and stood drying herself on a towel that smelled of salt, a worn towel—one of the light-green ones, brought out for the summer. She thought, as she dried, that she should shave her legs. . . . Maybe tomorrow. And she'd be shaving them now, only so no woman would notice she needed to.

A poor reason to do it. A poor reason to do anything.

Joanna went into the bedroom, sorted through her top dresser drawer for panties and bra—its right cup filled with her foam prosthesis—and while she was doing that, called absolutely without thinking.

"*Frank.*"

Hadn't even thought about it. It just came out.

But now that she realized, Joanna did it again, to hear the sound of it.

"Frank? . . . Frank!"

Waited for an answer. Waited for a sound. As if she might be discovering one of the great secrets of the ages—a new thing, a thing no one had ever thought of before. To simply call the dead and force them to answer.

"*Frank!*" As if she were angry with him for not answering. That would make the calling stronger. . . . And knowing it was so sad, so foolish, she nevertheless couldn't stop calling and walked out of the bedroom and called down the stairs. "Frank?" Soft inquiry, in case soft calling was what was needed, after all.

She went naked down the stairs to the entrance hall, walked into the living room, and called his name. And since he hadn't answered, it meant he might answer, might be somewhere else in the house.

She was afraid to go outside into the sunshine. If she kept calling there, she thought she wouldn't be able to stop, but would walk down the front steps and out into the street and go on down the hill to town past the cottages and fishermen's houses. Naked and calling her husband until the police or firemen came. Or women came out of the houses and put a blanket around her.

It was a shock to realize how much she'd loved him. She'd known it, but not how much. And he was only a man, not terribly special. Not terribly special. It was that tenderness of his not being special that she had loved. And now she knew it freshly, as if she'd felt no sorrow before.

Joanna called once more, just in case, then went upstairs to get dressed.

Chapter Two

"I just don't understand that language. I don't have any *feeling* for it at all." Rebecca put her books down on their study table. Spanish was her only early-morning class today; she didn't have another class until after lunch.

"You'll get it." Charis was sitting at the other side of their table, reading, making notes. She always made notes. . . .

"Meaning you'll help me get it."

"That's right."

"You shouldn't have to do that . . . spend time helping with my work."

Charis looked up from her book; her eyes were colored a complicated topaz. Beautiful eyes, of *course.* "I like to help you, Rebecca—and you've had a bad time."

"Well, I have . . . and you've really been a friend, Charis, not just a roommate." Rebecca sat at the table, and slid her Spanish textbook farther away. "—And I hear it gets harder the second year."

"What?"

"Spanish—and I have to take two years, and *then* Spanish Literature. I just think it's an unfair requirement."

Charis closed her book. "No, it isn't. If you go to the trouble of learning a language, then you ought to read the best that language has produced."

"I just don't want to do it . . . any of it." Rebecca thought there was no good reason to be crying—sure as hell not over fucking Spanish.

"Oh, sweetheart . . ." Charis got up, came over and bent down to hug her. "Come on . . . come on." Charis was wearing a man's white dress shirt and jeans and sneakers, and she looked like a goddamn model.

"And you look like a goddamn model," Rebecca said, and tried to catch her breath, stop crying.

"No, I don't."

"Yes, you do."

"Shhh . . ."

"I still don't believe it, that Daddy's gone. I forget it for a minute, and then I remember it and it's all new and terrible."

"It'll take time."

"Charis, there's *been* time, and it's still just as bad. —You have a tissue?"

"A bandanna. A week or two, isn't time."

"I don't want to use your bandanna." Rebecca got up and went to her dresser for a tissue. "And you've been really great—going to the memorial at the chapel, and then taking me out to Asconsett . . . when we scattered the ashes."

"I was glad to do that, Rebecca. The service, and going out to the island. I thought you and your mom did a proper thing, a good thing, out there." Charis sat down again, opened her notebook.

"Right, starting with a real treat for you at the chapel." Rebecca took another tissue, and went back to sit at the table. "—Getting to meet the summer faculty leftovers and a few friends, *and* my grandfather—who's the only man left in our family—*and* Mom's New York agent. Both of them really nice, but a little weird." Rebecca blew her nose. "My grandfather Louis is very eccentric. . . . Well, he's pretty old. He used to walk like a soldier, you know, striding around? And now he walks like an old man. And it's so sad . . . those little old-man steps."

"But he loves you. They all care about you."

"Charis, I know they do—but not the way Daddy cared about me. And I know I sound like some stupid child."

"No, you don't. And you still have your mother."

"Oh, tell me about it." Rebecca thought she'd start crying again if she just sat there, so she got up and went to her closet—what the college called a closet. None of the dorm rooms had big enough closets.

"Your mother's . . . formidable."

"That's the word." Rebecca looked through her clothes. She'd been feeling fat all morning in this ridiculous skirt and blouse. She'd like to wear chinos and just a T-shirt, but from the back—and most people didn't worry about what they looked like from the back—in those pants she'd look like a pigeon walking around. A five-foot-tall pigeon. The chinos had been another dumb purchase. . . .

"—So, I don't think you need to worry about her handling this."

"Worry about my mother? Charis, my mother . . . Joanna Reed was always able to handle anything."

"Including you?"

"Hey, absolutely." Rebecca moved hangers, considered her summer dresses. What was the problem? Why didn't she have just one thing that looked good on her . . . ? "Charis, you have to understand that Daddy was special. He was the one in our family who did the ordinary things that had to be done. My mother is the *extraordinary* one. She does the things other people are afraid to do."

"Can be scary, that kind of energy." Charis had filled a page with notes; she turned to a fresh page.

"It does scare me. It did, anyway, when I was a kid." There was a nice dress, short sleeves . . . and of course it was deep pink and made her look like a candy apple. "—My mother's not like other people, and she knows she's not like other people. And I think there's this sort of contempt, you know. She's very nice, she's kind, but there's this sort of quiet contempt for people who aren't . . . special."

"Meaning you, as not being special." Charis didn't look up from what she was doing—not being rude, just doing two things at once. When they started rooming together, first of the summer session— and Charis had come up to Rebecca at registration, and talked with her, and then out of the blue had asked if they could room together— Rebecca had thought she was rude when she kept working like that while they were talking, having a conversation. But it was just something she did . . . something most people *couldn't* do, probably.

"—Absolutely meaning me as not being special. Charis, she loves me, I know she loves me, but there's this 'And what is my plump, not very pretty, not terribly intelligent, and slightly disappointing little daughter up to now? Probably not much.' —And my dad just didn't think that way about me. I could . . ."

"Relax?"

"Exactly. I could *relax* with him, Charis. And now I don't have that, and I'll never have that again, and it—yes, it does scare me. You bet." She looked through the closet again. Nothing that did anything for her. And she kept buying stuff . . . it was ridiculous.

"You can relax with me, Rebecca."

"Not if you were my mother instead of my roommate, I couldn't. You're another one of those . . . beautiful achievers. It's just not fair."

"I'm not that at all, Rebecca. —And you *are* intelligent and attractive."

"Oh, sure." Rebecca closed the closet door.

"And as far as 'fair' goes, I've heard of that rare bird." Charis closed her notebook. "—But I've never seen it."

"Well, my father made up for a lot of that unfairness, for me. He was really a wonderful man—I loved him, and you would have liked him, Charis. People liked my dad; he was very *good.*"

"Tell you what I think." Charis stood, and gathered her books. "—I've got Engletree's class, and I have to stop at the library after that. But then we can meet at the Griddle for lunch, if you want to."

"Okay."

"—Tell you what I think, Rebecca. I think your dad's goodness lives on in you . . . and you should be proud of that, and not take advantage of his death to feel sorry for yourself." She slid her books into her old black bookbag, and touched Rebecca's cheek as she walked out of the room. Rebecca heard her talking to Grace Marcus for a moment, in the hall.

"I'm not satisfied," Joanna said, sat back and waited. He'd given her an uncomfortable ladder-back chair in a small sunny office— Asconsett Island's usual white-painted pine paneling . . . its usual big double-paned windows looking out to sea. The chief constable's office was second-floor back; his secretary's and deputies' desks below. Cells, she supposed, were in the building's basement.

"Well," the chief said, "—here's the thing." His "here" was Asconsett's down-east *he-ah.* "Here's the thing, Mrs. Reed—Professor."

" 'Mrs. Reed' is fine."

"Okay. Well, I'm going to be very direct with you. The Coast Guard is satisfied—the commander over at Post Port is satisfied, Commander Anderson. The state police are satisfied—you call in and ask them. . . . And what counts out here, is that I'm satisfied." Carl Early sat back in what seemed to be a much more comfortable chair, and looked at her across a gray steel desk.

The chief constable was almost startlingly handsome, an elderly movie star with elegant cheekbones, parchment skin, perfectly blue eyes—eyes a little bored, uninterested—and wonderful hair, thick snow, combed straight back. Very handsome, and had been tall and slender when he'd stood to greet her. Neatly dressed as well, in a light-blue summer sharkskin suit.

Joanna supposed the chief's wife must always have been uneasy about his off-island trips on business . . . duty trips that took him away from her to Boston, Providence, Portland. Mrs. Early must have had troubled visions of beautiful Carl in his hotel room with some woman he'd only just met. Just met that afternoon. . . .

"—I'm the senior law enforcement officer for seventeen islands along the coast, Professor—Mrs. Reed. For this whole county. It's an elective post, same as some mainland sheriffs. And I have not had this job, haven't kept this job for over twenty years, by being careless."

"I didn't say your people had been careless. I said I'm not satisfied. Frank never—and I mean never—sailed without a life jacket on. He's . . . he sailed since he was a little boy, and he always wore a life jacket. He never allowed anyone to sail with him unless they wore one. He was a fanatic on that; he *taught* boating safety for the squadron when he lived down in Gloucester."

Joanna felt herself getting out of breath, hurrying to say her say. "—And also, Frank sailed all his life and he never just fell off a boat—much less fell off a boat in good weather on a calm sea!"

Carl Early sat and looked at Joanna, an old man examining a woman who might have been his daughter. He sat for almost a minute without saying anything—a silence that must have been useful dealing with lobster-pot thieves and misbehaving tourists. . . . Useful dealing with bereaved women, too. Joanna was surprised to find she wished her father had stayed after the service and come out to Asconsett again, at least for a few days. The chief constable would have found Louis a tougher article to handle—a surly old French-Canadian, a retired lawyer, and unimpressed by handsome blue Anglo eyes.

"—So, that's why I don't believe it." Wrong thing to say. Chief Early made a patient face, must have heard other women say they didn't believe it. "I do . . . I can believe Frank—just once, just *once*—didn't wear a life jacket. I can believe he once, just this once, fell off his boat on a calm sea. But I can't believe he did *both* those things." Early's face still set in weary patience. "—You didn't know him. If you'd known Frank, you'd know it couldn't have happened like that!"

A sigh. "Well, if it didn't happen like that, Mrs. Reed—then how do you think it did happen? Your husband was found a mile off Little Shell, and he'd drowned and he didn't have a preserver on. His boat was found beached and busted, drifted way down the coast."

"I don't know. But not like that. Not that kind of accident."

The constable surprised Joanna by reaching across his desk—reached over, his hand held out. Joanna didn't know what to do, it was so odd. It was embarrassing, too embarrassing not to take his hand. He had a strong dry grip, a politician's grip.

"Now, Mrs. Reed, you listen to me. I worked on lobster boats, fishing boats, all the time I grew up and years after that. I still go out. I've been a seaman and known seamen all my life." He released her hand, sat back in his chair. "—I sailed from the time I was a little kid, everything there was to sail, and I can still run anything that floats, and that's a fact. And I can tell you *as* a fact that when a man is out by himself—especially, especially if he's sailed for a long time and never had any trouble—I can tell you that a man will sometimes take things easy, let things go a little, not bother getting into a jacket. It's just simple human nature." The handsome head nodded agreement with itself.

"—*I've* done it, and I've seen a lot of drowned people and I know better. But I've still done it. What a man tells his wife he does when his wife and kids are with him—is not exactly what he does when he's out there on his own. And that's a fact."

"Chief . . . All right. So, Frank—who never sailed without a life jacket on, no matter what you say—decided to do that. And then he just happened to fall off his boat—*another* thing that never happened before."

"—And that's exactly right, Mrs. Reed. What you just said is exactly right. Your husband made a mistake—and then there was an accident. And just that way is how men are drowned at sea. That's all it takes, and I've seen it many times. Things that might happen on land—a mistake, and then some dumb accident right after that—you get away with it. But not at sea." The chief shook his head. His hair was really remarkable, white hair so strong and thick, so perfectly white it seemed that that was what hair was meant to be, and any other color not quite right. "—That's how all men are killed at sea, Mrs. Reed, except in wartime. There's a mistake, then just one more thing happens, and that's that."

"All right. . . . All right. I happen to know that wasn't true with Frank, but you think I'm just being ridiculous."

"No, I don't. I think—"

"Oh, the hell you don't!"

Cold blue eyes, now. "If you'll just be quiet a minute, Mrs. Reed. I'll tell you what I *do* think. . . . I think you're trying to make some sense out of a tragedy. That such a terrible thing could have happened by just a little carelessness, by just a stupid accident. And what I've been trying to tell you is that most terrible things happen just that way."

"And that's it—that's the only way he could have died?"

"If you're talking about foul play, Mrs. Reed—unless you kept something back from my deputy when he talked with you about this case—if you're talking about foul play, because supposedly there was no *reason* for anyone to harm your husband. No money involved: no big inheritance; no big insurance; no gambling debts. And no known personal enemies." He shook his head at the lack. "And no . . . intimate involvement with another person by either of you to cause that kind of trouble. Now, is that right, Mrs. Reed? Or do you have something else to tell me?"

"No, I don't. I had no other 'involvements,' and neither did he. There was no reason for anyone to hurt Frank."

"All right. And the county coroner and a Coast Guard physician both examined your husband—and except for a bruise at the small of his back, probably from going over the cable rail when he went, there wasn't a mark on him—and also let me tell you something, Mrs. Reed. . . ." Joanna watched the chief's left hand, lying relaxed on his desk as he talked. Was there the finest tremor there? Notice that his handsome and formidable machinery was beginning to decay? There was certainly a fine tremor. . . .

"—Let me tell you, I attended the FBI Academy at Quantico. I have attended many classes and training programs with the state police. I have worked on a number of serious crimes out here through the years, very serious felonies—including homicides, you name it. They are not angels working these waters out here. And we don't always get summer tourist angels out here, either—"

"I'm sure—"

"So, when we get a death, we damn well check it out. I want you to understand that. —I do not take any drowning as an accident until my people have checked it out. You were asked right up front, day or two after we had to notify you—you were asked if there was any party at all who might have had an interest in harming your husband—"

"I said there wasn't."

"Well, if that's true, Mrs. Reed, then what are we talking about, here? Aren't we talking about an accident? Unless you want to change the statement you made."

"No, I don't."

"Well, then, where does that leave us, Mrs. Reed? You tell me."

"I suppose it leaves *you* satisfied about Frank's making a first-time mistake, followed right away by a first-time accident. And I still don't believe it. I just . . . I know it didn't happen that way. That's all. It's just something I know."

Chief Early stood up. "Then we're wasting each other's time on this, aren't we? And frankly, I don't have any more time to waste— no offense, now. I am—" Hand across the desk again. "I am real sorry for your loss. These things are never . . . never easy."

"I think," Joanna said, and stood up, too. Couldn't just stay sitting there. "—I think some are easier than others." She didn't want to take his hand, and was angry that she did.

Was still angry as she went down the station's steps—and furious with Frank. Also felt foolish for having put on a dark-blue business suit in the summer, for God's sake, to seem a proper widow for that cold policeman. —But so angry with Frank about everything. For not wearing his life jacket; for falling off his boat . . . if he had. But he hadn't. She'd tried to imagine that, Frank Reed managing to fall over a boat's cable rail in good weather, an easy sea. She'd tried to imagine it for almost two weeks now—and couldn't.

But if that hadn't happened, then *something* had happened, and the only thing she could think of—and not mention to Mr. Elderly Handsome Cop—the only thing she could think of was that Frank had been so secretly unhappy . . . that he hadn't loved her or Rebecca . . . and preferred to go into the sea with no life jacket, and drown.

But how could a man—although a secret person as all men were—even so, how could a man conceal such sorrow as that? Hide it for months . . . years? How could he have kissed her, and held her, fucked her? How been so constantly sweet with Rebecca, so alertly protective from the hour she was born? —Often more patient with her, more attentive than her mother had been.

How could he have gone for groceries, laughed so much—and still preferred death? And if he had, if he'd done that, it was such a betrayal it deserved death. If he had wanted to die, then he'd *deserved* his death and good fucking riddance. . . .

*   *   *

It seemed odd to Joanna to be walking alone through summer sunlight by the sea—the air sliding breezy and bright around her. People, tourists strolling along the harbor . . . their children trailing after, asking for ice cream. The tourists would go back up Ropewalk or Clamshell to Strand Street, to Eddie's—the soda fountain's marble table and countertops, its wireback chairs profitably unchanged since 1905.

Strange to be walking in dazzling light, when it was the cave she'd longed for for several days—its perfect solitude, its changes slow past any human understanding.

After Merle Budwing fell, Concave became known to every caver on earth. And what had been a treasure for the few members of the Midstate Grotto to be first to explore, to survey, to enjoy in lamplit darkness, had become instead public knowledge. News.

Howard Newcomb, who owned Whitestone Ridge—or most of it—had closed the cave entrance two weeks after Budwing's death, afraid of lawsuits from the families of careless cavers who might go deep under his land and kill themselves falling down the pit. Or suffocate in some one-foot squeeze below, where two walls of rock—becoming gradually closer together as a caver struggled between—allowed him finally only a last breath out, but no breath in. Those possible deaths—or another when the White River, risen after rain and spilling to roar beneath the earth in blackness, might trap a caver in some low passage, leave him to press his face up against rough rock for air, find a little but no more than that, and drown.

Newcomb closed the cave. But in the two weeks before its entrance was gated and sealed, the Grotto had gone all out, mapping, exploring. And had found a labyrinth of corridors, some only wide enough, high-ceilinged enough, for crawling—some much narrower, for wriggling through . . . and several with entrances under water, under the river still carving, shaping the rock in darkness beneath the ridge. —A web, a maze of miles of those passages, and long, long, curving galleries—gallery on gallery, passage on passage snaking through the stone to end several times in great chambers holding a million years of silence, and all the splendors of limestone carved by eons of running water.

These had flashed bright in the helmet lamps, chambers floored in fine mud dust sparkling with the sediment of ages, and decorated with gleaming white stalactites, helectites, soda straws and stalagmites, snowy limestone curtains, translucent fans of calcite, clusters of delicate stone flowers as white and finely wrought as snowflakes.

It was wonderful caving, and they'd managed to survey and map several miles of it with tape, compass, and inclinometer before Concave was closed, the narrow entrance barred with a steel gate, locked, and No Trespassing signs set on the access track up the ridge. The huge, deep, and many-storied paradise of perfect dark and coolness lay sealed again to its ancient stillness—broken only by distant echoes of water dripping, flowing, rushing through the earth. . . .

Gated and locked. —Frank had gone caving a few times. He disliked the perfect darkness always just beyond their small lamps' light, saw the stone's weight and closeness, felt the countless tons of rock above him in low places, and was uneasy. "Your thing, honey," he'd said.

Joanna paused to let people pass—a couple with three children trailing—then walked on down the South Dock steps. The harbor opened wider before her, Old Lighthouse Point curving out from the right, the breakwater from the left, to almost meet at the sea's narrow entrance. A small harbor. Frank must have imagined it packed in previous centuries with weatherworn whaling ships and sailing trawlers. Everything dark wood and tarred rigging, tangle and purpose all together, and smelling of sweat and the sea. . . .

Joanna went along the boardwalk beneath old warehouse pulley blocks, and past the ropewalk yard, trying to see it as Frank had, with the pleasure he took in all oceanic things. The odor of fish—not as many tourists strolling here; too busy, too smelly—the grinding scoot of forklifts down the wharf, shifting loads of catch. Busy men . . . but still not working as the men and women of the past had worked. Extraordinary, what must have been the labors of the past. And how different the men and women then, who'd worked so hard . . . and found no mercy if they failed.

Asconsett a fishing port still. But for how much longer with stocks so low? "The fishermen," Frank had said, after a few days on the island—he'd come in from one of his first sails in the leased boat—"those guys have fished too well."

More tourists. Three middle-aged women with schoolteachers' honorable and patient faces, walked toward her and passed. One of them glanced at her dark-blue suit, must have thought it odd, a peculiar thing to be wearing on a warm day in summer, out on the island. . . . Joanna thought of going up to the cottage to change, but it was too much trouble. —Men were such a pleasure in that way. If they weren't gay, they didn't give a damn what women wore.

Manning's, at the end of South Dock, had been a cannery once, now a processing facility for fish coming in. The Manning family had owned the big brick building, and the previous wooden buildings on the site, since 1734—according to their carved wooden sign along the wharf. Probably accurate enough, but not the oldest business on the island. The oldest was the bakery, Cooper's. Baking in the same tiny building off High Street, with two of the original wood-fired ovens still usable for special occasions, the Cooper family had run the business for more than three hundred years.

"An absolute record for family business ownership," as Mr. Cooper had told her when she'd first gone in to buy his bread. "—Though I suspect some of us was Coopers by courtesy."

A man and his wife walked past her, both a little plump, and stepping carefully on the slippery planks. A man and his wife. . . . Something that no one would ever say again, ever see again when she went walking. She would be alone, or with Rebecca, or a friend. It was a lesson of loss Joanna felt she was relearning every few minutes—as a person diagnosed with cancer was reminded so frequently, when they didn't want to be. . . .

She turned in at Manning's, went through a door with *Office* stenciled on it, and walked up a narrow enclosed ramp as four fishermen in coveralls and green rubber seaboots came down it, laughing at some remark, rumbling down the planking like heavy herd animals.

The office at the top of the ramp was very small, almost filled by dented black filing cabinets, a computer and printer, shortwave radio and microphone, and a large woman in a man's blue work shirt and oversized jeans.

"I wonder if I could speak with Mr. Manning."

"Business?" A no-nonsense woman.

"No."

"Well, you're lucky. He was gone to the mainland, but he's back. I guess you can go on into the plant." A dubious look at Joanna's suit and high heels. "—Or you want me to page him out here?"

"No, that's all right. I'll go back."

"Well, I think he's in the machinery room. You go all the way down the hall, keep going all the way to the end, and the machinery room is on the left. Just go out this door and keep going. It says 'Machinery' on the door."

Down the hall—the floor's dark wood planking stained and splintered—the summer's warmth grew less, refrigerated chill grew greater. The building shook slightly to the motion of shuttling fork-lifts, and there was a steady two-tone grumbling under the start-stop racket of their engines.

Through a half-open door off the corridor to the right, Joanna saw that the low two-tone note came from conveyor belts of wide black rubber, thumping over their rollers down the length of a huge high-ceilinged room. The belts carried intermittent silver pavements of fish, mixed with shaved ice the same shining silver. The door allowed a draft of colder air, smelling of fish and machine oil. The corridor's planking trembled beneath Joanna's feet.

The machine room's door was closed, and she knocked on it, but heard no answer. She tried the knob, and pushed the door open to bright light, the stink of refrigerant, and a deep, steady whining sound, as if a huge dog were unhappy.

Two men were bent over a large vibrating gray steel box—and another, older, his face sunken and drawn as a spoiled fruit, was leaning on a mop propped in a big rolling bucket. He noticed her, reached out and touched one of the others. That man, very big and broad in clean and pressed coveralls, stood and turned a flat, pale face to her. His eyes were small, and a true green.

"Yep. Can I help you?" A tenor voice.

"Mr. Manning?"

"That's right. What can I do for you?" A little impatience in his voice with a woman interrupting work. And an off-islander, some summer woman. . . .

"I wonder if I could speak with you for a minute, Mr. Manning. I'd appreciate it."

No expression on the moon face. His eyes were startling sea-green, suited to a more beautiful man. "Okay. We'll go outside." He drifted up to her, very large in gray cotton coveralls, drifted her before him out into the hall, and closed the machine-room door. "Refrigeration," he said. "A problem every day." The door opened behind him, and the mop man came out, towing his bucket.

"My name's Joanna Reed, Mr. Manning. I'm sorry to trouble you, but I wonder if you could help me with some information."

The round face calmly noncommittal.

"—My husband went out sailing almost two weeks ago. And he . . . he was drowned."

"Oh, sure. Oh, *sure.* That was a terrible thing. Reed. I heard he was lost." Mr. Manning made a massive grimace of sympathy. "My uncle exactly the same a few years ago. Uncle and one great-granddad a long time ago."

"What I wanted—I just wanted to talk to someone, one of the fishermen, and ask if they'd seen him out there that day. Seen anything wrong." The mop man went slowly sloshing past them—mopped more carefully past her pumps.

"Oh, right. Right. Out at sea."

"Yes, I wanted to ask if they'd seen anything at all. Anything wrong . . . unusual. So I need to know the names of the fishermen who would have been out there that day. And since they unload here . . ."

"Oh, yeah, I understand. You know, Mrs. Reed, the captains pretty much come in and out all the time. And they can stay out at sea a couple of days, maybe a week or two, they don't find fish."

"I understand."

"—So, a particular day is kind of tough."

"It was almost two weeks ago. The seventh."

"The seventh. Seventh. . . . Well, I know Tom Lowell came in, unloaded on the eighth, so he would have been out there probably, coming in. Unloading being when I get their business—which these days is a lot of trash fish each load."

"Lowell."

"Right. Tom's got the *Eleanor II*. Named for his mom. . . . So, there's him. And I think Billy Tucker's boat was out there. He was due in to unload, anyway. That boat's the *Circe*. —Bullshit name, you excuse my language. Some young guys like to pretend those are yachts they're fishing with."

"Lowell and Tucker. . . . Thank you very much, Mr. Manning. I really appreciate this."

"Happy to help. —But you know, Mrs. Reed, anybody out there saw something wrong, they'd have said so. And they're not going to leave a guy out there, leave a boat in trouble."

"I understand."

"—But you want to be sure, sure there was nothing weird, right? Maybe he was in a little trouble, didn't look serious."

"That's right."

"I can understand that. Tell you, though, nothing's easier than getting into trouble at sea. . . ."

* * *

Asconsett's fishing boats, fewer than they had been, tied up in the Pond past Manning's. They were ranked down nine long dock fingers—with many spaces between, where trawlers, draggers, longliners and gill-netters, the mainstays and steel uncles of their island families, had been scrapped, or auctioned and sold off. . . . The lobstermen, though burdened with right-whale protection, were doing better—lobster stocks were up. They moored their small boats the other side of the breakwater, in East Shelter.

Joanna, in suit and silk blouse, and made awkward by her high-heeled shoes, stepped down the docks over and around coils of line, rusting machinery, and fine cloudy green mounds of net.

The *Eleanor II*, a big trawler, black-hulled, her topsides painted white, was berthed stern-to at the end of the third finger. Several gulls—particolored dull gray, pure white—slid through the air nearby in slanting circles, but silent, not crying. There was a worn plywood gangway from the trawler's stern down to the dock. The boat's decking was battered gray steel, embossed in diamond-shape patterns for traction.

The *Eleanor II* moved gently under Joanna, with soft groans as she shifted, a faint rattling sound from below. The boat smelled of diesel and fish, and was bigger than it had looked from the dock. . . . A brute, and Frank would have loved to go out on her, would have been happy to work deckhand for a few days out in the Atlantic.

"Seasickness?" he'd said to her once. "A person getting seasick? All you have to do is vomit!"

Joanna walked along the port rail, careful to keep her suit's shoulder away from the boat's rust-dappled white superstructure. there was a steel ladder there, from the deck up to the boat's bridge, and Joanna hesitated, wondering whether to call or try to climb up. Her shoes weren't made for it.

"Just what are you doing? —And who the hell are you, lady?"

Joanna looked up and saw a dark face staring down. A beak-nosed, almost Arab face looking down from the bridge rail. "I'm sorry—"

"This is private property, Miss Whoever. And what you do before you come on a boat, is you call for permission to come aboard!"

"I didn't see anyone."

"You call *out*. I'm liable, if you trip down there and hurt yourself."

"Sorry. . . ."

The man swung onto the ladder, and came down it quickly as Joanna stepped back to get out of his way. —Coveralls, rubber boots, the fisherman's uniform. Black hair cut short, almost crew-cut . . . and when he reached the deck and turned, was a lean man, not much taller than she.

"All right, what can I do for you?" A dark face, looking sun-burned, windburned . . . with a high-bridged nose, and eyes so pale a gray that their black-dot centers seemed oversized.

"Are you Mr. Lowell?"

A nod. Lowell, having hurried down to her, now stood relaxed, leaning against his boat's superstructure—owner and captain, certainly. And not handsome; he looked like some fairy-tale fox who'd been transformed to a man.

"My name's Joanna Reed. Mr. Manning suggested I come speak to you . . . ask if you'd seen my husband out sailing."

"Sailing?" Eyes so pale revealed nothing, even in a male's automatic flickering glance down at her breasts. A gaze impersonal.

"—My husband was drowned thirteen days ago."

"Oh, right, that *Bo-Peep* boat . . . I'm sorry; that was real bad luck, lose him like that."

"And I was wondering whether you or another captain might have seen him that day. Might have noticed anything, seen anything wrong."

"Mrs. Reed, the constable already asked me and a lot of people about that. —I did see him out that day. We saw *Bo-Peep* a lot of times. He handled her all right, and that was a tubby old boat. Hope he hadn't bought her. . . ."

"Leased. We leased her."

"Well, he handled her fine. I saw her going south-southeast first thing in the morning, that day . . . maybe off a mile, mile and a half. So all I could tell, sail was set good, seemed to be going okay."

"Nothing wrong?"

"Nothing I noticed, Mrs. Reed. We were coming in—getting ready to unload. Saw him way out there, and we went on about our business."

"I understand."

This fisherman seemed to look people in the eye—was certainly looking Joanna in the eye. No uneasy wandering gaze, no attention paid elsewhere after that quick glance at her breasts. ". . . We see day sailors and summer people sailing around out there every day. That Kestrel ketch docks here. And a couple of Hunters, and a Swan. Bunch of boats. Gets to be a zoo out there all up and down the coast. Wouldn't believe the shit we see out there, fucking up our sets, everything. Picking up lobster pots, too, in autumn—see a guy's markers, go right for 'em."

"I know there are a lot of boats out there."

"Only reason I noticed *Bo-Peep* at all, is we know that boat and your husband was out a lot. He'd come out early, and we'd see him. He was up and down the coast." Lowell was an older man than he'd looked at first; there was gray dusted through the cropped black hair.

"Mr. Manning mentioned Bill Tucker. . . ."

"If he saw something? Well, when Bill fishes, that's pretty much all he does. Doesn't pay attention to much else. . . . You know, Mrs. Reed, if any of us had seen something wrong out there, looked like a boat in real trouble? We'd have done something about it."

"Well, thank you for talking to me, Captain."

"No big deal. Sorry for your loss."

"Next time, I'll call for permission to come aboard."

A smile from Captain Lowell—his first. "You do that, and I'll put coffee on. Be a guest, then."

But not, apparently, now. "—I wonder if I could ask you one more thing."

"Okay."

"I wonder if you could tell me what you—what the fishermen think happened to my husband out there. He was a very good small-boat sailor."

"—What happened out there, him falling off her and so forth? I can tell you exactly what happened, Mrs. Reed. What happened was some goddamn thing he never expected. That's what happened. That's what kills sailors."

"Yes. . . . Well, thank you very much for your help."

"Not much help," he said, and walked beside her, a strong impersonal hand at her elbow as she went to the gangway, and down it to the dock.

Joanna walked back up to the wharf and along it past the old chandlery, the ropewalk, and Manning's, to the street steps. It was a relief to climb up to Strand Street, to be getting away from the harbor, the sea—its salt smell, its sailing gulls and restless motion.

She walked through tourists down Strand to Slope Street. The warm day had become too warm to climb that steep lane comfortably in the suit, stockings, and silk blouse. Slope Street was narrow, cobbled, and had no sidewalks. The cobbles, brought in originally from a mainland quarry in the eighteenth century—replacements still imported from that quarry—had been kept for quaintness, apparently. Hard walking in high-heel shoes.

She climbed to the end of the street, high on Sand Hill, opened the cottage's low pine-stake gate, and went up the steps to the door. The cottage door was painted brown, and always had been. Joanna supposed those earth tones were a reassurance to returning fishermen that they had left the uneasy kingdom of the sea for the restful land. . . .

She went upstairs to change, came back down in jeans and a T-shirt, and sat to work at the little pine desk in the living room. . . . And what a relief not to have student papers to grade—attempts at poetry usually even grimmer than the attempts at prose. And White River students were supposedly an elite, cream of the crop. A chilling thought. . . . Of course, there was an occasional talent, a Dave LaPlanche. Very occasional; Dave had graduated three years ago.

This early would-be triptych, now—three illustrative poems concerning women's lives—had never *become* a triptych. Might be called a biptych, since this contributed nothing. Written so many years ago—obvious, superficial, in a didactic light-verse trot—as if, in writing the first two poems, she'd learned better than to write another. The first had prepared for the second, and the second, reluctantly, for the third. But the third, this clumsy puppy, had never been trained to follow.

It's to time's ragtime rhythm the young girl
Starts her slow stepping, swelling to unfurl.
This child who weaved the early lace of life,
What will she be after years make her a wife,
Whose hips appeared at twelve and slowed her,
Whose breasts came following lolloping after,
Whose blood then spilled in leak and spatter,
Whose childhood blurred then sagged to sugar?
What but her selfhood purchased this growing?
What spring of her past for future's flowing?
How wider her hips must straddle for seeding,
With accomplishment seen largely in breeding,
With what—in later, lonely years—to be left,
But her exhausted self, of even child bereft?
Would she better fitted for a life have been,
Living selfish, humorous, solitary, and slim?

Joanna worked all afternoon, rewriting, and didn't think of Frank very often. There was no background sound. They'd never had a television over in White River, and there was none in the cottage. There was a radio in the living room, but she wanted no noise or music—particularly no music. Silence was the least disturbing sound. . . .

She ate dinner in her bathrobe, standing at the kitchen counter. She had canned corned-beef hash, a fried egg, toast, and a glass of milk.

Dinner for one. And with no green vegetables, no yellow vegetables, no care for the health of a middle-aged husband careless of his health. All that had come to nothing. Wasted care. . . . Frank could have had all the country sausage and pizza, all the steak and buttered baked potatoes he wanted. Could have smoked his cigars. . . .

Joanna finished, with most of the corned-beef hash left over. . . . And had decided to get farther away, for a day or so, from the treacherous sea—the sea, its sailors and fishermen still alive, disinterested in a dead soccer coach, a lover who'd made her laugh so many years ago, first instructed—after a strangled Irish young manhood of swift drunken fucking—in the mysteries of her clitoris. Dead husband. Dead man. He was on that side now, and could never come over except in her dreams.

Joanna went down the kitchen steps, and around the back of the cottage to the garage's side door.

Her ropes and gear were hanging from pegs along the garage wall. A panoply of the elegant equipment necessary to travel and live beneath the surface of the earth. It was equipment a mountaineer or rock climber would use—but tougher, heavy-duty, made to accept unacceptable conditions of wet stone, crumbling stone, mud, fast water and abrasion.

These beautiful slender snake-skinned ropes, the gleaming links of aluminum or steel, the climbing and descending tools were, with courage, the keys to a world of darkness beneath the world of light, so she'd been able to live two lives, where most men and women lived only one. . . . Like many cavers, she'd been a concealing little child, happy hidden behind sofas or beneath the stairs, exploring the basement for what might be behind shadows, whatever found in darkness. She hadn't been afraid of the dark.

On vacation after her freshman year at Radcliffe, she'd gone with a young man to New Mexico—a golden boy, Curt Garry, she'd been too careless in loving. They'd met at a dance at Dartmouth—

both conscious of their cleverness, beauty, youth, and luck. Conscious even—at least she had been—of the picture they made together. A slender and active girl, dark-eyed, her long hair a rich and glossy black—and a tall lean hazel-eyed boy, old-fashioned in his angular good looks, his hair bright as sun-struck straw.

Too perfect a picture for them to fulfill.

Joanna had enjoyed the boy, the high-desert sun and sunlight, and had been invited by Curt's uncle down into the Lechuguilla cave, a very special favor.

Lechuguilla contained the most beautiful series of cave chambers yet found on earth. And in those glittering spaces—snowy, delicate, spun with frosted calcite lace and fantastic in limestone chandeliers, exquisite decorations jeweled by millions of years—Joanna had fallen in love with under-earth. With the earth's secrets, as a little child found comfort and mystery both, beneath its mother's skirts.

Muddy, exhausted, and badly frightened once—crawling through a narrow squeeze that seemed to contract its stone walls around her, press her breathless—she had found herself at home. . . . She found caving, and later in the year lost Curt Garry—who ran from her like a rabbit—and lost forever a certain regard for herself as well.

But after that, she had caved every chance she got. Below the earth seemed more important than above it, and she enjoyed the company of cavers—odd adventurers all, with that interesting combination of hard common sense and risk-taking seen in mountaineers, rock climbers, and pilots. Like poets, they saw life as a temporary opportunity, to be taken full advantage of.

—Curt's mother, who'd liked Joanna, had called her seven years later. Still single, an attorney with a Chicago firm, he'd died of lymphoma . . . had asked his mother to call, and sent love. . . .

Blue Water ropes, Pigeon Mountain ropes—all wonderfully light, slim, and strong—were hanging high on the garage wall in rich thick color-banded coils. Some of it static rope—tough and inelastic for long, long rappels down into darkness . . . and then the endless climbs returning, working back up that single thin, sheathed strand of nylon. Stepping up, rope-walking, with two or three cammed ascenders each sliding up the line in turn, then gripping . . . sliding up, then gripping . . . so the caver, attached to them, traveled like a great slow spider back up the hundreds of feet he'd sailed down so lightly.

Then a different rope for risk climbing, lead climbing, for rock climbing to depths beneath the earth. A dynamic line, more fragile, with stretch enough under shock to cushion a sudden fall. Giving . . . giving to prevent a smashed pelvis, a broken back, or snapped harness straps and a fall all the way.

A screamer, cavers called that fall, though Merle Budwing had shouted, and only once, as he went.

Hanging coils of rope, and below them the parachute-buckled black webbing straps of sit harness and chest harness. Her new harness—and her old set and helmet, brought out just in case she might persuade Frank down a shallow sea cave along the coast. . . . The bright red PVC equipment and supply packs hung from pegs to the side, one loaded with web-tape cow's-tails, tape slings, an *etrier*—that useful thick nylon strap sewn into a four-loop ladder— and batteries, flashlight, lighters, and Cylume sticks for emergency backup light—along with freeze-dried food bars, Super Leatherman multitool, and small hand-pumped water filter.

Another pack contained the neat machinery for movement up and down the rope. Cammed ascenders—yellow Jumars, Gibbses, and Petzl Crolls, with their nylon-webbing attachment straps and bungee cords—and the Simmons chest-harness rollers to run the rope through, hold the climber upright against the line. . . . Then the rappelling gear, to control descent by friction. A bobbin, with twin small pulley-wheels to slow the rope as it fed through. And, for longer drops, a rack—a fourteen-inch miniature steel ladder, with movable little aluminum rungs to cramp the rope sliding over and under them as the caver sailed slowly down.

The smallest pack held a Suunto compass, canteen and folding cups, pocket notebook and pencil, toilet paper, small plastic shit-sacks, and a first-aid kit.

. . . Ranked along higher pegs on their nylon-webbing slings, the carabiners jingled softly when Joanna lifted them down. Petzl Spirit 'biners, most of them, elegantly spring-gated links, D's and C's of fine forged aluminum to run rope through, to tie it to, or connect descenders and ascenders to her harness. The carabiners—and, ringing more brightly, three stainless-steel *maillon* connectors, strong screw-links in two half-rounds and a triangle.

There was nothing there—no carabiner or length of rope, no nylon-webbing tape in her packs, no cammed ascender, Gibbs or Petzl, no friction descender, bobbin or rack—that had not held Joanna's life safe many times suspended in lamplit darkness within chambers too deep, too huge, ever to be seen entirely. Great rooms beneath the earth and sunlight of America, of Mexico, of Jamaica, of Borneo.

In years of caving, she had learned to rock climb—lead or belay—to deal with stone-fall, packed mud, narrow squeezes, to deal with cave river duck-unders. To deal with fear. . . . She'd learned to rig, to prusik up the rope, rappel down it—and change, in mid-rope over emptiness, to either. She could, if necessary, do these things—and other rigging, for rescues, much more complicated—while beneath a cave's icy and battering waterfall, or in perfect darkness. She had learned to trust her gear, but back it up—and to dress and set every knot she made. . . .

Joanna opened the Volvo's trunk, laid the heavy rope-coils carefully far back, away from possible damage by spills or anything sharp or snagging, then lifted in the PVC equipment packs, two big rope sacks—to hold the lengths of line suspended beneath her, rappelling—her sit and chest harnesses, her helmet and its attached lamp—electric, not carbide—a spare helmet lamp and two spare sealed lithium battery packs.

Her boots—greased Redwing Red Setters—and her old jeans, work shirt, sweater, and blaze-orange ballistic-nylon coveralls were in the cottage hall closet with the sleeping bags. The evening ferry, the last ferry, left at dark.

Chapter Three

Charis, masturbating, pretended she was lying beneath Greg Ribideau. Beneath a boy, even pretending, was a good place to think. She supposed women often used beneath as a place to consider things.

Alone in the room, she lay under her sheet with her jeans and panties off. She lay with her knees up and spread as wide as she could, her socks on. "We do that, first thing," Mr. Langenberg had said to her many years ago. Said it only a few days after Margaret Langenberg had died.

Charis had had no real sex with Greg Ribideau. The only sex they'd had, and only once, she'd done. He'd just sat on the bed in her room, and she'd unzipped his pants and jerked him off into her other hand. Greg had been in heaven, coming in her hand.

He'd stayed for a while after that, and Charis had gotten her pint of Ben & Jerry's Chocolate Fudge Brownie from the common-room refrigerator. They'd had a mysterious ice cream thief in the dorm for a while, even though most of the summer students were graduates, and older, and should have been able to buy their own. —She and Greg had finished the pint of Fudge Brownie, then he'd kissed her and left, supposing they were serious lovers with a future.

But now he knew better . . . and it seemed to Charis he was relieved. She'd only known him the few weeks since she'd registered at White River for the graduate program, and started summer classes. He'd come over to her table at the cafeteria, said "Okay?" and sat down. "I don't know how to begin with you," he'd said. "I'm shy. And with a beautiful girl, I'm very shy."

Charis had kept eating her egg-salad sandwich.

"—But I've been watching you in The American Novel . . . and I finally couldn't help myself."

He was a nice-looking boy, maybe two years younger than she was. Tall, with pale-brown curly hair already hinting at receding. Soft blue eyes, almost a girl's eyes.

Charis had finished her sandwich. "What's your name?"

"Greg. Greg Ribideau."

"Well, I'm shyer than you are," Charis had said, then stood, picked up her tray, and walked away. She'd tried being with boys . . . with men, really. Just four of them in the seven years since Mr. Langenberg died. She hadn't enjoyed it.

Then, when she'd been thinking of killing herself so as not to be so lonely, she'd gone to bed with a girl, Margaret Gowens—but also for a purpose, for information from the agency. That sex, with the softness and slipperiness and hugging, had just been unbearable.

Charis lay back, lifted her knees, and was rough with herself down there. She was forceful with herself, but not enough so she bled.

She used to imagine she was submerged in a tank filled with dark-green water—and was slowly rotting in there, crumbling, with little pieces of her breaking off and sifting away. Spoiling under dark water in a tank made of glass. . . . Old glass, with dirt and streaks of green on it, so she could barely see people looking in, and they could barely see her.

Charis felt something beginning to happen; she was so wet she could smell herself. And she tried to be gentler. It was foolish to be so rough, when it was only her and her.

. . . It had been one afternoon last summer—while she was working at Birch Lodge in the Shawangunks in New York—that she'd realized she was going to kill herself because of loneliness, would have to kill herself unless she went back to basics and started again from the beginning. Unless she did the work, all the research necessary to find out where the beginning was, and then put right what had been so wrong.

. . . And doing that, starting over, was already beginning to help. For example, it had helped with Greg. She felt absolutely comfortable meeting him on the library roof for brown-bag lunches or takeout dinner when he worked late, Tuesdays and Thursdays. —He was a part-time book stacker for the summer, a good on-campus job. They'd meet up there, afternoons or evenings, sometimes with other students working in the library, and sit on the flat, tarred roof in old worn-out deck chairs, looking out over the campus . . . the hills.

She was even interested, now and then, in what Greg had to say. . . . So she was definitely getting better, socially.

People—Rebecca, for example—thought she and Greg Ribideau were close. Probably thought they had sex, which they hadn't, not after that once. Even though there was only a two-year difference, Greg was too young for her. He was a really young nineteen, like Rebecca, a baby. In fact, it was Greg and Rebecca who should be together. Rebecca liked him . . . did a little girl's restless got-to-pee dance when the three of them met on campus on the way to class. Rebecca, small, sort of cute but not beautiful, was a soft girl. A daddy's girl . . . without her daddy, now.

No more sex, no real sex, with Greg. It would be like being with a springer spaniel. Lots of whining and licking. There wasn't enough *to* Greg for anything serious. He wouldn't know what to do to her, whether she liked it or not. . . .

Charis turned on her side, and made a pressing fist between her legs. That was better. Something was happening.

. . . But still, she could date Greg sometimes, eat lunch with him and talk about their classes. He was in two of her classes, a regular student at the college, like Rebecca—in summer session to make up credits to save school time later. Greg wasn't stupid.

They'd talked about their papers, Thursday. He was doing Willa Cather. Charis was doing James Gould Cozzens.

"A choice out of nowhere," Greg had said. He was eating a cheeseburger, which was what he always had for lunch. "Why Cozzens?" It was hot, the library's tarred roof—the students called it Tar Beach—radiating heat from the summer afternoon.

"Read *Guard of Honor.* He's an adult and he writes about men who are adults."

"Cather writes about adults."

"She writes about girls and boys. Mainly girls. . . ."

Lying on her side was definitely better. Something was happening. . . . One night, Rebecca, across the room, had wakened when Charis was masturbating, had wakened and must have thought she was sick. She'd said, "Charis . . . ? Charis, are you okay?"

And Charis had said, "I'm masturbating, Rebecca. I'm fine."

Rebecca hadn't said anything after that. Probably embarrassed. Just lay there in the dark and listened. At the time, Charis had been using a hard rubber dildo called the Black Bomber, and it was big enough to hurt her. It hit something inside, which she'd felt before, and hurt her.

Rebecca had said nothing for a few days about that middle-of-the-night thing—then she'd said something to Charis about supposing that doing that, playing with yourself, was healthy. Just another experience, and she supposed Charis knew a lot about sex . . . had really been out in the world, not just a kid going to a college her mother taught at, for God's sake. From that, Charis knew that Rebecca had had no relationship yet. No serious fucking, for sure. Just a dreamer. Just hopeful dreaming. . . .

"Oh, I've been out in the world," Charis had said. "If you know the access codes and want to take the time, I think you can still find me on the Net."

Rebecca, sitting at her desk doing her first-year Spanish—a hard course—had said, "Find you?"

"Still see me on the Net, Becky. —I'm the six-year-old with the cock in her mouth."

Rebecca had stared as if Charis had just grown another head that didn't look like her at all.

"—See me doing that, and some other things. You'd be surprised."

Rebecca had looked surprised.

"I was there and in some magazine pictures, too. I was in *Daddy's Daughter*. I was in that one twice with just my white socks on—once with my father, Royce William Langenberg, and the next time with Philip and some other man. That time, I was eight."

Rebecca had bowed her head, said, "Oh, Charis . . ." looked down at her Spanish book and started to cry.

She was a baby; that's all she was. She'd been crying for her father, too. Crying at night. . . . Charis closed her eyes, drew her knees up and worked harder, pressing, turning her fist back and forth. Her vagina ached. She was hurt, and made a sound. Then she straightened her legs under the sheet and arched her back and came at last. . . . It was such a relief. Such a relief, it was worth the trouble.

The sheets smelled of her and sweat. Charis got up, changed the bed . . . then put on her robe and went down the hall to the showers.

When she came back, she dressed in jeans and a maroon T-shirt, her windbreaker and her running shoes. She packed an overnight bag, left a note for Rebecca—*Gone down to Boston, back tomorrow*—and left. It would be a long nighttime drive upstate.

. . . The Volkswagen's worn top was down for the first of morning air, blowing summer into the car. There were too many trees too close over the road for dawn to come quickly; it was easing in through the birches and oaks, so Charis drove gradually into daylight.

She'd stopped twice—at a strip liquor store for the pint of vodka, hundred-proof. . . then at Burleigh, at an all-night place, for gas and two chickenburgers—then had driven on up to Longford. . . . There was no summer traffic on the roads, so far upstate and inland. Nothing to bring in tourists, unless they liked blue-necks' trash trailers in roadside clearings, and some tacky farms. —She'd been careful, never stopped at Longford the other times she'd come up here. Never asked anyone for directions, so she'd gotten lost twice the first time up, and once the time after that. But now she knew the way.

The old man must have memories to keep him so far out in the boonies. A past—past love or whatever—to keep him at Lake Chaumette, which wasn't even much of a lake . . . keep him in an old fish-camp cabin with a woodstove, at his age. She'd seen him cutting wood for the last of winter, and now even for the summer evenings, cooled by the wind off the lake . . . his old man's blood running thinner and thinner.

He slept under a quilt, too, lying still most of the night . . . hardly moving, hardly turning at all, as if he were rehearsing for death. Charis had watched him sleeping, twice. He didn't snore, but moaned sometimes, dreaming like an old dog.

Charis had watched him from the woods in daylight, seen him walking around his place, doing something to a canoe up on sawhorses—repairing that, and doing other chores in brown corduroy pants and a checked flannel shirt. Daytime, he looked like a tough old man. —But at night, when she'd twice come into the cabin and stood by the bedroom door, he was only old, and moaned in his sleep. Didn't smell like pee, though. Not yet.

What in the world did he think while he was out there stacking the woodpile? —that if he turned suddenly, his wife might be standing behind him, smiling? His wife alive again, and as young as when he'd fallen in love with her?

Old men's dreams. Sad zombie dreams they must be, trying to magic back moments out of some hour years before—remembering them so well, so perfectly, so much more clearly than yesterday's trip to the grocery. . . . If there was a God, those memories wouldn't interest him at all. God would have seen all that, could go back and look again, anytime he wanted—trundle back down the railroad tracks of time. But people who thought he'd interfere with any-thing were kidding themselves. Strictly a spectator. Poor people down here were only TV for the angels—tragedy, comedy, porno, and farce. . . .

Charis drove on Peabody Lane, past an auto junkyard and a café, a diner that looked like something out of an old movie . . . shiny aluminum. The diner was closed. Peabody Lane ran right into Lake Drive, and Charis took a left there. The drive ran along the lake, past ancient dented trailers—parked on tiny lots by the water and never moved again—and a few cabins looking not much better. Chaumette was a tacky old lake now, however fabulous and beauti-ful it might have been back in 1950. Probably still was 1950 to the old man. Then, it must have seemed that 1950 was the way things would be forever. . . .

She stayed on the drive more than halfway around the lake, then slowed and turned right down an overgrown access lane cut through the woods. She pulled out of sight from the road into a sandy space where a cabin's basement had been dug and concreted years be-fore. . . . The project abandoned after that to encroaching tangles of berry bushes, birch seedlings, and the lakeside's weedy pines.

Charis turned off the VW's engine and got out of the car. There were two condoms in the pine needles beneath a tree. They lay gray, wrinkled, and collapsed, the only things new since she'd been in the clearing three weeks before, and twice before that.

Charis leaned against the tree's rough bark. She could see only a dawn-lit narrow reach of lake through its branches. No one was out on the water this early, fishing or boating. . . . She stood leaning there and closed her eyes. The morning sun soon would rise enough for its light to touch her. Then she had the whole day to wait through. But since she'd been a little girl, she had found wait-ing a pleasure, relaxing, corridors of time as long and narrow as the view of Chaumette Lake, as still, empty, and restful.

Joanna drove the narrow scrub-choked track up Whitestone Ridge—going slow through hill-shadowed dawn, the Volvo's head-light beams, barely useful as sunrise came, swinging slowly half around each rising turn. The Newcombs' farmhouse was a mile and more over the crest of the ridge; the car lights wouldn't be seen from there.

In the weeks after Merle Budwing's death, Howard Newcomb

and the Midstate Grotto had come to an agreement—far from satisfactory to the cavers. Their extraordinary Concave to be gated and shut to all further exploration, with the Midstate to have first go if and when it was opened again, with Newcomb's insurance company and lawyers satisfied. —The Grotto had supplied the gate, installed it, and kept two of the keys in case of a sudden change of mind, or an emergency rescue of some kids breaking the gate and going down and into trouble.

Chris Leong, president, had one key. Joanna—rescue chairperson—held the other.

Near the top of the ridge, she cut her lights, drove the last short stretch by increasing morning light . . . then pulled the Volvo up amid a stand of pine at the track's dead end, and cut the engine. The last nighttime crickets were still singing while a dawn breeze drifted through the birches below, the pines and hemlocks along the ridge.

There was no darkness left, up here.

Joanna got out of the car, went around to open the trunk, and began to unload gear. She took the static Blue Water out first—two big two-hundred-and-fifty-foot coils—broke the keeper knots, and slowly fed each line down into a separate rope sack.

It would have been convenient if they could have left a permanent rope rigged down, but that would have been too great a temptation to some break-in fools to try sliding down it, hand-over-hand. There was no man alive who could hand-over-hand down a forty-story rope, let alone climb hand-over-hand back up it. . . . She'd have to rig the top two-fifty feet, then tie on the second rope, transfer to that to get to the bottom of the pit.

She would certainly be out of the Midstate Grotto on her butt if they knew what she was doing. And be unacceptable after that to any cavers in the country, for breaking a gate agreement with a landowner, then going down into a major cave alone and scooping booty—discovering new passages, virgin chambers, on her own, taking all those pleasures for herself. That, and endangering the people who might have to come after her in trouble, find her and get her out of there, dead or alive.

But there could be no rescue now, anyway, with no one knowing she was here. No rescue if she got caught in a squeeze, or trapped in a drowning pool, or broke her leg in a far passage miles under the ridge. No rescue. And afterward, no recovery of her body until the distant day some hiker or hunter, climbing high, found the car. . . .

Joanna lugged the two rope sacks up through the pine woods, a steep climb with the bags' heavy weight among close evergreens that held and dragged at her. Burdened, it was easy to trip on roots risen out of beds of pine and hemlock fronds, small fallen branches.

One hundred yards . . . a little more than one hundred yards up, she smelled the cave's breath. Cool, cooler than the summer's morning air. Cool and damp, the setting-concrete odor of limestone wet with water. It was a clean slow breeze, with no smell of either life or death to it, and grew stronger as she climbed.

Soon she heard it, a soft hollow rushing sound as if the ridge were a beast of millions of tons, sleeping.

Joanna came out from under the low, brushing ceiling of foliage, and into brighter morning. The gate, in a crease of the ridge's stone shoulder, was made of steel rebar welded into a tall, narrow grid, hinged and set into concrete edging both sides of a ragged entrance more than seven feet high, slightly less than three feet wide.

The cave's cool breath came sighing through.

Joanna set the rope sacks down. . . . The gate's big padlock was a thick round of stainless steel. She unlocked it, hung it on a crossbar, and swung the heavy grid squealing open. Then she walked back down through the trees to the car . . . put on her helmet, lashed the sleeping bag, selected and stowed gear into one equipment pack . . . then slung the pack, the carabiners, and her harness over her shoulders. She closed the Volvo's trunk, and bent under the load, climbed back up to the cave's mouth, careful of her footing.

In two trips, she hauled her gear inside, and down a rough passage slightly more than two feet wide . . . piled the pack, sleeping bag, and rope sacks, then went back and closed and locked the gate behind her.

Hefting the gear again, Joanna moved farther down the passage into deeper darkness and damp, the daylight only a faint glow behind her. . . . She switched on her helmet lamp, and by that yellow cone of light, sorted out her webbing, then buckled on the sit harness, checked the adjustment—tight, but not too tight—and did the same for her chest harness. Then she buckled a one-inch-wide webbing strap up from her waist to connect them.

After Budwing fell, Chris Leong had bolted two steel rigging anchors into the low stone ceiling of the passage, just short of the mud-slide chute. Joanna tugged the Blue Water's working end out of one rope sack, snapped back-to-back carabiners up into each anchor fitting, then tied into one set with a figure eight on a bight loop . . . took the line over to the slightly lower anchor and tied another figure eight through the carabiners there. She examined the anchors' set by her helmet light, saw that the limestone they were bolted into was sound—not flaking, not cracked—then checked her rigging knots again, dressed and set them hard.

Joanna dug for the Blue Water's running end, tied a looped knot there to keep from rappelling off it into the pit—then began the routine of attaching her gear and herself to the rope. She snapped the web-tape runners of her pack and rope sacks to her harness loops with small bent-gate Petzl carabiners, then clipped her rack descender to the steel link at the front of her sit harness, and threaded the Blue Water back and forth through the rack's small bars.

She tested her harness buckles, snapped the safety shunt's runner to her waist link, and clipped the shunt onto the rope, for backup braking in case the rack failed. . . . Then she double-checked everything she'd done, looked along the passage's wet mud floor for anything she might have dropped, anything forgotten, overlooked.

When she was sure, Joanna backed slowly away from her anchors, feeding out rope through the rack, keeping tension on it . . . gripping the shunt with her left hand to let the rope run free. She backed down until the heels of her boots rested just at the edge of the irregular black mouth of the chute.

Then she stepped back and down—and instantly began to slide fast on slick mud . . . kept her feet straddled wide as she skidded backward at a steeper and steeper slant into darkness. She clamped the rack's bars in her right hand to slow herself, half sliding, half dangling from the angled rope . . . and looked up, trying to find the carabiner hanging from the chute roof. They'd rigged it suspended from a web-tape runner bolted to the chute ceiling, to pass the ropes through . . . run them high at the pit's stone lip, out of the mud.

Joanna caught a gleaming in her helmet's light, saw it was the carabiner hanging above her and to the left, and clamped the rack's bars to stop. She reached up with a loop of the rope in her left hand, unscrewed the carabiner's gate with thumb and forefinger, snapped the Blue Water in, and screwed the gate shut. —That was just done, and the shunt gripped again, when the pack and rope sacks, trailing on their tape runners, slid suddenly downslope past her, toppled over the rock's edge and into the pit.

Their weight yanked at her, and Joanna slipped and fell hard, skidded down the mud slope on her belly, and was over the lip and falling into blackness, emptiness.

She felt fear flash through her, bright and freezing cold. *The rack. Hold tight . . . hold tight.*

And she gripped it, gripped it with all the strength in her right hand, squeezing the rack bars together so the rope hummed, then whined running through them. She was too frightened to let go of the safety shunt, let its cam engage to halt her.

She hung frozen instead, gripping the rack with all her strength so the rope, as friction took hold, gradually . . . gradually ran through more slowly, until she was hardly falling, until she was only drifting down into darkness forty stories deep . . . her pack dangling beneath her with the rope sacks, the Blue Water line feeding out of the first one.

Embarrassed, grateful to be alone and have no one know how she'd panicked—gripping her rack in terror, instead of simply releasing the shunt—Joanna sailed down, sailed down the murmuring rope, its thin, sheathed nylon cording strong enough to hold anything but a fool.

She imagined Merle Budwing's ghost calling to her from below. A ghost eternally in darkness, coolness, calling others down to him at the bottom of the pit. It would make a poem. . . .

Now, after those moments of fear, the reality of Frank's dying came sharply, freshly to her. She'd thought of her loss, of his leaving her. She'd thought of Frank's death—but not his dying. She hadn't considered the moments of drowning, his exhaustion and agony.

Descending through an immense stone cathedral, hundreds of empty feet across, more hundreds of feet deep—its upper air lit after all, now that her eyes were accustomed, by two dim slender beams of light from minor cracks in the great dome of its ceiling— Joanna began to cry, and realized it was only the second time she had wept since Frank had died, as if she'd been waiting for this more proper place for tears. The cave, like the ocean, revealing so clearly how small, how minor they were, and in what a temporary way Frank had lived—and she lived still, and hung now on her little thread, a tiny, thinking spider with a poem in its head.

Joanna took a breath and stopped crying. She blew her nose on her coverall sleeve, eased the bars of her rack and fell a little faster, so the Blue Water's sound rose in pitch as it payed through the friction. Above her as she sank, the rope's thin strand ran up and out of her helmet's light into distance and vaulted uncertain shadow. Beneath her was a gulf of deeper, then perfect dark.

Joanna stood, her helmet lamp switched off, on heaped shifting slabs of fallen stone. She'd tied her second length of line on at two hundred and thirty feet . . . then attached herself to the new rope below the joining knot, to rappel down the last two hundred–plus feet to the pit's floor.

She'd turned off her helmet lamp to enjoy the dark, to stand in this great vault of darkness deep within the world . . . alone except for Merle Budwing's ghost. He'd struck this heap of spoil after accelerating second by second in his fall, breathless, out of shout, not knowing when he'd strike—or whether he'd strike at all, perhaps only fall and fall forever, fall endless miles in pitch darkness toward the center of the earth.

For him, the white smacking flash of impact must have been a fraction of an instant of relief.

Joanna looked up, searched for those two beams of light in the dome's great height, and saw, high and higher, almost out of sight, their hair-thin traces that by contrast made the cavern's darkness darker, as if it were flooded by a river of blackness flowing in, and bringing silence with it.

She lit her helmet lamp, and by that small bright cone of light fed the slack running end of the second Blue Water length into a rope bag, then weighted that with a heavy chunk of rock. Above the rope bag and its stone, the rest of the line rose up into cool damp dark air, up forty stories to the mud chute, the passage, and the gate. The rope, hanging slender as her finger, and moving slightly in the cave's cool breezes, was her only way up, her only way out.

She took her chest harness off and left it with the rack and shunt by the rope sacks, along with her sling of carabiners. Then she dug in the equipment pack and took out two nylon tape runners and the sixty-foot braid of Pigeon Mountain climbing rope—dynamic rope, with stretch and give to it to cushion a fall. She hunted through the pack again, found the folded plastic survival bag, took off her helmet and tucked the bag into it, then put the helmet back on and checked her chin strap.

It was odd to be alone in the pit, in darkness, alone in the tangled miles of the cave. Odd to be without the company of other cavers, their noise and occasional grunts of effort working passages in climbs and crawls, or lugging gear. Without their harsh joking.

Strange to be alone, and a relief. As if being beneath the earth in pitch darkness, coolness, silence, being here and all alone, were the truth of the human condition—and everything brightly lit, crowded, noisy and warm, were only a lie waiting to be exposed. Exposed by drowning and death. Exposed by loneliness and loss. The cave, like the bottom of the sea, presented the fact.

Joanna imagined herself as Merle Budwing was, and Frank. In stillness, silence, and the dark. The difference being that she still knew of death—and the dead did not.

She shouldered the pack and rope, took six carabiners from her sling and snapped them to her waist harness, and walked away from the hanging line . . . trudging, sliding down the long, unstable hundred-yard ridge of broken fallen stone. An insect crawling along the rough dark carpet of an enormous room. . . .

It took her half an hour to get off the ridge of fallen rock and onto the pit's stone floor—scored and ravined yards deep by ancient rushing waters, scattered with the rubble the currents had left behind them, boulders, gravel, megaliths larger than houses. The vaulting space around, above her, seemed to sing in Joanna's ears, then shrink to only the reality of her helmet's cone of light—a yard or two across, a yard or two distant as she traveled.

If she mistook a narrow trench in the pit's floor for a shadow in her light's beam, if she misstepped and broke her ankle, broke her leg, she could still self-rescue—crawl back to her distant rope in agony, rig her ascending gear, and struggle up, her bad leg dangling. It would take hours, it would be difficult, but she could do it, weeping, screaming if necessary.

But if she slipped and fell here and broke her pelvis, or broke her back, then there would be no getting up the rope, even if she could drag herself over the long ridge of rubble to it. . . . Then, she would lie licking damp stone for any moisture, and huddle dreaming, shivering, hallucinating as her lamp batteries failed, backup lights were exhausted, her rations were eaten . . . and she died of darkness and thirst, before she could starve to death.

Someday, after her car was found, cavers would come sailing slowly down through shadow for her body. They'd be very angry with her. . . .

Two hours later, Joanna had crossed the pit's floor, climbed a steep fifty-foot rise of rubble breakdown to its north wall, and stopped to rest a few minutes before climbing the forty feet of vertical limestone to the first passage entrance.

It was a sheer wall of fractured soft stone—chocks and aids useless to wedge into cracks that crumbled and broke away on strain. It was hand-and-foot climbing. The Midstate Grotto had a policy of avoiding permanent bolted anchors where it could.

"If you can't rock climb, don't cave—'cause where there're downs, there're going to be ups." One of Chris Leong's lectures. The Mad Chinaman—also known as Genghis Khan—Chris would be first down the rope, if they had to come for her body in a few months. He'd be absolutely furious. . . .

Joanna went to the wall . . . sidestepped along its irregular base, and found a deep crack that seemed to go. She stepped up to wedge her boot toe in, then reached up and found a grip to balance her for the next toe-in. She slowly walked the crack up at an angle to the right along the wall, keeping her body away from the stone, using her feet to climb, her hands only for balance. —Her helmet light was not much use; it threw too many shadows above her as she climbed. She did better with her eyes closed . . . relying on touch, running her fingers in slow sweeps above her, feeling for slight depressions, slight ridges to grip lightly for a moment as she went up.

The rock crack narrowed and vanished beneath her, and Joanna, committed, climbed with her feet turned sharply out, using the inner edges of her boot soles to boost her. It was a matter of keeping moving, not stopping—not hanging still on the wall.

Left step and right step up in darkness, in rhythm with her reaching, searching for finger holds to keep her on the rock. She began to notice the weight of the pack and rope braid on her back . . . notice the soft ringing of the carabiners as she rose. Her fingertips were hurting. Now she was twenty-five, thirty feet up, too far to allow herself to fall. There'd be no falling, now. Only climbing.

. . . At the passage ledge, Joanna had to mantle, brace her weight up on a stiffened arm to lever herself over the edge. She lay resting there a few minutes, then rolled to her feet, clumsy with the pack and rope—and walked over rubble into the passage. It was an ovaled tunnel, floored in a fine silted dust that sparkled in her lamp's light. Fifty to sixty feet wide, almost thirty feet high, its gleaming walls were dimpled by current swirls, the stone burnished by the White River's flowing through for two or three million years.

The river had flowed through for those ages before diverting to a lower level, slowly dissolving its way down. It had flowed through the passage and thundered out into the pit, an immense waterfall filling a black lake in pitch darkness.

This passage was the meandering mile-long walkway into the labyrinth—the maze of interconnected tunnels, chutes, squeezes, dead ends, river duck-unders, corridors, crawl spaces, waterfalls, galleries and great chambers of the cave. . . . The Grotto hadn't had time to map very much of it. Joanna had supplies for two days, two days to explore and rough-map a new mile, perhaps two.

Two days in which she had to think of nothing but staying alive—of caving, and its cold, harsh, and muddy labor, discomfort, danger, and exhaustion. Two days in which she had to think of nothing else, remember nothing else in a world of dependable darkness beneath the treacherous world of light.

Chapter Four

At dark, Charis reached into the VW's glove compartment, took out a small penlight, some Kleenex, and the flat pint bottle of vodka, and locked the car. Then she walked into the woods, unbuckled her belt, unzipped her jeans and pulled them down, pulled her panties down—and squatted, leaning back against a birch to pee.

She dried herself, tucked the used tissues under last year's fallen leaves, pulled up her panties and jeans, and began walking through the trees, working left along the lake shore. It was cool . . . a cool summer night. The breeze was off the lake.

She used the penlight sparingly, and only for a moment each time. The woods and brush were thick along the water, the ground soft, soaked to puddles here and there.

Music. Choir . . . a chorale came floating in the night. She saw house lights off to the right. They'd built on a low peninsula, cleared the trees. A few steps farther, and she could see the place, its lit windows. The music came from there, Benjamin Britten, or some modern romantic. . . . Classical-music people on a blue-collar lake. They, or their parents, must have built here in the good old days, and been annoyed when the trailers and mobile homes began to accumulate around the shore. . . .

Charis went carefully, quietly past, kept to the brush and trees—though these people hadn't had a dog when she'd been up before.

Then it was wet walking, her running shoes soaked squelching through puddles and muddy patches. The cool air smelled sweetly of pine trees and still water. There wasn't wind enough to build small waves across the lake tonight. Other times—one other time—

the wind had been blowing hard, noisy in the trees, and tiny waves had broken on the shore.

Charis could hardly hear the choral music anymore. —And just as that faded, she saw the old man's cabin. Small, much smaller than the other house had been. . . . There was light through the living-room windows. The bedroom window was dark and the kitchen window was dark. She doubted he'd eaten supper; she'd never seen him cooking any regular meals. Warmed soup, sometimes. She'd smelled tomato soup in the cabin, last time she was up.

An old man no longer interested in food. Eating and drinking his memories, and fading away. . . .

Charis walked out of the trees and went along the cabin's back wall. She'd heard the old man on the phone the first night she'd come up—raising his voice, saying "What?" every now and then. So she didn't take care to step quietly.

She circled the cabin—paused by the side of the porch to be certain he wasn't sitting out there, which he rarely did after dark—then went on around.

She saw him through the first living-room window. He was sitting in the rocker, reading. Charis had never seen him rock back and forth. He just sat still, with his feet flat on the floor, and read. He had no television.

There was a long bookcase against the log wall behind him, a bookcase of fine cherry wood, furniture from the house he must have had with his wife. No way to tell the title of the book he was reading—not from outside. But later, when she went in, she'd see. Last time it had been Céline, in French. A tough old man reading a tough book. . . . In a way, it would have been better if his wife were still alive. Then they would have tried careful trembling old sex, and Charis could have seen they weren't lonely.

She stood watching him read seven pages. He was a fast reader—it was the quickest thing he did. She watched him do that . . . watched a little longer . . . then went back into the trees to sit and wait.

. . . The moon was up when the living-room lights were turned off. Charis stood and stretched. She was getting hungry, and chilly in the breeze coming off the lake.

She walked around the cabin to the woodshed's outside door. The woodshed was off the kitchen, convenient in hard winters. She opened the woodshed door—lifted it slightly as she opened it, to keep its rusty hinges quiet—then eased inside in darkness, used her penlight to manage along the narrow aisle with rough birch and alder rounds and splits stacked on either side. It seemed to her the old man must not trust summer anymore; he already had his wood in, ready for winter.

Charis moved carefully to the door into the kitchen, put her ear against it and listened. . . . No sound. She put the penlight in her jeans pocket.

Then there was a faint noise—a chair or something being moved in the cabin . . . in the bedroom. A chair. He'd be putting his brown corduroy trousers over the back of the chair.

The old man had four pairs of corduroy pants—two brown and two black. He wore them winter and summer when he was at the lake, and washed them and his shirts and underwear in a tub over a fire behind the cabin. Really primitive and silly, because she'd watched him, one spring evening, try to wring a pair of those pants out, and he wasn't strong enough to do it right—so he'd hung them up, dripping, on his clothesline. It was sad, really, but it was his choice, since he'd been a lawyer and had had a practice and an office and so forth, and at least a little money. . . . An old man living in the past, every way he could. Eccentric, was the word.

Charis stood listening at the door to the kitchen, listened for a long time, and heard no more sounds at all but the soft mutter and tick of the woodstove in the living room.

Then she took the big Shrade jackknife out of her back pants pocket, opened it, slid the blade through the crack between the wooden door and jamb—old and shrunk to a bad fit—and carefully eased the latch hook out of its eye. She opened the door, lifting it slightly for silence, walked into the kitchen and stood by the refrigerator, listening, smelling food cooked a while ago . . . oatmeal . . . smelling the smoky odor of the living-room stove, the log-cabin smell of damp wood and old tree bark.

Charis opened the refrigerator. There wasn't much in it—half a loaf of whole-wheat bread; a glass bowl of what looked like mashed potatoes, with a plastic cover on top; a half-gallon container of milk; and some slices of salami on a small white plate. There was a big wedge of rat cheese in plastic wrap . . . and that was that.

She had never eaten any of his food. But now it made no difference. She took the bread and rat cheese out and put them on the kitchen table, then chose two pieces of bread by dim light from the open refrigerator—some of the bread was stale—and used the Shrade to cut a thick slice of the cheese for a sandwich. There was no mayo or butter in the refrigerator, so it would be a simple sandwich. . . .

Charis walked carefully to the door to the living room—avoiding two places in the plank floor that she knew squeaked—and stood in the doorway for a while, listening, and eating the sandwich. It was good, even without mayo.

When she finished, wasn't chewing anymore, she could hear the old man breathing in the bedroom. Not snoring as Royce Langenberg used to snore, but only heavy breathing . . . sounded like work.

She walked into the living room—dark, except for the Franklin stove's dull, flickering light—and went across to the bedroom door. Wasn't much of a bedroom, probably had been a storage space or spare room, ten feet square with a little half-window. The cabin's big loft was where people had slept. But the steep steps must have started to hurt the old man's knees. . . . She stood by the half-open bedroom door, listened to that slow, harsh breathing.

She slowly pushed the door open, stood watching as the old man slept. He lay on his side in soft moonlight shining through the half-window. Lay curled under his quilt like a child. He looked smaller than when he was awake and outside, working around the cabin. The moonlight was shadowed on his face. . . . Charis watched him for a while, then carefully closed the bedroom door and walked back into the living room. He'd left his book by the armchair, on the lamp table.

She took the penlight out of her pocket, held it in her mouth for light. It was a novel by Larteguy, in English translation. She leafed through the book, stopping to read here and there. She read for a while, several passages. . . . The central characters seemed to be foolish French army officers, all with beautiful-sounding names. No question French was lovely, when officers' names sounded like music.

She closed the book and put it down, didn't bother to keep the old man's place. Then she went to the Franklin stove, bent, and opened one of its small iron glass-windowed doors.

There was a long-handled ash shovel in a wrought-iron stand beside the stove, and Charis used it to scoop up a small heap of live coals, pulsing arterial red. She shook some onto the metal safety sheeting beneath the stove front . . . then scattered the rest out onto the pine-plank flooring.

She put the shovel back in its stand, left the stove door open a few inches. Then she stood well back, took the pint bottle from her windbreaker pocket, opened it, reached out and poured the vodka onto the floor . . . over the spilled coals.

A blue flash softly thumped and exploded several feet high and almost caught her—then hissed and ran out in blue and red runners along the planking.

Charis stepped back and went to the bedroom door again. She put her ear against it and heard the old man still sleeping, breathing his difficult breaths. Then she turned in brightening light to watch the fire exhaust the alcohol, turn it to fumes and gone . . . then learn to do without it . . . learn ordinary burning along the wooden floor.

It took a while. But finally the pine planks began to chuckle, smoke, and char in a large and larger circle. And when flames came up together, low and rolling, a gorgeous carpeting wave across the floor, Charis went back to the bedroom door, carefully opened it only a little—then walked back into the kitchen and out through its woodshed door. She closed that behind her, then went through the woodshed and on outside.

The night was cooler now, the breeze blowing stronger off the lake. She was glad she'd brought her windbreaker.

Charis walked around the cabin to the bedroom's half-window, and stood listening. She heard the old man still sleeping, breathing noisily. There was no other sound from the cabin. And outside, in the night, only the soft sweeping of the lake wind through the trees.

She stood by the window for a while, then walked around the side of the cabin to a living-room window. She saw blazing at the window's glass before she looked in—and there was no living room. Now it was a coiling furnace, and she could hear it. The Franklin stove, that had held fire captive for so many years, now squatted in the midst of fire that rolled free from wall to wall, and climbed the walls to follow its smoke. The smoke was black and slow as the fire was bright and quick. It made a rich contrast. . . .

Charis walked back around to the bedroom window and heard the old man calling. Definitely awake, now. She couldn't tell what he was calling. Maybe for help. —It was a sort of shouting.

She stood by the half-window, but not too close because smoke was coming out. It was pouring out of the window like black coffee poured from a pot. The old man was shouting in there. Charis supposed he must have opened the bedroom door and seen the living room was all fire, and no way out.

"Get out . . . *get outside!*" That's what the old man was shouting.

She could hear him through the little window. He was shouting as if he were calling to somebody else. Charis stood away from the smoke coming out, and listened. *"Get outside!"* was what he was yelling in there. Instructions to himself. Then he called out something in French, and she couldn't understand it.

Suddenly, the window screen came out, was broken and fell out, and startled her so she jumped back—and the old man was there at the half-window, staring out through the smoke. The smoke funneled past him, made a billowing dark halo around his face. Charis saw the old man's white face in the middle of moving black smoke that made his face whiter. It was the moonlight that was showing him to her. His face was nested in the smoke—and she saw him see her.

He put his arm out through the little window, his left arm, and she could see he was making small jumps, small hopping jumps in there to get up to the half-window, get out through it, somehow. She could see an edge of the fire behind him; it had come through the bedroom doorway like an animal made of gold.

He was reaching out with his left arm, and he got his head and left shoulder out of the window in stirring, roiling smoke. He was looking at her, and his mouth was moving but he wasn't shouting, anymore. He was trying to get through the window, but the window was much too small. He was wrestling in the window frame, his mouth open, breathing in smoke.

He stretched his arm . . . his hand out to Charis as if she could pull him free—and before she thought she reached up and took it. His hand trembled, big, soft, and cold. She held it—then suddenly let go when he screamed. The fire had found him.

Charis stepped back and stepped back again. His screaming was pushing her back. His mouth had become most of his face, a stretched black oval, and he screamed as if he were young again, making that terrific noise.

The old man seemed to shake and shake in the window frame—stuck half in and half out. There was brightness and blazing behind him. He breathed in smoke and shrieked it out—and in the smoke, Charis smelled cooking.

She turned and ran away as if he might get out after all, and come chasing her on fire . . . trailing fire after her through the night.

She ran by firelight, then by moonlight, ran through the woods hearing shrill failing noise behind her . . . then choral music ahead, sounding faintly from the house she'd passed before. So she was never in silence for a moment.

The first day and night had gone very well. Joanna had mapped almost two miles of passages no one had ever seen—low-ceilinged, wet, and tortuous ways winding beneath each other. She'd done a decent job of mapping—used the tape, inclinometer, and Suunto compass, made some small hasty sketches, too. A pretty good job of mapping to be working alone, with no one to run the tape end out and hold it, or anchor it with a stone.

The first day and night had gone well. This second morning would be more difficult—though she still felt at home, still was happier here, farther from Frank and his death than she would be anywhere else. But she was tired this morning, colder, weary with scrambling and climbing rope pitches, sore from stone bruises and cuts.

After she'd wakened—having slept in her sleeping bag under a mile of stone, alone on a patch of fine drift gravel in darkness deeper than dark—Joanna'd filter-pumped icy water from a small silver pool no one had seen since the world began. She'd drunk a quart of that stone-tasting water and eaten a protein bar and half a carbohydrate bar . . . then checked her equipment pack, her rope coil, lamp batteries, and gear. She'd sorted through everything, making sure nothing was lost, nothing would be left behind. . . .

She climbed from the graveled passage by a breezy squeeze, snaking up into it behind her helmet light's shifting yellow beam, feeling cool wind drafting down from chambers, crawl spaces beyond.

She started working her way up this narrow chimney that grew slowly narrower . . . climbed and twisted, writhed her way up, the equipment pack and rope coil—tethered with four feet of webbing—dragging up beneath her. The chimney took an awkward turn, up and to the right, and Joanna tried the turn . . . got into it with her right arm cramped down along her side as she pushed herself slowly higher. It was very hard work, because only that right hand—its leather glove worn through, so she was bleeding—only that hand and the toe of one boot had any purchase at all.

She moved up very slowly, her right side wedged in the angle of the stone. . . . Then moved more slowly; she could feel her boot toe scrabbling, scraping on the rock beneath her. . . . Then she couldn't move anymore. Couldn't take a deep breath, she was held so tight.

Joanna began to lie to herself—that she could keep climbing, that she was just resting because it was a hard vertical squeeze and now angling off, and she was lucky she was climbing . . . not caught crawling head down. Joanna lied to herself for several minutes, and pretended she was resting.

But the lie wouldn't last, and she had to try to move—not move up or down, just move a little, ease herself in the chimney so she could get a deep breath. A breath was really what she needed. . . . She'd crawled up, so there must be a way down. Or perhaps of continuing up. Plenty of choices, if she could get a really deep breath. There was no use wasting little breaths in grunting, murmuring for help, letting them know she was in trouble. No use in that. There was no "them."

And if she failed—couldn't get just one deep breath to start with; that would help so much—then no one would ever know where Joanna Reed was held, gripped, smothered in a million-ton coffin of stone. Someone might smell her one day . . . smell faint drifting rot in the cavern's air, and suppose some animal had come down for its own reasons, and died. No man, nor any god there might be, would be able to find her. . . . It was, in a way, the place she'd been seeking. Here, while she slowly writhed and twisted for any purchase—careful, careful not to begin to struggle desperately, to scream out air she would never be able to breathe back—here at last she forgot about Frank, forgot about loss and unhappiness. Here, caught hard and perfectly alone, unable to go up, unable to back down . . . caught hard in darkness that her lamp would only demonstrate as its battery slowly died, Joanna forgot about anything but getting out.

Secretly, she traded Frank's death for getting out. That dreadful thing having happened, seemed insurance against this dreadful thing happening. . . . And the cowardice calmed her, became very useful, so she breathed slowly out . . . and out again to make slight extra space where the stone clamped her so closely.

She decided to go up, not back . . . and quarter-inch by quarter-inch—using her chin once, stretching her jaw up against the rock, then slowly bowing her head with all her strength, so her chin caught on rough limestone, she added just that little bit to climbing. Added as much as her trapped right hand . . . and she twisted and slowly, slowly corkscrewed an inch . . . perhaps two inches higher. Her chest ached from effort where her breast had been, scar tissue sore across the muscle.

Joanna's left leg was numb; she couldn't feel it. Her left hand was free, but found nothing above her but limestone too wet, too slippery. She used her right boot toe . . . her right hand's fingers, and breathed out again and out again, worming, working, writhing up almost another inch . . . a cave snake, blind and slowly turning inside stone.

A rage began to grow in her like changing weather—a slow fury against all unmoving things, all things too hard, too solid, real and unchangeable. Stone, and death.

She took rapid small breaths, like the breaths she'd learned in her Lamaze classes years ago—giving-birth breaths that might allow her to live to leave this narrow passage. . . . She found that her right hand was doing the most, though it could curl, push against the rock in only a limited way. The hand was being hurt; she felt the stone burning the edge of her palm, wearing the skin away as she worked.

Joanna thought for a moment of trying to go back, trying to get down the chimney. If her left hand could grip above her, help her with leverage a little, she might be able to. Without that, not. . . . But rage, her anger, seemed to drive her up, drive her to complete what she'd started. She turned and turned her right hand, and felt the stone grow slowly wetter beneath, where the hand was bleeding. Wet, but not too slippery yet. She breathed in little sipping breaths, breathed them carefully out, worked her raw right hand, and scraped and scrabbled her boot toe against the rock beneath her. The scraping there seemed to uncover stone a little rougher than the surface . . . gave her a hint of purchase against it.

She rose an inch . . . then another. Her right hand—the side of the palm—felt as if she rubbed it on a hot stove, was scorching, cooking it as she climbed. The pain made her begin to cry—but only the pain. She wept for no other reason, and kept working.

She twisted, heaved up almost another inch—and felt with her searching left hand at last a chipped place, a tiny notch that misting water had corroded in the chimney's limestone through the centuries. She got a fingernail . . . almost a fingertip in it, hooked her hand into a claw and slowly, carefully on that fragile hold, began to lift a little of her weight, only a very little of it. If that fingernail tore off, she had four more. . . .

She wrestled, tugged, then twisted up a little more, and was able to breathe almost deeply. She rested there while feeling came tingling, stinging back into her left leg. . . . Then she had both legs, and was able to kick out a little and scramble, was almost free to climb. And in a while, when she was very tired, her left hand found a small round of stone to grip.

Slowly, as she climbed, the chimney began to open. It opened wider, and at last allowed Joanna—dragging her tethered gear up behind her—to haul out onto an easy crawl over mud to an upper passage's rubbled floor. She sat there, satisfied, dug in her pack and replaced her helmet lamp's battery. By bright new light, her watch displayed numbers near noon that made little sense to her until she thought about them, concentrated on them.

She'd been in the chimney almost two hours. And up had been the proper way to go. If she'd tried going back down the squeeze, conformations different, descending, she would have stayed in the stone forever.

. . . The afternoon was difficult because she was so tired. Too tired, too cold in cool air to map, stretch the tape, check the compass and inclinometer, get the readings right and noted. She rambled through an upper passage that turned and turned again, a maze she committed to memory as she passed, with a veteran caver's noting of lefts and rights, ups and downs. . . . She found a side crawl that had a breeze blowing from it, slid into that and down into shallow water, very cold—then stood and waded behind her lamp's light into a small chamber so bright with frost-white tapestries it hurt her eyes. Flashing from reflected water drops, from lacework and white ribbonwork in stone suspended from the little room's high ceiling, her helmet's light doubled and grew brighter in reflection, in rainbow refraction of roses, sulfurs, mauves and old ivory—chryselephantine. Miniature blizzard-white islands lifted from a shallow pool as clear as air, where her lamp's light shone down through perfect water to sparkle from quartzite pebbles on its floor.

No one had ever seen the small glittering room before—and likely no one ever would again. It had been waiting for millions of still and silent years of darkness for some living creature with curiosity and courage to search for it, and discover its loveliness. She had come, and it was hers.

For hours, as Joanna drove east toward the coast, early evening's falling sunlight forest odor seemed elements of a dream, an odd dream of roofless space and green of growing things. —Reality remained the coolness and darkness of the cave.

The cars approaching, then thumping past her, seemed driven by dream figures, two-dimensional, who had no notion how to find their way out of a dark labyrinth of miles of passageway, falls, and faults. No notion of how to do that—then climb four hundred feet of slender line out of a cavern's well of darkness, emptiness. To climb exhausted, stepping up as each ascender—one at her right foot, one at her left knee—slid up the rope in turn, and gripped. Up forty stories to the light.

. . . She drove east, the Volvo's trunk full of wet and muddy clothes, boots, mud-streaked coils of Blue Water rope and PMI rope, along with equipment needing cleaning, drying—and for anything steel, a light touch of oil. She'd poured hydrogen perox-ide over her right palm where the skin was gone, and that had hurt so much that spots swam before her eyes—tiny water-gray spots moving through a gray field. Then she'd taped on a gauze bandage.

Her legs and shoulders ached from rope climbing. Even with as-cenders, four hundred feet was four hundred feet. And her hands were sore—skinned palm, scraped knuckles, fingers bruised from gripping rock. Her hands hurt, cramped around the steering wheel.

. . . She came in on the nine-thirty ferry, with night unfolding like a bat's wing along the Atlantic's horizon. She drove along Strand, then up Slope Street and into the cottage's narrow graveled drive to the garage.

There were chores to do—the ropes to be hosed, coiled, and hung to dry, and all the other equipment cleaned and put away . . . equipment packs and rope sacks turned inside out to air. A couple of hours of chores.

Joanna was too tired, too hungry, to start working right away. She left the garage, went up the cottage's back steps and through the kitchen door, then almost called out that she was home—almost, but caught herself. After a few more weeks, she wouldn't even begin to call into empty houses.

She decided on a peanut butter and jelly sandwich and a glass of milk—put her purse on the kitchen table, and went down the hall to the entryway to check the phone. Its message light was blinking. Rebecca, probably.

Joanna pushed the *play* button and heard a voice she slowly rec-ognized. Mrs. Thurman, the president's secretary at White River. Very brisk old lady, and not friendly.

Mrs. Thurman spoke for quite a while, almost ran out the tape. . . . The president wanted to get in touch and was very, very sorry. The state police had been unable to contact her at her home in White River, and then her father's attorney, Ms. Dufour from upstate, had called. Terrible accident . . . woodstove door left open. Mrs. Thurman was anxious for Joanna to get back to her at the president's office, so they'd know she'd gotten the message.

Joanna put the phone down with the oddest sense of satisfaction. She felt almost pleased. . . . Besides that strange feeling of completion, she felt nothing at all. Felt no surprise, no sorrow, no sense of loss. Nothing more seemed to have been taken from her— as if she were an inner-city storekeeper who'd been robbed in such swift succession that the second theft didn't matter.

She walked back to the kitchen, and opened the refrigerator to take out the peanut butter, whole wheat bread, and jar of blackberry jam. She put those on the counter by the stove, then opened the refrigerator again to get the milk. Barkley's sold only whole milk.

She took a knife from the counter drawer and began making her sandwich. Peanut butter first, on the left-hand slice. Jam would be on the other slice—and not too heavy on the jam, or it would sugar over the taste of the peanut butter. . . . She supposed she would have to consider her father not only dead, but burned to death—as Frank was not only dead, but drowned.

It seemed to Joanna, relaxed in emptiness, that there must be a fact, a truth hiding, that explained it all. And to discover that truth? To explore these odd coincidences—Frank's improbable blunders at sea, her cautious father's carelessness with his woodstove—to search beneath, to map that dark labyrinth . . . who better?

Chapter Five

The Lake Chaumette Fire Department—volunteer—had sent its captain, Milt Duffield, out to meet Joanna at the cabin site. The fire captain, large and lumpy in slacks, jacket, shirt and tie, and with a baby's chubby earnest face, had been waiting when Joanna pulled into the cabin clearing after half a day's traveling up from the island.

The sun threw long shadows while they walked around a very large square shallow pit filled with charred planks, chunks of debris, and fragments floating on black water. A bitter smell drifted up . . . wafting on the lake breeze.

"We pumped from the lake," the fireman said when Joanna asked about the water. "But way too late. It was goin' too good for us to do anything about it, except keep it from startin' up the woods."

"You didn't find my father. . . ."

"Found his bones," the fireman said. "Some of his bones."

It seemed to Joanna that Captain Duffield—volunteer or not—must have dealt with relatives of the dead before. He was calmly matter-of-fact, no comments or posturing about loss.

"And it was the woodstove?" The early evening was growing darker, with clouds reaching west, in from the sea.

"Yes, Mrs. Reed; it was. I knew your dad, just to see him at the store, and he was gettin' pretty old to be out here alone. Tendency is to get forgetful, careless, that age."

"My father was a very careful man."

"Guess not enough," Captain Duffield said, "to be out here by his lonesome."

Joanna was walking around the fire pit again, looking down into the dark water as if something of her father might still be under it. "This is the way he wanted to live."

"Oh, sure. We got a bunch of old folks out here."

"And it was just an accident? Absolutely just an accident. . . ."

"Didn' say that. We don't say accident till the insurance guys say accident—but the police were out here last night, an' Ted Lujack from Beaconsfield FD came out, too—an' he's an ace. Said it looked like a hot coal thing, which is what we think, too, and we see a lot of 'em. —Stove door was left open just a little bit, some coals rolled out on the floor, and that's all she wrote. Nighttime, so your dad would have been asleep." Duffield closed his eyes for an instant, leaned his head to the left to illustrate sleep.

"I see."

"He probably woke up, came out to deal with it, threw a little water on an' that was no use. People . . . people live right through the woods there, they called it in. —An' you know, most cases, there isn't much sufferin'. Fumes'll get you before the flames."

Joanna was across the pit from Duffield as he was talking. She wondered how many families had been told fumes got the person before the flames.

"Are you saying . . . and those people who live nearby . . . are you saying he just died and didn't suffer so terribly?"

Captain Duffield looked at her across the ruin. Joanna could see his reflection beneath him, in the black water. His reflection seemed to open its mouth to speak an instant before he did. "No, can't say that for sure, Mrs. Reed. Wish I could."

His reflection seemed to want to add something more . . . to warn her not to inquire further about suffering. About being burned to death, and crying out.

Joanna walked back around the edge of the pit, but didn't look into it anymore. ". . . And nothing strange, nothing unusual? My father wasn't senile, Mr. Duffield. He'd lived here, starting with summers, and heated with that stove for almost forty years."

"Yeah, but it only takes one mistake. You foolin' with fire, one mistake is all it takes."

"And nothing—nothing at all strange about this?"

"Only thing was a small pour pattern in the char, what had been a couple of floor planks—the width of that charcoal is what tells us they were floor planks. That's why I said he probably threw a little water on there. Any liquid'll pattern like that, a wet stain. It'll burn that pattern right into the wood, charred doesn' make any difference."

"A pour pattern. . . ."

"Yeah, something just spilled there, and not much. An' Ted thought maybe an accelerant, you know, your dad got up at night, tried to jump-start his fire with a little kerosene or whatever?"

"He would never, *never* do that."

"Well, you're right. He didn' do that. Ted had that wood looked at first thing this morning, just to cover the bases, and it definitely wasn't a regular accelerant. You got esters and oils and so forth in that kind of liquid—those products are real complicated—and there was no chemical residue at all in those planks. Whatever it was just evaporated away real quick an' clean, so it was probably water. We think your dad woke up, found the fire an' threw some water on it, an' that didn' do any good."

Mr. Duffield—Captain Duffield; she was meeting captains now . . . sea captains, fire captains—Captain Duffield made a graceful dismissive gesture with his right hand, showing how little good the water had done. "You know, small amount of water's not much use on an advanced pine-wood fire, you get old dry-cured lumber. The water hits an' you get a little pattern an' it effervesces an' it's gone."

"But something was poured on the fire."

"Right."

"—Something."

"Probably water."

"Could it have been anything else?"

"I guess . . . umm . . . lab alcohol wouldn' leave any residue. But I don't see why he would do that, Mrs. Reed."

Joanna tried to imagine her father in his flowered boxer shorts—Fruit of the Loom—standing sleepy and surprised. Pale, large, and lumbering, his body welted, softened, melted by time like candle wax, he poured an improbable small vase of water on a fire—a fire young, beautiful, full of ferocious energy, and growing.

Captain Duffield, apparently with other things to do, turned from the site and walked away toward their cars, his shoes making no sound on pine needles. Joanna hurried after him as if she had another question she must ask, though she couldn't think of it.

He heard her coming and stopped, waiting for her.

"My husband," she said, surprising herself. "My husband was killed—drowned—a little over two weeks ago. This is the second person in my family." She said that as if this sturdy, pleasant man might be the one to do something about it.

"Jesus," he said. "That's just terrible. . . ."

Wanda Dufour kept her offices in the Gertner—an elderly two-story brick building on Second Street. Chaumette, a shrinking town, now had only seven through streets. The others had gradually gone to lanes and dead ends on the south side, lined with shacks, mobile homes, and sheds. Past the tracks to the north, New England's pines and hemlocks had returned to vacant lots, a slow, steady triumph over the lumbermen who had seemed to conquer them through the last two centuries.

The Gertner was still a fully occupied structure. A small corner café, a shoemaker, and a beauty shop on the ground floor, real estate and lawyers' offices on the second.

Joanna parked on the dirt lot in back, then had to walk around to the building's front. The back entrance had been nailed over with plywood. —The reason, the door's broken glass, still lay scattered on the steps.

She went in the front entrance, and through a heavy odor of chemicals from the beauty shop. Permanents being done. . . . She climbed narrow creaking wooden stairs to the first landing, turned and climbed again. It was always a little surprising to notice how high the ceilings were in these old buildings. Even small rooms had ceilings twelve feet and higher, as if the nineteenth century had expected its children and grandchildren to become giants.

On the second floor, there was no sound, no sign of activity behind the first office doors—they had the sleepy look of locked. The last office, at the end of the short hall and overlooking the street, had *W. Dufour—Attorney at Law* in gilt paint on its door's frosted glass.

Sleigh bells jangled as Joanna walked in, and a stocky young woman in a white sleeveless blouse looked up from a desk. She was smiling, seemed happy to have company.

"Hi. —Can I help you?" She was a little too plump for the sleeveless blouse.

"I called. Joanna Reed."

"Oh, right. I'm Bobbie Munn; I was the one who talked with you. Ms. Dufour is in her office and you can go right up."

"Up?" Then Joanna saw three shallow steps leading to another level, and door, across the office. "Oh . . . thanks."

. . . Wanda Dufour was bent behind her desk, searching for something in a side drawer. Only a thinning French knot of yellow-white hair was visible, and a small rounded hump high on her narrow back. Despite summer, she was wearing a black Chanel suit—an original, by the worn slate its black had faded to—and now too big for her.

"Joanna?" A reedy voice from behind the desk. There was a minor liquid sound.

"Yes."

"Sit down, dear." There was no aging quaver to Wanda Dufour's voice. It stayed on its notes, but as very thin sound with a whistle to it. Something, Joanna thought, to do with her teeth. False teeth.

Wanda shut the drawer and sat suddenly up with a glass in her hand that seemed to hold scotch or bourbon. She stared as if Joanna might have changed—as Wanda had certainly changed. Joanna hadn't seen her in five or six years, and those must have been harsh years into Wanda's late seventies. Her face, that in her youth had been big-eyed, blue-eyed, soft and neat, *retroussée* as a Persian kitten's—and that had, even when Joanna last saw her, remained a worn, softer, but acceptable version—had now collapsed. It was a sick old Persian now, its face fallen, blotched and crumpled. The blue eyes, watery, squinted out.

"I know," Wanda said. "Don't say it. —But you, thanks to that Indian blood, are still looking very good. You'll look good when you're sixty."

"Oh, I'll probably get fat. . . ." Joanna sat in the only chair facing the desk—an elderly straw-bottom bentwood. "Wanda, I'm sorry I didn't get your phone call. Sorry you had to go through the college and so forth."

"Well, your father was a reluctantly aging man. He hated it, took it very personally. He could have made sure his attorney had his daughter's vacation phone number in case of an emergency—but he didn't."

"I went out to look at the cabin—"

"Funeral pyre," Wanda said, as if she were correcting her. "It looked like that, and it smelled like that, and that's what I call it." She took a careful sip of her drink.

"Yes. . . ."

"You know, Joanna, children never understand their parents at all—never know the real people they were. It's all Mommy-Daddy stuff, and believe me that's not the real person."

"I suppose that's true."

"For example—if you don't mind a little digression, a slight delay in our doing legal business—if you don't mind a little digression, I can tell you you never knew your father. . . . Hell, your mother didn't know him. She thought your father was exactly what he seemed, a local lawyer with a local practice and two terms, a long time ago, as district attorney." Wanda swayed very slightly in her chair.

"—Well, let me correct that incorrect impression. Louis was a deeply unhappy man all his life; that's why he was so snotty to everybody but you—and me, because I knew the man. Louis Bernard did not like being a lawyer—which I always have liked, by the way. He absolutely hated it; he started hating it in law school. You'll notice he didn't care to do even his own legal work. . . . Speaking of which, I suppose we better talk a little will-and-testament business." Wanda lifted her glass, but didn't drink from it.

"—By the way, did you know your father wanted a career in the military? Does that surprise you? He wanted to be an officer in the artillery, of all things. He had a book about a young man named Pelham. He had books on firing tables, for God's sake—you know, how to time explosive shells and drop them right on some poor dopes thirty miles away? Called a 'guy thing,' these days."

"I think I've heard of firing tables, but don't computers do that now?"

"Honey, how the hell do I know? All I know is, he wanted to be an officer in the artillery—and the man couldn't even get into the Korean thing when he was a kid. Not with that hockey knee."

"That's so strange. That's . . . that sounds so *odd*."

"Oh, I know how bizarre it sounds, because I laughed at him when he mentioned it. . . . That was thirty-four years ago, and he never mentioned it to me again. That's how smart I was. Oh, I was very smart with Louis Bernard. It's called throwing your life away with both hands." Wanda sipped. "Okay, and so to business. . . ."

"Daddy never said anything about it. He never mentioned it. Never *ever* mentioned going into the Army, or anything. . . ."

"Joanna, let me give you some advice about men—well, it's a

little late for either of us to be giving or taking that particular advice, I suppose. Still, let me give you some advice about men, which you may not be too old to take advantage of, once you're over these catastrophes." Wanda paused to sip again . . . appeared to lose her thought, and sat looking at Joanna as if wondering what she was doing there. A few moments almost restful.

Then, as if her worn machinery had slipped back into gear, Wanda blinked, and said, "My advice is, pay attention to what men *don't* mention. And what I mean by that is, no man is ever really satisfied with what he's doing. There's always something else he has wanted to do, so there is always some sadness and unhappiness there, and of course we assume it's a love problem and we're the centerpiece and it's all about us or some other woman. —Wrong." She put her glass firmly down on the desk blotter.

"Frank loved to sail. I suppose that's what he would really have liked—something to do with the sea."

"Well, there you are. Frank was in that gymnasium or whatever down at your college, or out on the fields blowing his whistle at some muscular young idiots. Now, do you really think that is what he dreamed of for his life?"

"I suppose not. But he seemed happy, Wanda." Joanna wished the old lady would stop drinking while they talked . . . at least change the subject from men's questionable happiness.

"Don't be silly—and we do have some business to do here, and we need to get to it—but don't be silly. Men usually seem happy. They're not like us, at least the good ones aren't. They may betray, they may beat us, they may leave. But they don't whine. Your father was not a whiner. . . ." Having said so much, Wanda seemed to need to catch her breath, and sat softly panting, very much an elderly cat, and ill.

"Are you all right?"

"Oh, don't be an ass, Joanna. How could I be all right? I'm an elderly woman and I'm alone and Louis is dead and I've been drinking . . . I am drinking. You are such a talent—and by the way, I read your last book and I was enormously impressed with those plant poems; I suppose you have to call them plant poems—"

" 'Xylem.' "

"Yes. You could have had a better title, not something so botanical, but still those poems were beautiful. *'Stems never knot, pause only to push out thorns along their way, then keep right on to break in blossoms.*

After that splitting, spraddling for bees, only their death surprises them. And not much.'"

"'And that not much.'"

"Right—that's right. 'And that not much.'. . . All too apropos. Anyway, those poems made me want to garden, which I have never done and have no wish to do—but a poet ought to know better than to ask me if I'm all right. Okay? —Now, regarding Louis's will. . . ."

"Wanda, I'm so sorry. I didn't know that you and Father were even seeing each other anymore."

"We weren't. I suppose he finally just couldn't stand me—maybe didn't care for the aging alcoholic routine, the physical wreckage I represented for him. He wouldn't even nod to me on the street, and we only met for our very minor business, since I'm his attorney. —Was his attorney, though he used other lawyers, too. . . . But let me tell you—as I'm sure you're discovering for yourself—they don't have to be with you, to be with you."

Joanna, struck as if she'd never considered that, was embarrassed to find herself putting her hands up to her face to cry.

"Oh, honey," Wanda said, piped in her old lady's voice . . . and Joanna forced her hands back down into her lap. Her eyes ached with tears that would not fall.

"Cried out?" Wanda said. "Me too." She picked up the glass, finished her drink, then reached down to pull out the side desk drawer and put the glass away. ". . . I just miss that old son of a bitch terribly. It just seems—I'll tell you this and then I'll shut up except for business. I'll just tell you this: Louis would have left your mother anyway. Your mother bored him stiff. She was a nice woman and that's all she was. It's all I was, too, but I could tell that Louis didn't *want* a nice woman. He wanted a troublesome woman to keep his mind off how wrong his life had gone." Wanda puffed her cheeks, blew gently in and out. Joanna smelled scotch's smoky odor.

"—So, I gave him trouble. It was very funny, in a way. There I was—and what I really wanted was for your father to marry me and give me a child and a pretty house to live in . . . and wait for him to come home and cook for him and all the common rest of it. Isn't that funny? . . . And I suppose one of the reasons he finally got sick of me was he realized I'd been faking being the bad girl for all those years. . . . Oh, I gave him hell. Scenes, and then I wouldn't talk to him for weeks at a time, and I'd go out with some fool so he'd see us in town. And then, if you'll pardon me for saying it, Joanna, I'd go back to him and screw his socks off."

Wanda sat for a moment with her eyes closed, resting, or remembering. "I suppose there was some anger there too, for his making me go through all that when I didn't want to. Because I didn't want to play that game at all. —But I was absolutely crazy about the man. He was the coldest, most unpleasant person—then he'd do something so sweet. So sweet. . . . Just open himself up like a book, and then he was helpless, helpless and at my mercy. It just killed me."

"I'm sorry, Wanda."

"*You're* sorry. . . ." Wanda sighed in her voice's high pitch. "—Well, that's enough travel down memory lane. And we do have *some* legal business to conduct." She opened a manila folder, took out a four-page document, and held it away to focus on. "Your father's will was in order, and I do not anticipate any problem with probate. No problem. As the only child, only surviving relative, you receive his real property, which is the cabin—now, the lake lot the cabin stood on. You will also receive, after probate and my fee, approximately thirty-three thousand dollars in cash, and a small portfolio of extremely mediocre stocks—Louis didn't believe in stock funds—and dubious corporate bonds."

"I see."

"Your father was not interested in investment strategy, and would not take advice." Wanda was sitting up straight now, alert while she dealt with business, professional matters.

"No surprise."

"No. . . . Your father did have some expenses that lowered his estate's value. There was a trust arrangement he undertook, and other expenses that are no part of his will—and legally speaking, are now none of our business."

"Trust arrangement. . . ."

"Through another attorney in town—a *man*. From what I understand, your father decided to give some anonymous support to an individual in need of it. Which support, *not* a lot of money, ended two years ago when the trust arrangement wound up. And—so that attorney assured me—involved nothing discreditable. In fact, apparently a generous thing to have done."

"And nothing I should know?"

"No, nothing you need to know, and nothing I know details *about.* Your father's business, old business, and over with."

"All right. . . . Is there anything I need to do?"

"Other than wait for probate—which shouldn't be delayed, at least not more than usual in this state—and to pay my fee when I bill you, no. As to taxes due on the estate—and they shouldn't be much—I'll let you know."

"Do I need to come up again?"

"No. I'll call you when it's through probate, and I'll send the papers down to White River."

"I'm out at Asconsett for the summer."

"You're staying out there?"

"Yes. For the summer. Forty-seven Slope Street."

"I have that address. College called back and gave it to me." Wanda picked up a three-by-five card, examined it, and put it down. "—Do you mind if I ask if you need money, Joanna? I mean, with Frank gone. If you need money, I could advance you a sum, personally."

"That's very nice of you, Wanda. No . . . no, I don't need money."

"You get a portion of Rebecca's tuition off as a faculty member?"

"Yes, a percentage. Which is why she's going to White River instead of over to Dartmouth—where she was accepted and where she'd dearly love to be going, because it's a campus where her *mother,* for God's sake, doesn't teach."

"I don't blame her. I would have considered it a nightmare to have my mother at my school."

"I don't blame her, either. But frankly, Wanda, she's a very young nineteen. Dartmouth is pretty fast-paced."

"Party school."

"That, too."

"And how is she handling Frank's death—do you mind if I ask?"

"No, I don't mind. It hit her very hard. I don't think even the possibility of such a loss had occurred to her, and it's . . . hit her very hard. We babied her. She was always carefully protected, and she loved Frank. Loved him even more than horses."

"Oh, dear."

"Yes. . . . I've been very worried about her. She couldn't wait—we couldn't wait to get away from each other."

"Reminders."

"Exactly right. Wanda, we remind each other about Frank. We see each other and say, "Where is *he*?"

"Of course. —What happened to your hands?"

"What? Oh . . . I've done some caving."

"They're cut."

"Some little cuts." Joanna got up to go, picked up her purse. "Thank you very much, Wanda, for being so helpful. . . . And if it makes any difference at all—though I hated you when I was a little girl, and wished you were dead—now I think my father was a fool not to have grabbed you and held on."

"That's sweet. . . . Oh, hell, who knows." Wanda stood up behind her desk, slightly unsteady, and supported herself with a hand on the desktop. "Probably wouldn't have worked out at all. And you've been very patient, listening to my boozy nonsense. . . ." She came around the desk, small and very thin, and stood tall to peck Joanna dryly on the cheek, leave a hint of scotch. "This getting-old thing is just sickening . . . *sickening*. It means there's no God; that's what makes it so sickening."

At the office door, the door already open, Joanna paused and closed it again. "Wanda, I don't . . . I don't really believe that Frank's death was an accident. I want you to know that. I want somebody to know that. —I don't believe it was an accident at all, because an accident out there required two things that Frank just didn't do. He always wore his life jacket—*always*. And he did *not* fall out of boats—particularly in calm seas and good weather. I just want you—"

"Honey . . . honey." Wanda stared up at her, an elderly cat, startled. "—But that's why they *call* them accidents."

"I know . . . I know. I've already been given that line."

"Well . . . God. Well, let me ask you, Joanna, aside from the pain of it, the loss just because of something stupid, what reason would there be for anyone to do such a thing? Who would benefit . . . ?"

"I don't know."

"Did you go to the police?"

"Yes."

"And they said . . . ?"

"They said they see odd accidents at sea all the time—and no one would benefit in Frank's case, and besides, they checked it out."

"And nothing?"

"And nothing."

"Honey, it's easy for me to say, but I'll say it anyway. A loss is a loss." Wanda, unsteady, went back to her desk and sat down. "You don't want to be imagining it even worse than it was."

"Wanda, I have to tell you I think exactly the same about Louis's death. —I don't believe he ever in his life went to bed and left a stove door open with a fire burning in it. That is the last thing my father would ever have done."

"Louis was almost eighty, Joanna." Wanda seemed weary, shrunken behind her desk.

"I don't give a damn! Do you believe it?"

"I have to believe it, honey, because it happened."

"—And did you know that the firemen found a stain burned into the floorboards? They thought maybe Daddy put kerosene on the fire to restart it."

"Never."

"That's right. —Never. Then they said it wasn't an accelerant, at least not kerosene or gas. It was something that disappeared in the heat. They think he may have thrown some water on the fire."

"Oh, dear. . . ."

"I'm sorry, Wanda; I shouldn't even have mentioned this to you. I know it sounds ridiculous."

"No, it's just one more thing. . . . But Joanna, you know there's nothing *to* it. Because of just what the police told you. No one bene-fited from Frank's death—and sure as heck no one benefits from Louis's. You're the only beneficiary in each case, and for peanuts. So why? Why would anyone do such a thing?"

"I don't know."

"—Because there is no reason. Have you mentioned any of this to Rebecca?"

"No, not yet."

"Well, Joanna, please don't do that."

"I don't want to, but we're talking about her father. Hers—and now mine."

"Oh, God. . . ."

"But I'm sorry I troubled you with it." Joanna opened the office door again. "—Maybe I am just being stupid. Maybe I've lost too much, too quickly. . . ."

"I'd say that's probably so."

"Well . . . bye-bye."

"Bye-bye. . . ."

As she left the office, closing the door behind her, Joanna heard Wanda's desk drawer slide open.

The plump girl looked up from her keyboard and mouthed, spoke softly. "Is she okay . . . ?"

"I think so."

The girl shook her head. "I'm really worried about her," she said, barely above a whisper.

Chapter Six

Joanna went out to the island on the late-evening ferry. She sat in the cabin for the trip—not yet ready, she supposed, to see a lot of Atlantic Ocean.

They were mainly older people in the cabin, going out to the islands. Oteague, first. Then Parkers Island. Then Shell, then Asconsett. Older people, looking tired and staying in the cabin, perhaps also not ready to see more ocean.

The rhythmic grumbling of the ferry's engine, its vibration through the bench's weather-faded oak, were soothing ... so Joanna sat with her eyes closed and tried to think of nothing, tried to think of no loss at all. —She thought of an empty space where nothing was, nothing had ever been, so nothing and no one could be missing from it. It would be pearl gray, a space with no horizon, a room with no walls, a room of emptiness. . . .

Such a pleasant place to be. Heaven, she supposed, might be a perfect vacancy. —Only its gray was bound to become darker, shade to black as loneliness grew to fill it. Heaven becoming hell, she supposed, and perhaps that simple.

She sat relaxed, drifting almost to sleep. What vibrations soothed travelers before the internal combustion engine? Steam engines ... trains, of course. And before that, the less reliable beat of horses' hooves. Men and women pulled by horses, carried by horses, plowing with horses ... depending on those innocents for all civilization. And betting on their speed.

Even now, it seemed to her, people had what they had from foundations built by the sweat of horses. Their hoofbeats should echo in human hearts. But what statues had been placed in their honor? What horse-named streets and counties? What volumes of poetry . . . ?

The ferry came in fourteen minutes late, delayed by crosscurrents. Joanna drove off its ramp, along Bollard to Strand, then up Slope Street to the cottage as a crescent moon rose over ocean.

. . . She carefully thought only of horses, then tomato soup, tea, and toast. She did the dishes, then went upstairs, undressed, and took a shower—where other thoughts, memories crept in. She couldn't keep them out. They waited in the bedroom closet among Frank's summer clothes—time and past time to go through them, give them away.

The memories were there, hanging among seersucker sports jackets and slacks, a summer suit—light blue—and several pairs of jeans. His shoes, old Top-Siders, sneakers, and a pair of soccer shoes—for what, out here on the island? Why had he packed soccer shoes? Why did men do the things they do? . . . What sweet confusion in their minds obscured practicality? What different determination vaulted instead to inventions, to change, to long-term plans, to organization and the hunt? To possibly useful war? —It was odd that men and women could live together at all, and bear, long-term, such difference. Her father—wanting to be an artillery officer, of all strange things! And Frank . . . what had Frank wanted that he never had?

Joanna took off her robe, and looked at herself in the closet door's long mirror. It seemed to her she didn't look quite as she had even a few weeks ago. Her breast didn't appear perfectly the same—it seemed slightly smaller, shrunken, as if it were winter fruit, shriveled in storage . . . no longer a perfect match for the prosthesis. And her belly looked softer . . . her legs thinner, muscle showing wiry under the skin.

Death, coming once and then again, had touched her with age, lightly, as it passed by.

Joanna looked at her face in the mirror, saw concern there, shadowed by the closet's single bulb, and certainly the commencement of an older woman's face, a face from which youth's innocence was gone. A face that once suggested by her mirror, even hinted at, would become inevitable.

. . . Tired, of course. She was still tired from the cave. More tired from losing Frank, and now her father. —And certainly, even now, many men would find her pretty, a few find her beautiful if they liked slender older women with strong bones, black hair, and long-nosed Indian faces. But there was, behind her reflection, now a magisterial judgment only barely seen, but announcing the coming of age . . . to be in time more real than any sorrow.

Joanna peed, turned off the lights, and went to bed. Bed, the vault of memory. This summer bed, like all their beds, held history of every warmth, sound, and scent of sleep together, the companionable farts, the kisses, hard words and bitter silences, the effortful sounds, exercise, and oily odors of fucking—once grunting, moaning, then calling out to begin Rebecca.

In these soft vaults lay recollection. And no escaping it in dreams.

Joanna woke . . . then woke completely to breaking glass. Glass breaking, downstairs.

She'd heard it, but wasn't sure she'd heard it, and sat up in bed to listen. She already knew better than to put her left hand out to wake Frank. She'd learned better than that in only a few days.

More glass broke below, with a musical small crack and tinkle as pieces hit the floor. Something struck the back door . . . kitchen door.

There were tough boys, tough men, on the island. She'd seen them at Poppy's, downtown, when their boats were in . . . or when their boats were sold, and never going out again. Bored men lounging, staring at her and Rebecca once from the long bar, when they'd gone in to order fish and chips to go. Bearded young men, rope-muscled, tattooed, and perfect for piracy, if that were still possible.

And she was here alone—and of course everyone knew it. She was here alone, with only memories to keep drunken boys from her.

Something hit the back door again—harder—and Joanna got out of bed. She didn't want to turn on the lights, didn't want to see something bad. She put on her robe, and stood in the bedroom listening, hoping they would go away. Frank's shotgun, his revolver, were locked in the storage closet in the house at White River. There was nothing upstairs in the cottage to hurt anyone with, nothing to make them leave her alone.

It was too frightening to wait. Joanna went barefoot to the head of the stairs, then down several steps and paused, listening. The phone was in the entrance hall. . . . Moonlight cast banister shadows down the staircase wall. She could hear the sea wind, the ocean's distant conversation, and recalled her dream of Frank swept back to her by the sea.

A man called out, shouting in the backyard—something she couldn't understand. Shouted again, and hit the kitchen door. A stranger's voice, slurred and hissing.

But not Frank's voice—and Joanna, ashamed to feel relief, was no longer as afraid of the living. She went through the entrance hall and on back to the kitchen. Moonlight glittered on glass along the floor. The door's window had been smashed.

Careful of the glass near her bare feet, she crossed to the counter drawer, took out a filleting knife, then went to the other window and saw no one standing in moonlight on the back steps. No one in the yard. . . . If not for the cool sea breeze drafting through the damaged door, she might have dreamed it all.

Stepping around bright shards and bits of glass, she turned the kitchen lights on, and saw a minor spatter down the inside of the door, drops of fresh rich red against the white paneling. Whoever it was had cut himself reaching in for the dead bolt. Broke the door window, tried to get in, cut himself, and was gone.

Joanna got the broom and dustpan from the narrow mop closet, and carefully swept to pick up all the glass. She paid attention to what she was doing, close attention so as not to have to wonder who had tried to come in . . . and shouted, furious, when he was hurt.

She could have thought about that, but decided not to. It was one thing too many to think about—as if her world might tilt and turn over from the weight of additional trouble.

—And if she called the police now, other loud men would come. They'd park by the cottage with their lights going, and come into the house and talk and walk around and make her think of everything, try to make sense of it, when she was just too tired. Morning would be time enough. . . .

When she was finished cleaning, had checked the floor carefully for any glass sparkling, Joanna picked up her knife, turned off the kitchen lights, and went up the stairs, exhausted. She was tired as she'd been in the cave's close chimney, that tried so hard to hold her—as if that darkness, silence, and emptiness, weary of millions of years alone, had wanted her to stay.

She went into the bedroom and closed the door. There was no lock. She brought the ladder-back chair from the corner to tilt and wedge against the knob, then she put her knife on the lamp table and climbed into bed, grateful for a summer night cool enough for covers, a small and softer cave to rest in.

The phone woke her to a sunny morning.

Joanna got up, tugged the chair out from under the doorknob, and put on her robe as she went down the stairs.

"Mom?" A teary voice.

"Hi, sweetheart. I was going to call you this morning."

"I called yesterday, but you weren't there."

"I went up to Chaumette."

"Mom—what happened? What's *happening*—these terrible things!"

"I know. I know. . . . They think it was an accident, that Grandpa was careless with the woodstove. They don't think he suffered."

"Oh, that's just such bullshit! Didn't *suffer?*"

"Well, Rebecca, they may be right."

"—In a fire?"

"I know. I know. . . ."

"And he was just careless with that woodstove?"

"That's what they think. . . . But I have to tell you, sweetheart, I really don't believe it."

"You don't—"

"I don't believe it. Louis Bernard was not careless—just the reverse, he was an obsessive pain in the butt."

"No, he wasn't careless, Mom. —But I don't understand. What was it, if it wasn't an accident? Why would anybody hurt Grandpa?"

"I don't know, sweetheart. —And I could be wrong, absolutely wrong. Wanda thinks I'm crazy."

"But it doesn't make any *sense*. Why would anybody want to do that?"

"I don't know, Rebecca . . . but I think I should tell you, I don't believe what happened to your father was an accident, either."

"What? Mom, I don't understand. . . ."

"I think neither was an accident." And having said so much, she decided not to mention the broken window, the shouting man.

"But nobody would hurt Daddy. He had an accident on the boat!"

"Maybe he did. —And maybe your grandpa had an accident, too, just a couple of weeks later. But I don't believe it."

"Does anybody say that? Does anybody else say that?"

"No. They don't."

"Mom—oh, Mom, please don't be crazy. *Please* don't do that! We're all that's left. It's just the two of us!" Crying . . . crying now.

"I know, darling. Don't be afraid. . . ." Was there ever an end to this caring for a child? This need to guard her? What turned in a woman's brain to leave this black egg of worry in her head for a child old enough now to have children of her own? It was a god-damn bore, and there was no end to it.

"Mom, I *am* afraid. Everything terrible is happening. . . ."

"Rebecca, there's something I want you to do. Will you do something for me?"

"What—what do you mean?" Sniffling. Needed to blow her nose. . . .

"I want you to be careful, Rebecca."

"Mom—"

"I want you to be careful! Is that too much to ask?"

"No. . . ." Sullen little-girl's voice.

"Then do it. Do it for me. Don't go out with some boy you don't know very, very well. Do you understand? Don't . . . don't take chances, Rebecca, just in case I'm right, just in case I'm *not* crazy."

"Mom, please—"

"Goddammit, will you just do what I ask? Two members of our family, half our family. . . . Your father is dead! My father is dead! Two men who were very careful and knew what they were doing and did it for years are dead, one right after the other! And suppos-edly ridiculous accidents—and I don't fucking *believe* it!"

"Mom—"

"So, just in case your mother is not going mad, will you please, *please* do as I ask and be careful!"

"Okay, I will. I'll be careful, Mom."

"Sweetheart, I know it sounds weird. And I could absolutely just be . . . be shell-shocked. I could be completely mistaken. I try to convince myself I am. I tried that—and I just can't believe it."

"Mom, I said I'll be careful."

"Thank you. That's all I want. Just . . . you know, cautious. Be cautious."

"Is there going to be a service? Are we going up to Chaumette?"

"No, I don't think so. Grandpa pretty much—he really was just gone, disappeared in the fire. And except for Wanda, there isn't anybody still up there who was a close friend. His best friends were Elise Brady and Edward and his brother . . . and Elise and Edward are gone. So, there's really no reason to go up."

"All right."

"Also, Rebecca, I've had all the memorial service I want to attend for a while."

"I know. I just . . . it's so hard to understand."

"Sweetheart, I know it's hard to understand."

"Well . . . listen, people keep asking me for your number out there, Mom. You know, they call me at the dorm? A lot of people have phoned—Francie, and Brian called, too."

"Rebecca, I don't want a lot of people calling me out here. I don't want to have to talk to anyone. So don't give them my number."

"Not even Francie? She called me from New York four times."

"Nobody. I just . . . I just don't want to hear from people about Frank or my father. I don't want to hear any of that yet."

"Well . . . I understand."

"So—so, what's new at school? Did you have your Spanish exam?"

"Mom, exams aren't until next month."

"Right. That's right."

"I'll do fine. Charis is helping with my Spanish, and I don't have any problems with math at all."

"All right. I can't tell you how sorry I am, sweetheart. All this . . . all this loss. Your daddy loved you very much. Did you know, when you were a little girl—do you know how jealous I was of you sometimes? He loved you so much, I was just part of the furniture."

"Oh, sure. That'll be the day."

"No, it's true. And you're young—you're still very young to have lost your father."

"I think so. I think so . . . but we both lost him."

"Yes. So—you'll be careful?"

"Yes, I will."

"No accidents. No more accidents, Rebecca. —And if they were something else . . . just be cautious. Don't be so trusting. It's okay to say 'no' to people, Becky. It's okay to just say, 'No, thanks,' if it feels wrong to you."

"Mom, I understand. You know, I'm really not a baby."

"I know, and I wish you were. If you were small enough, you'd be in a carrier on my back and there damn well wouldn't be any more accidents."

"Mom, you're too much."

"Well, it's true."

"Mom . . . you know, it is possible—I mean it's most likely that

Daddy and Grandpa had accidents, that that's all those things were."

"I know. I know that, sweetheart. I know that's possible. . . ."

The constable's outer office was bright with morning light, its white-painted wood looking sea-washed in summer air. A deputy, neat in starched khaki behind a gray steel desk, looked like a boy—too young, too slender in his uniform to be a policeman. He observed Joanna with the disinterest of the young in anyone much older—and this despite her careful dressing.

No dark suit today. Instead, summer casual in a foam-green print dress, showing some leg for that icy old man—still good enough legs. The impression intended to be of a sensible, attractive, and determined widow who had now accepted summer—not of a snotty mainland business-suited pain in the ass.

And all wasted on this very young policeman—almost young enough to be her son. A good-looking boy, brown eyes and carefully cut thick red-brown hair—run-your-fingers-through-it hair for some pleased girl. *J. Spruel* was engraved on a small steel nameplate pinned to his right breast pocket.

"Mrs. Reed, the chief is off-island this morning, and I have no idea when he's going to be in. If you want to leave a message for him, I'll take that."

"All right, I will leave a message for him."

The young cop sat politely receptive.

"Are you going to write this down?"

"Oh . . . yes, ma'am." He took a pencil and yellow legal pad from the desk drawer.

" 'To the chief constable: To remind you, my husband was drowned in a dubious accident over two weeks ago. Now—' Have you got that?"

". . . Yes, ma'am." A left-handed writer, his hand cramped on the paper.

" 'Now . . . night before last, my father was burned alive in his cabin upstate, at Lake Chaumette. A second *very* dubious accident.' "

The young policeman looked up at the news of Louis's burning, giving Joanna a moment of real attention—also glancing at her breasts. She had become someone.

"—Do you have that?"

". . . Yes."

"Okay. Then take this down: '*Last* night, someone—a man—

tried to break into my cottage while I was asleep upstairs. He smashed the kitchen-door window, I suppose to reach the dead bolt—and he cut himself when he did."

The young policeman was scribbling away. A crime, at last.

"—There's a little blood down the inside of my kitchen door. I cleaned up the glass last night, but I left the blood."

Officer Spruel looked up from his legal pad. "How did you know it was a man did it?"

"Because he yelled something, I suppose when he cut himself, and I heard him upstairs."

"Why didn't you call it in?"

"Because he was gone when I came downstairs—and I'd had enough shit for one night."

Spruel seemed slightly uncomfortable with an older woman in a summer dress saying "shit." Apparently a nice old-fashioned island boy, behind the times.

"So, Mrs. Reed, you're making this report now. . . ." He drew a line under his notes.

"You bet. This report, and my father's burning to death. —And I think I'll report my husband's death again, too, since that hasn't been taken very seriously out here. . . . Supposedly he took his life jacket off—which he never did—and then jumped out of his goddamn boat into the ocean!" Joanna felt herself getting angrier and angrier, but it was important not to become some crazy in a green dress. . . .

The boy kept his head down, probably worried about a scene— a furious woman shouting, yelling. Voice carrying right out the windows.

"And that," Joanna said, "is my report. Now, my suggestion . . . my suggestion is, that the chief constable get off his ass and check into my husband's death *again*—and my *father's* death—and my *break-in* last night, just in case they weren't three fucking accidents in two weeks after all!" . . . Language and temper. Control that temper.

The boy's head was still down, concentrating on the legal pad. Probably hoped the worst was over, all the bad language.

It seemed to Joanna that the light . . . the white sunshine light in the office was unpleasant. Nothing could be hidden in it. "—The worst *is* over," she said, as though the deputy had complained aloud. "I apologize for my behavior, for getting so angry. I didn't mean to embarrass you. I just . . . I suppose I'm just desperate. And

I also know I could be making a complete fool of myself and I'm very sorry." She felt so restless, tired of standing still to talk—as if she might say it all more clearly if she were moving. "—But, Officer, doesn't it seem strange to you? These things happening? And I'm very worried about my daughter, even though there isn't any reason for anyone to do any of this! I'm worried because there *isn't* any goddamn reason." She ran out of breath, stopped talking. Her heart was beating as if she'd been running in place.

"Well, sure looks like somebody did something last night." The young policeman finished writing, put down his pencil. It rolled toward the desk edge, and he stopped it. "Uneven legs," he said, "—couple of glides are missing." He aligned the pencil at the side of his legal pad. "Chief'll get this, and somebody'll go up today, take a look at the damage, check around. You're in that blue house top of Slope, is that right? Light-blue house?"

"Yes, I am."

"College professor. . . ."

"Yes."

"Chief says you write poetry."

"Yes, I do."

The boy sat thoughtful in his perfect uniform, digesting that oddity. "And the window was broken out?"

"Yes, and part of the frame."

"Tell you what, Mrs. Reed: I'll call Mrs. Peterson tonight; her kid Jerry does glazing and stuff. Jerry's okay, and he'll come over tomorrow, cut some glass, and put that frame back together for you. Probably cost maybe thirty, thirty-five bucks."

"Thank you."

"You have Jackson Fix-Up do it, they'll charge you fifty. Summer people get billed pretty good out here."

"Thank you very much. And I apologize."

"No need. Everybody's real sorry about your husband. —Didn't know about your dad, and now this guy last night. I'll tell you what, we'll have a deputy go by this evening, and tomorrow evening, keep an eye on the house."

"Thank you, I'd appreciate that. . . . But as far as what I said, I meant every word."

"I understand. —And I'll give it to the chief just exactly like you said it."

"I don't want to get you into trouble."

"Can't get me in too much trouble. Married to his grand-daughter. . . ."

Joanna walked down Strand Street, her body feeling happy as she did not—bone, muscle, and skin pleased with striding in sunlight and warmth, her dress hem breezing, curling around her legs. Her body, like a foolish and amiable dog, pleased with only going for a walk . . . looking around, breathing the scents of summer.

Tourists were drifting along, pausing just ahead of her to look into Scrimshaw's window at small models of sailing ships and fishing boats, wooden whales and dolphins, rope knots, and little boxes carved from wood, soapstone, old ivory, or—more authentic, much more expensive—carved and polished dried salt beef as hard and rich in color as cherry wood.

Frank had bought her one of those salt beef boxes, the first few days on the island. "Get hungry enough, we can soak it for a sandwich. . . ." He'd stood in the cottage kitchen, smiling, pleased by her pleasure in the odd little thing.

She'd put her earrings in it. . . .

Walking along, Joanna could, by listening carefully in imagination, hear her father's footsteps coming up the sunny sidewalk behind her—his long, heavy, deliberate stride of years ago. His had been a sort of military way of walking, she supposed. . . . The poor man, a small-town lawyer with knees damaged by youthful hockey. What caissons must have rolled through his dreams, what flashes of nighttime gunfire. What long thunder behind the hills where his army lay. . . .

Frank had moved quite differently, ambling along in an athlete's easy collected gait. —Who knew, what woman could know that just to see her men move, to see them walking, was a privilege to be withdrawn, and never enjoyed again.

Her father's footsteps sounding behind her, with Frank's footsteps now—but only as long as she didn't turn to see. Then they would be gone, and she bleaching to the pillar of salt that women became, looking back in regret for a past irrecoverable. . . . What woman did not taste that sea salt on her tongue?

—But if she didn't turn, and if she closed her eyes, Frank and her father both might come to walk beside her, stroll along, dance around her in dear awkward passages. . . . How sensible for the mad to speak in the street to those they saw, though unseen by others. Why not speak to friends invisible?

And if she had the faith to begin dancing herself, to whirl and whirl, dancing with her lost men along this ordinary sidewalk in ordinary sunshine—stepping, spinning, weaving through startled tourists—would motion that eccentric settle them to stay? Why should she pay attention only to the living? What good were they? What comfort?

How easy it would be to go quietly mad, if that would bring her husband to her . . . bring her father back. Madness seemed a small price to pay for loving company.

Joanna walked, and disliked the strangers walking past, most blind to what catastrophe awaited them—perhaps at the next corner, perhaps further on. Until that event, what did she and they hold in common? She was torn, and they were not. It was she who'd been reminded of the fragility of happiness. . . .

At Barkley's, she went in and was oddly soothed by stands of vegetables, shelves of canned goods, and in the back, the meat case's wide chill white. . . . Prices were really outrageous, way too high to be explained by transport from the mainland. Summer prices, was what they were. —You could forget asparagus. Forget any citrus except seedy little oranges and bruised lemons.

Had mangoes though, which she hadn't seen in the store before. Where Barkley had found fairly ripe mangoes for a dollar each was a mystery. Probably fell off a hijacked truck down in Providence. . . . Blueberries; Frank had loved them. Five dollars a box— and no need to buy them, now. . . . The meat was pretty good, not too out of line, not quite highway robbery. And almost always good pork chops—very good pork chops today. Fish, of course, really excellent out here. . . .

Joanna bought too much for one person, not quite enough for two. She gave Hanna Barkley a check for the groceries—waited while the check was examined—then hugged the heavy paper bag like a baby, and lugged it down Strand Street to the car. . . . Her imagined men, bored with shopping, had left her.

. . . At the cottage, she parked in the street, not wanting to see the broken back window again, and went up the front steps and through the door, grocery sack in her left arm. She put her purse on the telephone table, closed the door, and was walking down the hall when she heard two sounds. *Tock . . . tock.* Wooden sounds from the kitchen, as if someone had put something—two somethings—down.

She stood in the hall, listening. . . . It couldn't be Mrs. Peterson's boy, Jerry. He wouldn't have been called yet.

Nothing more from the kitchen for almost a minute. . . . Then a sliding sound in there, a long soft hushing. Whoever it was, hadn't heard her come in.

—But if she turned and ran back up the hall, whoever it was would hear that. They'd hear it and come fast from the kitchen and into the hall after her . . . come rushing, rushing while she stumbled in high heels, spilling groceries, trying to reach the front door.

To have someone . . . to have sudden trouble in daytime, in this bright and sunny light, seemed much worse than trouble at night. What happened would be so clear, too clearly seen . . . whatever was done to her.

She could call out, say, "I was just down at the police station! They're sending someone right now!" She could do that. She could do that. . . .

Joanna took a careful backward step. It seemed a loud step. She listened, and heard nothing.

So stupid. A woman in a summer dress, standing alone with her groceries in the hall. A woman—a widow; the word was her word now—a widow with ice cream melting in her grocery sack. Two pints of Häagen-Dazs, expensive. . . .

Joanna imagined herself running, screaming for help, to the front door. She imagined that and couldn't bring herself to do it. She felt too tired to do it.

She said, "Hello?"—and heard a man in her kitchen. A man unmistakable, that low discontented grumble. And something was put down with a thump.

"*Pain in the ass,*" he said, and Joanna knew that tone, the familiar complaint of a man annoyed by a task. It was only a man working . . . doing something in her kitchen.

"Hello . . . ?" She walked down the hall, and saw a man with red-rimmed eyes squatting on her kitchen floor.

Chapter Seven

Name's Moffit. . . ." The man stared up at her, eyes bloodshot, his face darkly veiled and streaked with dirt. "—Just fixin' your window, here. Bought this glass out of my own pocket, since I was the one busted it to begin with." Said in the down-east accent of the island, an accent dulled by alcohol, or its damage. He heaved up, got to his feet to face her.

Joanna stepped back. "You get *out* of here!"

"Said it was my fault. . . ."

"You just get out of here!"

"I come up to fix it, that's all." The man's eyes were a blurred avoiding brown. An odor of spoiled sweat drifted off him.

". . . You broke my window, scared the hell out of me—and now you come mumbling up here to fix it?"

"Yes, ma'am."

"You can pick up that glass and stuff and just get out of here. You understand? *Out.* —You can tell the police all about it, Mr. . . ."

"Moffit."

"Mr. Moffit."

"Well, ma'am, that's what I'm askin', for you not to call those people." Moffit swayed slightly back and forth, like a circus bear.

Joanna saw he was drunk, at least a little. She was meeting with captains and drunks. . . .

"—I'm askin' you not to do that, because I'm goin' to fix this little window up just fine, an' I'm real sorry if I scared you. I bought this window glass out of my own pocket. Nine dollars an' thirty cents."

"I don't care if you're sorry, Mr. Moffit."

"Wouldn' have done it if I wasn' drinkin'. Liquor was doin' it, not me. . . . Saw you down at Mannin's."

" 'Mannin's'—I don't know what you're talking about." Joanna's left arm was aching. She put the grocery bag down on the kitchen counter.

"Mannin's fish processin'."

"Manning's?"

"That's right, saw you down there the other day."

Joanna thought she remembered him now, outside the machine room—a grimy specter with a mop and rolling bucket. "Just, please . . . Mr. Moffit, just get this stuff together and get out of here."

"—Heard you down there, askin' about your husban' an' that *Bo-Peep* boat. Worked on that boat myself; worked on her more'n once. Good wood in that boat. . . ."

"Would you please leave? Right *now*." Moffit's odor was making her feel a little ill. And there was a faint smell of urine.

"Don't blame you a bit, Mrs. Reed. Wouldn' want me in my house neither. That's what you earn—drinkin' earns contempt. I been told that many times, and it's right." Moffit suddenly sat down on the kitchen floor again, began fiddling with two short, thin, unpainted sticks, and small squares of glass. His hands were black with dirt.

"A police officer is coming up here."

"I guess I don't mind," Moffit said, bent over his material as if it were a jigsaw puzzle. "—I get in trouble, it'll be because I deserve it. Long ago gave up blamin' anybody but me for my own misfortune. Mark of bein' an adult." He raised his head, looked around the kitchen. "You have any glue—wood glue? Needs to be good glue."

"No, I don't' have any glue, and I want you to get up and go!"

Mr. Moffit picked up one of his paper bags, opened it and looked inside. "Here we are. I got the glue . . . got all this stuff together. Never mind about the glue."

"All right. Okay. . . . A police officer is coming up here. If you want to go to jail, you can damn well go to jail."

Mr. Moffit nodded, sat bent over, piecing broken sticks of framing together on the floor.

Joanna started out of the kitchen, then turned and came back in. "Why did you come up here?"

"Fix this window I broke, drinkin'."

"I mean, why did you come up here last *night?*"

". . . Had business. I'll tell you, I hate to ask, Mrs. Reed. I'm—I'll tell the truth; I'm a poison alcoholic but I haven't had a drink since this mornin'. I'm short of cash is what the truth is."

"You want me to give you *money?*"

"I sure do." He picked up a square of window glass and looked at her through it, apparently confirming its transparency. "I cashed my month's check to buy the glass an' glue an' compound. Charlie Marks kept just about every bit of that check. I rent over his garage. But I spent almost fifteen dollars of that money on glass an' glue an' stuff. So, if you could give me that back . . ." He made a child's grimace of distaste. "—Sure hate to ask."

He had the wooden pieces of broken window almost reassembled on the linoleum. ". . . Need it for breakfast. I eat a regular breakfast every day. Scrambled eggs an' toast. No matter what, I have that." He took a plastic bottle of glue out of his shopping bag, pried at its tiny cap with mottled trembling fingers.

"Why in the world should I give you money, Mr. Moffit?"

"Bobby's okay."

". . . Bobby, I don't know you, and I don't want you in my house—I'd like you to get out of my house right now. I already have someone coming to repair the window."

"Charge you an arm an' a leg." Bobby Moffit got the cap off the glue bottle, bent to apply careful drops to a break in a slender crosspiece. "Busted muntin." More drops of glue. "—Nobody'd want to sniff this stuff . . . got no kick to it."

"Right. Will you *leave?*"

Moffit paused in applying glue. ". . . Okay. I'll go, and you have a promise I won't bother you anymore."

"Fine. Good-bye, Bobby."

He recapped the glue with some difficulty, put it down, and hauled himself up to his feet. ". . . Why I came up last night is I heard you askin' about the *Bo-Peep*—down at Mannin's? I was cleanin' up; I clean up down there. I'm the mop man. An' it's a shame to say so, but I was hopin' for money out of it."

"Money? Money out of what?"

"Out of me seein' her when she went out."

"Seeing her . . . ?"

"That *Bo-Peep* boat."

"Are you—you saw my husband that morning?"

"Darn tootin'. Handled her pretty good, too. Not exactly right;

he kept her too close, you know. Fat little boat like that, you got to give her some ease off the tiller or she'll walla'. . . . Hoped there was some money in it, I'm ashamed to say. Takin' advantage of you, was what I figured to do. Last person saw him alive, I'll bet. . . ."

"You saw him in the morning? And it was that *day*?" Joanna pulled a chair out from the kitchen table and sat down. "—You're sure it was the day he died?"

"Could I ask you again could you give me just a little money? An' I'll tell you, it kills me to ask it. It just kills me, but I lost my pride."

"I'll—I suppose I could give you something, but how do I know you saw Frank that day? How do I *know* that?"

"Lady, I do lie, but I'm not lyin' now. Ain't so far gone I don't remember a day a man drowns out there an' don't come back. Had a calm sea an' a south-southwest breeze blowing maybe four, five knots. That was that day. . . . An' your husband was carryin' a beer cooler, too. Blue beer cooler. An' when he sailed out in the bay, he had a boy in the boat with him. Must have took him off that lease dock."

". . . Are you—are you saying there was someone *with* my husband? With him the day he drowned?"

"Darn tootin'. Some kid wearin' a baseball cap. Red cap. Too far to make out who. Some tourist kid, I guess, because I ain't heard no island lady missin' one. . . . Your man was up trimmin' sail. Kid was just sittin' on his ass wearin' that cap. Young people these days don't work at nothin' they can help."

Joanna's heart seemed to accelerate to some music too faint for her to hear. "You . . . Bobby, you didn't tell this to the police?"

"Didn' ask me—an' they wouldn' give me any help with my rent, neither. Wouldn' help *me* with groceries—"

"For Christ's sake . . . !"

"Wouldn' believe me, anyway. Figure I was just shittin' 'em, wantin' some money. Wouldn' give me any."

Joanna got up, left Bobby Moffit standing, went to the entrance hall and called 911.

A quick answer—*"Nine-one-one Island Emergency. Police."* The young policeman; she recognized his voice.

"Officer Spruel?"

"Yes."

"This is Mrs. Reed—"

"Right. You okay?"

"I'm fine. I'm just calling to let you know that . . . that a neighbor has come over. He's fixing the window for me, and I wanted to let you know you don't have to send Jerry—Jerry Peterson—to do it."

"Okay, Mrs. Reed, I'll cancel that."

"But I do appreciate your help."

"No problem. One of our people will be up pretty soon to take a look at the scene. I'd leave that blood alone up there—blood on your door?"

"I will. I haven't touched it."

Joanna hung up and walked back into the kitchen. Bobby Moffit was down on the floor again, sitting cross-legged on the linoleum, muttering over another join . . . squeezing out wood glue.

"A police officer is going to be coming up," Joanna said. Bobby paid no attention. He got his angle to fit—difficult, with the steady tremor in his hands—then fixed the join to cure with a small red-handled spring clamp.

"I brought this clamp with me. . . . I didn' take nothing out of your kitchen."

"That's all right."

"Everything I need, I brought right up here myself. Clamp's Charlie's, out of his shop. . . . Real lucky, window wasn' double-hung. Just fixed in the frame."

"Bobby, would you . . . would you tell the police, the chief constable, what you told me?"

He looked up at her. "Well . . . if I did, could you help me with some money? I hate to ask, I really do, but even ten bucks would take the pressure off. An' if you could go for twenty dollars, you'd have made an unfortunate and weak person very happy. I admit the weakness there."

"Mr. Moffit—"

"Bobby's okay."

"Bobby, if you will just tell the police what you told me, I'll . . . tell you what: I'll pay your rent. I'll help you any way I can. I promise that. I promise you!"

". . . You know, even ten dollars cash would really help me out. The cash thing is important, an' I promise I won't use it for alcohol. But just ten dollars would really help me out—an' it's a rotten thing to ask a lady lost her husband. I'm well aware what a rotten thing it is."

"Stay right here, Bobby. You stay right here. I'll get my purse." Joanna hurried out of the kitchen . . . walked faster and faster to the staircase, then went up the stairs two and three risers at a time.

"I'll be right here," Moffit said to the kitchen, the noise of the lady running through the house. "I'm fixin' it. . . ."

Joanna came back into the kitchen, relieved to see him still there. "—Fifty-three dollars. It's all I have. Or I can give you a check."

Bobby reached up from his work, took the money, then examined it . . . shifted the bills in his palm with a forefinger as if it were a currency he hadn't seen before. "That's a lot of money. . . ."

"And you'll stay here, and tell the police? There was somebody with my husband; someone sailed with him that morning."

"Oh, I'll tell 'em. —I saw that kid for sure. Skinny kid way out there in a baseball cap. Red baseball cap. Kid was out there just sittin'. Your man was the one doing the work sailin' that boat. Needed to ease her off. You got a broad boat, you need to trim it easy. . . ." Mr. Moffit folded the bills, put the money in his shirt pocket, and bent to his work again. He began to murmur softly, what seemed instructions to himself about joining . . . gluing . . . clamping. "Sash an' busted muntins is the easy part, an' fittin' the glass is the hard part," he said.

Joanna sat in the kitchen chair again, and tried to imagine Frank befriending some boy at the docks; she tried to see that picture . . . see him taking a boy out sailing without checking with his parents. It was difficult to imagine Frank doing that. And if he had, what happened to the boy? "—It doesn't make any sense."

"Huh?"

"Mr. Moffit, it doesn't make any sense. —That a boy went out with him."

"Can't help that. Saw the kid out there, and that's a fact. Your man had that blue beer cooler, an' he had that . . . that zipper jacket on. Green jacket."

"Yes. . . . Yes, he was wearing that."

Moffit murmured to himself, adjusted the small clamp. "I don't remember everythin'. I do forget some things because of my dependence on alcohol." The clamp was tested, left in place. "—But I remember a man drownin' out there. I remember that day pretty good."

Silence seemed to thump in rhythm with Joanna's heartbeat. Soft beats sounding in a sunny kitchen . . . with this sad oddity crouched at her feet. So strange a moment that she felt herself and her kitchen and Mr. Moffit become features of a dream that might last forever—she sitting waiting, the summer light unfailing, the broken window never quite repaired.

Burdened gravel sounded outside her dream, a car rolling into the drive. Joanna saw the light bar, the cruiser's official white and green. A woman officer, small and slight, stood out of the car, slammed its door shut, and came trotting to the kitchen steps and up them. Her thick-soled polished black shoes seemed too large for her . . . the broad black belt, its equipment pouches and heavy, holstered automatic seemed to weigh too much, as if she'd had to wear her husband's shoes and gear today.

The policewoman knocked on the kitchen doorframe with a small hard fist, then stepped inside smiling, a neat, wiry woman in her forties, her narrow face slightly withered from smoking, hair a dyed dark red.

"Mrs. Reed? I'm Officer Lilburn." The smile was a general encompassing smile; the pale-gray eyes were more direct, examined Joanna with little interest . . . looked down at Moffit with no more. "Window busted in last night, right?"

"Yes. About midnight, maybe a little later—"

"But no entrance into the dwelling."

"No, he cut himself . . . I guess reaching in to unlock the door."

"Homeowner's best friend," Officer Lilburn said, and squatted to look at dried drops of blood down the inside of the kitchen door. "Homeowner's best friend is untempered glass. Be surprised how many goblins get cut breaking glass." She leaned forward, looked closer, as if the spatter of blood might speak to her. "Bobby," she said, and didn't turn to look at him. "Bobby, what have you been up to? Been behaving yourself?"

Silence from the floor.

"—I asked you a question, Bobby." She stood and looked down at him.

"Mr. Moffit saw my husband sail out," Joanna said, "—the day he died. He says there was definitely someone with him in the boat. Said it looked like a boy, a boy wearing a red baseball cap."

"He did? Is that what he said? . . . Did you say that, Bobby?"

"Yes, I did, and it's true. Long way out, but I saw that kid."

Officer Lilburn smiled and shook her head. "And what day was that, Bobby?"

"Day that man drowned out there."

"What day of the week was that, Bobby?"

"Day of the week . . . ?"

"That's right. Monday? . . . Tuesday? . . . Wednesday? What day of the week?"

"Ummm . . . Tuesday."

"No, it wasn't. Bobby, was Mr. Reed lost last week, or the week before that?"

Bobby Moffit sat silent on the floor, picked up his work, and rubbed his finger along the narrow wood to wipe excess glue away.

"Bobby, what month is this?"

Bobby put his work down. "I don't see what that has to do with any damn thing."

"What month is it, Bobby?"

"It's summer, goddammit! It's June . . . or July. It's early in the damn summer." His hands were shaking; he folded them together.

"Did he ask you for money, Mrs. Reed?" Officer Lilburn was smiling. "Bobby, did you ask this lady for money?"

"None of your business, just because she was nice to me. . . . My people been on Asconsett when your people wasn't anywhere near here."

"Did you give him money, Mrs. Reed?"

"I did, but I don't think that has anything to do with it."

"Oh, I bet it does. —Our Bobby, here, will do and say just about anything that gets him money for a drink. —Isn't that so, Bobby? You tell the truth, now."

"I never said I was better than anybody else. I have a weakness with alcohol, but that doesn't mean I'm a bad person. Lots of people around here do real bad stuff for money—an' you know that's true. You know what they're doin', an' I know what they're doin'."

"If I were you," Officer Lilburn said, "I'd keep my mouth shut about what other people may or may not be doing. —So, you're saying you just came up to help this lady . . . just came up to fix her door window here, and tell her you saw her husband sailing with somebody."

Nod.

"How did you know her window had been broken last night, Bobby?" Officer Lilburn squatted down beside him with a creak of burdened gun belt. She was still smiling, still looked pleasant. "—You going to answer me? I don't think I need to take a sample of those blood drops dried on that door, do I? You going to show me your arms, Bobby? Going to let me look at your arms? —where I'll just bet you got cut last night."

"I don't have to show you nothin'. It's not fair. . . ."

"Officer, he did break the window last night," Joanna said. "He told me so, and he apologized. He came up to fix it this morning."

"That so? Apologized. . . ."

"I wouldn't want to press charges."

No more smiles for Joanna. "Well, that's up to you. Our Bobby's been in trouble before, drinking."

"I'm not a bad person," Bobby Moffit said from the floor, and put his face in his hands like an upset child.

Officer Lilburn sighed and stood. "He's a very sick alcoholic. Been in treatment . . . been out of treatment."

"But I think he knows what he saw."

"Maybe . . . and maybe not. Trouble is, who's going to know? He said a boy went out with your husband—is that what he said?"

"Yes. A boy . . . wearing a red baseball cap."

"Right. But you know, we have no report of a missing young person, or a missing child. We have no report like that anytime the past three months, near-mainland or the islands."

"Maybe that young person *isn't* missing."

"You saying some youngster could be involved in your husband's death? What boy? Why would he be in your husband's boat at all? —Do you know any such person? Did your husband?"

". . . No."

"—And I have to tell you, Bobby is not a credible witness, even if he wanted to be. Even if money wasn't involved."

"Not fair," Bobby Moffit said from the floor.

"Bobby," said Officer Lilburn, "I think you've said enough—and you darn sure have done enough, breaking this lady's window and then coming up here for money to fix it. That's real cute, and it's an offense, a criminal offense."

"Isn't."

"Yes, it is. And even if this lady won't sign a complaint, I can take you in for an examination of your health and competence. And you'll go right to the hospital in Post Port."

"Will not."

"Yes, you will."

Bobby Moffit just shook his head no. He picked up one of the squares of glass, but his hands were trembling so he couldn't hold it. He put it back down, and tucked his hands in his lap.

"What a shame," Officer Lilburn said. "Isn't this a shame?"

"He can fix the window," Joanna said. "And he can keep the money, too. He won't bother me again."

"You hope. —Let me give you some advice. Don't adopt Bobby; don't try to help him. It's been tried before."

"Has not," Bobby said. "That's not true."

"Hell it isn't," Officer Lilburn said. "Bobby, didn't Mrs. Johnston let you stay free in her side-porch room?"

"No."

"Yes, she let you stay there. And you sold her floor lamp for money to drink with."

"No, I didn't."

"Yes, you did."

"Officer," Joanna said, "—thank you for coming up. And I would like it if you'd mention what Mr. Moffit said about somebody—a boy in a red baseball cap—sailing out with my husband."

Officer Lilburn sighed and stepped to the kitchen doorway. "I'll report that. I'll report it, but you don't have . . . you really don't have much of a witness here." She went out and down the steps, then called over her shoulder. "—Bobby, you finish up that window and then be on your way. Don't you be bothering Mrs. Reed anymore. Did you know she just lost her dad, too? That her father was killed in a fire the other day? —And you come up here giving her this trouble."

Bobby Moffit sat unmoving, head bowed, for the few moments until the police car's door slammed, its engine started. Then he reached out for a square of cut glass again, and after two attempts, was able to fit it to the frame. "Glue's got to dry," he said. "Then the glass is goin' to fit in there, put in new points an' glazin' compound. . . . Sorry about your daddy."

Joanna stooped, to be more on Bobby's level. He smelled like a baby who hadn't been changed. ". . . Bobby, the police asked them, and none of the fishermen saw anybody in *Bo-Peep* with my husband. One of them saw the boat way out that day. . . ."

"That's a laugh."

"What do you mean?"

" 'Fishermen.' That's pretend fishin', is all that is. I know what I saw." He turned, tilted the glued window frame against the kitchen wall . . . then dropped his glue bottle into the shopping bag and stood up with a grunt of effort, staggered a half-step. "—I'm goin' now. Glue dries, I'll come back an' putty tomorrow."

"Okay. And thank you for coming up to fix the window, Mr. Moffit."

"Hell, I was the one busted it. I busted it under the influence. . . .

But don't be scared; I'll be up here sober in the mornin'. I don't have to drink. People think I can't control myself, but I can. I just don't want to."

"I understand—and Mr. Moffit, I believe you did see someone out with my husband that morning. I believe you."

"Well, that makes two of us—you an' me. People say I'm just a lyin' drunk, when it's them that's doin' the big-time lyin' around here."

He went out the door, carefully down the kitchen steps, and walked away along the drive, swinging his shopping bag. He had an odd walk, a walk drifting at an angle, so he was facing slightly to the right as he went along. . . . Joanna supposed that was due to damage from drinking.

Late in the evening, she sat at the kitchen table, eating a second slice of a small delivered pizza. A gentle sea breeze was drifting in through the broken window. —A more collected repairman would likely have left the window boarded up.

She'd asked the pizza delivery girl if she knew an island boy who went around wearing a red baseball cap.

"Baseball caps, sure," the girl had said. She hadn't seemed to think it was an odd question. Thin, dark, and very tall, so she already stooped slightly, she'd stood on the front steps, considering the question. "Baseball caps . . . but not red, particularly."

A boy in a red baseball cap. . . . But seen by a sick man and from a distance, so perhaps not a boy. Perhaps a slight, slender man. A wiry, friendly person met down at the dock. An amiable, amusing man who talked sailing, who talked boats—and wanted one.

The pizza was very good . . . good crust. But if ghosts might be fed, her father wouldn't be pleased with pizza. —Frank would; she'd ordered extra cheese and ripe olives. His favorite, not hers. So he could come into the kitchen out of the dining room's shadows— and come not as ashes; ashes had no appetite. . . . He could come in as she'd dreamed him, soaked, wetting the kitchen linoleum. Come sauntering in, smelling of the sea, and sit down beside her. —All that would be allowed. Everything would be allowed except looking into his eyes. Their color would have changed to a color never seen, a fourth primary color.

Frank might come in for dinner, if she called him correctly. And her father drifting in behind him, gusting into the yellow kitchen light as swirling ash, as turning smoke that wanted no pizza . . . that disdained his drowned son-in-law, eating pizza though dead.

"An amiable young man—is there anything more?" That question of her father's, after he met Frank.

"Love, and the strength of love," she should have answered. But she hadn't. She had stood on the porch of the old Chaumette house with her father smiling down at her, and she'd been slightly embarrassed by Frank's revealed simplicity and sweetness.

"He's very kind," she'd said, knowing that was not enough, betraying Frank in complicity with her father on her father's porch. And that little treachery, that small betrayal, had lingered years afterward in Louis's courteous contempt for a man who only coached soccer—who had no fierce temper, no hard and adamant withholding in him, who suffered no considerable loss.

What else might she have said on the Chaumette house's porch? It had been evening, and warm, a summer evening like this summer evening. . . . She might have said, "He's strong enough to take care of me. He's strong enough to take care of me without letting me become a tyrant and sicken. There's no poetry in him, and that's a great relief, and will help me not to kill myself if I discover too frightening a truth in poetry."

What if she'd said that to Louis Bernard?

The embarrassment then would have been his, and would have cost her his smile as he turned cold. . . . It was that smile she'd paid for by betraying Frank while Frank was in the side yard, playing hardball catch with the neighbor's tomboy girl. What had that wild girl's name been? An unhappy child, nail-bitten, scabbed, and odd. . . . Gloria. Absolutely the wrong name for her. Gloria Dittmer. Gone, now, killed by a car. But she'd been, of course, one of the oyster seeds of the last poems. . . . Odd to realize that so late, and prompted by the vision of Frank's ghost sitting down, soaked, to eat from the pizza's other side. He'd take the extra slice. Why did men eat so much more? Was it only their size—or appetite unashamed?

. . . But no ghost came, actual enough for dinner. So when Joanna was finished, there were slices of pizza left to be plastic-wrapped and put in the refrigerator. And only one plate to wash.

That done, she turned out the kitchen light, walked down the hall and climbed the stairs. The bedroom, yellow in the bedside lamp's mild glow, was as empty as if no man had ever seen it, ever slept there, or ever would—as if it had been built for her to be alone in.

. . . But deep into night—interrupting drifting conversations with her mother—was a commencement of dreamed lovemaking so sudden, so specific, she heard their liquid noises, felt soaking at her sex—and so real she underwent the heave and buck, the oily delicious ache of penetration as she was fucked. Joanna felt Frank and saw him braced above her in dim light, frowning in pleasure's concentration as he worked on her, into her.

"Oh, fuck me," she said to him, groaned and felt wonderfully relieved, so happy about something she'd misunderstood. . . . She had almost come, but not quite. And being steadily driven, driven in bittersweet in-and-out from sleep to waking, had just said, "My darling"—when the blade of recalling, that shone as morning light, sliced between them and woke her, bereft.

Joanna groaned, kept her eyes closed, and reached under the sheet to finish with her fingers what was started. She managed, by insisting, a cramping conclusion that allowed her to say, "Ohhh . . ." And finished, she drew the sheet away—slowly as if a lover watched her—and lay naked, knees up and apart, so the sunlight at least could discover her wet and openness. Not absolutely wasted.

Chapter Eight

Joanna waited almost three hours after breakfast—Cheerios and a tangerine—for Mr. Moffit to come up to finish glazing the broken window.

She waited . . . waited a little longer, then took her purse off the entrance-hall table, went out the front door, and locked it behind her. A useless precaution, with the kitchen's door window out.

She went down Slope Street—her sandals uneasy on the cobbles—walking into a perfect summer morning, a summer's bright and rolling sun. A beautiful morning but still, with no breeze from the sea. Beach weather, walking weather, but not fine for sailing. . . . A woman in T-shirt and jeans—a neighbor whose name she didn't know—was coming up the hill as Joanna walked down, and smiled as they passed. Shared pleasure in a sunny day.

. . . The chief constable was in, and looking older, more tired than before—particularly in the island's summer light, pouring so perfectly cool and bright into his white-painted office.

Joanna supposed the light must make her look older, too.

"Sorry about your father," the constable said from the other side of his gray steel desk. Looking very tired, and wearing a different suit today. Sharkskin—but cream, not blue.

"Yes, I left a message with your deputy."

"I got that message, Mrs. Reed. And I have to tell you, I really didn't care for the language."

"Too bad." Tough talk; it startled Joanna's heart into thumping.

". . . Mrs. Reed, I take into account that you have had two tragedies in your life, one right after the other—this . . . your father's death—

but let me tell you, it is not a good idea to try to harass law officers, talk like that." Tired, and angry. It didn't hurt the old man's looks.

"Language is my business, Chief Constable. I say what I mean. And I mean to have you check again into my husband's death—*and* my father's death. You may be used to people being afraid of you out here, impressed by your professionalism—"

"Now—"

"But I can tell you that I'm not afraid of the police—and I am not impressed, so far, by your professionalism."

"I don't think we have anything more to talk about, Mrs. Reed." And he stood up, cold . . . coldly angry. Really was a handsome old man. A tall, cold, tough beauty—and when young, must certainly have been every woman's dream and nightmare. His poor wife. . . .

Joanna stayed sitting. "Yes, we do. I'm *not* going to run out of here, Constable!" Heart calming . . . getting used to confrontation. "I want to know what you think about what Mr. Moffit told me. And . . . and I want to know what you know about the fire that killed my father—who, by the way, was a very careful man, a *neurotically* careful man, who had used that woodstove for almost forty years! How many very improbable accidents must my family suffer before the police get interested? I'm . . . worried about my daughter."

The chief constable made a suffering face and sat back down behind his desk, apparently a gift sitting, an example of heroic patience. ". . . I did call up to Chaumette, and spoke with the fire chief there. He said they do not regard that cabin fire as suspicious. They do not regard that wood staining they found as very suspicious, since there was no accelerator residue, as there would be with gasoline or kerosene."

"Not *very* suspicious."

"Not suspicous, period."

"Just another accident. . . ."

"Mrs. Reed, that's exactly right."

"And Mr. Moffit—"

"Please, *please,* don't take Bobby Moffit seriously. Bobby is a sick man, and we have dealt with him for many years out here. He's been an alcoholic since he was sixteen years old—and for quite a while was a violent offender, a brawler very lucky to stay out of prison."

"He—"

"He is not the man you want as a witness, when you've had a tragedy like yours."

"Constable, he was very specific, very *specific*. A boy—or perhaps a young man—definitely out sailing with my husband the day he died! A boy wearing a red baseball cap."

"Oh, Lord. . . ." The chief, exasperated, was looking less perfect. "Of course he was specific. How else was he going to get some money out of you? . . . Listen, I had Bobby brought in here first thing this morning, very first thing. I went over that testimony— and he initially denied breaking your window, denied everything. Then he said that was right; he did see some kid out with your husband that particular day—and let me tell you, Bobby Moffit doesn't know what the hell *year* it is."

"So he made all that up, just for a few dollars."

"That's right, so you'd give him some money—which I understand you did. He took advantage of your loss."

"Even so—"

"Just the same, just the same, we looked into that . . . we're still looking into that. We're talking to some local people; we'll talk with kids. And we'll also check with the ferry crews to see if by some very unlikely chance they recall a particular boy in a baseball cap coming onto the island, or leaving, within a couple of days before and after your husband's death."

"Well . . . I do appreciate your doing that—"

"And let me tell you, Mrs. Reed, I consider all this a complete waste of time. Complete waste. It is time and effort that my people could use on other cases, other duties."

" 'A waste of time.' "

"That's exactly right. Because, Mrs. Reed, you have given us no motive—not one—for any person wishing to injure your husband. And let me ask you this: Do you know any motive a person would have to cause your *father's* death? Do you?"

". . . No, I don't."

"You bet you don't." The chief constable stood up, a conclusive standing up. "—And for a very good reason. Both of those deaths were accidents." He walked over to the door, stood waiting for Joanna to get up and get out of his office. "Now, we'll look into this boy . . . this kid thing. And that's going to be it, you understand?"

"Yes, I understand, and I appreciate your efforts . . . your people doing this."

"I hope you do, Mrs. Reed."

. . . Out on the street, and standing in sunlight that now seemed too bright, Joanna thought how Frank would have enjoyed hearing the discussion in the chief constable's office. He would have made some remark about inevitable handcuffs, if she kept on. If she kept on. . . .

A soft late-morning breeze had begun drifting off the sea, stirring her dress's skirt against her. The green dress again, and not particularly successful with the chief constable. The old man, apparently used to deference and cautious respect out on the islands, was not to be won by a summer dress and fairly good legs.

. . . And might the constable be right? Perhaps be dealing only with a shocked and foolish woman, a woman poet—deep truths her business, but now unable to accept the truth of loss? . . . It certainly might seem so to anyone who never knew Frank Reed, never went out sailing with him. And might seem so, too, to anyone who'd never seen Louis Bernard fuss and fiddle with his cabin stove— selecting his twists of newspaper for starters, then carefully his sticks of tinder, then the perfect quarter logs—all ritually arranged in the Franklin stove. Then lit with one Blue Tip match, and the two small iron doors swung smartly shut, and latched.

A husband and father, both careful men, though otherwise so different. The wrong men for their accidents.

But what reason . . . what possible reasons could there be for anything *but* mischance? To begin with, what reason for a boy— or perhaps a slight man who might have looked, from a distance, like a boy—to sail out with Frank Reed and somehow manage his drowning?

Reasons: Hate. Love. Money.

Not hate. Another man, perhaps, but not Frank. There had been nothing in him dark enough to provoke it.

Love . . . ? Only a little more likely. A few women must have loved him, been very fond of him, no doubt. Susan Thom, and probably one or two others through the years. Perhaps even now, another faculty wife . . . a student. Perhaps one of his athletes—some young man, gay, might have loved Frank, might have been the boy in a red baseball cap. . . . But all so improbable.

—And no man had approached her, at least not for years, in such an obsessed and furious way that murder might seem possible. Men had asked . . . had suggested. Some had always done that, making their pass at the Poet—because of the poetry perhaps, or her very minor celebrity. Perhaps for her legs, her ass, or her single breast and its foam twin. Perhaps dark eyes had sparked them, a Mohegan nose. . . . But none of those men had been frightening, none seemed to have loved so that no husband—perhaps not even a father—could be allowed to live to share her.

Michael Jaffrey, drunk, had exposed his modest penis to her in the den during Lianne's party, almost two years ago. "Please," he'd said, his chinos unzipped, holding it up in display. "I'm desperate for you."

"Sorry," Joanna had said to him. She'd come to the den for the silver ice bucket. "Sorry, Michael; it's just too small."

A phrase she'd regretted afterward. So much better to have simply kept her mouth shut, and walked away. Later, miserable Michael had vomited on Lianne's carpet runner—and on Monday, in Lufton Hall, had come up to Joanna and said, "For God's sake, tell me what I think happened at the McCreedys' didn't happen."

"Sorry," she'd said.

"Oh, jumping Jesus. . . ."

"And it isn't too small," Joanna had said. "It's perfectly okay. Looked very sturdy."

No . . . not likely Frank was murdered by a jealous professor of physics.

Which left only money. . . . But where could money be found in Frank's death? His insurance would be enough to pay off the mortgage on the White River house, and that was about all. No serious money would come to anyone from his death—not nearly enough to reward a carefully planned murder. And if not from Frank's death . . . then from what, the wreck of the *Bo-Peep*?

What insurance had there been on that small boat? Surely not much. . . . .

Joanna walked back on Strand, threading through tourist families wandering, and turned up Slope Street. The sea wind, rising, gently assisted . . . pressing cool, soft, and salty against her back as she climbed to the cottage.

She walked down the driveway, went around back and up the steps to the kitchen. No Mr. Moffit. His window frame still leaned against the wall.

Joanna walked through the hall and went up the stairs. Perhaps because of the light—streaming sunlight that stirred and slowly rippled across white-painted pine walls as if the sea were reflecting everywhere—the upstairs seemed emptier than the rooms below.

She went into the bathroom, peed and wiped, then stood at the cabinet mirror, washing her hands. Looking into a widow's face. A widow's face, already seeming older, preparing to be older still.

"Middle-aged," Joanna said to her reflection, and wasn't answered it wasn't so. Her reflection stared at her like a stranger, a person who'd had bad news.

After a late lunch of tomato soup and toast, she drove down to Strand, then turned left out Beach Road through sunny afternoon, past Trudie's and on along Asconsett's northern coast. A two-mile coast, the island's weather side, and dotted with half-million-dollar beach houses stilted twelve feet high on tarred telephone poles over sand and sea grass. Houses with Land Rovers, Jeeps, and dune buggies parked alongside, and bright banners and flags—many the American flag's candy colors—fluttering from their several decks, their carports. There were three . . . four fishing boats in line far out on a whitecapped ocean.

The sea wind wandered through the Volvo's open windows as Joanna drove. She was driving left-handed, her right hand resting over along the passenger seat, so she could pretend Frank was sitting there, thoughtful, silent, holding her hand. —And he might be, if she didn't glance that way.

Asconsett's roads were minimal, narrow blacktop tracks with sea-bleached sand sweeping over here and there. Roads that dipped and broke where the wind or winter storms had blown dune from beneath their edges, so the car rose and fell in rhythmic memory of those storms' striking. Everything here was by the sea's permission, and with its mark.

A spark flashed on the road ahead : . . flashed again and became the sunstruck windshield of a Jeep coming toward her . . . rising and falling with the road.

It rose out of a dip, came to her on the left, and buffeted past, going fast. It left an impression of youth behind it—four or five tanned grinning boys and girls in bathing suits. Packed in, merry and traveling fast—heading for South Beach, its small marina, and shallower slightly warmer water. Children of money and good times—descendants, most of them, of old mainland families grown rich dealing in the spoils of a continent and the sea.

Beautiful careless young people. Joanna had seen them in town, cruising through the wandering summer tourists, yachts passing barges.

. . . She drove another half mile, saw the tilted signpost for Willis Street on the left, and slowed for the turn. Willis was Asconsett's only cross-island road, and it was narrow, pavement often broken and half buried in sand as it went along. Low dunes, furred in sea grass, rolled away on either side.

Mid-island sand was too unstable to build on. There were no houses on Willis Street for almost a mile; the island's center had been left a state bird sanctuary. Plover and terns due to come kiting along the New England flyway later in the season.

Willis Street went southwest, and ended at the island's original settlement, the sandbarred reach where the first fishermen had built driftwood homes four hundred years before. The stretch of coast, like the street, had been named Willis, and had been the island's village capital until whaling and a deeper harbor had created Asconsett Town.

The Willis people had been the island's first fishermen, lobstermen. Joanna supposed Mr. Moffit's family were Willisers.

The bird sanctuary ended in a handsomely carved sign—a tern in flight—and the first sheds and shacks appeared at once, all on the left side of the road, all facing west to the mainland channel. The mainland was too far across to see.

Shacks, sheds, and wind-worn cottages set into sand, each with a battered pickup truck or car or brace of rust-spotted motorcycles resting in the sun beside it. Most trucks held clouds of green trawler net.

Willis ran on for a stretch, to a small gas station, bait shop, and closed ferry dock. Only the distance from the mainland, only the slow ferry's successive stops at inshore islands, had kept this ancient settlement from transformation into massive ranks of time-share condos and strip stores.

Joanna took her hand from what should be Frank's, and slowed to read the mailboxes along the road's left side. The name was Wainwright. Murray Wainwright had leased the *Bo-Peep* to Frank—he and his boat suggested by the marina office. . . . Wainwright had been elderly and crippled, squatting fat in his wheelchair on the Willis dock. A cheerful old man, missing several front teeth, which loss had given his singsong down-east speech an occasional flatulent accent. . . .

The mailboxes in Willis were damaged goods, apparently targets for passing boys. Joanna, driving slower and slower, was able to read *Cabot, Lindsay . . . , Shallowford, Wilson. . . .* Then two mailboxes destroyed. Then *Wainwright.*

Their cottage was set farther back from the road than most, seemed to rest on a double sandy lot, and was fenced with rusty chain-link five feet high. . . . Joanna pulled over to the left, half onto the road's soft shoulder, and parked.

There was one of Asconsett's rare trees—a molting, lean, and knotty pine—in the Wainwrights' wide front yard. A thick rope was attached to its largest limb, a car tire was suspended from that, and a medium-sized red dog hung from the tire. The dog seemed content to have the tire's heavy rubber in its jaws; it dangled clear of the ground, relaxed, still, and smiling.

Joanna got out of the Volvo, went to the cottage's fence gate, and paused. The red dog hung comfortably from his tire, and only rolled an eye toward her. . . . Joanna hesitated at the gate. She couldn't see anyone at the house, only the dog hanging in the yard. It was an odd-looking dog, ginger-colored—almost orange—and short-haired, its heavy muzzle and thick shoulders laced with a pale spiderweb of scars. It seemed to have had an accident. . . . The dog watched Joanna as she watched it. Its body, a compact cylinder of muscle, was completed by a head as massive, red, and rectangular as a brick block. The dog, its eye considering her, swung very slightly with the sea breeze as it hung.

"Hello . . . !" Apparently no one home. *"Hello . . . !"*

And as if he'd waited behind the door for her second call, a stocky young man in ragged jeans and a black T-shirt came out of the house, slammed the screen door behind him, and trotted down the steps. "What do you want?" His hair, cut short, was the color of sand. He had a neat mustache.

He walked fast across the yard to her, short, muscled arms— sunburned dark over complex tattoos—swinging as if he were easing them for a fight. "Well, what do you want?" He had an unpleasant face, an old-fashioned pugged tough-boy's face. He looked like his grandfather—but young, very strong, and less amiable.

"My name's Reed, Joanna Reed. We . . . my husband leased Mr. Wainwright's boat."

The young man—a boy, really, barely in his twenties—stood behind the chain-link fence, looking at her. He had pale-blue eyes— round as a child's eyes, but not wondering, not gentle. "Oh, right. Reed. And you wrecked the fuckin' boat. . . . Think maybe you owe us for that? I mean, I just wonder if that occurred to you summer people—lose our boat and don't even give us a call about it? What was that, three weeks ago?"

"My husband was drowned."

"Hey, I know that. And if he couldn't sail, he shouldn't have taken her out."

"My husband was a good sailor. Now . . . now, is there someone I can talk to—"

"You're talkin' to me, lady. Gramps is sick over at the mainland, and my dad's fishin'."

"Bud . . . !"

The boy didn't answer, stood staring at Joanna. She could smell him standing so close, just across the low fence—a pleasant odor of clean young man, tense and lightly sweating. She was surprised how she'd missed the smell of a man. The pleasure was embarrassing.

"Bud—goddammit!"

Bud turned away, and Joanna saw a woman on the cottage's roofed porch. She was a tall woman, and broad, with no waist. Her hair was iron-gray and loose down her back, and she was wearing a sleeveless light-blue house dress, her pale arms heavy, lumpy with fat and muscle.

"Bud—you get in here."

"Shit. . . ." The boy went back into the yard, stood beside the hanging dog, and said, "Get down."

The red dog yawned and dropped from his tire. He landed in an odd, springy undoglike way, and sat. He turned his head to keep watching Joanna, and she saw his right eye was white and blind.

"What do you want here?" the big woman called to Joanna as if she were a hundred yards away.

"Mom, she's the people wrecked our boat."

"You be quiet. *I asked you a question."* The big woman, so bulky elsewhere, had a man's gaunt face and beaky nose.

"I'm Joanna Reed. I wanted to talk to Mr. Wainwright," Joanna said. Then, thinking the woman might be deaf, called, *"—Joanna Reed. I wanted to talk to Mr. Wainwright."*

The apparent Mrs. Wainwright didn't answer, only stood on her porch, watching Joanna standing in the road. The cottage's paint, that had been white, was peeling everywhere off its wood in delicate patterns of curling chips, so standing in shadow, the woman seemed to be nested in old lace. "Granda's gone to the hospital at Post Port," she said conversationally, without shouting.

Joanna, tired of standing in the road, went to the fence gate, opened it, and walked into the yard. "Then I'd like to speak with you," she said—and stopped walking because of the dog.

As she'd come into the yard, the ginger dog had risen and gone to her, so they met in the middle. The animal was not big at all, but looked extraordinarily dense, solid with muscle, and carried a head so massive it seemed to belong to a bigger dog. Its white eye was not troubling, but the other, a light topaz to complement its coloring, had an odd expression—so though the animal hadn't growled at her, or threatened in any way, Joanna stopped and stood still. She wished the boy would call it.

This close, she could see the dog had no ears—only trimmed stubs. A piece looked to have been bitten from its lip. . . . But it was the dog's good eye that held her still. The animal watched her, head cocked for one-eyed sight, looking up with no expression of either threat or friendliness, no sort of exchange at all. There was nothing in the topaz eye but study, and stern purpose.

"Would you call your dog, please."

The boy stood smiling at her. "You got a problem?" he said. "—Comin' in our yard?"

Joanna could hear the sea behind her . . . the soft ruffling of its breeze over the mainland channel. She looked up and saw the big woman watching from the porch. Not helping her.

. . . *Frank is dead,* Joanna thought. She almost said it out loud. *He won't be here to help me. No one will be here to help me, anymore.*

She went to one knee in the sand. Knelt there in her green dress before the dog. It watched her as it had watched before. This close, at the animal's level, she saw how savage were its scars. Saw tumors of muscle bulking at the hinges of its jaw. Of course—a pit bull, and this a true fighting dog, participant in that ancient pleasure of the poor.

"Hello," she said to it, and slowly put out her hand.

"Don't," the woman said from the porch. "Don't do that. —Call him, Bud!" But the boy didn't.

The dog paid no attention to her hand, and Joanna saw it was watching her throat. Joanna put her hand down in the sand, and leaned forward a little, turned her head so her throat was there for him.

"Percy," the boy said, "Percy . . . *down.*"

The dog stayed standing.

It was odd. Joanna hadn't thought of killing herself for so many years, not since the baby. —Hadn't thought of it later, during the cancer and her surgery—or in caves, or rock climbing, hours when death leaned ready at her elbow. It had seemed such a hackneyed thing for a woman poet to do. So expected and tedious. . . . Yet here she was, kneeling before a maimed fighting dog, and waiting for his bite.

Then he moved . . . moved to her, but slowly. She smelled him. Clean dog. Clean master.

"Percy," the boy said. "Down . . . *down.*" And took a step, then stopped. "Lady—back away. Just back away from him!"

Joanna, kneeling, closed her eyes. The sunlight was too bright. She took a breath, and felt cold at the side of her throat. Coolness pressing. The dog stood with its blunt muzzle closed, pressing against her throat. It pressed hard . . . then the cold nose drifted up to touch her ear, then slowly down and across to her mouth. The animal sniffed, smelled her there, and she opened her eyes to its inhuman face, its single jeweled eye, and it licked her once, delicately at the corner of her mouth, as if it were a lover changed by a witch, but come back to her.

"Shit . . . lady," the boy said.

Joanna sat back and put her hands on the dog's head, cradled that heavy harsh-coated wedge of bone and muscle . . . rubbed gently behind its ruined ears. The animal stood under her stroking, made no further demonstration.

"Dumb," the big woman said from her porch. "I call that real dumb, fool with that dog." She came down from the porch, bigger and bigger, and put a hard hand down to help Joanna up. "Dumb. Dog's not the kind of dog you want to be pettin.' Shouldn' be keepin' him at all."

"Mom . . ."

"Don't 'Mom' me, Bud." Mrs. Wainwright, slow and shambling, led Joanna up the porch steps. "That Percy dog ain't no good at all, and he's real costly. Eats meat like a damn tiger in the zoo. . . ."

"Not good . . . ?" Joanna followed the woman through the front door into the house—a house, like the woman's son and dog, surprisingly clean. Its linoleum floors smelled of wax polish, and collections of things—minor groupings of tiny decorative cushions, still-boxed Barbies, and German figurines of rural flute players, dancers, and shepherds—were set out on little tables in the small living room.

"Not good no more. You see he's got a blind eye. . . ."

"So he can't fight?"

"I don't know what you're talkin' about." Mrs. Wainwright led the way down a hall paneled with family photographs—most of children, grandchildren—down the hall and into the kitchen, another small room, and very clean. The appliances and sink counter crowded close around a scarred wooden table, an old hatch cover. It was the only nautical note in the cottage. "—Don't know what you're talkin' about. Dog's just not no good anymore, that's all." She pulled a chair away from the table, and sat with sigh of relief. "Go on, sit down. Mrs. Reed, right?"

"Yes." Joanna sat, and saw the heavy tabletop was roughly carved in intricate patterns. Flower patterns. Flowers and vines. "Pretty carving. . . ."

"Oh, sure. You don't have to keep this damn table clean, so all that carvin' looks pretty. Mr. Wainwright, Junior, did that. He's been cuttin' on my table all the years we been married. It's a habit, an' he won't be broke of it. He's been out a week now, long-linin'."

"Well, I came—"

"My name's Beverly."

"Joanna. . . . Beverly, I came to ask about the boat, the *Bo-Peep*."

"I named that boat after the nursery rhyme."

"I'm . . . I'm trying to find out what happened to my husband."

"Honey," the woman said, "—everybody knows what happened to your husband. He drowned out there . . . and not the first to do it, neither."

"I don't believe he just drowned. He was very careful. He always wore a life jacket. *Always*. And they found him without it."

"Shit, if it was Mr. Wainwright, Junior, got drowned, I'd be surprised they found him wearin' one. Most fishermen don't wear that stuff."

"My husband did; he *taught* boating safety when he lived near Gloucester. —And he didn't fall off boats, either. Especially not in good weather."

"Didn' fall off boats?"

"No, he didn't."

"Well, my man wouldn' do that, neither. That'd be the day. He'd be ashamed to come home, he did that, 'less it was one hell of a storm out there." Beverly heaved herself up. "I'm goin' to have a glass of apple juice. You want some?"

"No, thank you."

"It's real cold an' good. It's Mott's apple juice."

"Well . . . all right." Joanna wanted to sit quiet for a moment and think, but she found she couldn't do that, couldn't stop talking.

"—And also, I lost my father. He was . . . burned to death up in Chaumette day before yesterday."

Beverly Wainwright, at her refrigerator, bowed her head slightly, as if under such a storm of misfortune. "My, that's terrible news. Both your people gone like that."

"Yes, it was terrible news—and I don't, I simply don't *believe* that that was an accident, either. My father was very careful with his woodstove. He'd heated with that Franklin for years, and they said he left one of the stove doors open when he went to bed, and I don't believe that for a minute."

"Both your men gone." Beverly poured juice into two blue plastic glasses.

"—So, I'm trying to find out what *did* happen. The police . . . the chief constable thinks I'm a fool. Just a hysterical woman."

Beverly put the juice in the refrigerator, brought the glasses to the table, and sat with a sigh. "—That Carl is the meanest old son of a bitch. Always lookin' to cause trouble for Parsonses an' Wainwrights an' Armstrongs. Can't please that good-lookin' son of a bitch, no matter what."

"He hasn't been helpful to me at all. . . . He is a handsome old man."

"Oh, an' don't the old scut know it, too. . . . Honey, you should have seen that Carl when he was younger. Looked like a damn movie star. Isn't it a crime, havin' looks like that wasted on a man?"

"It is a crime."

"Married a second cousin of mine—Marilyn Osborne. And has he led that poor woman a chase? I hope to tell you. An' Marilyn is as sweet as candy."

"Well, he thinks what happened to Frank was an accident, because no one had any reason to hurt him."

"Nobody?" Beverly seemed surprised. "—Shit sure couldn' say that about my husband. Lots of people would like to kick my Murray's ass, if they dared to. Lot meaner than that Percy dog out there. But you know, that man never touched me except with love in our whole life together. Always talks nice around me, too. . . . I'm crazy about my Murray. We're just a couple of old love bugs."

Beverly smiled, and Joanna saw her as the girl she'd been—large and lumbering even then, coarse, tough, and unlovely—and wondered how it was that the probably even tougher Mr. Wainwright, Junior, had been wise enough to see her value, love her, and take her for a wife.

"You're lucky, Beverly." Joanna drank some apple juice, very sweet and cold.

"Yes, I am."

"And I *was* lucky."

"Lucky with that dog out there. Could have bit you real bad, maybe killed you. Sure scared the poop out of Bud."

"Yes. . . . Well, the police have been no help, so I'm looking into it myself."

"Lookin' into it. . . ."

"That's right. I believe something may have been done, that someone may have killed my husband. And I think my father, too. —And I suppose that sounds crazy to you."

". . . Well, honey, you know stuff goes on out there. I don't know about your daddy—but men get in trouble out there at sea, an' there's not a damn thing women can do about it." She shook her heavy head at the unfairness.

" 'Stuff goes on'?"

"You know, just *stuff.* Fishin' an' whatever. Men can get in trouble about anythin'."

"But what trouble could Frank have had out there? —Except the weather, or if something went wrong with the boat and she began to founder."

"Wasn't nothin' wrong with that boat. Period."

"Well . . . well, Beverly, what I was wondering was whether anyone had a reason to sink the boat—and maybe that was what happened."

"You know, you owe us money on that boat, that *Bo-Peep.* That would be fair, 'cause your man had her out and let her go wreck."

"I'm sure that wasn't his fault, Beverly." Joanna drank some more apple juice.

"He was the one had her out. He was captainin'. So you bet it was his fault. Who else's fault was it?"

"I don't know yet. I don't know. . . . Could you tell me whether the boat was insured?"

"What? Whether she was insured?"

"Yes, that's right."

"You lost your man—and it was on our boat and our boat got wrecked. And you're askin' if we had her insured?"

"Yes, I just—"

"Just nothin'." Beverly put down her apple juice, and looked grim. "Tell you, Mrs. Reed, I'd say you are real lucky my Murray is out at sea, workin'. Because if he was here, guest in our house or no guest in our house, he would pitch you right out on your fancy rich-lady ass!"

"I wasn't accusing—"

"Now you listen to me." Beverly's face almost a man's face in anger. "—Wainwrights an' Parsons have been fishin' out here since forever. And the Parsons may have done some of this an' that be-side fishin', but that was a long, long time ago." Beverly paused for breath. "And since that long *long* time ago, there hasn't been any-body said anythin' criminal about us—period. We don't do nothin' that a lot of people aren't doin' now, just to get along."

"I didn't—"

"You just shut up and listen to me, now. Who do you think you're talkin' to? We been doin' boats forever. You come out here with your fancy clothes an' bullshit airs and so forth, all you sum-mer women—and here you are in my house talkin' about barratry an' sinkin' and so forth. I won't say some men haven't put a big fisher down they couldn' pay for, but we don't do that. That's the last thing we'd do unless we had to."

"I'm sorry."

"So, you just mind your fuckin' manners or get out of here. . . . Invited you in my house, an' served you juice an' everythin'."

"I didn't mean to insult you, Beverly."

"Better hope not."

"—But my husband's dead, and now my father's dead, and something was wrong about both of those deaths. And I'm going to find out what, no matter who I piss off asking. Do you understand that?"

"Just don't insult me."

"I'm not insulting you."

"Sure sounds like it—an' I don't hear nothin' about payin' for our boat, neither."

"I don't owe you for the goddamn boat, Beverly. —Was it in-sured or wasn't it insured?"

"You call five thousand insurance. You call that insurance, it was insured. Through the co-op."

"Only five thousand. . . ."

"An' let me tell you what Mr. Wainwright, Junior, would tell you better—there's no way at all you're goin' to replace a fine wood sloop like that *Bo-Peep* for five thousand dollars. No way at all—build *or* buy. It's a loss, an' how are you goin' to make that loss up, is what I want to know." Beverly had her son's eyes, pale, slightly bulging, and hard as aggie marbles. ". . . Didn' even call us about it. Just let it go."

"Oh, for Christ's sake, my husband *died* out there! Would you people please just give me a few weeks before you start asking for *money*? —Which I don't owe you at all, anyway."

"Yes, you do."

"No, I don't."

"Do so."

"Do not."

"Do *so*."

"Do *not*," Joanna said, and began to laugh. She tried to stop, and did for a moment. Then she thought of herself out in the yard with the dog, and started laughing again. It felt wonderful.

Beverly Wainwright had a laugh like a man's, a deep *huh-huh* that shook her in her kitchen chair. "Doesn' mean, now," she said, when they'd stopped laughing, "—doesn' mean you don't owe us money, just because we was chucklin'."

"Do not," Joanna said.

Beverly Wainwright looked at her, obscurely pleased. "You want some cookies? Oreo cookies?"

"No, thank you."

"You sure? They're the vanilla cream ones, an' they're really good. I'm goin' to have some." She stood up with a grunt.

"Well," Joanna said, "then I'll have some, too."

. . . Out in the yard after apple juice and several Oreo cookies— and dazzled by summer sunshine past the house's shade—Joanna nodded to Bud Wainwright, received no nod in return, and bent to pat Percy as the red dog came up to her. It was like stroking furred bronze; there was no give beneath her hand.

"Do you miss fighting?" she said to him. ". . . I'll bet you do."

Chapter Nine

Joanna drove up her driveway, and around back—and saw Mr. Moffit's face, dark with dirt, at the kitchen door window. She got out of the Volvo, went up the kitchen steps, and he opened the door for her.

"I'm puttied, an' I'm gettin' ready to fit her in." Moffit smelled of urine.

"You didn't come this morning." Joanna put her purse on the kitchen table.

"Couldn' do it; couldn' come up. Constable wanted me . . . and then I had two drinks despite real good intentions." He bent and picked up the door window to show.

"Looks nice. . . ."

"Damn right. Good as new . . . except I can't tack her in as neat as original. I don't claim I can do that."

"Good enough will be good enough, Mr. Moffit."

"Bobby's okay. You can call me Bobby."

"And if Mrs. Evanson wants me to get a new window, Bobby, I'll just do that."

"No, no. No way. If Nancy Evanson wants a whole brand-new window, I'll buy it because I was the one broke it. . . . But I'll have to owe you."

"That won't be necessary." Joanna sat at the kitchen table. "Bobby, do you know the Wainwrights? They're over in Willis."

"Wainwrights? Oh, yeah, you bet." Bobby turned the completed window in his hands, peering along the sashes and muntins. "Set straight as a string."

"They leased the *Bo-Peep* to my husband—"

"Yep. Thousand bucks for the summer."

"That's right. How did you know that, Bobby?"

"Everybody at the docks knows what people lease for. —Could have got that *Bo-Peep* boat for six, seven hundred. That wasn't a fancy sailer."

"I was talking to Beverly Wainwright—"

"Bev's real rough. All them Wainwrights is rough." He tried the glazed repair in the window's empty frame.

"They have a rough dog, too. But a nice dog."

"You talkin' about that pit bull?"

"Yes. . . . Percy."

"Made a lot of money with that red dog. —Still do make money, studdin' him out."

"They have dogfights on the island, Bobby?"

"No, not out here. Fought that dog over at Post Port. Fought him all the way down in Boston, once. Made a lot of money with that dog. . . . But don't say I was the one told you."

"I won't. . . . You know, Bobby, I was talking to Beverly Wainwright, and she said they had only five thousand dollars insurance on the boat. And I was wondering if that was true—that they'd have so little insurance."

"Oh, sure. That's a *lot* of insurance on that old boat." He tried the window again, thumping its sashes for a fit in the frame. "—Plenty of people out here don't pay insurance at all, unless the bank makes 'em. Figure those insurance men just take advantage." More thumping on the window. "She's goin' in, fits just right—an' them jambs wasn' real square, neither!"

Joanna got up to examine the work. "It *does* fit. Thank you, Bobby. Looks as good as new."

"Well, I got to tack it in . . . an' caulk it, an' it needs some touch-up paintin'. I got paint I'm usin' on a dory; I'll bring a little of that up. White oil paint, an' it'll do just fine."

"I appreciate this, Bobby. You broke it—and you fixed it."

"Damn right." Bobby stooped, slightly unsteady, to collect his tools and glue . . . put them away in his shopping bag.

"I'd like to ask you about the boy you saw out sailing with my husband."

"Yep?"

"It was a boy—you're sure of that?"

"Kid. That's right."

"Could it have been an older person? A young man?"

Bobby stood thinking about it. "Pretty skinny if he was. Didn' look as big as your old man, out there on that boat. But, you know, Mrs. Reed—"

"Joanna."

"You know, they was pretty far out. Out there in the offin'."

"A boy—maybe a young man—out there with Frank. And wearing what, besides a baseball cap?"

"What was he wearin'?"

"Yes."

"Mrs. Reed—"

"Joanna."

". . . Joanna, I just couldn' tell you what that kid was wearin'. I'm sorry. I never noticed, exceptin' the cap." Bobby picked up his shopping bag, and went to the door.

"And this boy, or this young man, he was just sitting in the boat—wasn't helping sail her?"

"Just sittin' in the cockpit on his ass. Not doin' nothin'. Your man was doin' the work, takin' her out. . . . Holdin' her a tad close to the wind too, fat little boat like that." Bobby swayed slightly, leaned against the doorjamb.

"You know, Bobby, when I spoke to Beverly Wainwright, she said something about fishermen doing 'stuff' out there. 'Stuff.' "

"Right about that. Some of them captains'll do anything for a buck."

"Do what, Bobby?"

"Ask me no questions, an' I'll tell you no lies."

"Okay. —Do I owe you any money for the window supplies?"

"Nope, you already gave me a lot of money." Bobby shifted like a restless child, anxious to go.

"Well . . . then maybe you'd like to stay to dinner."

"Thanks, Mrs. Reed, but I'm not much for eatin'. Drinkin' is my style, sad to say."

"Well . . . then I could offer you a drink, but I don't want to do that if it would harm you. Do you think one drink would harm you?" That had been said to Joanna's surprise—as if by another person, remote, ruthless, and determined.

". . . I guess one . . . just one wouldn't hurt too bad. I can handle one okay. Second one is what does the harm. Then the rest of those drinks after that—they do some harm, you better believe it."

"Okay, then we'll only have one drink, Bobby, just to thank you

for fixing the window." Joanna looked into the cabinet over the refrigerator. There was a half-empty bottle of vodka and an unopened
bottle of Gordon's gin. Almost a full bottle of Chivas Regal. "—You
sure you don't want something to eat?"

"No, thanks. I'm a light eater. Food don't taste like anything
to me."

"Well, why don't you sit down and relax, Bobby, and I'll get you
that drink."

"One. One drink."

"One it is. You can have vodka, gin, or scotch." Joanna felt the
oddest sureness, as if some carnivorous part of her had been waiting for a sacrifice. Criminals, she supposed, felt the same—setting
caring aside.

". . . Don't like scotch." Bobby settled gingerly at the kitchen
table, as if uneasy sitting up off the floor.

"You know, Bobby," she took down the gin bottle, "—it occurred
to me that both my husband and my father went out on the *Bo-Peep*.
They went sailing together almost a month ago, when we first came
out. My father was fishing."

"Fishin'? Fishin' off a little sloop?"

"My father would fish off anything—particularly if it annoyed
Frank . . . my husband." Joanna took two tumblers from the cabinet
over the sink.

"Fishin' off that boat." Bobby Moffit shook his head at the picture. "Summer people. . . ."

"You want tonic, or ginger ale?"

"Don't need neither one."

Joanna twisted the cap off the gin bottle, and poured a tumbler
half full . . . then much less into the other glass. "You said something, Bobby, when you were up here before—said the island captains were 'pretend fishing.' What did you mean by that?" She put
the fuller tumbler on the table in front of him, and sat down opposite. She'd never drunk straight gin in her life, not without ver-
mouth . . . an olive. Had never drunk hard liquor in a kitchen in
daylight, either.

"Didn' mean nothin'." Bobby sat looking down at the glass of
gin, looking into it as if to see his reflection. "—I didn' mean
nothin'. They want to do that, that's their business."

"Do what?"

". . . What they do." Bobby picked up his glass and drank like a child, with attention, holding the tumbler's rim so firmly to his mouth that his cheeks were dented by it.

Joanna sat and sipped her drink. She felt the oddest tenderness for Bobby—as if by damaging him so contemptibly, she was making him her responsibility. A stranger, and being broken for her purpose, he was becoming something more by it—as, just as surely and in perfect balance, she was becoming less.

Bobby, having swallowed several times, put his glass down, and Joanna could see that was difficult for him. She sat watching, watching over him, and sipped her drink. The gin, unmixed, tasted like a complex garden in which nettles, roses, and herbs grew together, pungent, vigorous, sweet-scented, and harsh.

Bobby left his glass on the table for several breaths, then looked up at Joanna as if for permission to lift it.

. . . The second drink she poured seemed to break a cord within him. Later, the third made additional difference.

"Smuggling?" Joanna had had one more minor drink. She appreciated Hogarth's ruined subjects of Gin Lane. For those sad, buckle-shoe'd brutes of slum warrens and cold weather . . . what a splendid floral fountain gin must have brought to warm them, make them jolly. "—Smuggling? Like running cigarettes down from Canada?"

"You got . . ." Bobby seemed to lose his words, then recovered them. "You got to be kiddin'. *Canada*. Nobody runs nothin' out of Canada since Pro . . . Prohibition."

"Then what?"

". . . Nothin'. I don't have no boat; don't ask me." He looked across the room as if someone else had come in—stared with such attention that Joanna glanced over. There was nothing to be seen in that corner of the kitchen, except the last slanting light of day.

"What if you did have a boat, Bobby?"

"Shit. Mrs. Reed . . . I'm an alcoholic." He took a deep proving swallow. "—I can't get insurance even if I had a boat. An' I can't get a boat anyway, because I don't have the money." He cupped the tumbler in both hands, cradled it. "—An' if I *could* get insurance . . . an' I *did* have a boat, I couldn' run it anyway. You got to be real responsible, or you can't run a boat. Now, that's pretty . . . pretty much how things go." He closed his eyes, sat holding his drink, keeping his eyes closed.

"But if you could run a boat?"

"I don't give a shit—pardon my French. I don't give a shit; I don't trust a Russian far as I can throw him. An' I sure as shit don't trust those Russians . . . out there. Not even Russians—people used to be Russians."

A ghost's cool breath seemed to drift up Joanna's arms. ". . . What people, Bobby?"

"Ask . . . ask me no questions, an' I'll tell you no lies." He opened his eyes, and took a drink like necessary medicine.

"What do Asconsett fishing captains have to do with those people—with Russians, Bobby? What do they do out there?"

"None of my business."

"Is it *my* business? Did my husband see something—did my husband and my *father* see something?"

"Damn if I know. Don't ask me. . . ." Bobby drank again, then set his glass down too hard.

Joanna sipped more of her gin. There was a comforting rhythm to serious drinking with someone, a rhythm the alcohol accompanied like a melodic line. "—If the captains aren't fishing out there, then what are they doing?"

"They're fishin', fishin' for trash. Cat food is all that's out there now."

"Then how are they making a living, Bobby?"

"What . . . ?" Bobby Moffit was collapsing as he sat, the gin slowly breaking him to pieces. Sections of his face and body seemed ready to slide away, as slabs of ice toppled from glaciers and fell into the sea.

Joanna started to reach across the table, pour more gin into his glass. —And she intended to do it, was willing to do it, but her hand wouldn't. Her hand felt pity, and wouldn't pour. It put the gin bottle down. "How do the captains and processing people, the people on the island . . . how do they make a living now, Bobby?"

"Captains an' processin' people. . . . You ask Mannin' how he's makin' a livin' . . . processin'."

"Manning?"

"Right. You just . . . ask him. You ask him what he's holdin' down there, makin' a *real* good livin'—an' he pays me shit for doin' all that moppin'. Goin' around with that mop an' bucket like a damn woman." Bobby emptied his tumbler as if he were terribly thirsty, as if the gin were cold water, and saving his life.

"Bobby, did my husband get into some kind of trouble when he and my father were sailing out there?"

"Hey. . . ." Bobby sagged in his chair, and yawned. "Askin' the wrong guy. Askin' the wrong guy. . . ." He took a sudden gasping breath, then put his hands on the tabletop and pushed himself up to his feet. His face was flushed scarlet. "I better go . . . outside."

Joanna stood up. "Can I help you?"

"No . . . you can't," Bobby said. Then said, "Oh, dear," and staggered away from the table toward the kitchen door. "Oh, dear," he said, and stumbled as Joanna got to him to help. He was heavy and she couldn't hold him—he fell against the stove . . . then swayed, stepped across to the door, and began to vomit as he groped for the knob.

The vomit, gritty and dark with blood, spattered and drained out of him down his clothes, splashed on the floor, and Bobby made an odd shoving motion with both hands, slowly sat down on the linoleum, then slumped over onto his left side, his knees drawn up like a baby's.

"Oh, God . . . oh, Bobby . . . please forgive me. Oh, *Christ.*" Joanna bent over, wrestled awkwardly with Bobby as if that might help. She was in the vomit. It was all over the floor, stinking spoiled blood and gin. "—Bobby . . . Bobby!"

His face remained dull maroon—but printed pale around his mouth. He was breathing bubbles of vomit.

"*Oh, God* . . . " Joanna pulled and tugged him away, out of the worst of the mess; his clothes were soaked with it. She unbuttoned his shirt, turned and heaved him from side to side to peel it off. The blue cotton was black with dirt, soaked down the front with vomit. She got him out of that, out of the shirt, and stood up to get a dish towel to wipe the floor around him.

"Oh, God. *Please* . . ." The "please" was for the gift of Bobby's living and being well—the gift of her not having killed him.

She took his arms and hauled, dragging him after her along the floor. There was a trail of bloody vomit. She tugged him past the kitchen table, then stopped, and bent over him to be sure he was still breathing. —And he was, but very strangely, a liquid sort of breathing. She was able to lift his shoulders a little, turn his head to the side . . . and that seemed to help. He still breathed, but not as badly.

"My fault," Joanna said it to herself aloud, for the relief of saying it.

She took a deep breath. The smell was dreadful. Bobby's smell, and the vomit. She bent over him, unfastened his belt, and unbuttoned his trousers. They'd been good trousers once, dress slacks. Now they were stiff, dark with dirt and caked in the seams. There was vomit only down the left leg . . . but all the way down to the cuff. Some of it was pooled in the trouser cuff there.

Trying to hold her breath, Joanna knelt astride Bobby and tugged and worked at the trousers to get them off. They wrinkled and folded down. He wore no underwear, and displayed a grimy belly, a sad sagging penis the same congested color as his face.

Joanna gathered the trouser material and pulled the pants down his legs—then had to stop to untie laces, get his sneakers off. He wore no socks, but the smell was very bad.

When he was naked, Bobby lay still, sprawled in smears of vomit and breathing noisily. His body, streaked and cloudy with dirt, was mottled the color of bruises.

Joanna, calmer now, didn't think he was going to die—didn't think she had to call an ambulance. . . . She supposed Bobby had done this many times, drunk himself sick. This once more wasn't going to kill him, just because she was responsible. . . .

She stood, and rinsed the kitchen towel in the sink. Rinsed it, soaked it in hot water, then wrung some out and knelt to wash Bobby's face, scrub it clean. She used a corner of the cloth to get clots of vomit out of his mouth so he could breathe more easily. She was afraid he'd breathe it in and strangle. . . . She did that, then got up to rinse the towel again, rub Ivory soap into the cloth.

Joanna cleaned Bobby's face, his neck and ears, and behind his ears. She saw herself frantic as a frightened cat with a sick kitten. . . . It seemed essential to clean him, necessary for forgiveness. She wanted to wash his hair—it was filthy—but there seemed no good way with him lying on the floor. And having started to clean this collapsed man, found she had to continue doing it . . . getting up again and again to rinse dirt from the towel, soak it in more hot water, wring it out, soap it, and kneel to Bobby again to rub and scrub. . . .

. . . After a long time, having bathed his torso, his groin, his sex, his legs and feet . . . having heaved him over to clean his back and flaccid buttocks, Joanna found she couldn't leave Bobby's hair unwashed. She stood up once more, her knees aching, filled a pan at the sink, swished the diminished bar of soap in the hot water, and went to sit on the wet linoleum beside him. He was breathing long slow breaths, eyes tight shut as if light would hurt them if he woke. . . . She soaked his hair, soaped and scrubbed it, rinsed the towel in the pan water and soaped his hair again, getting more water on the floor.

. . . When Joanna finished, she was stiff and sore from so long kneeling and scrubbing. She stooped, took Bobby's wrists, and dragged him slowly out of the kitchen and into the dining room. Then she stood, stretched to ease her back, and went upstairs for towels and blankets.

She took them from the hall closet—the blankets were Mrs. Evanson's—and went downstairs. She dried Bobby as thoroughly as she could—he was mumbling—then laid one of the blankets, folded lengthwise, on the floor, rolled him over and onto it, and covered him with the other. Then she went down the hall for a cushion from the living-room rocker, came back and put it under his head. . . . Naked, and clean—or fairly clean—Bobby lay swaddled in his pallet, breathing heavily, but breathing.

Joanna, very tired, gin buzzing in her ears, stood watching him —her accomplishment. A sick man deliberately made sicker, then cared for and cleaned. She supposed other women had done things similar. . . .

She stood for a while, watching Bobby breathe, listening to him. Then she went upstairs to the bedroom and selected a pair of Frank's jeans, one of his blue work shirts, an old tan windbreaker, a pair of Jockey shorts, and white athletic socks. She brought the clothes down, folded them into a little stack with the socks and underwear on top, and put them on the floor next to Bobby. . . . Everything should fit him, if not very well, except the jeans; they'd be a little short in the leg, but not much. —If there were ghosts, if Frank was a ghost and watching her, he certainly wouldn't regret the jeans and shirt. He would regret her giving gin to Bobby Moffit.

There were freedoms, advantages after all, to having your loved ones dead, and no longer watching. . . .

Joanna wandered through the house, walking in failing light to Bobby's sleeping music, hoarse and harsh, and the distant rhythm of the sea easing through open windows.

Drinking. . . . Neither she nor Frank had been big drinkers. White River's faculty—with exceptions—wasn't the alcoholic faculty of a few decades earlier. People, most of them, sipped wine. Less vomit on carpets, and fewer of alcohol's harsh revelatory truths. —And what truth had alcohol now offered her? That Beverly Wainwright . . . that poor Bobby Moffit knew of something spoiled, something wrong on the island? Something for which she had no evidence, no proof of any kind, so she could only play the bereft woman still acting her sorrow out, to the fatigue and boredom of official men.

Bobby moaned on his pallet, shifted under his blanket in search of comfort.

"You ask him," he'd said. "Ask that Mannin' what he's holdin' down there. . . ."

Joanna stood by the dining-room window, looking out into darkening night. The sea sounded clearly up the hill, salt breeze bringing its voice to her. The moon was rising, stretching the cottage's faint shadow over the yard. . . . There was the sleepiest, most smothering pressure to do nothing. To do nothing odd, foolish, and possibly— even probably—mistaken. She had gone to the authorities, spoken to a lawyer, made a continual fuss. . . .

Would Frank, would her father mind if she did nothing more? Did nothing foolish? Would they mind if she just let it go? . . . They were dead; there'd be no bringing them back, whatever or whoever had caused their deaths. —And they might have done it themselves; might have had accidents after all. In a few years, there would only be sadness when she thought of it. Only sadness and dark poetry when she thought of Frank, thought of her father . . . and their accidents.

Bobby Moffit was almost snoring, breathing in slow huffs and puffs, so he sounded like a worn train working uphill . . . weary, unhappy machinery.

Joanna went to him, saw he'd turned onto his side, the top blanket slid off his shoulder. She bent, tugged the blanket up to cover him, then walked into the kitchen, took the slender-bladed fillet knife from the sink drawer, and went out the back door and down the steps.

Moonlight lay like platinum webbing, rippling, moving as the breeze moved the sea grapes edging the yard.

Joanna opened the garage's side door, went in, and turned on the light to select what she needed.

Chapter Ten

Charis sat studying on her side of the room's table. Art of Poetry, a course that all the jocks—as jocky as students got at White River—attended and depended on for summer credit. Chris Engletree taught it, and it was an easy course to pass, a hard course to get good grades in.

Engletree, very gay, had little good to say about most traditional poetry, and thought less of Joanna Reed, colleague or not. "—Reed's work tends to be painfully old-fashioned and form-cramped. Personal *interactions*, moral *homilies*, concentration on structure and beautiful *language*, including little narratives and *events*, and often rhymed. —Read poetry that is truly of today, and you'll see exactly what Reed's work isn't. It isn't of the moment; it isn't structure-free; it isn't culturally inclusive; it isn't all-race-referenced."

Engletree loved Japanese poetry. "Perfectly minimal, accurate, and cruel . . . in haiku, seventeen precise syllables. I forgive structure that is ethnically determined."

Charis, second row center, had raised her hand. "But how does it sound when you speak it?"

"Ugly, and so what, Ms. Langenberg? Japanese is an ugly language—and so is German and so *what?*" Chris Engletree, tender with handsome soccer or track men, was tough on women.

"So, there's no music to it at all," Charis said. "It's limited to evocative observations— '*Mount Fuji is very small, seen in my mirror, as I shave my forehead, on the first day of winter*'—observations the reader is intended to internalize in response. That's a pretty restricted art."

"Bullshit," Engletree said. "Is that your rule or something? Are you making up rules about art?"

"I'm commenting on yours," Charis said. "Japanese paper-making is more intricate than their poetry."

"That's so cute," Engletree said. "Aren't you clever? But Japanese culture and poetry may be a little too sophisticated for some American *coeds.*"

He really disliked her. . . . Charis had imagined cutting her hair very short for his class, then using no makeup and wearing breast-hiding sweatshirts, wearing shorts, hiking boots, and thick socks just to watch his attitude slowly alter as she became more boyish to look at, more brusque, her voice lowering until she was a strutting casual lithe young man, the finest blond down decorating long un-shaven legs. Tough and beautiful, with only a cock necessary to complete him.

It would have been amusing . . . but too much trouble. Engletree wasn't worth the trouble. He didn't like her, but he wouldn't grade her down because she cared for poetry, because it was important to her. . . .

"Charis?" Rebecca, across the table. She was supposed to be do-ing her Spanish. "Charis . . . ?"

Charis hadn't spoken to Rebecca all day. Hadn't said a word to her, hadn't answered anything she'd asked.

"—Charis, if you're angry, I really don't know what I *did.* I know I've been upset about Daddy and now my grandfather dying. I guess I've been a pain."

Charis looked up. "I do have two words to say to you, Rebecca. The words are: Greg Ribideau. Okay?"

"What do you mean?"

"Don't give me that shit—roommate, *friend.*"

"Charis, really, I don't know what you mean." Round little face gone pale. "—I haven't even talked to Greg except once!"

"Just . . . Rebecca, just study and don't try to talk to me, all right? I'm not interested in hearing a lot of lies."

"What are you— Charis, really I haven't *done* anything!" Sitting confused in pajamas and her pink terry-cloth bathrobe.

"You are just a little bitch, and that's all you are. Greg says it's you, you, you he likes and finds interesting—and he just realized it and so forth, all that crap! You're both a pair of goddamn *liars.*"

"What are you talking about? Greg doesn't like me. He never said anything to me!"

"Oh, right, Rebecca. Sure. He thinks you're 'really interesting,' a 'special person,' and he feels as if he 'knows' you—and you two haven't even *talked*? Please don't waste my time with this shit, Rebecca. Greg likes you; you like him—and that's great. . . . Just leave me alone and stop treating me like some goddamn fool. I'd really appreciate that. Just cut out the 'I'm a little mouse and I wouldn't fuck anybody else's boyfriend' bit. —And I will move the hell out of this room just as fast as I can arrange it."

Charis closed her book, got up, and walked out, leaving Rebecca startled, upset, and pleased. —Charis went down the stairs to the dorm entrance and put three quarters in the snack machine. A small bag of barbecue Doritos rattled down.

She went out the dorm door, down the steps, and strolled away into a summer night lit by starlight and occasional lamps along the paths. Charis ate the Doritos as she walked; they were deliciously salty.

Mr. Langenberg had eaten only healthy food—fed her healthy food. Turkey breast and steamed carrots, steamed new potatoes, steamed green beans. He'd hated Doritos, chips, dips, anything like that. . . . Mom—Mrs. Langenberg—had been a good cook, and made peach pies. Charis could still remember the pale gold of a peach pie cooling on the kitchen table in the house on Edgar Avenue, in Cincinnati. She remembered having to stand on tiptoe to see along the tabletop. And she remembered the taste.

After Mrs. Langenberg had a kidney infection, then had more kidney trouble a year later and died—died swollen and itching—after that, there were no more peach pies.

Mr. Langenberg became very concerned about diet and health, being healthy in mind and body. "Is this a perfect little body, or what?" he asked that whenever certain men came over. "—Is this a perfect little body or what? And not a feather on her." The visitor always agreed that she was perfect. "Bend over and show him," Royce Langenberg would say.

And the man would make the sound "Mmmm . . ." If there were two of them, they'd both make that sound, "Mmmm . . . ," and take her picture.

When Charis grew older, and had feathers, Mr. Langenberg would go with her into the upstairs bathroom, and shave her after she took her shower. But she could tell he didn't like having to do it. . . .

Charis came to the Fork, and turned up the high walk, wishing she'd gotten two packages of Doritos. —What the college cafeteria served as dinner was pretty grim, even for institutional food. Supposedly, things improved in the fall, when they had a full staff cooking.

. . . It was difficult for her to remember much in the way of conversation with Royce Langenberg—though they were together until she was sixteen, and it was time for him to have his accident. . . . She did remember driving with him back and forth across Ohio. The first few years, she'd sat on a pillow so she could see out the passenger-side window. But it was difficult to remember the individual days, individual conversations. The days and conversations seemed to have fallen out of shuffle, like a dropped deck of cards.

"A district sales manager is either God almighty—or the goat." He had said that to her once, while they were driving. Mr. Langenberg had four salesmen under him, getting market orders for frozen-food products, prepared meals, and instant mixes. "—Give me a biscuit, give me any baked or prepared food, and I'll tell you the producing corporation." And he could; did it often in restaurants.

Otherwise, especially when he was driving, he didn't like a lot of conversation. He did say, "Daughter-mine, you just don't know how much I care for you. I care for you just as if you'd been born our own little baby." Said that to her more than once. —But when Charis disobeyed, or brought bad grades home from school, or was rude to a man who'd come to see her, then Royce Langenberg would put her in the cedar chest to think about it.

"Are you thinking . . . ?" He'd ask that several times during the day, bend down and ask it in a loud voice so she could hear. Then he'd ask her again, just before he went to bed at night. *"Are you thinking . . . ?"*

And she'd say "yes," and he'd say, "I am *so* glad," and take her out next morning in time for the bus, if it was a school day. And at school, a girl sitting behind her once said, "You smell like moth balls."

. . . Charis ate the last Dorito. And as she passed under a maple's lamp-lit leaf ceiling, murmured one of Joanna Reed's poems.

> *I wait, and you wait with me,*
> *Expecting   different   visitors.*

I wait, and you wait with me,
But one visitor will not come.
I wait, and you wait with me.
Who comes, will be unwelcome,
So must be greeted with a lie.
You are the visitor I wait for.
You may go, and return welcome.

Chris Engletree was an idiot.

Joanna, wearing old cotton coveralls and her caving boots, drove down the hill by headlight and moonlight, then turned right on Strand Street, its sidewalks empty to the night. She went three blocks, then took a left down Ropewalk. There was no one in the alley. The only light, filtered green-yellow through sea fog, shone down from a streetlamp on Strand.

Joanna parked the Volvo between two battered pickups at the foot of the alley, by the docks. She got out of the car, and crossed Ropewalk to Manning's. . . . The warehouse and processing plant was a big three-story brick building, half a block wide and a full block long, its bulk backing up from the waterfront to Strand Street. Huge—and old, built in 1870 . . . 1880. There were no windows on the alley side except a row of wide glazed window vents beneath the third-floor eaves.

It seemed to Joanna it would have to be here. —The front entrance up on Strand was impossible, with streetlamps, alarm tape on the windows and doors, and people certain to be passing by, even this late at night. The dock entrance, below, was almost as bad—alarms on the windows, office door and loading dock . . . and security lights all along the pier.

It would have to be here. . . . She leaned against the building's brick, stroked it, ran her fingers along the masonry. Ancient mortar, crumbling from sea air, its dampness and salt. Still, she could bolt between the brick runs, haul herself up from anchor to anchor. But it would be noisy—too noisy—and take too long. So, wall-climb whatever was handy, quietly and quickly, with no driven bolts or aids.

It was a great comfort to have so limited, so familiar a problem.

Joanna walked up the alley along the wall, and saw a drainpipe down the building's side. It ran a straight line from the warehouse's roof gutter to the street.

She tried it, gripped the wet metal and tugged left and right for motion. It was very old and rusty cast iron—would be brittle, easy to crack and break, especially where narrow iron straps, almost weathered through, fastened the pipe to the building's bricks.

An old length of rusted pipe, but a straight run up to the roof . . . thirty-five, forty feet above the cobblestones. Quiet, and quick.

Joanna walked back across and down the alley to the car, checked to see that no one was passing up on Strand Street, then opened the trunk and took out her helmet and lamp, a thirty-yard coil of PMI dynamic rope, a short nylon tape sling of carabiners, and a small belt pack. The fillet knife was in the pack, with a butane lighter, small flashlight, her gloves, and the Leatherman multitool.

Joanna closed the car trunk, checked the street again for any late-night passerby, then rigged up—draped the tape sling and rope coil over her shoulder, belted on the pack, put her helmet on and tightened the chin strap.

Quietly . . . and quickly.

She crossed the alley, walked up to the drainpipe, gripped and tested it again, then took a deep breath, reached up on the fog-wet iron as high as she could, jumped off the cobbles and began to climb.

She leaned away from the wall as she went up, frogging—reaching above her with one hand, then both, for a grip on the pipe . . . then tucking her knees, digging her boot toes into the brick courses, and straightening her legs to drive herself up.

Easier top-roped, with ascenders. . . .

Twenty, twenty-five feet up, she stopped on the wall to rest. Her fingers hurt, cramped from gripping slippery round metal. . . . She could loop a nylon tape under the pipe, make a sling to hang from for a rest. Could do that—and if there'd been another fifty or hundred feet of climbing, would have had to.

She hung there, pulled in close to the wall, and looked down into the alley. No one . . . nothing but sea mist drifting in dim lamplight, dampness, and dark.

Joanna took a deep breath, relaxed her shoulders, reached up and began to climb again. The rope coil was cramping her right shoulder; she had to pause and shift it slightly. Right shoulder, right arm—neither quite the same after her surgery. Something cut in the chest muscle or the armpit, limiting just enough to be noticeable. Noticeable during great effort.

She frog-climbed another ten or twelve feet, saw the roof gutter overhang only a little higher, and reached up to the pipe for another grip.

She had it, held it hard—and the pipe made a celery sound, cracked, and the piece broke away.

Joanna swayed back, the chunk of pipe still in her hands—and she might have fallen, felt that sudden urge to disaster, to let go . . . let go and fall back and down through darkness.

She refused to fall, let the piece of pipe go instead, so it dropped away—and as if she were in love with the building's wall, slumped into it, curved her belly into it, and let herself relax against its brick as the piece of broken iron rang, then rattled on the cobbles below. Her boot toes, at a mortar line beneath her, supported her for that moment . . . and her hands, turned to claws, set their fingernails into the brick.

Only for a moment. —After the moment, if she didn't climb, she would fall.

Joanna bent her knees only slightly, and as if she had a solid ledge beneath her, jumped . . . reaching for the section of pipe just above the break.

Her boot toes slipped as she went up. She missed the hold with her left hand, and seized it with her right. She had the jagged end of wet pipe in her grip right-handed, and hung there for less than a second until her left hand could join it.

With both hands holding on, she knew she wouldn't fall. She could hold on forever . . . never fall.

She hung from her sure grip, hung in the air against the wall. The darkness below, the waiting cobblestones, no longer called to her. . . . She carefully, lightly, stepped stepped stepped, her boot toes found their momentary purchase between brick courses, and she started climbing the pipe again . . . gripping as lightly as she could, so as not to break the rusted iron.

The roof, its gutter overhang, was now only a few feet above. Joanna went up, and up . . . then stretched to touch the overhang. Old iron—but thick, crusted with layers of crumbling paint. The fat, rough, curved metal edge was a comfort to her fingers, a good hold.

She hung there, brought her other hand up to the gutter, and rested a moment, swinging slightly to ease her shoulders.

The nearest vent window was six or seven feet to her left, and a couple of feet down. She began to swing a little more, side to side—setting up a rhythm to help her hand-over-hand along the gutter's edge to the vent.

There was a sound in the alley beneath her. A soft thud, thud . . . thud, thud.

Joanna stopped swinging and hung still, her fingers aching . . . then slowly, carefully, turned her head to look down.

Someone was walking down the alley from Strand Street—a man in dark shirt, jeans, and black rubber boots. It was too dark to see more detail, make out his face.

Joanna dangled from the gutter, hanging still as a cave bat, and watched the man walking along the cobbles . . . walking beneath her on his way to the docks. She allowed her fingers to hurt, as long as they kept their grip—and slowly, slowly turned her head to follow him down to the end of Ropewalk . . . then a turn right, onto the pier and out of sight.

A fishing-boat crewman with some nighttime chore to do. . . .

Joanna shifted her grip from one hand to the other to ease her fingers—the rope coil was weighing heavy on her shoulder—then began to swing left to right and back again, gathering momentum.

On the end rise of her third swing to the left, she went quickly hand-over-hand three or four feet closer to the vent window . . . then took a breath, began to swing again, her hands hurting, and went hand-over-hand three feet farther to hang from the gutter just above the vent.

The low, wide window, its thick frame hinged at the top, was crusted with peeling white paint. Its bottom edge was canted open four or five inches. —Joanna, stretching down, was just able to get a toehold on the sill beneath the window frame's outward angle. Not stance enough.

It was very bad practice to fall—even for two or three feet—to a hold. It was a question of acceleration forces. . . .

Joanna kicked her foot free of the sill, let go of the gutter's edge, and fell down the wall. . . . Almost past the canted window, she reached with both hands, gripped the sill, and caught herself with a grunt. Her wrists wrenched at the leverage; her hips and legs swung hard into the wall.

She had the sill, but not its inside edge. She held with her right hand, scrabbled at brick with her boot toes . . . then reached in farther with her left, found the sill's inner edge, and had her hold.

Joanna hauled herself up and against the window, and tried to pull the bottom of the sash frame out and open. It didn't budge. The vent must have been left ajar for years . . . been painted open just this far. There was a steady slight draft blowing out, stinking richly of fish.

She was getting tired . . . tired of clinging to the wall. She held with her left arm jammed under the window, hand gripping the inner sill—and with her right hand reached behind her for her pack, tugged the Velcro open, and dug into it for the multitool.

Opening the Leatherman with only one hand and her teeth was a chore . . . to open it, and fold out the serrated knife blade. —When she had the blade out and locked, Joanna began to work on the paint plastered in brittle layers along the upper side edges of the vent window's frame, where their angles narrowed to the hinged top sash above.

It was hard work, hard to do clinging to the wall almost forty feet up. . . . Difficult to do one-handed, and in darkness only a little relieved by lamplight from Strand Street. If she dared to use her helmet lamp, it would have been so much easier . . . so much easier.

She worked and worked the blade along one side of the window, and then the other—sawing, slicing through old paint down the window frame's edges. Then she paused, tucked the tool into her coverall pocket, and tried the window again, heaving at it, trying to force it up and wide enough to crawl through.

Her left hand, deep under the window, was growing numb from holding.

She took the tool out and went to work again . . . carving into the painted-over joins, prying thick strips and chips of old paint away. It was becoming very difficult. . . . After a while, she stopped and hung at the window, getting her breath. There was no feeling in her left hand and forearm.

She braced her boots against the brick below, tucked the tool into her pocket again, and hauled up on the window's bottom edge, yanked it. She struck the sash frame with her fist, then hauled and heaved again. . . . The window moaned softly, and swung up and out two or three inches.

"*You son of a bitch,*" Joanna said, and wrenched at it again. The vent window made another soft noise, then something split or splintered slightly along its frame's left edge, and the window swung up and open all the way.

She reached in with her right hand to relieve her left from holding . . . then crawled under the open window frame and inside, to straddle the wide sill and crouch there in darkness, safe from falling.

Chapter Eleven

Joanna rested for a while, head and shoulders bent under the canted window frame. She exercised her fingers, easing their soreness and cramp. . . .

Then she leaned out over the well of darkness to her right, reached up and switched on her helmet lamp.

This was the warehouse's main processing space. Wide, deep, and two stories high. She'd seen it before, from the side passage, when she'd come in to talk with Mr. Manning. . . . The huge room below her was filled with machines, tubs, and parked forklifts. And there was a complex stepped pavement of wide conveyor belts down the length of the space, supported on series of huge rollers above steel frames, drive chains, and shafts.

Joanna lifted the rope coil off her right shoulder, and passed the working end of the line through the narrow slot between the hinges at the top of the window. She fed a short length of line through, brought it around under the window, tied a bowline and backed it up with an overhand knot. Then she let the rest of the rope fall free down the warehouse's inside wall.

She dug her gloves out of the pack, put them on—bare hands to climb, gloves to rappel—then wound the rope's slack between her legs and around her right thigh . . . then up and over her left shoulder and down her back to be held firm in her right hand. She switched off her helmet lamp to keep its beam from the open window, swung off the sill, set her boot soles against the room's wall . . . and leaning against her rope, backed slowly down into darkness. . . .

More than thirty feet lower, her boot soles hit the floor. She stepped out of the rope . . . a trespasser who'd listened to a poor alcoholic's mumbling. If she was caught, the handsome old constable would come down on her, jail her in a minute.

The odor of fish lay like fog along the room. Fish and machine oil. It was a big space, silent, its tons of hulking machinery bearing down on a floor of heavy splintered planking. There was only a dim night-light far across the processing room, a small red bulb above a door to the passage beyond.

Joanna switched on her helmet lamp, ducked under the conveyor belt, and worked her way beneath it, snaking through the complex of gears and rollers. The floor planking was wet under the wide belts, soaked from hosing down and the workday's melting ice. The wood was wet, and slippery with slime the hose had missed.

Joanna climbed and crawled through the maze of machinery by the light of her helmet lamp . . . a questing hunter, searching for whatever might be strange, wrong, and out of place.

She traveled the length of the room, from a wide brick fireplace in the west-end wall to the office along the east—weaving under the machinery, then climbing up onto the belts and load trays to check the work surfaces.

It took time . . . a long time to search the machinery, the loaders, the floor and corners of the warehouse space. —And there was nothing there. Nothing but fish smell, and fish-transporting machinery, and fish-processing machinery.

Joanna tried the small front office. She searched through the desks by helmet light—used the Leatherman to pry two locked drawers open—then went through the file cabinets. . . . Bills of lading, receipts and requests for receipts, utility bills, payment slips, and canceled checks. Shipping journals, waybills, and mainland truck drivers' mileage records and delivery schedules.

Two cabinet drawers of tax forms, tax records—federal, county, and state.

It took her more than an hour just to skim through it. And she found nothing to suggest any business but the fish business. Preliminary processing, icing, small-lot freezing, and shipping. . . .

Joanna tried to leave everything in the office as she'd found it, but couldn't fix the broken drawer locks. . . . She remembered Mr. Manning's great bulk, his round flat face oddly set with handsome green eyes.

She went down the hall passage to the back of the warehouse, opened the machine-room door, and searched through the equipment there, the tool racks and heavy rubber hoses, the battered cooler cabinets and their ducting, dented and taped.

There seemed to be nothing at Manning's that shouldn't be there . . . except for a very foolish woman.

Joanna went through a thick heavy door across the hall from the machine room—and walked into hard winter. The freezer space was smaller than the processing room, and packed floor to ceiling with icy crates of frozen whole fish, gutted and headless fish, small boxes of fish roughly filleted.

It was very cold—colder than any cave. Joanna shivered in her coveralls, sorting at random through a few of the smaller boxes . . . several crates.

Frozen fish.

Weary, fingers aching from the cold, she left the freezer room, made sure the heavy door was closed behind her, and went on down the passage. There was a small bathroom on the left—very dirty, smelling of fish and urine—and beyond that, a door with a heavy padlock on it.

She took the multitool from her pack, unscrewed the Phillips-heads holding the lock plate, and when that came free of the jamb, swung the door open with its lock assembly dangling, still attached.

. . . Burglary was if you took something. Otherwise, it was breaking and entering. That seemed right; that seemed to make sense.

Her helmet light wavering before her, she went through the doorway and down a narrow flight of stairs—very old, worn, and creaking—to a small landing, then down the next flight, descending into a terrific odor of rotted fish . . . almost unbearable.

An open barrel stood against the wall past the bottom of the stairs, a big rusting steel drum resting on concrete blocks . . . and there was apparently garbage, a slurry of fish heads, fish guts rotting in there.

Bile rose in Joanna's throat—she turned aside, bent and retched, trying not to vomit. She pinched her nostrils shut, breathed through her mouth . . . and that helped a little.

There was a door to the left of the barrel, and she opened it and walked into a low-ceilinged corridor, its walls hung with various machine parts, drive chains, tools, oil cans, rags, and long-handled scrub brooms. . . . Her helmet lamp cast odd, moving shadows as she went through that space, and down seven or eight steps to a small dirt-floored basement room. Deep—a story and a half, at least, below the building's main floor.

There was an ancient furnace crouched there, bulky as a hibernating bear. It had been converted to oil-burning; a big plank-sided coal bin, empty, flanked it.

Joanna, very tired now—wishing she hadn't come into this place at all—climbed up the furnace-room steps and walked the narrow aisle between racked and hanging equipment . . . back to the foot of the stairs.

The smell coming from the garbage barrel seemed even stronger. . . . Her helmet lamp printed a hollow frame of shadow above the steel drum.

She stood still, then slowly turned her head . . . and the lamp threw the shadow again, outlining a framed panel over two feet square. She went closer, despite the stench . . . and saw there was a shallow box frame set into the wall above the barrel—inch-thick wooden framing.

Joanna stretched to reach over the rusting drum, shoved the panel, and felt it move. An old framed-in access trap. An access likely to nowhere, now.

. . . She'd been in this place for at least two hours. Two hours of criminal activity and wasted effort. It was time, and past time, to go.

"Oh, Jesus *Christ.* . . ." Joanna climbed up onto the open barrel's rim on all fours, bracing herself with her hands . . . the steel edges digging into her knees. She didn't look down at what was waiting beneath her, waiting for her to slip.

"Frank, you son of a bitch." His fault in some way, no matter what. . . .

She pushed against the framed woodwork—definitely had been an access hatchway of some sort. It moved a little, then caught. She reached down behind the back of the steel drum's rim . . . feeling for whatever was holding the trapdoor closed. —She felt a hook down there, swiveled into an eye on the door's frame to hold it shut.

Her knees were in agony, the drum's rim cutting into them. . . . Joanna tried to unlatch the hook, wedge her hand down behind the barrel to get to it. *Goddamn thing.* . . .

She got a two-finger grip on the hook, and tugged it. It resisted . . . then snapped free. She straightened with a grunt of relief, shoved at the access door—and it swung open away from her so suddenly, she lost her balance. Her right knee slipped off the edge of the barrel, and she fell half into it. Right leg plunged down into it.

"*SHIT!*" Joanna kicked and wrestled her way up and out of the stuff . . . and stood away from the drum, stomping to get the soup of garbage off her leg. Wet . . . soaked to her thigh. "Oh, my God. . . ."

The odor, the thought of what the stuff was—nasty rotting crap—was nauseating. And now there was a new smell with it, a draft of air along with the fish stink. A draft smelling of new-mown hay.

Joanna forced herself to lean over the garbage barrel, her helmet light shining through the half-open hatchway behind it. . . . Breathing through her mouth, she still smelled that odd medley of fish rot and sunny summer pasture. The cut-hay odor was breezing through the trap.

She climbed up onto the steel drum again, balanced there, shoved the small square door wide open, and crawled straddling over the barrel's open top to look through. There was a sort of chute . . . a narrow wooden chute crusted with white. White crystals glittering in her helmet's light.

Joanna rubbed a gloved finger across the white . . . carefully tasted with the tip of her tongue. —Salt. Before ice-making . . . mechanical coolers, they must have used the access hatch and chute to send salt down into a basement storage area. Packed the new-cleaned fish with it.

She worked her way into the chute, slid down it headfirst for ten, twelve feet . . . and ended on her hands and knees in damp dirt. The farm smell, country smell, was very strong. Pastures . . . hay.

Joanna stood, and slowly turned her head—sweeping with her helmet lamp as she'd done countless times in deeper places, darker than any basement. . . . This was a big rectangular space, high-ceilinged, beneath the warehouse's long processing room. A wide brick fireplace was set into the cellar's west wall.

When Joanna looked up, her lamp picked out massive old wooden beams—each almost two feet square—crossing the ceiling.

Heavy timber uprights marched away down the basement in long ranks.

The only storage in this nineteenth-century space was modern—several long rows of nearly yard-square bales stacked side to side and three or four bales high—each neatly bundled in thick shining black plastic marked with a few scribbled white Cyrillic letters, and double-bound with wide silver strapping tape.

Joanna walked down a narrow aisle between two of the stacked long rows, her helmet light shining right, then left, as she turned her head. The big bales were set on wooden pallets, off the cellar's dirt. At a rough count, perhaps five . . . six hundred bales.

She stood beside a wall of them, took off a glove, and reached out to touch, stroke smooth heavy black-plastic wrapping . . . run her fingers along the strapping tape to be certain all this was real, and not imagined.

The saturated odor of cut grass was overwhelming. Down here, there was hardly any smell of fish. And that, of course, had been the reason for the garbage barrel above, the rotting offal meant to cover any odor rising from this stored cargo.

What was the street price of say eighty- or ninety-pound bales of marijuana leaf and seed, grown in dark Russian earth? What was the price of a huge basement full of it, all neatly wrapped? Wrapped for transfer at sea, of course. . . .

Joanna walked down to the end of the cellar, and found a very wide iron double door, rust-streaked over peeling red-lead paint. The loading door. She supposed the cargo must come in over one of those second, lower docks, directly beneath the main warehouse piers—built originally so fish could be unloaded from a boat into a warehouse's first floor and basement at the same time, for quicker turnaround, less spoilage.

Old construction, the lower dock not really secret . . . not perfectly hidden from view, but still handy for unloading under cover and into the basement, particularly at night—particularly while fish were being unloaded on the pier above it. And must have been a very useful arrangement during Prohibition, when whiskey was smuggled down from Canada.

A different contraband today. . . . What was the price of a cellar full of it, ferried to the mainland in fish trucks—then delivered direct to Portland, Providence, and Boston? A near and handy New England source . . . with none of the hassles of long and complicated transshipments from the South and far West.

What was its price these days? The value of so many big un-processed bales? A million dollars? Much more than a million dol-lars. . . . Part of the cost, of course, having been the life of a man out sailing his summer boat—and the life of an old man who'd gone with him, fishing.

. . . Frank and Louis must have sailed too early one misty morn-ing, sailed by bad luck too far or in the wrong direction, and seen the transfer . . . seen something and perhaps not even understood it. And their lives, thereafter, had become part of the cost of doing business, of ensuring Asconsett's secrets.

Joanna, smelling—under a climate of marijuana—the stench of rotting fish soaked into her coverall leg, paced the basement aisles behind the bright circle of her helmet's light. She said, "Oh, Frank, I know it now," and began to cry, weeping with relief at finding the reason, something less frightening than chance. And the foolish widow not, after all, a fool.

Reason, and then the bittersweet satisfaction of being proved right. —Now everything was explained, and was bearable. Even if the constable, if the fishing captains, caught and killed her—if all the island rose to silence her and keep its secret—she would die al-most satisfied. She wept a little longer, returning to the chute through corridors of bales, wiping her eyes with her glove's coarse leather.

. . . Getting back up the chute was easy—climbing through the hinged trapdoor and over the fish-gut barrel was hard. Joanna didn't try to fasten the hatchway shut behind her. She crawled over the open steel drum, dropped to her feet, and started up the cellar stairs.

They wouldn't hold the shipment long; in a few days the base-ment would be empty. But if she left tomorrow on the morning ferry, she'd be in Post Port by noon. No phone calls, sounding im-probable . . . and no more talking to old Carl Early and his island deputies—who must know, must at least have suspected.

The Coast Guard commander's office was at the Port, and the state police. And if they didn't move, she'd call the federal drug people. —Then they would all come out; they would come out and begin to destroy the island fishermen. . . . Revenge only a sad sub-stitute for Frank and her father—but much, much better than nothing.

Joanna opened the door at the top of the basement stairs—

and saw bright light shining at the far end of the building, shining through the glass-paned door and office windows from the pier outside. A big fishing boat just come in. . . . Breathless, suddenly weary, she went to the left, weaving her way through the machinery toward the north wall, toward the length of hanging rope.

The light from outside was very bright. The boat's searchlight beam threw streams of white-gold along the plant's floor. Joanna snaked under the conveyor belt, working her way over to the wall. —There was noise. Noise outside.

She reached the hanging length of rope as the warehouse door opened, men talking . . . trooping in, rubber boots thumping up the short ramp to the office. The office lights went on.

Joanna lay down along the wall, stretched on the floor in the machinery's shadow. No one could see her from the office. She could barely hear the men . . . talking, laughing in there. The front door opened again and someone else came in, stomped up the ramp. Joanna lay still, safe in her shadow as long as it stayed a shadow. . . . The rope's running end hung only ten or twelve feet away. She could get to it, and with great effort climb hand-over-hand—boot soles stepping up the wall—the thirty or more feet to the vent window. Climb it in a minute or a little more. . . . Still a long time to be hanging against a white-painted wall, a long time rope-climbing when men were in the office, perhaps coming into the warehouse.

Joanna lay still, listening to the men's faint voices. . . . How wonderful it would have been if women, like the female hawks and eagles, were the large and powerful sex—owned layers of muscle and heavy bone, and had that instinct to apply effective force. How wonderful if men had cocks as their only advantage—as cunts were now for women—and men were the ones required to be shy and careful, to smile even when no smile was called for, to propitiate, supplicate, and scheme to every end. . . .

A man said something loud in the office. Said something louder—a sort of shout. A door opened, and Joanna heard a voice she'd heard before but couldn't recall. Whoever it was, that man said, "Turn on the fucking lights in there!"

No rope-climbing now.

Joanna got to her feet and started back through the gears and rollers of the conveyor belt's machinery. She worked her way through as fast as she could and was halfway across the space when the overhead lights came on.

"Been in the office...." More talk. Men were coming down the passageway beside the processing line.

Joanna got out from under the machinery and ran—her heart thumping, driving her faster and faster—ran down to the end of the processing room, and past the bathroom to the basement door. She shoved the door open as someone coming down the passage saw the motion, yelled after her—and she was through and leaping down the first flight of cellar stairs in the dark.

"You're not getting out of here . . . motherfucker!" And they were at the end of the passage and after her in a sudden surge of motion, chasing, chasing . . . boots hammering across the plank flooring.

It was so odd to be pursued, hunted. It was real and unreal at once. —And the men made hunting noises, hunting calls, shouted curses and encouragement as they came after her through the basement door.

At the bottom of the stairs, Joanna reached the garbage barrel in darkness, and wrenched and wrestled with it as men crossed the landing above her. She heaved it rocking on its concrete blocks— then hurt her back and hauled it tipping and over with a heavy flooding gush of rotten liquid that spilled and foamed stinking over her legs.

She splashed through that as the men came down the last stairs— and she was up and into the hatchway—shoved it wider and slid down the chute while men bayed, milling, stomping in the dark behind her.

As she got to her feet on the basement's dirt floor, lights came on along the ceiling, first one rank of hanging bulbs, then another.

Joanna ran down an aisle of bales, reaching behind her as she ran, fumbling in her belt pack for the fillet knife. The first one to find her would get the blade in his eyes. . . .

She ran down to the iron loading doors, saw them impossible, dogged and heavily bolted shut—and as she heard the first man slide down the chute, doubled back behind the farthest stack and ran between it and the basement wall, running frantically up that aisle to anywhere.

One man . . . two men were in the cellar now, trotting down other corridors of bales toward the iron loading door. She heard a third man calling as he slid down the chute—and she came to her aisle's dead end at the fireplace. She slid the slender knife into the deep side pocket of her coveralls—then ducked down into the wide hearth, down and under . . . reached up into narrow gritty blackness, bent her elbows for a first wedging hold . . . and writhed and struggled, hauling herself up and in.

She lifted her feet, jammed her left hand down beside her, and shoved, shoved herself up into another wedge for her elbows. —And knees now, her knees in and bracing so she could pull her feet up after her, cramp them into the flue. . . . It was narrow, very narrow.

She was up.

And kept climbing rough abrading inches in darkness . . . a measuring worm in an old brick chimney. A slow worm so as not to break ancient carbon deposits loose. Climbing inch by squeezing inch as men's roaming bootsteps, their angry voices, echoed more and more softly beneath her.

"*. . . Hidin' in the goods. Go through the fuckin' bales. . . .*"

The flue was coarsely mortared and very old, and its edges bit and gripped, worried and tore at her as she worked slowly up. Slowly, so as not to be heard below, not cause a sudden shower of soot. . . . She climbed a little higher—and came to a place almost closed with sharp and crumbling cinders.

It felt bad, obstructed and bad, to her left hand, and would need careful passing. Her left glove was already cut across the palm; she could feel she was bleeding into it. And the belt pack was giving her trouble; the chimney flue was too narrow. She'd have to hang the pack from a length of nylon tape, tie that to her ankle, and drag the pack up behind her as she climbed.

Joanna rested, listening. Heard a man's voice . . . but faintly. Wedged in, she bent her helmeted head and could barely see beneath her . . . see only with her left eye. The dim light entering the fireplace below was not broken by the shadow of someone bending to look in and up.

It had not occurred to them.

She felt a terrible urge to laugh—it was all so dreamlike, so bizarre—as if hearing her, the men would also laugh, wait for her to come down, and be too amused to kill her. . . . But then she imagined them being serious, instead, and beating her to death in the basement. She listened, and heard distant voices beneath—shouts, men calling. They'd be going through the hundreds of bales, pulling the stacks apart to find her . . . then backtracking up the wooden chute, checking under the staircase, searching the tool-room, the furnace room.

She was safe from them. Safe in the warehouse's body, buried in its bones. —And as she climbed higher, if she came past a bend in the flue to a trapping angle, or even the slightest additional narrowing, she might be kept there, and rest in the brick forever.

Chapter Twelve

Parsons Hall, across the campus, was White River's oldest dorm, three-story stone with a slate roof. Only a few students were assigned to it during the summer. Girls roomed on the first floor, but the upper floors were for boys—with, supposedly, no closed-door visits. . . . White River, otherwise anxiously politically correct, had bowed to parents in the matter of boys and girls rooming together. A number of midterm pregnancies and a recent boozy rape had turned the argument.

Charis had gone up the stairs to Greg's room over an hour ago. He roomed alone, summer assignment luck, and she'd climbed the stairs to random music—Pearl Jam being played loudest—along the halls.

She'd gone up, and heard someone else in his room, a girl talking . . . sounded like Lauren Gomez. Charis had listened at the door, then gone back down the stairs and outside. She'd strolled around Parsons several times . . . thought about her paper, about Cozzens's fondness for the dilemmas of responsible men . . . then walked around the building one more time, went inside, and climbed the stairs again. —It was late. Greg was going to get laid, or he wasn't.

He wasn't. Lauren was sounding coy, mulching relationship.

Charis knocked once, and walked in. "Hi, Lauren—sorry to interrupt."

"Oh, hi. . . ." Lauren didn't look pleased. She was sitting in Greg's armchair in white punk shorts and a long blue T-shirt, barefoot, her legs drawn up.

"May be *de trop*, but I need to talk with Greg."

"What about?" Greg was sitting on the side of his bed, looking sleepy.

"Just stuff," Charis said, and went over and sat on the bed beside him.

"Well," Lauren said, "—we *were* having a sort of private conversation."

"Sorry." Charis leaned over and kissed Greg on the cheek. Sisterly kiss. "You okay, guy? You look tired."

"I am tired. . . ."

"Paper done?"

"It's done and that's why I'm tired." Sleepy, Greg looked even younger.

"Poor boy." Charis kissed him again. Another sisterly kiss.

"Like I said, we were talking—you know, privately?" Lauren Gomez, dark, black-haired, and very thin, affected Latina waif as her social presentation. She was not friendly with other girls. Definitely not friendly with Charis. . . . They had one class together, Sociology—a bogus course in every college, and particularly feeble at White River. But Gomez was into class participation and sat front-row, representing the Third World. Her accent grew heavier in that class, to the amusement of other Hispanic students.

Charis put her arm around Greg, gave him a little hug. "I understand. 'Private conversation.' " She smiled at Lauren. "—And believe me, I wouldn't have interrupted except it's something really important."

"Oh, sure. —*Greg . . .* ?"

"What?"

" '*What?*'—Oh, just forget it, man. You can just forget it!" And Lauren was up out of the chair, and going. "I don't give a fuck what you two do."

"*Chica,*" Charis said as Lauren went, "—get some bleach on that mustache. You look like an Airedale."

A failed attempt at door-slamming. The piston closure slowed the swing.

". . . Jesus, Charis."

"Sorry—you think those scrawny thighs were going to introduce you to paradise?"

"Well, I had hopes . . . I had hopes before you showed up."

"Didn't want to see me?"

"Charis, I always want to see you."

"Nice to hear. . . . If you want Gomez, just talk me down hard—I'm crazy, sick with jealousy because you love her."

"I don't love her. . . ."

Charis, really fond of him, gave Greg another one-arm hug. "Sweetie, everybody likes being told someone loves them. They always like it, and they always believe it. It's one of life's great mechanical manipulating arms."

"I'll keep it in mind."

"Do that. —Don't waste my lessons, Greggis. They were learned in a hard school."

"That I believe."

"Now, speaking of love, we have a problem. . . ."

"What problem?"

"Don't look so worried—your little face is all scrunched up. The problem is that *you* are loved, Greg. You are the object of my poor roomie's affections."

"Come *on*. . . ."

"No, I mean it—and unfortunately, it's not funny. We're not dealing with a skank like Lauren Gomez."

"Hey, I haven't even talked to Rebecca." Greg was awake now, alert. "I *never* talk to Rebecca."

"Maybe that's what did it! As long as you kept quiet, she could imagine you were something special—not just fairly cute."

"You *are* a bitch."

"No, I'm busy. And I have a very, very troubled little roommate."

"Hey, like it's my business, Charis! It isn't. I never even talked to her!"

"Makes no difference. She thinks you're wonderful. And the reason this is very serious is that she is very serious *about* it. —And we're discussing a young girl who has just lost her father and grandfather, and who is probably looking for even a pitiful substitute for those men."

"Thanks a lot." Greg reached over into his bedside table drawer, found a midsize roach, and lit it with a transparent orange lighter. "But don't, please don't tell me I'm supposed to pretend—"

"No, no, no. Absolutely not. That's the *last* thing." Charis held out her hand for the joint. "What's needed is a very gentle correction—you really like her, she's a pretty girl, a really nice girl, but you're just not ready for a serious relationship." She took a toke.

"Oh, thanks, Charis. That's great. —But what about just ignoring it, letting it go away in its own good time? What about that?"

"Well." Charis passed the joint. "The problem with that is, she has mentioned killing herself."

". . . Are you fucking *kidding* me?"

"Wish I were, Greggis, and don't give me the college-clinic-and-counseling routine. I already tried that one—professional help—and I got a fit of hysterics in return that really scared yours truly. And I'm not an easy scarer."

"What about her parents?"

"Her father's dead, Greg. Remember? Died about three weeks ago?"

"What about her mom?"

"Well, I'll tell you . . . I've met her mother, and I can't quite see myself calling Joanna Reed and saying, 'Hi. I'm your daughter's roommate—Charis? We met when I drove Rebecca out and you scattered your husband's ashes? —Oh, by the way, I was really sorry to hear your dad was just burned alive. . . . Anyway, the reason I called is, I think your daughter might be going to kill herself.' "

"*Man.* . . ." Greg pinched out the joint. "Shit won't stay lit."

"I haven't figured out a really good way to make that call, Greg. I also have a feeling that doing that—telling Mama—is just what might push my roomie over the edge. So, I thought we might be able to defuse the situation, let Becky down easy, and allow truth, common sense, and caring to do their work."

"I don't know. . . ."

"Because, I'll tell you, I'm terribly worried about her. I know that's not cool to say, but it's the truth. I just wish to God she didn't go absolutely nuts when I mention seeing somebody at the clinic."

"Not good. But I don't know. . . ."

"I want—what I want to do is go to the clinic myself, talk to somebody there about it. It's getting too fucking *serious*, Greg. I mean, that's all she talks about . . . that then she could see her dad again and so forth. I mean really weird sad dangerous stuff."

"Charis, you need to go talk to somebody."

"And if she finds out? *When* she finds out—what then? . . . I don't want to be responsible for a girl committing suicide! I couldn't . . . I couldn't stand it, Greg. I know I'm supposed to be the older woman and tough and so forth. . . ."

"Well, you are."

"Oh, thanks. But I'm not tough enough for this. I'm worried sick, and I thought if she wouldn't let anybody else help, at least we could try. . . ."

"I guess I could tell her what you said—you know, that I think she's pretty, that she's a great girl, but I'm . . . I'm just not ready for that kind of serious relationship."

"Greg, I think we have to do that. —Are you going to re-light that joint, or what? . . . It may not help her, but at least we're trying, because Rebecca's just making herself sick over it. She's really, really going absolutely off the wall about you, about the whole thing."

"Oh, boy." Greg fell back on his bed. "I really hate to do this kind of shit . . . this kind of embarrassing shit."

"What a sophisticated dude. —Greg, you're going to have to learn to let a lot of girls down easy."

"Oh, right. That's really funny, Charis. I'll be doing that a *lot.*"

"Well . . . could happen. Rebecca fell for you."

"Right. A nut case."

Charis stood up. "Just give her a call—*don't* say a lot on the phone, *don't* go into detail when you call her, or she'll know I talked to you and it's a plot and so forth. . . . Just be nice, just say you'd like to talk to her, like to meet her somewhere."

"Oooh, Jesus—talk about embarrassing. . . ."

"Greg, please try to sound older than twelve—okay? Now, I've got to go; I haven't printed out my damn paper. Just call her, be friendly, and ask her to meet you . . . meet you after work. She could meet you up on Tar Beach, meet you on the library roof when you finish work on Thursday, day after tomorrow. —You work that evening, right?"

"Yes. . . ."

"When are you off work?"

"Depends . . . late. Sometimes nine-thirty. Sometimes ten."

"Well, call her at the dorm and ask her to meet you up on the beach, Thursday. If she gets there early, if she gets there at nine, she can wait for you. It'll be private that late; nobody else will be up there, and you can talk."

"Man, this just sounds terrible. Talk about a *drag.* . . ."

"Greg, have I asked you for any favors?"

"No, you haven't asked me for any favors."

"And you like me?"

"Well . . . I still jerk off thinking about you, so I suppose we do have a relationship."

"What a guy. —Then do me this favor. I'm *worried* about her, Greg."

"All right. . . ."

"—And for whatever foolish reason, she has decided you're Mr. Fabulous."

"I said I'd do it."

"You'll call the dorm tomorrow?"

"—I'll call tomorrow."

"Greggis, you're becoming really cool." Charis bent over the bed, and kissed him on the lips.

"Oh, absolutely."

"I'm starting to find you attractive—almost attractive."

"Thanks. But I'm beginning to think it would be safer to be gay. I'm definitely going to check that out. . . ."

The night air hummed softly with insects' songs the moonlight had persuaded them to sing. Charis walked back across the campus, tired and ready for sleep, pleased with a stroking night breeze, gentle and cool. The maple-leaf ceilings were moving now, and whispering . . . whispering tree talk as she walked under them. The air smelled of stronger winds to come by dawn, of rain and changing weather.

For a time past time of slow and painful passage . . . of writhing up through a narrow maze of rough brick and black soot, Joanna had followed the small wavering orange circle of her helmet light. . . . It had occurred to her that young boys had once been driven to crawl through chimney flues, with ropes and brushes to clean them.

She had taken a wrong turn once, working to the right along a dead-end run, and had only barely been able to return, inching back, feet first. That mistake had left her lying trembling . . . squeezed, gripped, compressed in darkness, waiting for her courage to come back to her.

. . . For the past while now, Joanna had been seeing an elusive silver reflection high above. And that soft small slice of light held steadier now, as she struggled up through a long cramped choke of rough mortar, small clouds and falls of soot. It was difficult to breathe.

She climbed—hands, knees, and elbows scraped and seeping blood—climbed holding that occasional reflection as her mark . . . until she paused to rest, looked up again, and saw the silver was a slice of the setting moon, obscured by shifting clouds.

Joanna switched off her helmet lamp, then managed slowly up—more frightened now to be so close to freedom, afraid she would panic at last, so cramped, and begin to scream and thrash, a mindless animal. . . . She wriggled, wedged her way up a little more, then reached to touch the chimney's capped edge and the open air. She kicked, kicked and climbed, then hooked her hand over and dragged herself up and out, arms . . . . helmeted head . . . shoulders. Up and out into the sea's night wind, a spatter of salty rain.

She clambered down from the chimney top to stand trembling on a slant of roof . . . reached back to drag her small tethered pack up behind her. The wind's fine-blown rain was in her eyes, its salt stung her hands, hurt her where her skin was scraped. Smears of blood, through torn cloth at her elbows and knees, showed black under an obscured moon.

Joanna stood exhausted, legs shaking, and looked out into the night. . . . Far below, on the dock past the foot of the alley, a small group of men were gathered in the bright pool of a fishing boat's lights.

She watched them for a little while, then took off her helmet and let the sea wind, murmuring over the roof's cracked and ragged shingles, come combing through her hair, lifting it—soot-caked, damp with sweat—separating it with cool fingers for the gusting rain to rinse.

Joy flowed into her and out of her, as if she breathed it in and out. Pleasure as specific as a trumpet's sound. . . . She'd felt nothing like it before—and supposed men knew such sweetness after risking, bleeding, to win a battle. Their wars fought for the chance of this reward.

"We have them," she said, as if Frank were standing with her, angled against the roof's steep fall. *"Oh, dear heart, we have them. . . ."* Joanna stood resting a few moments more, then stepped up to the wet roof's high ridge in clouded moonlight, balanced, and began to dance a slow dance of triumph along it, holding her arms out to the sea wind as if it might lift her as it lifted its gulls, to swoop and slide and rise again.

Chapter Thirteen

Sand Hill was hard climbing in the rain. The sand, lying steep, and soaked here and there as the rain came blowing in, sagged away from under Joanna's boots as she labored up the slope. . . . The patches of sea grass helped, gave better footing.

It had been an easy slide down to the warehouse eaves—a more difficult swing in to the roof's downspout and the drainpipe. . . . Then a careful descent, her hands, arms, and back muscles aching, to the alley's darkness.

There'd been men still gathered down at the docks—several of them, in yellow sou'westers, standing in blowing rain under a lamppost too near the parked pickups and her car. So, carrying her helmet and pack, and staying in shadow, Joanna'd limped up the alley. Strand Street had been almost empty. But there'd been three men, fishermen by their boots and coveralls, standing in a storefront beside the police station, the next block down.

She'd waited until they'd turned away from gusting wind, then had crossed Strand quickly under rain sleeting gold past the streetlamps . . . and gone between the hardware and Michael's Antiques to start up Sand Hill, and stay off other streets fishermen might be searching.

Climbing wet collapsing sand in darkness was hard as climbing a wall. Weary to nausea, Joanna worked up the slope, grunting with effort, tending to the right to reach the cottage. There was no moonlight now, so the rain sheeted down out of darkness, drenched her by surprise, then slackened and blew away.

The sand made a soft rasping sound, spurned from under her

boots, and Joanna chanted to it softly to keep herself from being sick, or lying down to sleep. *"I am justified. Justified. Justified."*

Then she supposed she was taking too much pleasure in having proved herself right, proving others wrong—as if Frank and her father had died so she might show off, demonstrate her skill and courage. Prove what a personage she was. . . .

It was an unpleasant thought, and Joanna considered it as she struggled up yielding steeps . . . dropping to climb on all fours for a while, her hands' scraped skin burned by the salt and sand. —That burning seemed an answer to her, and she decided to make anonymous phone calls, take the chance they wouldn't be heeded. Call the mainland tonight, the Coast Guard, state police, and federal drug people. Pay-phone calls, information from no one known— so justice would be less infected by herself, and self-satisfaction. . . . Then she would have done what needed to be done, and nothing more.

She was able to stand and climb crouched, then walk upright as the hill's slope rounded to the ridge. The cottage, and Slope Street, were still off to the right. The rain, come with the wind, was easing as the wind eased.

"Tired," Joanna said aloud, as if to confirm it. "Tired. . . ." She stumbled along the sand crest, and had a growing urge, almost compulsion to lie down, since the sand, wet or not, was so soft.

There was nothing to prevent it. She could lie down and sleep through the rest of the night, then get up with the sun in the morning, sand-caked and stiff . . . go on to the cottage for a hot shower . . . then walk back down to Strand, to the pay phone to make her calls. The captains would not have had time enough to clear all those bales, get them out. There was more than a night of unloading and loading there. . . .

Joanna thought of that—dropping her pack and helmet, lying down in the sand—then decided not. She took a deep breath of wet and salty air, kept walking, hobbling along, and after only a little while saw a streetlamp on Slope. Near enough . . . near enough. There was only a last labor through wet sand, wet sea grass—shaking from fatigue, her heart thumping—exhausted, and all glory gone.

No lights in the cottage. No cars parked there. . . . Joanna trudged across the yard to the side door of the garage, took her keys from her pack pocket, and unlocked it. She left the light off, and went in to hang her helmet and pack on wall pegs, unzip her torn coveralls and step staggering out of them.

Beneath, her jeans and shirt were torn as well, certainly blood-stained at knees and elbows. . . . She took her kitchen knife from the coveralls—the blade's point had cut through the bottom of the side pocket—and slid it into her belt.

She locked the garage, limped to the back steps, and climbed them with deliberate effort . . . then opened the kitchen door and stepped into the dark, and the pleasant tobacco-and-work-sweat odor of men.

—Joanna was startled by her body. It spun around while she was still considering, and leaped with her out the door and down the back steps. Her body ran away with her like a frightened horse, as if it had not been worn and wearied at all, and now was ready to run.

She stretched across the yard in darkness, into a spatter of rain—thought of the street, then decided the hill instead and ran through sea grape and out onto the sand.

She reached to her belt as she went, felt the fillet knife's handle—and as if that minor interruption in perfect running had cost her dearly, heard footsteps—bootsteps coming behind her.

Now her body realized how tired it was after all. Those swift strong steps behind had reminded it. Joanna stumbled, and kept running.

She ran and pulled the knife free—it was surprising how that slight motion unbalanced her. Heavy steps behind. Heavy and quick . . . muscle mass. Too worn for fear, though her body seemed terrified, Joanna drew in a breath deeper than the running breaths, and used that to scream.

It was a wail . . . almost trilling, not the tearing shriek she'd hoped for. The night, the occasional gusts of wind and rain, seemed to swallow her sound . . . so she screamed again as she tripped, then almost fell down a steep pitch of sand. She went into the sand up to her knees, and whoever it was almost caught her. She heard his breathing, the churning of effort just behind.

Joanna heaved and kicked out of the sand, leaped down through sea grass, and gripped the knife as firmly as she could. Running through the grass, sobbing with effort, she felt him close and closer—he was almost running with her.

She took the last longest strides she could, all in darkness plunging—then turned, turned as she ran, and as he reached to take her, swung the knife up and into the pale indication of his face.

Almost his face, but something stopped it. His arm, he'd put up his left arm, and the knife stuck in and then slid in farther, a greasy sliding, and he said, *"Jesus!"*

For a few seconds, they swayed and staggered together in darkness and slipping sand as if they were drunk and dancing—and Joanna knew she should pull the knife blade out of him and stick it in again and again as hard as she could until, in the dark, it reached where he wasn't guarding and killed him.

She should, but to do it meant she'd have to tug it free, pull the blade out of his arm, and she didn't want to feel that. She hesitated only that instant, and the man took her wrist and twisted it so the knife was pulled out and gone—and she kicked him, tried to kick up into his groin. He hit her, slapped her . . . something, and she fell down, seeing sheets of bright tiny dots parading and marching up and up in her sight.

Joanna tried to stand, but he came to her in the dark, gripped her and shook her as if she were a child, and she turned her head to where he held her, found his wrist with her mouth, and bit as hard as she could.

He grunted, yanked his arm away, then came again, grappled with her and suddenly lifted her up into the air, did something, turned her in some way, and she was over his shoulder . . . being carried over his shoulder.

He began walking up the sand slope, holding her over his shoulder like a sack, a duffel bag. He had both her hands gripped in one of his at the small of her back.

Nothing had made their difference in strength as clear as this walking up Sand Hill with her over his shoulder. It was such . . . such a caveman cliché, it would have made her laugh if she hadn't been so frightened.

And a terrible thing happened—because she was so frightened, so tired. She peed a little . . . just a little bit in her jeans. And it was as if this was the worst that could happen, that nothing—even being killed—could be as bad, as humiliating. And another attempt at screaming would only add embarrassment, before she was clouted to silence. A woman reduced to peeing in her pants . . . to wailing like a frightened baby as she was carried along.

Better to be silent, until she could bite again.

He carried her back into her yard, and Joanna writhed to turn on his shoulder, bent her head to catch flesh on his upper arm, and bit deep.

"For Christ's sake," the man said, a voice she just recognized as he

yanked his arm away, so she lost the mouthful of shirt and skin. Joanna wished she had the red pit bull with her—wished she were the red pit bull, could change to a weredog. Then there would be a serious bite. . . .

He went up the back steps as easily as if she weren't on his shoulder—pushed through the kitchen door into bright light, and swung her down, dumped her on the floor so suddenly she almost fell, staggering against the sink counter.

Captain Lowell, in rain-wet jeans, gray shirt, and black rubber boots, stood staring at her. His sharp fox face was flushed with anger, and blood was running along his forearm, soaking his shirt-sleeve and dripping from his fingers to the floor.

"What did you do to her?" Mr. Manning—bulky in a khaki windbreaker—stood by the stove, his broad, padded face calm as pond water.

"Not a goddamn thing, except bring her in."

"Didn' do enough." —Joanna hadn't seen this man. He was standing behind her at the kitchen door, a younger man, crewcut . . . and short, almost squat, his torso slabbed with muscle under a worn blue work shirt. His jaw was too heavy for a small-nosed face. "Didn' do enough to this bitch." The young man had dreaming un-focused brown eyes.

"She's bleedin'." Manning shifted by the stove.

"She's bleeding? I'm the one who's fucking bleeding. Took a knife to me. . . ." Lowell went to the sink, rolled up his sleeve, and exposed a neat, small cut in his forearm. He turned his arm over and an identical cut bled on that side as well. "—Through and through, and hurts like sixty. Thank Christ it didn't get an artery. . . ."

"Need to put a knife to *her*." The young man behind Joanna.

"Take it easy, George," Manning said.

"I just want to know what we're goin' to do. Need to finish up right now."

Joanna heard snoring from the other room, the dining room. Bobby Moffit was still in there, sleeping.

Captain Lowell was rinsing the blood off his arm in the sink. "—Shouldn't have parked your car down by the docks," he said to Joanna. "Blue Volvo. We know people's cars, out here."

"No asking permission to come aboard—to come into my house?" Joanna was pleased at the sound of her voice. It seemed important they not know she was afraid, as if knowing that would make it easier for them to kill her.

"Apologize for that, for not asking," Lowell said. He stopped rinsing the wound, still held his arm over the sink, and began searching through the counter drawers. "—Sure wish you hadn't done what you did. And you look tired, Mrs. Reed. How'd you get out of that building?"

"The chimney," Joanna said. "I want you all out of my house."

"The *chimney*. . . ." Lowell shook his head, examined her. "Will you people look at this? Woman went up a damn three-story chimney from the basement. Chewed herself up doing it, too." He checked through another drawer. "Where the hell are your dish towels?"

"Top drawer, on the other side." Joanna wished she didn't look so bad, dirty, wet from the rain, and bleeding where her clothes were torn. If she looked nicer . . . was prettier, younger, they might not hurt her.

Lowell took out a dish towel, bound it tightly around his forearm, and using his teeth to hold a cloth end, knotted it. "—Then, I suppose, you climbed off the roof . . . but not down that rope of yours." He nodded to the kitchen table, and Joanna saw the length of PMI there, neatly coiled. "—Beautiful line," Lowell said. "Had to go up an extension ladder to get it untied from that vent. Really fine. What is it?"

"It's . . . a kernmantle climbing rope," Joanna said. The kitchen light, dull yellow, seemed to vibrate . . . fix her and the three men in their places.

"Cost an arm and a leg, I'll bet. So you got off that roof what way?"

"Drainpipe."

"Drainpipe. . . . And climbing is how you learned to do that chimney stuff?"

"Caves. I'm a caver." An odd last conversation. Joanna supposed most last conversations were odd.

"Caves." Lowell seemed amused. "I bet you're a pistol down in those caves. . . ."

"I want you to get out of my house."

"You shut your mouth." The young fisherman shifted behind her. Joanna knew, as she'd known when men wanted to touch her, sexually—knew he wanted to put his hands on her, but for a different pleasure. And she felt an odd melting, as if it were her proper role to be taken into these strong men's hands. To be taken and held . . . to be done to, whether she liked it or not. She felt she might like it in a way, even to death. It was a dream feeling, frightening, sickening, and sweet.

"I just talked to the deputy, downtown," Joanna said, and remembered saying the same thing to Bobby Moffit, when he'd come up to fix her window.

"You dirty liar," the young fisherman said behind her. An enraged boy's insult, and all the more frightening.

"*George. . . .*" Lowell adjusted his towel bandage. It was spotted with blood. "—We know you didn't do any such thing, Mrs. Reed. Had a couple of people over by that station, and one inside, visiting with the duty man, and you didn't call or go in there tonight, and nobody else did either." He pulled out a chair, and sat down at the kitchen table. "So we came up to settle some things before you made any phone calls, talked to anybody."

"What did you do to my husband?" Joanna looked at Lowell, not at the others. . . . She'd spoken to him on his boat. And he'd glanced at her breasts, and taken her arm to steady her off the *Eleanor II* . . . walked her past winches and gear, and down the gangplank to the dock.

Tom Lowell was all she had in the kitchen.

"You people," he said, and rested his injured arm carefully on the table. ". . . Tourists, summer people, come out here every year. You take pictures of us working, take pictures of the boats and so forth, and you eat a lot of lobster and clams. . . . Consider us very quaint out here."

"Right," the young man said behind Joanna. "Fuckin' quaint."

"—Now, we've been fishing off this island almost four hundred years." Lowell paused, considering centuries. ". . . Maybe we got too good at it. Maybe with the Japanese and Russian factory ships, and the Canadians. Maybe we all got too good at it. But whatever, we can't make a living fishing anymore."

"Shippin', processin' either," Manning said, by the stove.

"—We had two men kill themselves last couple of years. Boat captains that couldn't pay their crews, feed their families."

"My *husband*—"

"I'll get to your husband, Mrs. Reed. . . . Now, we had a choice out here. We could sell our boats for next to no money, and then we could get off the island and take our families into a city—Portland or Providence or Boston, in some neighborhood not too good. And we could take a job in a gas station or doing roofing or cleaning up construction sites, if we could get apprenticed in the union."

"Welfare," the young man said.

"—That's right," Lowell said. "We could get on welfare, tide us over a few years in those cities. Real bad for men with families. . . ."

"You murdered my husband and my father," Joanna said, and couldn't imagine why she'd said that, when they might not yet have decided to kill her. She couldn't imagine why in the world she'd said it.

"Her father?" There was still no emotion visible on Manning's round face. No expression in the striking moss-green eyes. Joanna wondered how his wife knew what he was thinking, whether he was pleased or not.

There was a sudden blatting, brassy noise from the dining room— a very loud fart, Joanna realized, after a moment. Then a muffled shout, *Wow . . . wowowow.* Sounds of stumbling, a chair scraping on the pine boards.

Bobby Moffit, looking grimly ill, came staggering into the kitchen, naked, barely wrapped in the brown blanket.

"Hey, people," he said, and stood blinking, blear-eyed, in the light. He looked as if she hadn't bathed him at all.

"You motherfucker," the young man said. "You're the bigmouth around here."

". . . Am not."

"We can settle all this," the young man said. "Paul an' me can settle it."

Joanna thought she might take a chance—get past the young man and out the kitchen door again. Run out into the island night—and this time, hide. . . . And if they didn't find her, wait until morning and attempt the police, or the ferry.

She thought of trying it, but some part of her refused. Her body refused; it had done enough, tonight. —Besides, these were fishermen; this was their island. They would net her, tangle her, and winch her in. And she was afraid of the young man; if she ran again, she would give him the excuse he wanted.

"—Me an' Paul can take care of it like it never was."

"George," Lowell said, "—you just take it easy." He picked a loop of the PMI rope up off the table, tested it in his hands, and winced at the sudden pain in his arm. "Line like this must cost a fortune. . . ." He set the rope back into its coil.

"Am not a bigmouth." Bobby tried to adjust his blanket, hitch it up. "—Am not."

"Bobby," Lowell said, "we don't need to hear anything out of you. Sit down and shut up. I think you said enough to this lady already."

"It wasn't his fault," Joanna said. "I made him drunk."

"Am *not* what he said." Bobby pulled a chair out from the table and sat. The blanket slipped to his lap.

"Tom," the young man said, "—listen, Paul an' me can take care of this, an' there never will be a word about it."

"Why did you murder my husband?" Joanna asked Lowell. She didn't think the others would tell her. They would take her and Bobby out to sea on the *Eleanor II*, and never tell her. —And certainly she and Bobby wouldn't be the first to be taken from Asconsett Island in four hundred years, taken out to sea. . . .

"We didn't kill your husband, Mrs. Reed," Lowell said. "—And no *way*, George. We already decided that doesn't happen."

"Mistake," the young man said. "Real bad mistake."

"It's decided, George," Lowell said. "And that's that—unless you want trouble with me and Murray Wainwright, and I don't think you do."

"*Big* mistake," the young man said, and Joanna realized they weren't going to kill her. It came as change, rather than relief—a change so sudden and important it was difficult to comprehend. The kitchen light seemed to alter with it, become part of a different spectrum, more orange—as if that were the color of a future.

She needed to sit down, she felt a little sick, but there was no place to sit but at the table, and she hadn't been invited. She leaned back against the refrigerator, instead. . . . The young fisherman turned his head and stared at her with a bull's dull murderous gaze, thwarted by fencing.

Bobby Moffit began to snore sitting up, then slowly slumped forward until his forehead rested on the table, and slept . . . as if to demonstrate that possible tragedy was turning to only melodrama, and perhaps farce.

"Look at that," Manning said, from the stove. "Sound asleep."

"My husband. . . ."

"We didn't hurt your husband," Lowell said, and checked the towel around his forearm. More of the cloth was blotched with red.

"Some people came out from Providence," Manning said. "Asked if we were interested in pickin' stuff up for 'em."

"Ten years ago," Lowell said, "we'd have told those clowns to get off the island real quick. Even five years ago, maybe."

"Not now." Manning shifted by the stove, too big, too heavy to be comfortable standing for long.

"No," Lowell said, "—not now." He retied the dish towel tighter around his forearm. "Hurts like a son of a bitch. Middleton's going to have to take a look at this, give me a shot. —She bit me, too."

"I'm sorry," Joanna said.

"Don't be sorry. You were scared. . . . Tell you what goes on, Mrs. Reed—what some of us do is go on up the coast and meet factory ships out there, maybe once in the summer, once later in the year. Most of those vessels are from one of the republics or whatever was left when the Soviets broke up. We go up there, meet them early— in fog, if we can—and take those bales of marijuana off them."

"Why tell her everything?" the young man said.

"George, she was in the basement, and that's that. But it may be helpful if she knows the *why* of it. —Anyway, those bales get trucked out of here on the ferry . . . three, four trips, with whatever fish we've been catching."

" 'Whatever fish' is right," Manning said. "Then people from the mainland take the stuff from there."

"For fuckin' short money, you bet," the young man said.

"And," Lowell said, "what that does for us, is give a lot of fishermen and processors out here enough extra, with their catch, so they can salary their crews, or make boat payments, or maybe just feed their families."

"I want to know about my *husband*." A courageous Joanna Reed now—who would live, and was demanding answers.

"Mrs. Reed, about four weeks ago, that *Bo-Peep* came up the coast in the morning—all the way to Nattituck Cove. She must have got a real early start."

"Too fuckin' early," the young man said.

"—Came sailing up there," Lowell said, "and the first we saw her, she was out of that fog and right in our laps while we were loading. Maybe three, four hundred yards off." Lowell sat stroking the coil of PMI rope with his good hand as if it were a pet, some calm, slender, perfectly patterned snake from South America. "—We meet and load in those early fogs. That's . . . just the way we do things, ducking the Coast Guard. And I have no idea what the hell your husband was doing coming up so far."

"Told Hollis Porter he was fishin'," Manning said.

"My father was fishing," Joanna said. "My father was with him."

"Didn't know that." Lowell paused, recalling. "Knew your husband had the *Peep*; didn't look close to see anybody else on her."

"Fishin'?" the young man said. "Fishin' from a fuckin' sailboat?"

"Why not?" Lowell eased his towel-wrapped arm; more of the cloth was stained red. "Our great-granddads did it—and on back before them, out whaling."

"What did you do to him?"

"Not a damn thing, Mrs. Reed." Lowell apparently exasperated by the question. "We didn't do a damn thing to your husband!"

"Hollis talked to him," Manning said.

"That's right," Lowell said. "Hollis Porter spoke to him next day, after he came on us out there. Spoke to him at the Hatch."

"Spoke to him. . . ."

Manning, tired of standing, pulled a chair out from the end of the table and sat with mild grunt. "Hollis mentioned to your man about seeing him up at that cove—and Mr. Reed told him he must have been mistaken. Said he never *was* at Nattituck that morning, had sailed south an' didn' know what the hell Hollis was talkin' about."

Lowell smiled. "Your husband didn't tell you any of this, did he?"

"No. . . . No, he didn't."

"Good man. . . . So, you see, we weren't concerned about your husband, Mrs. Reed. He was a person who minded his own business. —Good sailor, too, except he held her a little close on the wind."

"A 'good man'? Then you tell me how Frank *died* out there."

Lowell seemed surprised by the question. "Why, he drowned, Mrs. Reed. Not the first and not the last going to do it, either."

"And what about my father?"

"What about him?"

"My father was burned to death a few days ago. Killed in his cabin in Chaumette."

Lowell stared at her. "Listen . . . listen, we wouldn't do anything like that. We didn't even know your dad was *on* the boat!"

"No, of course not. You people are smuggling and making money smuggling. And my husband caught you at it—and he's dead. And my father saw you—and he's dead. And I would like to know why I should believe your bullshit!"

"Tell you one good reason," Lowell said, pushed his chair back and stood up. "You can damn well believe us, because you're still standing there, talking. We decided up front we weren't going to do anybody over this venture. . . . Decided after some argument, I will say." He stood, cradling his injured arm. "—You think, in the old days out here, captains wouldn't have wrapped some anchor chain around you and put you in the sea?"

Manning leaned over to shake Bobby Moffit awake. "Bobby . . . you get up and come out of here."

Bobby sat up, yawning. "I didn' do nothin'."

"You're goin' to do something," Manning said. "You're goin' to be cleanin' holdin' tanks off Gloucester. An' you don't keep your mouth shut, you'll stay doin' them tanks till you rot. . . . Where're your clothes?"

"In the other room—the clean things," Joanna said, and Manning scraped his chair back and heaved to his feet to get them.

"Real serious mistake, Mr. Lowell," the young fisherman said. "You're takin' a shitload of responsibility here."

"That's right," Lowell said. "Get on your horse, George, let's leave the lady's house." He came over to Joanna, standing near and not much taller. He smelled of tobacco and fish. "Up to you, now," he said to her. "You wanted to know something—and now you do."

"Mistake. . . ." The young man, George, went out the kitchen door. Joanna heard his heavy seaboots down the back steps. Odd to think he'd have killed her. Perhaps the catching and killing of tens of thousands of swift silver fish had prepared him for it.

Manning came back with the clothes. "Bobby, you come on out of here." He took Moffit by the arm, lifted him out of his chair, and marched him to the door. "You can change outside."

". . . Am not goin' out from Gloucester."

"Yes, you are." Manning pushed him outside and down the steps.

"Am not. . . ."

"It really wasn't his fault," Joanna said. "I gave him the liquor."

"So you said. We're not going to hurt him." Lowell's eyes were a very light gray, the mercy in them invisible. "—Now, if you want, Mrs. Reed, in the morning you can go and talk to Carl Early. Up to you, and we won't stop you. Old Carl will *have* to come after us, then. . . . Or you can call over to the mainland and talk to the Coast Guard, tell 'em what's down in Manning's place. That was two nights unloading off three boats, so no way we could get that cargo out of there and stowed before daylight—and we won't even try."

Something about these forthright confessionals made Joanna angry. Now that she was going to live, she felt she could afford anger. "—And I'm supposed to believe that you've told me the truth, told me *everything* . . . and you're just an honest smuggler who saved me from bad young George, and has nothing to hide."

"That's . . . that's right." Lowell seemed to regret the "saving" part. He looked pale; the arm was hurting him.

"Blanket." Manning opened the kitchen door, stepped in, and put the folded blanket on the table.

"Thank you."

"Okay." Manning went out again, and down the steps.

"—And of course," Joanna said, "such honest smugglers would never have murdered a man just to protect themselves and their friends."

"If we had, you'd be out at sea right now, weighted down and going under—instead of us giving you every chance to hurt our people, put some of us in prison. . . . Now, you do whatever the hell you want."

Lowell went out the kitchen door, and closed it behind him. . . . He'd left several bright spots of blood on the linoleum.

Chapter Fourteen

Still alive in a silent and empty house, Joanna wandered at first enormously relieved, grateful she hadn't been taken away to drown. . . . But after she'd washed both blankets, mopped the kitchen floor—and straightened the dining-room throw rug and chairs from Bobby's awkward rising—she felt an odd regret that the men were gone. Gone with their harsh voices, their boots and heavy odors, their disagreements and dangerous company. For a moment, she imagined herself making coffee for them so they would stay . . . serving them sandwiches.

But in the entrance hall, she found the phone with its cord torn loose and neatly wrapped around it, a useful antidote to that fantasy of companionable men. . . . Weary, her knees and elbows sore, raw where they'd been worn on the chimney's brick, she went up the stairs too full of things discovered, claimed, and explained to sort them out, consider them. She was sick of all of it . . . all of her loss and rage and adventuring.

Joanna undressed, left her ruined jeans and work shirt on the closet floor, and went naked to the bathroom to take her shower. Her knees and right elbow were badly abraded, crusted with dried blood.

She sat sleepily to pee, then wiped and rose, flushed the toilet, and turned the shower on. She tested the water's temperature, then stepped into the tub and shifted within the spray as if it were a sliding, ever-falling translucent beaded garment, stinging her knees and elbow, but comforting. The soap burned more.

. . . Rinsed, she climbed from the shower dizzy, a little nauseated with fatigue. She dried herself, then walked into the bedroom, turned off the light, and went to bed.

Windborne rain tapped softly at the windows. Joanna's bones and muscles ached in relaxation between cool sheets as smooth as the chimney had been rough. She lay still, still as a dead woman. Not moving even slightly, as a dead woman—just drowned perhaps, wrapped in anchor chain and sunk fading into the sea—might slightly move, her long black hair shifting as the sea currents stirred it, even so far, far down. . . .

When she woke in the morning, her period had come—as if it had been waiting to be certain of her future.

Joanna sat on the toilet with a Tampax, her right foot up on the rim of the tub, and enjoyed the minor masturbatory comfort-discomfort of insertion.

She thought of breakfast. She had the eggs and cheddar cheese, and could make a three-egg omelette. An omelette and two pieces of buttered toast—the bread buttered before it went into the toaster oven. And coffee.

She stood, and smelled her fingers before she washed her hands. Fish blood, an Asconsett odor.

Breakfast took some time . . . cooking, then eating in a sun-flooded kitchen, breathing rain-rinsed air through open windows. She had a second cup of coffee, then washed the dishes, put them away, and never concerned herself with questions, judgments, decisions. —These seemed to slowly stream beneath her like a flooding basement spring that would have to be dealt with, but not quite yet. . . .

Swinging her red canvas tote bag, Joanna started down Slope Street in summer-weight khaki slacks and a white silk long-sleeved shirt, the cobbles uneven beneath her sandals. Her knees and right elbow were sore, and scabbed. The muscles at the small of her back ached a little. . . . The ferry was in, lying miniature down at its dock. She saw it through dazzle as the morning sun flashed off the sea's smashed mirror, forced her to lower her eyes.

The ferry grew larger as she walked down . . . then sank from sight behind the chandlery roof when she reached Strand. Tourists, only a few, were strolling the street, and she threaded through them to the public phones on the corner of Strand and Ropewalk. These old-fashioned phone booths—painted maroon, their narrow doors set with glass panes—seemed to demand a decision.

Joanna stood on the corner beside the booths as if waiting for a friend. . . . She held the island in her hand. For only several quarters and minutes of her time, she could set into motion the heavy machinery of law. Two calls to the mainland—to the state police and Coast Guard—then perhaps one more to the Drug Enforcement people. Three phone calls to bring them out in their helicopters and launches, eager to use federal money, anxious to demonstrate how serious the problems their budgets had to meet.

They would display for television the goods at Manning's, then sink their teeth into the men and women of Asconsett—a harder bite than Percy's ever was. And the island families would crumble under it, the fishing captains and their mortgaged boats fading away, gone for bail, for attorneys' fees. . . . The island, under that grim pressure, would sicken, develop tumors of those informing, those indicted.

The quarters were in her purse, her purse in the red tote bag, and no one to stop her.

Had the fishermen lied? Had they been clever enough to see that one more killing might be one too many . . . and so presented their case, then let her live to prove it? That might be so—though George, the young one, had certainly wanted her gone, and been eager to see to it.

Perhaps the fishermen *had* been clever enough to lie about murdering Frank—but they'd been genuinely startled to hear of her father's death in fire, to be accused of that. That had not been acting. —And there was the fisherman they'd said had mentioned the matter to Frank at the Hatch, when he'd walked down for his evening beer. Supposedly the fisherman had spoken to Frank there, under the noise of bad music and men's voices, and Frank had said he'd seen nothing—had sailed south, not north, and didn't know what the hell the man was talking about. . . .

And that sounded so like him, and like him to keep only that sort of secret from her. Men's risky business. —It was a question why men's business so often caused women pain. . . . But given that conversation had happened, would Frank have wanted her to inform on these fishermen for their pot-smuggling? He'd been very Irish on the subject of informers.

It came down to belief—and Joanna found she no longer believed they'd murdered anyone. She didn't believe Tom Lowell had planned and carried out the drowning of a decent man, a man who would never have betrayed them.

Joanna paused beside the phones for a while longer. Then, an accessory to a crime, certainly at least a person with guilty knowledge—and possibly a credulous fool as well—she walked away down Strand Street to Barkley's, for salad greens, apples, and lean ground beef.

She crossed the street, and as she passed the chandlery, noticed the boater supplies stacked in the display windows and remembered the raw wood of Bobby's window frame. . . . Poor Bobby, gone on his way to exile off Massachusetts, hosing out fish-holding tanks in some friend-of-a-friend's trawler.

She turned back, went into the store—its generous two-story space, painted bright white, had been one of Frank's pleasure places—and was surrounded by gallons of marine paint, coils of salt-water line, inflated yellow rubber boat tenders and more formidable Zodiacs. There were ranks of bins and wall shelves of fishermen's heavy tools and equipment, and boaters' less sturdy gear—decorative chronometers, navigation electronics, gaudy pennants, and anchor-engraved glassware.

The odors were linseed oil, new rope, machine oil, and fresh-sawn wood, though little woodwork was visible except for prelacquered stern counters, rudders, and dinghy paddles gleaming dull gold.

"Yes, ma'am." A tall long-faced boy in white T-shirt and jeans, looking just out of high school. *BOAT BUSINESS* was printed across his T-shirt in ocean green.

"I need some paint. Just a little . . . for a window frame."

"Busted window?"

"That's right."

The boy held out his hand. "Hi. I'm Jerry Peterson. Jack Spruel—deputy?—called my mom about your door . . . window in your door."

"Oh, yes. I remember." Joanna shook the boy's hand. Strong wiry hand.

"Did Bobby do okay with fixing that?"

"Yes, I think he did a good job, but he didn't paint it."

Joanna watched the boy withdraw into that masculine reverie so familiar from watching Frank consider some material problem. It touched her, a bittersweetness, as men and boys, she supposed, would now always touch her in reminiscence.

"White door?"

"Yes."

"Lots of whites. . . ."

"I think the same white paint they used on the cottage trim."

"Evanson's," the boy said.

"Yes."

"Then you'll want Cargill's Satin Cream-white. That's what that paint was. Lot of people out here use it; takes weather real good, and it'll do fine on the frame, front and back."

"That sounds all right, but I only need a little."

The boy drifted toward an open double door, and Joanna trailed after. "You're going to want a half pint, and a number-two brush . . . real small brush. Paint's self-priming, *supposedly.* Wouldn't trust it self-priming on siding, but I guess for just a window sash, it'll do." He led her into another, even larger room, the hardware side. — Passing by when they'd first come out to the island, she and Frank had seen a plaque by the store's front door commemorating the businesses joining, in 1865. The two brothers owning the hardware store had been killed on the *Kearsarge* the previous year, when it fought the *Alabama* off Cherbourg. Their widows had sold to the chandlery.

. . . A stroll down the shelves, the boy reached up for a small white can, then turned and selected a slender brush from a jar on the store counter. "—Cheap brush, but it'll do the job. Be sure and stir that paint real good."

"Thank you." Joanna followed him to the register, paid a total of $6.43.

"Sorry for your trouble, Mrs. Reed," the boy said, and handed her change from her ten, and the paint and brush in a small brown paper bag.

Joanna nodded and smiled . . . but out on the sidewalk she wondered which trouble he'd meant. Frank? Last night's adventure and fright—or simply her broken window?

She put the small sack into her tote bag, and walked on to Barkley's. The vegetables grim as usual, the fruit fairly good, but except for the apples, expensive. The beef was excellent—Asconsett people, routinely fed on fish, were choosy of beef, pork, and lamb as delicacies. The chicken was local, yard hens raised on feed, salty grass, and sand bugs.

As Joanna and a few other women shopped, Mr. Barkley, tall, elderly, and sullen, drifted through his small store keeping an eye on them as if, at a signal prearranged, they intended to plunder his counters and bins and run out into the street with vegetable booty, quarts of milk, and live lobsters from the ice tub.

Joanna shopped carefully, buying for one, moving with the others through the market in slow circling hunt-and-gather. An ancient feminine pleasure of small discoveries and decisions. . . . And considering there was no man, no Frank to please with red meat, she decided instead on chicken—a small fryer. She brought her basket to the counter and paid Mrs. Barkley, a shadow retired behind her cash register, for the chicken, a bunch of slightly wilted spinach, a half-dozen early yellow pippin apples, one pound of new potatoes, and a bottle of Gallo Hearty Burgundy—Barkley's only habitual wine.

Her groceries just fit into the red canvas tote bag. Joanna lugged that back along Strand to Ropewalk, then went down the alley to dockside parking. The Volvo was where she'd left it. She unlocked the car, put her tote bag into the backseat, and opened the driver's-side door to get in—then paused and stood looking up the alley. Manning's warehouse seemed higher in its three stories than it had last night, when much had been lost in shadow. At the third story, just under the eaves, the farthest vent window was still canted open . . . space enough for a mistaken heroine to have slid through on her quest.

Two couples, tourists, came walking down the alley. One of the women was carrying a large sketch pad under her arm, prepared to capture fishing boats along the wharf, their complicated reflections. . . . These tourists would stroll past Manning's—its big basement loaded with black bales of green cargo—then go on along the docks, perhaps imagining harsher and more colorful days, whaling days . . . harpooners, ape-armed sailors with their palms tattooed by ground-in tar, and the no-nonsense captains, with voyage shares and faces grim as any arctic sea.

The couples walked past her—Southern accents, Southern people up to see gray cold Yankee water, hear swallowed down-east speech, notice the men whose great-great-grandfathers had manned the Federal fleets blockading their Confederacy from Charleston to the Mississippi, starving them of grain, guns, and victory.

. . . Except for Whitman and Stephen Benét, who had written the poetry of that war? It had been too big, too much of a matter for minor poets. A family feud—richer, more tragic than struggle between nations, so Homer's verse was needed, or Shakespeare's plays. The scope and wry oddness of those armies of strong, humorous farm boys fighting . . . sewing a landscape quilt of banners, gunfire, band music, and blood.

The tourists went on their way. There was little doing at Manning's wharf. Joanna saw no loading or unloading—top dock or basement dock beneath it. Nothing doing at Manning's this morning. . . .

She drove up to the cottage, pulled into the drive, and climbed the kitchen steps to put the groceries away, all but the chicken and potatoes. —She'd forgotten milk. Should have made a grocery list. . . . Food. It would take a while before she settled on what groceries, what meals only she enjoyed—preferences that had been set aside for Frank's taste over the years. She really didn't know yet what she wanted to eat. Breakfasts, of course, would be easy. But dinners . . . once this chicken was gone, what next?

Joanna went upstairs and changed to old jeans, sneakers, and a blue work shirt, for possible window-frame painting. Then she came down to the kitchen, unwrapped the chicken, put it in the sink, and began to cut it apart, clean the pieces in running water. She had to use a small utility knife. The other knife—the fillet knife—was out on Sand Hill. Probably findable, if she searched. . . .

The chicken came apart in the rubbery light-pink helpless way birds had under a primate's steel. "These are all my parts," the pieces seemed to say. "See? I keep nothing from you—except my bowels and odd feet, my narrow witless head and lidded eyes. And those you do not want to see. They are too much me; my head would spoil your appetite."

In time, Joanna thought, she'd learn the mechanics of solitude, how to keep private all she used to share—no shared observations, no shared jokes, no shared memories anymore. And no disagreements; no one would argue with her from one day to another. She would always be right.

She finished the chicken, took the two-pound sack of flour from the pantry, and shook a cupful—and pinches of salt and pepper—with the chicken pieces in Barkley's big brown-paper grocery sack.

She poured four tablespoons of olive oil into the big frying pan—weighty old-fashioned iron—turned up the left front burner, and set the chicken pieces in to b wn. Now they'd become food, no longer bird parts. It seemed there was no essential that couldn't be transformed by use and point of view. . . . And it might be the same with loneliness.

Joanna washed the new potatoes, scrubbed them with the vegetable brush, and cut each in half . . . then peeled and sliced an old onion into chunks. Used a fork to turn the chicken pieces over.

There was one large pot—battered aluminum. She rinsed it with hot water, poured four cups of cold water in, and set it on the stove's big back burner on low. She spooned in two tablespoons of olive oil, added a pinch of dried rosemary, a pinch of dried thyme.

Then she forked out the browned chicken pieces, set them into the pot, and instead of the Hearty Burgundy, struggled to open a bottle of merlot, the last of three they'd brought when they came out to the island. —Uncorking wine had been Frank's job; he'd used an old-fashioned corkscrew, requiring strength to haul stubborn corks free. . . . Joanna found this one difficult, had to hold the bottle down between her thighs, then wrench up with both hands on the corkscrew's handle. It was a struggle, took anger to finally get it done with a juicy *pop* and small spill.

One of the little reminders of his absence. Those would recur through the rest of her days, in one way or another.

She measured a cup of wine into the stewpot, dumped the potatoes and onions in. —It occurred to her then that she hadn't bought mushrooms. She liked them; Frank hadn't.

Joanna stirred the vegetables in restless seething water, then shook in pepper, added two dried bay leaves, and checked the burner heat, turned it lower to simmer.

Then, she had nothing more to do except minor housecleaning. Nothing else to do for the rest of the day. . . . She washed her hands at the sink and thought she might go down to the pay phones again, and call Rebecca, let her know that her mother had descended from the heroic to the sensible, which might be some comfort. —But the call would also bring up what didn't need bringing up again—would involve denying everything she'd insisted on before, involve offering explanations for that change of mind that couldn't be complete without betraying the fishermen.

Better to let it go . . . let Rebecca rest for a few days from dealing with her mother, the widow's song and dance.

Joanna was considering mopping the kitchen floor when the doorbell rang. She thought of not answering, then went up the hall to the entrance and opened the door.

. . . Beverly Wainwright, massive in outsized stretch jeans and a yellow cotton pullover, stood on the steps. She was holding out a quart jar.

"Chowder. An' you're not gettin' any better anywhere."

"Beverly, that's really kind. . . ."

"Don't mean to intrude on you—"

"You're not. Come in. . . ." Joanna led the way down the hall to the kitchen. The jar of chowder was very warm, almost hot in her hands. Behind her, the old pine flooring creaked beneath Beverly.

"Sit down. Would you like some tea?"

Beverly pulled a chair out from the kitchen table and sat—the chair vanishing beneath her, so she seemed to be sitting in midair. "Don't have time for any tea. I'm catchin' the ferry off to Post Port—just stopped by to bring that chowder. You think you tasted chowder before, but you didn't, not like I make—from diggin' 'em up to doin' 'em."

"It looks wonderful."

"You just stick that right in your icebox. It'll last just fine."

"Thank you, Beverly; I'll enjoy it." Joanna put the chowder in the refrigerator, then sat at the table.

"Guarantee you will." Beverly looked around, examining the kitchen. "Nancy Evanson changed this kitchen—had a woodstove in here, and she took it out. *Her* mother, Pauline, used to cook on that woodstove, sometimes. . . ."

"It's a nice little house. I really like it."

"Evansons always did keep a good house, kept a good boat—but they're gone. An' now Nancy's more a mainlander. She's the only daughter, married a dentist over in Peabody, had a little boy an' lost him to a disease."

"I didn't know that. I only met her once."

"—Has one brother, an' he's an officer in the Navy."

"You sure you won't have some tea, Beverly, or coffee? I don't have any juice."

"I would, I would have some tea, but I got to get goin'. The old man—Mr. Wainwright, Senior?—he's stoppin' in the nursin' home over at the Port, an' I guess he's stoppin' for good. So I'm goin' for a couple of weeks to see him settled."

"Oh, I'm sorry. My husband . . . Frank liked old Mr. Wainwright."

"Well, Senior's mean as a serpent, but folks like him anyway. Like the old fool myself . . . damn if I know why."

"Well, it's nice of you to visit."

"Wouldn' have bothered you, Mrs. Reed—"

"Joanna."

"Well, wouldn' have bothered you, Joanna, except for an item of business."

"What business?"

"Business is, Mr. Wainwright, Junior, and I discussed payment for the loss of our boat, takin' account of the meager, real meager in-

surance . . . and the long an' short is, we will not require any payment from you on the *Bo-Peep*."

"Well, that's . . . that's very nice. That's a relief."

"Mmm. . . ." Beverly smiled, her harsh face transformed. "Not all
that much of a relief, considerin' you wasn't goin' to pay nothin' any-
how. But we figured to set your mind at ease from worryin' about it."

"I know, and it's kind of you. Will you please thank your husband
for me, tell him I appreciate it?"

"Yes, I will. . . . You bearin' up?"

"Yes, I am."

"That's good, that's what you have to do. Bear up, or go under—
that's what we all have to do." Beverly grunted with effort, and
stood.

"Sure you have to leave, don't have time for a cup of something?"

"I'd like to stay, honey, but the ferry's not goin' to wait—not as
long as that jackass, Andy Ford, is captainin'."

Joanna got up, walked with Beverly down the hall. "And how's
Percy?"

"Oh, God—that dog. He is eatin' us out of house an' home, an'
not bringin' in a dime."

"So, one-eyed dogs can't fight."

"Now, you said that, Joanna, an' I didn' say a word, don't know
what the hell you're talkin' about."

"You interested in selling him?" Joanna opened the front door.

"Honey, I would love to sell him—but not to a lady. That is no
lady's dog."

"Just thinking about it. . . ."

"You're 'thinkin' about it' because Percy likes you—and that is
the weakness of women: anybody likes us or comes to love us, and
we melt soft as butter. That's our weakness." Beverly went down the
steps. A big black pickup, loaded with fishnet and floats, was parked
at the sidewalk, her son behind the wheel. The boy looked at
Joanna, nodded politely.

"Bear up!" Beverly called from the walk, climbed into the truck,
and was driven away.

. . . Joanna went out back and sat on the kitchen steps in sunshine. The backyard—fenced from the hillside dune by thick sea-
grape shrubs and, on one side, a short remnant section of ancient
sagging wood palings—was an enclosed little meadow grown wild.
The mixture of flowers and weeds, clustered where beds had been,
looked even so early in the season like weary soldiers, worn with

battle in soil too sandy for them. . . . Nancy Evanson's mother—
Pauline—had lived here and been a gardener, busy with tiger lilies
and other bulb plants that needed seasonal culling when winterkill
became spring's recovery. There'd been no culling now for several
years, and the summer had brought a tangle of overgrown grass,
odd lilies, dwarfed tulips, and what looked like asparagus greens.

Tom Lowell had trampled through them in darkness and rain,
with her over his shoulder and ready to bite.

Ready to bite, and had bitten. Had stabbed the man and bitten
him, a terrified cat with a kitchen knife. Recalling, it seemed clear
now that Lowell's mild reaction to all that—patient with pain and
bleeding, calm at the notion she might have killed him, hacking in
the dark—now it seemed clear that he and the other captains had
had no intention of murdering her.

. . . As it was, there'd been only a chase and brawl that seemed to
have happened some time ago, not last night. Seemed to have happened a month or two ago, and have nothing to do with her now,
sitting on her kitchen steps and looking out into the backyard. . . .

Frank would have loved it, would have thought it wonderfully
funny, once she was safe. If amusement could bring back the dead,
then he would have appeared this morning, laughing. . . . The
poetess in arms, full of swagger and tragic self-importance, clank-
ing with gear to climb into a fish-processing plant—to discover the
illegal last sad hope of the locals, and not a damn thing to do with
her or hers.

Was there an end to vanity, to vanity's foolishness? How badly
had her poetry been marred by it over the years, how much damage had she done to her work?—and not even noticed self-regard
smearing the words, altering a poem's tone to self-congratulation
and the satisfied second-rate.

Joanna Reed and her poetry. Joanna Reed and her breast.
Joanna Reed and her husband. Joanna Reed and her father. Too
many possessives. After swollen pride of ownership, what room had
been left for her poetry, for Frank, for her father—how much room
now for Rebecca?

She had gone into the warehouse enraged because someone
had been taken from her. A loss that could not be accident; accident had been too trivial, too random a cause of loss for Joanna
Reed. —But now she was left with it. Accident . . . ill chance . . . bad
luck. Bad luck and possible blunders were what she was left with—
poor clay to turn to tragedy.

She stood, and went down the steps into the yard. The flowers seemed ragged under their summer colors. Sea wind and sandy soil—or the salt sifting from the air—had pinched them, pressed them to produce their blossoms, their pollen, soon as possible. Decorations of the mainland's deep soil, woods-sheltered and gently rained on, here they grew fragile at the sea's apron, in the sea's washed sand.

But they seemed good company for her, providing an example of doing the best one could. Joanna knelt—her knees very sore from chimney climbing—then lay down in tall grasses among the flower stems. She stretched out amid them and closed her eyes, felt the earth firm beneath her, and sighed deeply as if she were weeping. Breathed in . . . and sighed again so her bones seemed to slowly settle, clicking into place, her blood begin to run more freely through her. She felt, lying there resting in the sun, that she could make do with loss in place of a husband and a father—that she could manage loss and learn from it, work through the days alongside it, then take it with her to bed.

She lay resting awhile longer, and almost fell asleep. It was a pleasure to have only ground and grass and sky to consider—the ancient trinity of the natural world. A trinity unconscious, with no interest in time, time's changes, with no interest in itself. . . . She lay for a while in a haze of grass stems, small-blossomed flowers, and sunshine . . . then she got up, went to the garage, and sorted through rusting tools and implements lying on the workbench and stacked into a corner.

Joanna hadn't liked to garden, though she'd done it to keep the White River house lot neat. The careful attention to witless living things, the responsibility for them, had seemed to be poorly rewarded with only temporary blossoms. . . . Now it had occurred to her the work might be reward in itself—the flowers' colors only a sort of seal. She selected a hoe with cracked handle, a trowel, and a small white weed rake with one tooth missing. There were no gardening gloves.

She walked back out into the yard, and decided to begin at the west corner, where weeds and flowers fought a silent slow-motion battle for a patch of sunlight between sea-grape shadows.

It was heavy hoeing. The sandy soil, moving so easily underfoot, was a different proposition laced with roots and matted undergrowth. Joanna enlisted with the flowers, and fought the weeds. . . . Her cave-hardened hands helped. And the climbing muscles laced through her shoulders took to the hoe as if hacking weeds and rootlets were another sport and adventure. As she worked, she learned one by one the tricks to hoeing—slid her left hand farther down the handle and raised the blade with a scissoring motion of her arms, her right hand levering against the fulcrum of her left, and lifting the cutting head not too high . . . only a foot or two.

Only that high, then letting it drop—but drop where she wanted it, no fiddling for position once it was down. Letting it drop, adding a little power, then tugging it back only a few inches through the soil.

And up again.

After almost two hours working, Joanna was satisfied with a section of backyard, roughly three feet by ten, thoroughly weeded and the earth turned at least a few inches down. She had killed several flowers too, at the beginning, victims of friendly fire. —The hoeing in warm sunshine had oiled her with pleasant sweat, made her callused hands only comfortably warm, and eased the muscles of her shoulders, the long muscles of her arms.

The section done, she straightened and stretched in a ghosting veil of summer gnats, then stood leaning on the hoe, considering. It would take three or four days to hoe the backyard into order . . . days more to reconstruct the original beds, decide on new plantings, perennials. Hot work in dirt, with green creatures that could never know her—but only sun, water, growth, and death.

The hoe's long handle seemed to keep her too separate from her work, standing away and striking at it. Joanna put the hoe down, went to her scabbed knees, and began to work her border with the trowel and little rake. . . . This way, she killed no flowers. It was a closer combat. She saw the small weeds she killed up close, their slender stalks, odd with shreds of greenery along their length, no two nearly alike—and with flowers of their own, small, undecorative, ragged and stippled, useful only for sex. . . . If she hadn't already made the accepted choice, she might have championed them, and killed flowers so the weeds could grow.

Well past noon, she stood, brushed sandy soil from her jeans and work shirt, and put the hoe, trowel, and small rake away. Then she went up the steps into the kitchen and turned the burner off. The *coq au vin*—or almost *coq au vin*—smelled very good . . . lacked only mushrooms.

Joanna made space in the small refrigerator, used washcloths to hold the stewpot's hot handles, and fitted it in. She was hungry, but didn't want to spend the time indoors to make a lunch; the sunshine had been such a pleasure for her.

She took her purse from the kitchen table, then went down the back steps and around to the car, started it, and backed down the drive and out into the street. The Volvo's tires rumbled down Slope Street's cobbles to Strand—and Joanna turned left, to follow Strand around the end of the harbor, then along Beach Road, out of town.

Trudie's Hotdoggery—a shabby plywood shoe box, and painted pink—was perched at a slight tilt on the slope of a dune along Beach. Trudie's had been built on the sea side of the road, but a combination of savage storms, sand slides, and island road repair had resulted in its relocation to the other side of the street.

Trudie, very old, freckled, thin, and apparently frail, was still competent to run her restaurant, aided by mirrored sunglasses and a nasty temper. The restaurant served only milk shakes, Cokes, hot dogs, peach pie, hamburgers—seared half-pounds of round steak ground—and lobsters steamed out back and presented, huge and whole, on too-small paper plates with large paper cups of peppered melted butter. Nutcrackers were loaned with the lobsters, and Trudie kept a close count of them, reacting with a snake's rattle of insults if one proved missing.

Joanna parked among motorcycles and dune buggies waiting in Trudie's small sand-and-gravel lot, got out, and went through the front screen door to a row of broad tanned bikers' and beachies' backs, ranged along a twenty-foot counter covered with naileddown burnt-orange laminate. There were plywood booths along the right wall, but Joanna looked for counter space, and saw an opening large enough to stand in by the cash register.

Trudie permitted no music in her place, so the noise was loud voices, loud laughter, food orders and demands for payment over the sea's soft thudding reminder down the beach across the road. Sea wind, drifting through wide windows' rusted screens, cooled the grills' heat, dried the sweat on the foreheads of the three girls serving. All three were Trudie's grandnieces, as sweet as she was sour.

Joanna, wedged into her space, waited for a girl to ring up a biker's bill, then shouted her order. *"One hot dog. One Coke. No fries. To go."* The girl nodded, went back to place it at the grills, and Joanna saw Trudie stop her and say something.

A young surfer with fisherman's tattoos was sitting on the first stool beside her, his girl to his right. The boy—long hair red-blond, his skin coffee'd by an early-summer tan—seemed to radiate the perfect heat of youth.

He and his girl were talking as they ate, and Joanna could almost understand what they were saying amid the noise of all the others— their minor melody threading through. The surfers, the bikers, were almost all from Asconsett or the other islands. Trudie's was a local place; the tourists usually ate at Bucanne's, in town, or the Lobster Trap at the Willis marina.

. . . Trudie's grandniece, sturdy and smoothly fat, brought Joanna's order in a large brown grocery sack, stained with grease along one side.

"Looks like too much," Joanna said, then had to raise her voice. "—Too much. I don't think it's my order."

The girl checked the ticket. "Strawberry shake, two hot dogs, fries, one piece peach pie."

"Not my order. *Not my order.*"

"Yes, that is your order." Trudie, in mirrored sunglasses, had stepped behind the register.

"No, I just ordered one hot dog and a Coke."

"I said, that is your order. Now you take that food an' make room for another customer there, if you're eatin' out."

"But I didn't order this!"

"You're gettin' it just the same," Trudie said, plucked the ticket out of her grandniece's hand and tore it in half. "No charge for this lady. —Now honey, you go out and give us some room here at the counter, and you eat all that good food and God bless you." And was gone with a turning reflection of light in her mirrored glasses.

The girl made a face of astonishment for Joanna. "That's a first, for sure," she said.

. . . Tears in her eyes over kindness—perhaps to a recent widow, more likely for silence concerning the captains' trade—Joanna went outside, climbed into the Volvo, and put the sack of food on the seat beside her. Too much food. Trudie's split and grilled their fat frankfurters, toasted the long buttered buns. . . .

She ate far down the coast, sitting in solitude amid sea grass where two small dunes met shoulder to shoulder. All the island's other beaches were proper New England—short, shelving, and stony. Only the north shore ran to sand, piled up out of shallows by driving Atlantic storms.

. . . She looked out to sea and into an afternoon sun, mature and blazing. About half of the milk shake, creamy rich, thick with chunks of early strawberry, was gone—and more than half of the fries, salty and still smoking hot, blistered with fat. She'd eaten one hot dog with mustard and relish, and had started on the second, plain, only the grilled sausage—spiced red meat, juicy and edged with char—resting in the toasted bun.

The harsh sunlight enriched the food, sharpened its colors so they burned. . . . Joanna decided to save the slice of peach pie for dinner, and wrapped it in a napkin. Then she sat eating until only a portion of hot dog and some french fries were left for the gulls and the little shorebirds scissoring along the surf's scalloped hem. . . . She stood, brushed sand from her jeans, and went down to the sea's edge to set out the scraps for them . . . then walked back up to take her trash and piece of pie to the car.

She left the Volvo, and walked farther north down among the dunes, slowly wending her way through low sand hills whose slopes, when slumped to certain angles, flashed and sparkled under bright sunlight. She walked through patches of sea grass, past occasional sculptural antlers of driftwood, angled and weather-worn soft gray, brought far up by sea storms, and left.

She walked along, then down through the last of the heaped sand, furred with wind-bent grasses, until the damp hardpack of the beach was firm beneath her feet. Then she stretched out to walk herself weary, striding in quick counterpoint to the rollers' slow rhythms as the surf came in. A mile offshore, a white fishing boat rocked sunstruck . . . and farther out, a small rust-red freighter sailed south along the horizon.

As Joanna walked, the sea's sound suggested poetry to her—perhaps had provided the primal impulse to poetry and music. *"I sing the wrath of Achilles, Peleus's son. . . ."* The regular crash and murmur of that grand unconscious and its winds indicating an immense imbalance—all the magnificent and witless universe weighed against the living few, and fewer still who could consider it. The living sentient few—temporary growths, collections of trillions of tiny animals that had found, over ages, better feeding in clusters. And these, now glued together in walking watery heaps, believed they thought and were aware, even supposing similar gods to keep them company.

But still, even such self-deluding creatures could observe in a limited way, could speak, scribble down description, and dream of mysteries—their poets' business.

Joanna began to speak aloud over the sea's sound, walking along

. . . calling out in her near-contralto. *"There are mountains steep beneath the sea, in dark and singing silence, desirous of no company. . . ."*

But even these, heights and depths at once, vibrated to the distant drumming on the shore. The whales' tunes as melody line, the chirps and grunts of smaller lives, the susurrations of great sharks swimming . . . all were measured out by rollers beating beaches far away. There the sea struck at the land, whose air no basic thing can breathe—but only oddities discontented, that had crawled from resonant depths into distant, bright dry days.

Frank had died in the ocean, as so many others—their huge and senseless mother reclaiming them, extinguishing the accidental life she'd allowed so long ago. Holding them dear as ever, floating or sinking, as everything between her green breasts must do.

. . . Joanna walked along, murmuring pieces of what might become a poem to deep and tide-won water, and its mate, the wind. She walked on—muttering to herself, occasionally calling out over the ocean's toppling noise—walked on until she was weary, then turned and made a slower way back down the long beach to the car, and home.

. . . In the evening, an almost tropical sunset stretching away over the sea in streaked black, painted rose, and gold, Joanna walked around the cottage, examining its shrubs and stunted flowers . . . the light-blue paint checking along its clapboards, the white paint flaking from the palings of the front yard's picket fence. —It seemed to her the cottage required better care. Dumb, helpless in its worn fatigue and solitude, however charming and perfectly set high and apart on Sand Hill's crest, it seemed needy as a child. Nancy Evanson hardly visited the island. . . .

Tired from beach walking, her face windburned, halations of bright sunlight still seeming to linger in her sight, Joanna started to sit on the front steps, and saw a white envelope tucked half under the black rubber welcome mat. It was a short plain drugstore envelope, unsealed. There was a folded piece of ruled notebook paper inside. *THANKS*, printed in large letters, was the only word on it.

An appreciation, from Captain Lowell she supposed, for the absence of any federal agents today, swarming on Asconsett's docks. . . . She wondered how the captain's arm was doing. —And even with this courtesy, of course, Manning's goods would certainly be off-island as soon as that could be arranged.

Joanna put the note in her jeans pocket, and sat on the front steps looking down Slope Street—gazing down the cobbled lane past other cottages descending the hill . . . looking out over the docks and harbor, out to the sea and its sinking sun.

She imagined a life here, on Asconsett, imagined never going back to White River to stay—only to sell the house, or rent it, to get her things and dispose of Frank's. There would be just enough money to rent this cottage year round—or buy it, if Nancy Evanson would sell.

She could live here, perhaps get a part-time job teaching or assistant-teaching at the school. Could live out here and write. And perhaps, if the Wainwrights could be persuaded, buy Percy for company.

A widow and her one-eyed dog, sharing island summers and the long, cold, stormy winters, when sea sleet hissed folding and unfolding over Asconsett. They would take walks in that windy weather, she in Frank's duffel coat—and Percy wearing a dog sweater, blue to set off his short red fur.

They would walk together, companions . . . and age, year by year, would come for them both on the Atlantic's tide.

Chapter Fifteen

Tar Beach was empty under a rising moon.

Rebecca had come up the library's south stairwell—the heavy door out onto the roof unlocked as usual. The administration had given up trying to keep students working or studying in the library off the only flat roof on campus—and big, perfect for sunbathing on breaks during the day, or just hanging out, scoping the landscape . . . some people smoking.

She was almost an hour early; it was just past nine o'clock. Greg was supposed to finish work and come up at ten. . . . Rebecca walked over pebbled asphalt to the south parapet—only a couple of feet high—and looked out over the campus. Some graduate students were leaving Glaser Hall, walking under the light from the lampposts along the paths. Math people just coming out of evening classes—so she definitely was up here early, and wished she hadn't come at all.

In the first place, the whole thing about Greg suddenly liking her was absolutely surprising, because he hadn't ever said anything *to* her—except "Hi," which was the same as nothing. . . . And then there was the question of why he would like her better than Charis, anyway, since Charis was very pretty—well, beautiful—and was also an adult, not just another college kid who wasn't especially good-looking, and didn't even know who she *was* yet.

It seemed to Rebecca the whole Greg thing—the Greg Thing—was just another oddness, as if her father's death and her grandfather's death had changed everything the last few weeks, twisted the whole world out of shape—and changed her, too, so she could never be the same as she was. And also, her mom was acting absolutely bizarre, so there was nobody she could depend on.

And there was the weird but definite feeling that *she* was changing a little day by day, waking up slightly different, a slightly different person each morning. That, and everything else, was becoming very peculiar. . . . A perfect example being this sudden really off-the-wall thing with Greg. When Charis mentioned it to her—and Charis was still very angry, hadn't spoken to her for three days—but when she'd mentioned it, it had been upsetting . . . but, face it, exciting too.

Now, however, a couple of days had gone by—and maybe she was just growing up, getting too grown up to stay excited and think it was going to be a great thing with Greg. —And that this nice guy, and really nice-looking, had secretly liked her so much he was dumping Charis for her. Dumping *Charis.*

Did that make sense? No, it did not make sense. So now, what had seemed to be so surprising and great had just become strange. . . . In a way, it was like her father suddenly dying, being gone forever—it didn't make *sense.* The Greg Thing was like that, could almost be a sort of cruel joke—except that Charis didn't have much of a sense of humor.

. . . The moon. It was a beautiful moon. You could see it better up here, without the lights. Moonlight on the tops of the hills all around—like snow, summer snow.

The roof door squeaked open behind her, and Rebecca said, "Oh, God," to herself . . . to somebody. But when she turned to look, it was a girl, not Greg. The girl walked out of shadow, her face and hair shining pale in moonlight. It was Charis, in jeans and a gray sweatshirt, walking across the roof toward her. —Charis didn't seem angry, didn't look as if she was there to make some grim scene when Greg showed up. She didn't look upset at all.

"Hi. . . ." Rebecca hoped Charis wasn't going to keep on with the not-talking. "—Greg told you he was going to come up?" She started to say something more, about how weird this whole thing was—but Charis just smiled as if she understood all that, and it wasn't important and she wasn't angry anymore. She came up to Rebecca at the parapet, and kissed her cheek.

"Forgive me, Rebecca," she said, and was definitely smiling. Then she hugged her, a big hug; Charis was very strong, for a girl.

It was such a relief things were okay. Before Rebecca could say anything, Charis asked, "Do you forgive me?" and she held Rebecca's arms, stepped back a little, and began to turn them both, whirl them around as if they were dancing. They spun, and Charis leaned back, turning, and swung Rebecca around and around so fast that Rebecca's feet weren't touching the roof. ". . . Forgive me, Rebecca." It was so much like the way Daddy had done it when Rebecca was little, that it wasn't scary when Charis suddenly let her go.

It was just surprising to be over the parapet, out so far. . . . Then she realized . . . and saw Charis watch her fall.

Joanna slept as if her bed were warm sand that smoothed and stirred and turned with her through the night, so she was always comfortable. In this softness and support, she dreamed of weather, of being able to call up clouds to shadow a landscape she'd seen from the mountain, but had never descended to.

She drifted through leafed greenery in her dream, peering down through its foliage along the slope of her mountain, to see the cloud shadows she had called by name—names she'd already forgotten in her dream—to see those shadows slowly shade the valley below . . . turn its fields to forest green, darken its sinuous river from silver to bronze.

Joanna woke still seeing a veil of rain, distant drapery, sweeping slowly across the valley she knew so well, though she'd never gone down from her mountain.

She stretched—her muscles slightly stiff from gardening, her knees still a little sore—then got up and went to a window, stepping into a rectangular block of white-gold sunlight to look out at a perfect morning, and the distant sea.

She went into the bathroom, peed, and changed her Tampax. Though she'd showered the night before, she showered again to wash her hair . . . stepped out to towel . . . then stood blow-drying at the sink, combing her hair up for the hot air, and studying her reflection. Her face was still a little flushed from yesterday's sun and sea wind. There were familiar lines at the outer corners of her eyes . . . at the corners of her mouth. Sunblock—foolish not to use it.

Joanna brushed her hair, pulled it back and through a maroon elastic tie into a ponytail, then went to the dresser for underwear . . . the closet for worn work pants—caving pants till the knees gave out—an old T-shirt and weary sneakers. Paint clothes.

Dressed, she went downstairs considering breakfast, and decided on cold cereal. There'd be island blueberries with it, later in the summer. . . . In the kitchen, she made tea—Russian Caravan—then sectioned an elderly orange for eating out of hand, and used the last of the milk on a bowl of shredded wheat.

She ate sitting at the kitchen table, looking into the backyard . . . looking past the sea grape out along Sand Hill's irregular crest, the dune ridges lit various colors of toast by the morning's slanting light. . . . The orange sections were seedy but sweet, the cereal richly coarse.

When she was finished, she sat awhile longer, sipping the dark, complicated tea, and trying to remember her dream . . . what the names of the clouds had been, that came when called. When she finished her tea, she got up and went to the sink, washed the cup and cereal bowl, and put them in the drainer.

Then she spread pages of last week's edition of *The Islander* out on the table with a half-roll of paper towels and an old mixing bowl full of water, for cleanup. She brought her small can of paint and the brush from the counter and set them out.

The paint can was hard to open. Joanna pried the lid up with a table knife . . . then stirred the paint carefully to keep from spilling any. The brush was not a great stirrer; paint got on the handle. . . .

She started with the inside members of the window frame, standing holding the small can in her hand, and dipping and wiping the little brush for every two or three strokes. . . . She covered the slender sticks with great attention, enjoying the paint's perfect white—brushing lightly up and down—dressing so nicely the fir's coarse grain. As she painted, and as if the smooth white were smoothing over her, perfect as a field of snow, Joanna began to imagine at least the possibility of limited happiness.

She painted carefully . . . dipped a little twist of paper towel into the bowl of water to clean the few small streaks of white smeared onto the window glass.

Finished in the kitchen, Joanna took her paint out on the steps, and closed the door behind her to get at its window's other side. She begin again the careful dipping into paint, neat strokes to cover the whatevers . . . what Bobby had called them. The *muntins*.

. . . She was sorry when the job was done. The window frame, fresh white, looked better than it had before Bobby broke it. —Poor Bobby. She'd have to check with Tom Lowell, make sure he hadn't been mistreated, only sent into exile. . . .

Joanna was cleaning the bowl and little brush at the sink when the doorbell rang. And of course her hands were wet and she still had paint on them.

"Shit. *Just a second. . . .*"

The doorbell rang again. She rinsed the brush once more, left it in the sink, and called *"Be right there. . . !"* Drying her hands on her trousers, she went up the hall to the door, and opened it.

Chief Constable Carl Early, in a gray summer suit, was standing on the front steps. An elderly woman—short, plump, and plain—was standing beside him. She was wearing a dark-blue dress, white shoes.

"Mrs. Reed . . ." The constable was looking older, less handsome.

Trouble, Joanna thought. *Trouble over that goddamn marijuana. I should have called the police. . . .*

"I'm Marilyn Early," the plump woman said. "People have been trying to call—I think something's wrong with your phone."

"I brought my wife." Early was wearing a shot-silk tie to set off his suit.

"What is it?"

Neither of them answered her.

"Is it . . . am I going to be arrested?"

"Oh, my dear," Marilyn Early said. "Oh, my dear, it's your girl."

"What do you mean, 'my girl'?"

"Mrs. Reed," the old man said, "I received a call this morning from Captain Fetterman, with the state police. . . . Your daughter was found last night. She fell from a building on the campus over at White River. She fell three stories, and was killed." He stopped talking, to clear his throat. "—Apparently, people have been trying to call you all night, and I can't *tell* you how sorry we are. Everyone out here is just terribly sorry." He took a clean, squared handkerchief out of his suit pocket and wiped his forehead. "It is the worst goddamn thing on top of everything else."

"Carl," his wife said.

"Well, it is. It's outrageous."

It seemed to Joanna that she was dreaming and they were speaking a dream language she didn't understand. She supposed she looked like a fool, standing looking down at them.

"I'm sorry to be so stupid," she said. "Rebecca . . ." She turned her head to stare down the cobbled street at the sunny cottages descending, their small yards bright with what seemed strange flowers. It was all part of a new world, not the one she'd known. The air was different, hard to breathe. The light hurt her eyes, pulsed in slow rhythm.

"What's happening?" she said, and was asking what had happened to the world to change its air, its light and colors.

"Oh, you poor thing," Mrs. Early said. Joanna understood that—and as if it were the signal she'd been waiting for, leaned out from the doorway to darkness, and fell into the constable's arms.

Waking to light that hummed, she sat up shouting *"Oh . . . Oh . . . Oh,"* until someone came and stung her left arm so she slowly slid away . . . and when next she woke, it was night. Joanna woke, but drove herself back down into sleep as if a wakeness-tiger would catch and kill her, otherwise.

She didn't rouse again until fading afternoon. And when she did—careful to open her eyes slowly, so as not to see too much, know too much—a girl was sitting by the white bed in a white room. A pretty girl with dark-blond hair was sitting in a white chair beside her bed, holding her hand.

"Are you awake?" the girl said. "Are you awake . . . ?"

And there was no answer to make but yes . . . to nod yes. Of course she was awake; her eyes were open, and seeing. . . . The girl was stroking Joanna's hand. She seemed very sad, very concerned. And familiar, Joanna knew her from somewhere.

"Do you remember me? Charis Langenberg?"

"I think so." Joanna was surprised by her own voice. It was a hoarse and harsher voice than she was used to hearing.

"I came out with Rebecca that time. I'm . . . I was her roommate."

"I remember," Joanna said, drew in the deepest breath she could, and used that to dive . . . dive suddenly and deep into sleep. She did it so quickly that nothing could catch her—not even the girl who bent from her chair to look into Joanna's eyes and watch her go, as if to follow her down.

Two days later, Charis sat through the morning watching Joanna sleep—lying with her long black hair, threaded with ash gray, spread smoky on the pillow. Her face was drawn, fine lines carved into it across her forehead and at the corners of her mouth. Charis watched her sleep for a long time before bending to kiss her cheek, then sat back in the chair to watch longer.

"I'm a friend of the family—I was her daughter's friend," she'd told the nurses. "I don't think she has anyone else, close." And they'd let her stay.

That had been the evening of the first day, after they'd brought Joanna in from the island. They'd brought her in by helicopter. . . . She'd slept, drugged, and when she woke, the doctor had put her to sleep again. Charis had sat by Joanna's bed, watching.

The second day, she woke and Charis spoke to her, and she went back to sleep until late at night, when she woke again and refused to use the bedpan, confused, querulous as a child. Charis had helped her out of bed, and stood by the toilet holding her hand. . . . And toward morning, when Joanna cried out in her sleep, Charis had wakened her from that dream, and sat on the bed to hold her until she slept again.

But today, flowers had come and people had come. —A while ago, Charis had gone to get orange juice, and seen White River's dean and his wife, and one of the professors, McCreedy, and his wife, at the nurses station. Charis had stepped into the hall bathroom, and stayed there for a while.

When she'd come out, the White River people had left, and left Joanna dozing, tired by the visit.

Charis sat watching a long time, holding Joanna's hand. Then, in early afternoon, she got up from her chair and was careful to be quiet as she took her purse and safari jacket from the closet. She felt now was the time to leave for a while. —And knew she'd been right when she heard Joanna wake and call her name as she walked down the hall. . . . Knew again she'd been right when she passed the nurses station and heard still another visitor—an old lady in an ancient Chanel suit—asking for Mrs. Reed.

It was time to be gone for a while. There was a rhythm to things, like dancing. A rhythm even to contentment.

. . . The first feelings that happiness brought with it were comfort and weight. Charis felt those during the long drive back across the state to White River. She'd put the VW's torn canvas top down, and drove one-handed, her left arm resting on the top of the car's door. The wind of driving touched and plucked at her hair, trying to get it loose. Touched her blouse front gently, as if it wished to open its buttons to reach her breasts. . . .

The results of happiness were not what she'd expected. She'd thought it might make her lighter, ease her over things like an airy high-hurdler. —But now that it was here, now that she was starting over at last and had her place prepared, she felt heavier, more solid rather than less. . . . So, happiness seemed to mean settling into things, resting comfortably, as if the world were fine furniture and she could be at ease on it. A strange sensation; it made her smile, driving along, and explained the smiles she'd seen on others.

Chapter Sixteen

I wouldn't call it a nervous breakdown. Don't know what that is, anyway." Dr. Chao was young—tall for a Chinese-American—and impatient, though he'd been gentle with Joanna. "I'd just say you had a hell of a shock. A series of personal tragedies, and the last one was one too many."

"One too many," Joanna said. She knew she'd been repeating people's phrases. And that must be annoying. "—I'm sorry to always be repeating what you say."

Dr. Chao reached down and patted her hand. "It's a way of anchoring yourself dealing with people, while you're so distraught. . . . You know, we have a psychiatrist coming in part-time on staff here, and we've discussed your situation. She's really nice, might be a good idea to talk to her."

"I'd rather not talk to her. —And I didn't mean to repeat what you'd said. 'Talk to her.' That was just part of my own sentence."

"I know," Dr. Chao said. "Don't worry about it. Strictly your sentence." He smiled, seemed to think she was amusing.

"Where's Charis?"

"Charis?"

"The girl who was here with me."

"Oh . . . she left. You were feeling better, so I suppose she thought she could go."

"Is she coming back?"

"Well, I suppose she could—but you're not going to be with us much longer, Mrs. Reed. You're much better; it was just a matter of shock, collapse due to shock . . . call it battle fatigue. And a hospital is not the best place to recover from grief. Continued medication isn't going to be good for you, either."

"I'm better."

"Yes. . . . So I don't see any reason why you couldn't be released tomorrow."

"I can be released tomorrow," Joanna said, made a baby's face and began to cry. "This is so ridiculous," she said—tried to say that, and had to put her hands up to cover her face so she could speak through her fingers.

". . . Maybe day after tomorrow," said Dr. Chao.

Greg was in Charis's room when she went up. He was sitting at her desk, reading, and looked as though he'd been waiting there a long time.

"Jesus, I've been coming up here the last two *days*. Where have you been?"

"I was with Mrs. Reed."

"Wow. With her mother?"

"That's right." Charis opened her closet door, put her overnight bag in—reminded herself to do a wash—and hung up her safari jacket.

"Better you than me, man. . . . Well, what are we going to do? I don't know what to say to anybody."

"Have you talked to anyone about this, Greg?"

"You said not to."

"That's right. We don't need to say *anything*, Greg. It would be really smart just to keep quiet about it—because believe me, people are going to be asking." Charis sat on her bed, kicked off her loafers. "—It's a death. Campus cops and plenty of people are going to keep coming around." Tired from the drive, the nights sitting up at the hospital, she stretched out and closed her eyes. She could do the wash when Greg left, take a hot shower, then sleep. "—There's nothing to say, anyway. You never even got a chance to talk to her, try to make her feel better."

"She was gone—I mean, I went up on the roof and it was dark and there was nobody there . . . just people yelling down on the sidewalk."

"I know, Greggis." She could take a nap now, shower and do the wash later. "—Not your fault. If it was anybody's fault, it was mine. I should have gone to the college clinic, no matter what Becky said. I should have told them she was just so . . . sad, so desperate." Charis yawned; it was hard to stay awake.

"What did you tell her mom?"

"Like as little as possible." She could do the wash tomorrow; it was just underwear, socks, jeans, and a sweatshirt. "—And when the campus cops get around to you, you do the same. I'm damn sure going to keep *my* mouth shut."

"Why? We were trying to help her."

"Why? Listen, if you tell people about our being so concerned and trying to help . . . and she was in love with you and so forth? If you do that, Greg, then believe me—long after the details, the facts of Becky's suicide, are forgotten, *your* part in it is going to be remembered. You will be the guy who had something to do with a young girl's death—period."

"Shit. . . ."

"You just let people know you were personally involved with her at all—and thanks to campus gossip, *and* the dean's office, *and* the net chat rooms, that will follow you all the time you're at White River, and right into graduate school. For the rest of your life, Greggis, you'd never know when Becky's death could rise up and bite you."

"Oh, man. No good deed goes unpunished—and I never even talked to her!"

"I know. —Anyway, I intend to keep my mouth *shut* about having anything to do with this, except being shocked and saddened—and that's true enough. I've done my crying for Rebecca."

"Okay . . . okay. You know, I never knew anybody who killed themselves. It's extremely unreal."

"Yes, it is. —So, no matter who asks us, we were really surprised, and we're very sad about it because Becky was a nice girl. But she did seem pretty upset by those deaths in her family. *Period.*"

"Period. . . . You know, this is the first tragedy I've been involved with."

"What a lucky guy. . . ."

Joanna lay in summer light made brighter by reflection of her room's cool white. The window blinds slatted sunshine to fine stripes across the walls.

She lay resting, reflecting on being alone—with no one left to love or be loved by. Her family now stood separate, on the other side of everything. They were there—or nowhere—and she was here, solitary as a wandering animal, with only food and shelter as necessary concerns. A cheeseburger, a clean motel room, some pleasant landscape view . . . those sorts of limited pleasures, like the coolness of her bed's sheets as she lay, lunch over.

She could do as she pleased—and had to please no one, wonder about no one, worry about no one. Now she was alone in the castle of herself, free to wander from room to room, view to view . . . and had to let no one in, admit no guest, no intruder, and no messenger, since there would be no news to receive that might concern her . . . until at last, after many years, a doctor at the drawbridge confirmed her sentence of death.

A "sentence" of death . . . as if there were some written phrase— with subject, adverb, verb, and object—that *was* death. Death described so perfectly, so completely, that the description became the thing itself, a phrase that if spoken, killed all who heard it.

She, a poet, might have made that perfect sentence, a sentence of death. She might have written it in rough draft, or spoken it by chance—not realizing its accidental perfection. But those nearest, closest to her, had heard or read, and died.

These losses seemed part of a pattern past rational cause or interruption. She'd tried action to break open and reveal its secret machinery—tried that, and exposed only the fishermen's desperation.

Small wheels squeaked in the hall. Some patient being borne past, to hope or hopelessness.

. . . The fishermen, rough innocents. Of course the Russians, or whoever, must be taking advantage of the Asconsett people in the trade—as the dealers and thugs of Providence and Boston were certainly taking advantage of them. Even as criminals, the captains— clumsy and old-fashioned in their seaboots and sou'westers, their heavy hands net-scarred and scored by salty weather—even as criminals they would eventually lose their boats, as their time was already lost to them.

In Manning's, she had accomplished only an adventure, an incompetent bandage for her injury. Poor protection against savage ill chance, ill chance again, and inconsolable regret. —And proved so swiftly, in only the time it took a young girl to fall three stories onto stone.

. . . Now, there was only dinner to look forward to. This evening's dinner, supposed to be chicken, peas, orange sherbet and a roll. A solitary animal had dinner to look forward to, and sleep.

*   *   *

There was that dinner, the chicken dinner, yesterday evening.

And today, breakfast, sunshine at the window, and another visitor. Francie, up from New York and doing more than an agent's duty to a fiscally very minor author.

Francie Pincus didn't look New York publishing at all. She was large, easy, flushed, and freckled, with soft brown curls—an Iowa farm woman out of place. Francie's calm and good nature ran all through her, so bad news seemed to bruise only for a day or two, then vanish.

This news, Joanna's news, had overpowered those defenses, so it was a pale, large, damp-eyed agent who wandered into the hospital room as if it must be the wrong one, and Joanna not her published poet after all.

"Oh, Jesus . . . Jesus, Joanna." And this heavy woman, in a badly fitting blue suit, sagged onto the bedside and put out a strong, plump hand to pat Joanna's. Francie scented with strong florals. It was lavender today; she smelled like a linen closet.

"It's all over," Joanna said, and couldn't think why she'd said it. Perhaps she'd meant she had no one else to lose.

"Rebecca," Francie said, china-blue eyes slightly popped and glaring with a rage of loss. Childless, she'd loved Rebecca—been happy to offer her apartment for overnights, happy to escort first the child . . . then the young woman to museums and Broadway musicals on her infrequent visits to the city.

Joanna wanted to join her in anger, and speak Rebecca's name—but that seemed impossible to say aloud, so she only nodded and gripped Francie's strong freckled hand.

Francie sat and said no more for a long time—time enough for the sun to shift the room's shadows slightly. Then she said, "What a fucking shame," and bent over Joanna, her bulk breezing lavender, to kiss her loudly on the cheek, an almost comic smacking kiss.

After that, she sat silent another while—her weight affecting the shape of the mattress. She sat for those slow minutes more, a soft blue monument . . . then suddenly got to her feet with a large animal's swift heave, squeezed Joanna's hand, let it go, and walked to the door and out.

Then she ducked back in, only her large head showing, said, "No business to speak of—nothing important. Oh, *Christ. . . .*" And was gone.

Joanna lay in her white bed in her white room, and feared more visitors, but no other visitors came. She lay and waited for lunch . . . found herself smiling once. The weight of tragedy, grown too great, might tilt the balance to comedy. She had lost too much—almost a pratfall, a blow with a bladder, a shove over the back of a surprise clown. She felt she was drifting away into only observation, and might see humor in the Auschwitz ovens.

Only the pain kept her human—the bright hook of agony was in her mouth, it had driven through her gum and jaw, so there was no point beside that point. The shoals of silver fish taken off Asconsett and dead, now were revenged by their absence. But she still lived.

Lunch was ham salad, succotash, and a roll. Desert was a little square white cake with brittle frosting.

She dozed through the afternoon, with half-dreams bright and patchworked as a child's in its midday nap. Graham-cracker dreams, cup-of-milk dreams in which there was not enough knowledge to spoil the colors.

They woke her for dinner, and it was Swiss steak, mashed sweet potato, string beans, and lemon sherbet.

After dinner, when they took the tray, said something, then left her alone, Joanna took deep breaths to be ready for the night—she stretched and eased her muscles in the bed, and did a little shifting dance beneath the white covers, as Greek warriors had stretched and danced their rhythmic steps in slow circles with spear and shield, the sun gleaming on bronze armor, brightening their helmets' nodding crimsoned horsehair.

Joanna prepared for the night as if for battle, or some dangerous cave. She armed herself, stretched her muscles, and prepared to stay awake to avoid the realities of deep dreaming, in which anything or anyone might come to her.

Exhausted when morning came, though successful against the night, she welcomed a last breakfast—Cheerios, grapefruit juice, a miniature apricot Danish.

A little while after breakfast, a farewell visit by Dr. Chao, very breezy, jovial. —And then, in a flurry of attention, Joanna was up and dressed in khakis, a white shirt, and a natural cotton sweater she recognized—all brought over from the island for her, she supposed, by Marilyn Early. And must remember to thank her for those and her purse and robe and toothbrush and makeup, though they hadn't given her time to put her makeup on.

They placed her in the departure wheelchair, all extra items bundled in a small white plastic sack in her lap, with her purse.

She was in the chair and ready to go, when she turned to look up at Mrs. Laval, the morning-shift RN. Laval was standing at the wheelchair's handles.

"Where am I going? I mean, I don't think there's anyone to meet me. . . ." She meant that it was too soon for her to leave, that she would be left alone in front of the hospital, with no way to get to the ferry, no one to be with her, help her. How was she to do all that? . . . And what was she to do when she reached the island? And when she got to the cottage alone—what then?

"There's someone to meet you, dear."

"Who . . . ?"

But they were rolling out of the room and down the corridor, and Laval was talking about towels with Connor, the aide. Connor was late, collecting the towels.

Someone, an elderly woman at the front desk, smiled and said good-bye when she gave Joanna two pages of health insurance forms and receipts, but Joanna didn't remember her—and was wheeled away before she could say thank you.

Laval pushed the chair out through heavy automatic glass doors, and down a sunny curving ramp to the sidewalk. There was no one waiting there except a girl, a young woman standing beside an old VW convertible. . . . Then the girl smiled and came to her, and it was Charis.

"I was worried you wouldn't want to see me when you were better. I was afraid I'd just remind you of everything." Charis reached down and took Joanna's hand. "—Is it okay that I came to get you?"

"Yes," Joanna said. "It's okay." She began to cry, but only a little, because she was tired.

Laval started to assist her out of the chair, but Charis helped her instead, and said, "I'll take care of her."

. . . On the long trip out through the islands, Joanna didn't want to talk, and Charis was silent, too. They sat side by side on a deck bench in the sun, and watched the colors of the sea, watched seabirds swing past the ship in ellipses that brought them by again, after a while.

The ferry's ponderous slow dancing motion eased Joanna slightly. Sitting silent, silent and swaying to that minor rise and fall, made her feel better . . . as silence and swaying might quiet the agony of a wound.

Charis sat beside her, a golden girl in jeans and a tan safari jacket—tall, slender, and beautiful, beautiful as Rebecca had never been. Charis's face was made of elegant angles, almost too extreme, and tilted hazel eyes. It was an oddly familiar handsomeness, like some young actress's face seen in a film before, and remembered. . . . Sitting by her side, their arms lightly touching, Joanna could smell the scent of the girl's youth, mingled in the sea's warm fluttering breeze, the ferry's faint diesel—could smell the perfume of young womanhood, delicate as the odor of a risen cake drifting down the hall from a kitchen.

. . . The cottage appeared to Joanna a garden of ease and restfulness. The short drive up from the dock had seemed as tiring as walking would have been, and she had yawned and yawned like a sleepy child.

Charis, very quiet, hardly speaking at all, had gone upstairs with her and helped her undress . . . then had found the blue nightgown and put her to bed. It was only afternoon; the sunlight through the window shades seemed too bright for sleeping. But Joanna slept, and had no dreams after all.

She woke in darkness, confused, and thought for a moment she was still at the hospital, but Charis heard and came upstairs, turned on the bedside lamp, and asked if she wanted to go down to dinner or have it on a tray in bed.

"I'll go down," Joanna said. But she didn't get up. She lay with the covers pulled up to her chin, looking at Charis as if waiting for another, more important question.

Charis smiled and said, "Do you *want* to get up?"

Joanna had the feeling—foolish, she knew—that bad news would be waiting downstairs. "No."

"Well, you don't have to. I was afraid your chicken stew, in the big pot, might have spoiled—and something in a jar, too. So I'm making beef-barley soup—warming it, anyway—and toast. A glass of milk?"

"Yes."

Charis smiled again, and left the room. She had a quick light step; Joanna could barely hear her going down the stairs.

Joanna had time to lie still, and think of very little . . . notice the stillness of the room, its odors washed faint by sea breezes. She was reminded of her grandmother's house in Boston, which had smelled strongly of age, its high-ceilinged rooms darkly furnished and completed in sepia wallpapers of dim roses and faded vines.

Rooms seeming to belong to oddly dressed men and women who might come into them at any moment, alive again, smelling of tobacco or perfume, and casually loud as they called . . . looking for a missing collar button or one of a pair of French silk stockings.

But her room, this room—furnished with common painted pieces—though dark now, was bright in daytime. Then, the flooding summer sunlight seemed to lift it free of the house, so it floated slightly, out over the front yard.

Joanna, her eyes closed, was lying imagining it was daytime, when Charis came back upstairs with a tray.

"No milk," she said. "I'll get some, tomorrow."

She bent to prop Joanna up, fluff her pillows, then settle the tray on her lap. Tea, a bowl of beef-barley soup, a piece of whole-wheat toast, a spoon and two paper napkins. "Butter on the toast," Charis said. "Would you like some jam?"

"No. Thank you very much."

When the girl had gone downstairs again, Joanna sipped the soup slowly. She felt that she had been sliced in two, and it had been done swiftly and properly, with no ragged edges. There was Joanna, who'd had bad news—and there was this body, which was not interested. The body, intelligent in its own way, was where she'd stayed for the last two days. Now it sipped and swallowed; it ate a bite of toast and had some tea. It didn't care who was dead.

. . . When she was ready to lie down, tired of the tray, Joanna called Charis. Called her once—but that business of calling out disturbed her. Calling out a name, calling for a person who would answer.

Charis came upstairs, took the tray in silence, and went away. Afterward, there was soft singing from downstairs, of no particular song. The girl's voice was slender as she was slender, and wavered in pitch—the sound a cracked bell's, beautiful and imperfect.

Joanna got out of bed, went into the bathroom, and took off her pajamas. She had slept so much the last few days that she staggered a little, stepping into the shower, as if wakefulness required better balance. She ran the meager water very hot—steamed herself, soaped herself, and rinsed. Then she stepped out to dry . . . and felt dizzy, sick to her stomach, and had to sit naked on the bathroom's little white stool. She sat, her head bowed, taking deep breaths to keep from vomiting.

Something touched her shoulder, and she looked up to see Charis standing beside her, a handmaid with a towel.

"Shhhh. . . ." Charis made the soft hushing sound as if to quiet nausea, then stooped and began to dry Joanna gently and with reserve. She hesitated and was delicate along the scar where Joanna's breast had been—then stroked strongly down her back, helped her to stand . . . and dried between her buttocks and down the length of each leg, then up again, deftly at her crotch and belly. Did her arms, armpits—Joanna lifting her arms like a child to facilitate—then lightly patted her throat and face.

Charis seated her on the little stool again, found the hair dryer in the cabinet, and stood behind her, raising banners of long black hair with a rat-tail comb to funnel the warm air.

Finished, Charis brought a different nightgown, the peach, helped Joanna put it on . . . and led her back in the dark bedroom to the bed, as if she might have forgotten where it was. Then tucked her in.

"If you can't sleep," Charis said, "I'll take you for a drive. We can drive somewhere along the sea."

"All right," Joanna said, turned on her side, and slept.

She woke to morning sunlight freshly golden, and smelled oatmeal cooking . . . and cinnamon.

Charis came upstairs. She was wearing jeans and a white summer sweater. "Breakfast," she said. "You need help?"

"No, thank you." Joanna supposed Charis would want her to go downstairs.

"Then get dressed," Charis said, "—and come on down."

. . . Oatmeal. Charis, lacking milk, had served it like a vegetable, with butter, salt and pepper. Oatmeal, cinnamon toast, and tea.

"I'd like to thank you, Charis—for breakfast . . . for everything you've done."

"You don't have to thank me, Mrs. Reed." Charis finished her tea, stood and began to clear the table.

"Joanna. —Yes, I do." Joanna hadn't thought she'd be able to finish her toast, but she had.

Charis stacked the dishes in the sink. "Are you going to be all right?"

Joanna sat startled as if by a gunshot. " 'Be all right?' "

Charis began to wash the dishes, her hands' motions economical as a cat's. "I have to go. Summer midterms."

". . . Of course," Joanna said. "Of course you have to go." She used both hands to steady her teacup, put it down on the saucer. "It was good of you to come to the hospital, Charis, and stay with me. I know I was a mess."

"You weren't a mess, Mrs. Reed."

"Joanna."

"—Joanna." Charis came to the table, began cleaning it with the washcloth. "Want another piece of toast, or more tea?"

"No, thank you. . . . It was very kind of you."

"It wasn't kindness," Charis said, and took Joanna's cup and saucer to the sink. "Rebecca was younger, and my roommate—I *asked* her if she wanted to be my roommate—and we were friends. I didn't pay enough attention to her after she'd lost her dad and grandfather that way." Charis rinsed the cup and saucer. "—I was careless with her."

"No—"

"I didn't do what I should have done to try to help her over it. I was too busy for Rebecca." Charis put the cup and saucer in the dish drainer. "—Thought I had more important things to do."

"You weren't responsible. . . . I was responsible." Joanna hoped Charis wouldn't say the name again.

"I could have talked to her, listened to her. I could have helped a little more." Charis folded the washcloth, draped it over the sink faucet.

"It wasn't your fault, Charis." Joanna got up from the table. She needed to get out of the kitchen, where this talk about it was smothering, crowding the room's air. "—Not your fault." She went out the kitchen door and down the back steps to stand in the yard, free of the talking about it still drifting through the house.

"I don't know what I am," she said to the bed of flowers she'd fought the weeds for. "But I'm not what I was." It was an exhausting notion, that she would have to learn to know a strange self. She stood in the yard, examined the scattered remnant flowers and ragged border of sea grapes. Over years, the dune hill's sand must have slumped beneath the picket fencing here in back. Swallowed it, buried it, swept it slowly away. . . . Charis was finishing in the kitchen; the legs of a chair scraped as it was pushed into place.

A little later, while Joanna was still standing in the yard alongside her morning shadow, and looking out over Asconsett Town, Charis came down the kitchen steps with her black backpack and overnight bag. She walked along the driveway past the parked Volvo, dropped the pack and bag into her little convertible's backseat, then came out into the yard.

"I shouldn't have said anything about it," she said. "Forgive me."

"I'm not the only one in the world," Joanna said. "I'm not so important that other people—especially you, who were her friend—that you don't have necessary things to say."

Charis, hazel eyes studying, had seemed to listen carefully to that, her elegant dark-blond head cocked slightly to the side. She appeared, in the flood of morning sunlight, too vivid, too brightly symmetrical for ordinary purposes—some almost-angel, stopped by to comfort. "Yes, but necessary things didn't have to be said so soon. . . . And now, I guess I need to be going."

"Well, thank you again for helping me, Charis." Joanna leaned to kiss the girl on the cheek . . . kissed skin smooth as sun-warmed glass.

"I needed to come." Charis hugged her—slender arms quite strong—then went back to the VW, got in, started its engine and slowly backed down the drive.

"Be careful," Joanna said—then was suddenly afraid the girl hadn't heard her, and hurried after the car and called out again over its engine's harsh buzz. "Be careful. Drive carefully!"

Charis, backed into the street, smiled and nodded, then started down the hill, going slow over Slope's cobbles.

Joanna thought Charis had heard her . . . but wasn't absolutely certain, so she went out into the street—saw the girl was already too far down to call to—and began to trot after her. She went faster, almost running to catch up, to be sure Charis was reminded to drive very carefully, so that nothing terrible would happen.

Almost down to Strand, Charis must have seen her in the rearview mirror. She stopped the car as Joanna ran down to her, unsteady on the cobbles and oddly out of breath.

"*I just wanted* . . . just wanted to remind you." She supposed someone on the hill, some woman in her kitchen, had seen her running after the car. "—Please drive carefully. Be very careful."

Charis smiled, and reached out to take Joanna's hand. "I will. Don't worry, I'll be careful."

"Thank you," Joanna said, and meant thanks for agreeing to be careful. She held Charis's hand for a moment, a living girl's hand, then let it go.

"Good-bye." Charis started her car.

"If you want to come out again and visit," Joanna said, raising her voice over the engine's sound, "—if you want to do that, Charis, you'd be . . . you're really welcome. There *are* things to do out here—

the beach, and we could go lobstering. And boys are out here for the summer. It's . . . there really are things to do."

"I'd like that. I'd like to come out, but I wouldn't want to bother you."

"It wouldn't bother me! You could come out anytime, come right back after your exams—I don't know why the hell they have summer midterms, anyway; it's ridiculous. Oh, but you still have classes. . . ."

Charis put the VW in gear. "I only have five weeks left. I think I can finesse that—just write papers for them."

"Well, then please think about it."

"You're sure you want me hanging around?"

"Yes. Yes, I do."

"Okay. Well, I'll see if I can. . . ." And she smiled and drove away, put up a hand to wave good-bye at the bottom of the hill . . . then turned right on Strand. There was plenty of time for her to make the ferry.

Chapter Seventeen

Joanna climbed the hill, and walked down the drive into the back-yard. The house seemed too empty to go into. She was so glad she had the whole day before night . . . and the backyard's struggling flowers, its tough little weeds and countless threading insects to keep her company. Here, in a small green handkerchief draped across a dune, was life enough for a city. Life enough so death made no difference, and could never catch up.

The world outside was full as the house was empty. Out here, she'd miss no voices, and no one would think it strange, in such sunny summer weather, that she stayed in her backyard.

She went up the back steps and into the house, then upstairs to change into old clothes—and did that as quickly as she could, humming to fill the silence.

When she came out, she collected her few gardening tools from the garage, then went into the yard and lay down along the flower-bed border . . . sinking into soft grasses, volunteering again to be commander and commando in the war against the weeds. —She had wondered why so many men enjoyed at least the idea of war, and now she knew. It was a second, separate, and simpler universe, much less cruel and arbitrary than the first.

. . . She worked through the morning, and into early afternoon, her right shoulder aching from digging and pulling roots. And it was an odd thing, but the more weeds she came against, dug up, de-feated, and destroyed for the flowers' sake—the more she admired the little plants' determination, their slender rough-stemmed courage. And as she honored the dying weeds, she began to doubt

the flowers—that had nothing to offer but slavishly colored pleasure to the people who had planted them.

. . . The telephone rang in the house just after three, and didn't
stop ringing. Joanna had thought it was still broken, disconnected,
but they must have come into the cottage and fixed it while she
was gone.

Reluctant, her muscles sore and stiff from working lying down,
Joanna went into the house . . . walked up the hall to the phone.

"*Mrs. Reed . . . ?*"

"Yes?"

"It's Marilyn. Marilyn Early?"

"Yes. . . . Oh, yes. I believe you brought my things over to the
hospital, and I'd like to thank you."

"You don't have to thank me, dear—and I don't want to trouble
you; I don't want to be a nuisance. But I would like you to know that
I'd be happy to help in any way I can. Some friends and I—if you do
want something done, housecleaning or shopping, we'll be happy
to do that for you."

"Thank you. That's very nice. But I don't think I need
anything. . . ."

"All right. But now listen, Joanna—may I call you Joanna?"

"Yes."

"Well, listen, now. If you do need help—maybe just some prepared dishes so you don't have to cook—if you do need help, or just
want company for a little while, you call me. The Earlys—we're in
the island book."

"Thank you very much . . . Marilyn."

"Well, I won't trouble you any longer, dear. But if you need
something, you *call.* Okay?"

"Okay. . . ."

Joanna put the phone down, and got out of the house.

Too hungry and tired by the end of the day to stay out any
longer, she cleaned the tools and put them away, then went into the
kitchen.

Still no milk. . . . There was a can of B&M baked beans in the
pantry—easier than making spaghetti, easier than making a sar-
dine sandwich, or peanut butter and jelly sandwich.

Joanna opened the can of beans, and turned back the lid. She
took a spoon from the counter drawer, went to sit on the back steps,
and looked out over the yard . . . out along the ridge of the hill as

she ate. The baked beans were good, cold; she could taste the molasses in them.

. . . Joanna had just finished, was scraping the bottom of the can with her spoon, when the phone rang again. She got up, went into the kitchen and down the hall to answer it.

Someone said something she didn't understand . . . then her name.

"Yes, I'm Joanna Reed."

"Mrs. Reed—I deeply regret troubling you at this time. My name's Gosden, Jack Gosden of White River Memorial. We've been called by the County Clinic, and I've checked with the police and talked with Dean Widdner, and the dean suggested I get in touch with you out there."

"Why are you calling me?"

"This is really difficult. . . . I am very sorry, but some decision is required about your daughter's remains. The law enforcement people have released them, and County Clinic also has released them. —If you prefer, Mrs. Reed, some other funeral home could handle the matter. And there's also the question of any service or memorial gathering you might wish to be held. Dean Widdner has offered the college chapel. . . ."

"What's your name?"

"Gosden, Mrs. Reed. Jack Gosden."

"Do what you want. Do what's fastest. I don't want her to be dead there any longer."

"Well . . . cremation would be the most . . . it would be quickest."

"Then do it. Do that."

"Would you like any service, any viewing—"

"No."

"No service?"

"No."

"Well, on cremation, Mrs. Reed—the costs there would amount to . . . to approximately one thousand, five hundred dollars, with a small bronze urn. That would be pretty much the total cost."

"I know what it costs—you're the people who did that with my husband."

". . . Mr. Reed? When? —Oh . . . that's right, we did. Another person handled that—I'm sorry."

"So, just go ahead with it."

"All right, then. We will."

"Wait, let me get you my credit card number." Joanna went

through her purse on the entrance-hall table, found her wallet, and took the card out.

"Are you ready?"

"Yes. . . ."

Joanna read out the numbers, and expiration date. "Do you have that?"

"Yes . . . I do. And Mrs. Reed, I'm very sorry to have had to call you with this."

"That's all right. . . . And pretty soon I will come and get her. Just keep her, and I promise I'll come and get her." She hung up, put her credit card away in her wallet, then reached down to grip the telephone cord—gripped it with both hands—and yanked as hard as she could, but it wouldn't come out of the wall. Hauling on it only hurt her hands.

She looked down behind the table to see if the wire's connection was that little plastic fitting that clicked into place—but there was a small round thing fastened to the wall, with no way to get it free.

Joanna went to the kitchen and searched in the top counter drawer—regretting the fillet knife lost on the hill. She selected a paring knife, went back to the entrance hall, picked up the phone cord and sawed at it. It was a tough cord, with metal in the middle, but she cut it through.

She took the knife back to the kitchen, drank two glasses of water at the sink, then went outside to sit on the back steps again. . . . It was startling to be so perfectly alone; a constant reminder seemed to flow under every minute like groundwater, recalling her solitude to her.

The summer evening was slowly coming on, softening light and easing the brilliance of every color. The quality of air changed as the light changed—Joanna could feel it by rubbing her hands together. She held them open—aching, dirt-grimed—then clapped them together in slow motion to capture a texture of the air. Rubbed them lightly together. The evening's air was more manageable than the afternoon's—it felt like soft cloth . . . almost gathering, pleating between her hands.

Joanna sat on the back steps for a long time, until the last of light had risen up, and the dark came down. Then, by starlight, she got up and went into the house. She walked to the staircase, climbed halfway up—then turned and came down again, took one of Bobby's blankets from the hall closet, and went outside. She wrapped herself in the blanket, lay down in the grass beneath the sea grapes, and went to sleep.

She dreamt that the moonlight woke her . . . found that was so, and slept again.

Joanna woke to morning sunlight and the odor of earth, turned her head, and saw a pair of shoes—brown tasseled loafers.

"Mrs. Reed. . . ." Carl Early, in a tan summer suit, bent over her. He was still handsome, viewed from the ground. Joanna saw what she supposed was the bottom edge of a pistol holster—black leather—under the hem of his jacket. . . . And he was carrying something in his left hand, something small in plastic wrap.

"Too warm in the house . . . decided to sleep out," she said, so Early wouldn't think she was crazy to be lying in the yard. She wriggled out of the blanket and stood up.

"You all right?"

"I'm fine. Fine."

Early looked her up and down, blue eyes taking in the caving pants, smeared with dirt . . . her grimy work shirt and torn sneakers.

"—Gardening," Joanna said. "I've been gardening." She put her dirty hands behind her back.

"Your phone's out again—did you know that?"

"Oh, yes. Yes, I did. I'm going to town today; I was going to stop at the office and have them come out."

"I'll do that for you."

"No, really. I'll take care of it."

They stood together in the sunshine, silent a few moments, like friends too familiar for constant conversation.

"Chief, before the phone went out? Your wife called . . . to see if I needed anything. It was very good of her. Will you thank her for me?"

Early nodded, seemed to be waiting for something.

"Do you . . . do you want to go inside?"

"I guess we better," the old man said, and followed Joanna across the yard and up the steps into the kitchen.

He pulled out a chair, and sat at the kitchen table. Joanna stayed by the sink.

"Got something here for you, Mrs. Reed. My wife sent it over—some of her banana bread; it's very good."

"I'm sure it is. Please thank her; I know I'll enjoy it. . . . Would you like a cup of coffee? —Tea, I'm out of coffee. Get some when I go to town."

"No, thanks, Mrs. Reed. I already had my coffee." The chief suddenly tilted his chair far back—a boy's or young man's move, careless of accident. Apparently a coordinated old man. It made Joanna nervous to watch him balancing that way.

"—I do have some things to tell you . . . let you know, Mrs. Reed. First thing is, I need to apologize to you for my brusque manner those two times you came to me. That was out-of-line behavior with a lady who'd lost her husband and then her dad. I'm sorry for it."

"No, no. I knew you were busy. . . ."

"No excuse for rudeness. What happens to a man been a law officer a long time, is he sometimes confuses himself with God almighty. So, you have my apologies for that."

"Not necessary. . . . You don't want any tea?"

"No, dear, I don't." He leaned forward, brought his chair upright, and folded his hands on the table in front of him. "—Now, let me tell you what I've done the last few days. When I got the call that your girl died like that . . . well, that really tore it. I never in my life heard of anything so bad, that a person's family would go like that—one, two, three. About the worst thing I ever heard."

Joanna nodded and smiled. Then, so as not to listen anymore, she turned to the sink and began to wash her hands.

Early sat and watched her soap her hands, scrub, and rinse them. Watched as she dried her hands with a dish towel taken from a counter drawer.

". . . So, what we did was review everything we have on your husband's drowning—and we rechecked the Coast Guard's findings, and the coroner's, looking for anything out of the way, no matter what. . . . Then I sent a deputy down to Gloucester, to interview Bobby Moffit again—man had to rent a helicopter, go out to the Banks to find that boat, then go down a rope ladder at sea."

"That . . . that was a lot of trouble."

"Wouldn't believe what they charge to rent those machines."

"Thank you, Chief. It was good of you to do that."

"Then I went up to Chaumette," Early said, and Joanna couldn't think of anything to do so as not to hear. "—Went up to Chaumette and talked with the officers up there—checking on possible harassment of old people out at that lake, vandalism and so forth. And an officer and I went out and we reinterviewed the people living two, three houses each side of your dad's cabin. . . . I also went to see your dad's attorney of record—lady was home, sick—but the secretary, paralegal, assured me there was no amount in the willed estate worth a serious felony."

"I see," Joanna said, because she thought she should say something.

"Went out to the lake again that evening, and had a talk with the fire people. And they just do not have evidence of arson. —Checked on the stain. Their opinion, it was a drink of some kind spilled the evening of the fire, or a glass of water thrown *on* the fire. There was no residue of any flammable usual in arson cases."

"I really appreciate . . . I really appreciate your doing all that." Joanna wished she had a radio in the kitchen. Early probably wouldn't mind if she turned on a radio while he was talking, kept it low.

The old man looked down at his folded hands. "Am I helping you here, or hurting you?"

"Neither one," Joanna said, and smiled so he wouldn't feel she was ungrateful. "I don't know why—but it doesn't hurt and it doesn't help. I suppose that's strange. . . ."

"Well, then I went over to White River, yesterday. . . ." The chief stopped, sat uneasy as a child unsure his tale of yesterday's adventures was welcome.

"Yes?"

"I can . . . I can just send you a written report of all this stuff."

"No, Chief—go ahead. It really doesn't bother me that much."

"Okay . . ." The chief began to speak faster, apparently anxious to be done—and seemed to edit for brevity as he talked. ". . . Went over to White River yesterday, and talked with the town police, a Lieutenant di Simone—just checking whether they'd had a complaint filed on some student or person bothering girls, threatening people on campus. Stalking girls, and so forth. . . . Last complaint was over a year ago, no reference at all to your daughter." Early cleared his throat, refolded his hands, left over right. "I then spoke to the college security people—seemed to know their business— and they also had no current report of any harassment, strangers on campus, students being too aggressive with girls, and so forth. Last case of that was two years before—Egyptian boy, just come over here, was bothering a girl, sending letters to her and so forth."

"Ab Nouri."

"That's right! That's the boy."

"I remember that. I don't think he was really dangerous."

". . . So, campus police had nothing current, nothing referring to your daughter. No evidence whatsoever of anything but suicide. —And I spoke to two of her instructors. They hadn't noticed anything out of the ordinary, except her being much quieter, obviously very upset over losing her dad." Early paused, looked up at Joanna. "I'm almost done."

"No, go ahead, Chief."

He drew a deep breath. ". . . And I did check with some students, summer students. Spoke to kids in her dormitory—definite odor of pot smoke, by the way. I don't think they even go after the kids for that, now. Just let them smoke that stuff and the hell with it." He shook his head. "—Anyway, talked to a couple of friends of hers. Talked to her roommate. And everybody pretty much agreed your girl was badly shocked by her dad's death—and then her grandfather on top of that apparently hit her real hard. . . . Friends were still surprised at what happened, hadn't realized she was . . . so upset. —Well." The old man pushed his chair back, and stood up. "Well, fact of the matter is, all of this comes out just like it did before. Two terrible accidents, one right after another—and more than a real sensitive girl like yours could take."

"Yes. . . ."

Early went to the kitchen door, seemed anxious to be gone. "—Young girls, young women are delicate that age, they bruise so easy. I had a girl myself, then a granddaughter. You catch them one way, they're strong as iron. Catch them another . . . if they're already troubled, some female stuff bothering them—and they break."

Joanna tried to think of something to say, but she couldn't.

"So . . . so I'll be on my way. I'm sorry to have brought all this up again, but I thought you should know we went back and double-checked everything, just in case."

"I do appreciate that, Mr. Early. —And remember to thank Mrs. Early for the banana bread."

"Will do."

". . . Good-bye." Joanna watched the old man go out the door—relieved to be going—and down the steps to the backyard. He'd wrinkled his suit jacket, sitting down. Early's age, concealed by his neat movements when seated and stable, was betrayed in the almost tentative way he'd descended the steps . . . the slight hesitation for balance down each riser.

She watched his handsome head—white hair gilded faint gold by the sun—as it passed the kitchen window . . . then listened to his footsteps along the drive. A few moments later, she heard his car's engine starting in the street.

Joanna sighed with great relief—and to avoid any recalling of what he'd said, all reminders, she picked the small paring knife up from the counter, and stuck it . . . pushed it through the skin and down into the muscle of her left forearm. Dull-pointed, it didn't want to go in—but she made it, and a blurt of blood came out as if it had been waiting, then ran down to her wrist.

It was a sickening feeling, but so specific—and the blood so bright, even in the kitchen's shadows—that it left little room for re- membering. Even less, when she tugged the paring knife free and dropped it in the sink. . . . How dreadful, when men had fought with edged weapons. How personal an invasion, when the steel went in. . . . Tom Lowell had felt that when she'd stabbed him. Now, they both had sore arms.

She stood holding the wound out to bleed in the sink. It was a small steady welling flow—not broken jets of blood coming—so she'd only stabbed through muscle and little veins, not sliced an artery. But it had helped tremendously, though anyone watching wouldn't think so. It was keeping everything in three dimensions . . . instead of flattening to two, like folded pieces of paper.

Joanna let the cut bleed awhile under running cold water. It hurt and felt pleasant at the same time. There was gauze, medical tape, and antibiotic ointment in the upstairs bathroom cabinet, but she didn't want to go up there. The kitchen was far enough into the house, where those other people used to be.

She dried her arm, and wrapped it tightly with a clean dish towel—the second dish towel used as a bandage in her kitchen. She wondered if it had felt good at all to Captain Lowell, when he'd been injured. . . . Probably not.

And since she was in the kitchen, Joanna felt she might as well eat some banana bread, and drink a lot of water. She opened the wrapping, and cut a piece of banana bread. When she picked that up to eat, she saw a slight smear of blood on it from the paring knife, but she ate it anyway, since the blood was hers. She chewed that piece, swallowed it, and drank three glasses of water at the sink.

Then she was very reluctant to go to the bathroom, even though the first-floor toilet was just off the hall. She was reluctant, but she did it, and was surprised to see what she looked like in the bath- room mirror.

She came back through the kitchen, and went out into the backyard. Outside seemed where people should spend most of their time. . . .

Joanna gardened through the long hours of the day, weeding, clearing beds, her wrapped dish towel marked maroon with drying blood. She slowly worked her way, troweling and uprooting, crawling across the yard and back again, hands raw and aching, sore arm very sore. She wove through passing time, and only paused now and then to lie still and rest awhile, before resuming.

The sunset, after so long a time of light and heat, came as great relief . . . and weary, reluctant to go inside just for banana bread, Joanna wrapped herself in her blanket, lay down in the grass, and went to sleep.

Chapter Eighteen

What are you doing? What the hell do you think you're doing?"

Joanna first thought she was dreaming, then was roughly shaken.

"What the fuck are you *doing* out here?" Rage in a woman's voice. "Get up! Get the fuck UP!"

Her sheltering blanket was pulled away to morning light, and Joanna saw a gold-and-ivory Medusan mask—fury—and Charis hauled her up to her feet and shook her. Strong girl. . . .

"I've been sleeping outside," Joanna said, still waking in that grip. "It's . . . it just felt better."

"You get in—you get *in* here!" And Charis, an angry mother with a foolish child, chivvied Joanna across the yard and into the house.

". . . Charis, I'm glad you could come back," she said a while later.

No response from a girl pale with anger, lean and beautiful in gray slacks and a man's white dress shirt. The kitchen table was cluttered with scissors, bandage tape, ointment, gauze pads, and hydrogen peroxide.

"Exams went okay . . . ?"

Charis had nothing to say. Her hands spoke for her, mopping crusted old blood away, squeezing new blood running from the cut . . . then wiping that with cool peroxide.

"Strong hands," Joanna said, pleased to be done to, even hurt. "Have you ever done any climbing, caving?"

"No caving." Her first words in some time. "—But I know you do that."

"Well, if you're not claustrophobic . . . and not afraid of the dark or falling, you might try it."

"I've rock climbed. Last summer I worked five-two leads in the Shawangunks."

"Then you can come caving with me! If you want to. When I'm better." —Joanna considered what she'd just said. *When I'm better.* Which must mean she wasn't better now. . . .

"If this gets infected, we'll have to go to a doctor. It's deep."

"Accident," Joanna said. "I was prying up a can lid, and the knife slipped."

"That's a lie," Charis said. "Don't lie to me."

". . . Okay. I did it because it kept me from thinking about things. Chief Early was here, and he went over everything, and there was nothing new. . . . He said he talked to you."

"The old guy? He talked to everybody. . . . Must have been great-looking when he was young."

"He is handsome."

Charis finished with Joanna's forearm—handling it gently now—placing the gauze pad, taping it, then bandaging lightly, neatly over that. . . . She finished, and sat holding Joanna's hand. "I'm sorry if I hurt you."

"You didn't hurt me."

"You hungry—ready for breakfast?"

"Yes, I suppose I am."

"Good." Charis stood up. "Why don't you go take a shower, and wash your hair. —Try to keep this bandage dry; if you can't, we'll just do it again. . . . Breakfast'll be ready when you are."

"I don't . . . I don't really need—"

"Joanna, you need a shower. You need to wash your hair. —What is it? Don't you want to go upstairs?"

"I can go upstairs. . . ."

"Then come on." And as if Joanna were a stranger, unfamiliar with the house and reluctant, Charis led her out of the kitchen, encouraged her up the hall to the staircase . . . then went up behind her, insisting.

In the bedroom, she helped Joanna out of her dirt-caked trousers and sweated shirt . . . sat her down on the edge of the bed to tug off old sneakers and soiled socks. Then she offered her arm for balance as Joanna stood to step out of her panties.

Naked, Joanna put her hand up to cover the scar where her breast had been. "I know I look terrible. . . ."

"You don't look terrible; you have a beautiful body. —You look dirty." Charis went into the bathroom, started the shower—tested the water for heat—and folded a clean towel and Joanna's robe on the little white stool.

"Thank you."

"You don't have to thank me, Joanna. —Don't forget to do your nails."

"I was gardening."

"I saw you've been gardening. . . ."

Joanna came downstairs into mingling odors of coffee, frying bacon, and buttered toast.

Charis was at the stove, forking the bacon strips over in the big iron skillet. She was cooking a lot of bacon.

"Good morning—now you look great."

"Good morning." *Great* apparently resulting from the shower, washed hair and clean nails, along with moccasins, old khakis, and a short-sleeved plaid summer shirt.

"I had to make a quick breakfast-stuff run into town. We can make a list, do the main shopping this afternoon."

"Okay." Joanna sat at the kitchen table, both uneasy and pleased with such energetic company.

"I know this is really nutritionally incorrect, but I think we need it." Charis transferred the bacon—eight strips, fat and smoking—onto a plate. And cracking their shells in swift succession, dropped four eggs hissing into the pan. "Got toast going, too—regular, not cinnamon. Butter already on them."

"Yes," Joanna said, amused by how difficult it would have been to say even an unimportant *no* to the young woman at the stove, radiating light through a faint haze of smoking grease. The house seemed bearable now, filled, vibrating to this handsome creature . . . a distraction offering greater relief than the paring knife had given her.

Charis leaned over the skillet, harassing her eggs as they cooked, poking them into conformity with a steel spatula. She stared down, intent, gave them a few moments more, then ran the spatula under them and served two onto each plate—swift movements—divided the bacon slices four and four, and brought the plates to the table. Then to the oven for four slices of toast—each with yellow spots of melted butter—and back to the stove to pour the coffee.

The coffee mugs came to the table, and Charis sat down, salted and peppered her food, and began to eat.

Joanna recognized the energy and task-concentration, the pleasure in a produced result. It was the way she worked . . . when she worked. It was the way she'd handled classwork and grading papers—the way poems came to her, the ideas like stray puppies to be taken in.

"Charis, your classes. . . ."

"I'm doing papers for them, instead. Professors have agreed I can do that, so everything's okay. —Now, you eat."

Joanna broke the yolk of her first egg with a corner of toast, caught some sunny spill on it, and ate the piece runny. Started with a bite of bacon, then slowly chewed it all, greasing, oiling her throat for more eating, for the rhythms of eating.

Halfway through her breakfast—still an egg left, almost a whole piece of toast and two strips of bacon—Joanna glanced up and saw Charis looking at her, watching her with pleased affection.

"It's very good."

"Eat it all," Charis said, and began finishing her own food. She ate as she'd cooked, swiftly, neatly, absorbed as a hungry child or fastidious animal, only glancing up from time to time. There was no conversation.

A vaporous, uncertain tail to Charis's comet, Joanna sat in the little convertible's passenger seat as the girl rowed through the VW's gears at the bottom of Slope Street—then took a fast left turn to drive out Beach Road at Joanna's direction.

"This is your island," Charis had said, washing the breakfast dishes. "Take me on a tour. —We'll pee and hit the road."

. . . They'd peed, and hit the road.

They went out Beach, past the last of the town's weathered gray houses, to ride the slow rise and fall of sandy blacktop along the sea, the morning's heat and cool ocean breeze weaving together over the car's open top. The VW, an elderly metal turtle, its worn black shell sun-dazzled here and there, bucketed over the road's sandheaves past Trudie's, and went on.

"Good food, there," Joanna said.

Charis nodded, smiling. She was hardly talking now, was only present, a companion, as if silent company was the medicine Joanna needed most.

They drove up the beach, past stilted beach houses staggered along the dunes, past drifts of sea grass stirring to sea breezes. Joanna sat with her head back, resting, her eyes half shut to glittering light. She sat moving only to the car's motion, content to be carried and cared for.

They drove all the way to the end of Beach Road, then turned back a mile to go right on Willis . . . and continue touring as if the island were Joanna's own estate, its heat and light and beauty enough to recompense any loss, and be bound to heal her.

They drove down through Willis, its sheds and shacks and rusted machinery—came to the Wainwrights', and Joanna saw Percy sitting alone by his tree in the front yard. Slightly smaller, stockier than she'd remembered him, the red dog sat watching as if he'd been waiting for her.

"*Percy*. . . . *!*" Joanna called as they went past, and had time to see the stubs of ears alert, to catch a glimpse of his grim one-eyed stare.

They drove to the Willis marina, where the sportfishers rocked at their moorings, and sailboats—anchored out—seesawed gently to a southwest wind.

"Beautiful," Charis said, pulled in beside Chester's Bait 'n Tackle, and stopped the car. They sat for a while, silent in a glass-and-metal dish of heat, looking out over the channel. The mainland shore was lost in heat haze and sun-mirrors flashing off a slight chop.

"Beautiful now," Charis said, "—and I bet more beautiful in winter, when you have to look for color."

"Probably so. . . ."

They sat watching a while longer, then Charis started the car and drove out the only road east of Willis—South Sound Road. And as they traveled along that hard-shelving stony coastline—so different from the island's north—the ocean came in booming, fetched for three thousand miles to foam and fountain against the rock.

They stayed on South Sound around the island's southeast tip— the lighthouse, built of blocks of granite, the last object off the Point—then drove almost two miles north into Asconsett Town.

. . . At Barkley's, carrying one of their two baskets, Joanna trailed behind as Charis shopped. Cans of tuna and sardines. Cans of corned beef. Saltine crackers and cans of pork and beans. Oatmeal, bran flakes, raisins and prunes. Peaches, a dozen lemons for lemonade, and three grapefruit—spelled *greatfruits* at Barkley's.

"I'll pay today, then we can start splitting the bills. . . ." Charis shopped very directly, no wandering; she sliced through the other women to the counters and bins she wanted, and picked out quickly. Two small yellow squashes, two yams, a bunch of carrots, string beans, six onions, a garlic bulb, broccoli, and the best head of romaine.

Two women—one Joanna recognized, had spoken to coming out on the ferry once, though she couldn't remember her name—these two women were stealing constant quick little glances at her as she followed Charis from one side of the store to the other. Quick looks, as children watched frightening movies, glancing, then looking away. The women were curious what catastrophe accomplished in a woman's face, what sores marked such a leprosy of loss.

Other women must be looking at her too, but Joanna kept her head down as she followed, so as not to notice.

"What the fuck are you staring at?" A clear snarling cavalry trumpet. The bustle and conversation stopped in Barkley's. A plastic blue basket swinging from her arm, Charis glared past others at the two women . . . and they did as Joanna had done, and looked down as if for something in the sawdust, a dropped plum. *"You keep your fucking eyes to yourselves!"* It was the kind of order that promised enforcement, and prolonged the silence.

Then Charis said, "Lamb chops," to Joanna in an ordinary voice, and went over to the meat counter. Other women there, all silent, were examining the trays with great attention. The lamb looked very good, beef very good. Pork less attractive.

. . . At home, Charis set a kitchen chair in the backyard, then brought out the string beans in a big blue plastic bowl to be snapped, stripped of their small threads, and put into a smaller blue plastic bowl, part of the set.

"You do this," she said to Joanna, "while I put things away and make lunch. Then we can garden."

"Okay. . . ."

Joanna sat in the sunshine, snapping string beans; she needed a paring knife to cut the sharp little ends off. She was listening to her heart—could barely hear it thumping, moving her blood around—and sat listening until Charis brought the paring knife from the kitchen as if Joanna'd called for it.

They had sardine-and-chopped-onion sandwiches for lunch. Peeled peaches, banana bread, and glasses of milk. Charis enjoyed the banana bread, had two slices. "But coconut cake is really my favorite. . . ."

Joanna had been anxious to lie in the backyard grass—see what she'd done, what she had left to do . . . see how the weeds were managing. She hurried her lunch and tried to leave some of her sandwich and the peach, but Charis asked her to eat them, so she did. Then she had to wait while Charis finished—eating in that neat, deliberate way, and looking up from time to time as if to prevent surprises.

It was such a relief, afterward, to change to clean caving clothes—then go outside and lie down in the grass, feel things she might remember draining out into the ground . . . and then the hot sun slowly putting something back into her, something simpler and more bearable.

Charis came and crouched to work beside her, using a foot-long flat pry bar and large screwdriver—both rusty from lying on a garage shelf—to dig out the weed roots so she could pull them, since Joanna was using the trowel.

"I'll get my gardening tools in the morning," Charis said, and seemed happy to join Joanna in this safari—giants laboring over a miniature jungle more savage than the Mato Grosso, a patch where a thousand thousand hunters roamed, six-eyed spiders, searchers and small spinners and more tens of thousands of others less theatrical . . . smaller and smaller. The grass was full of deaths dreadful beyond consideration, but none with malice. Deaths innocent as ice cream.

It seemed to Joanna that she and Charis were soldiers, volunteers against the weeds, but lacking a lethal enemy to give them honor. "We need a giant weed," she said, "to come hissing along the ground into the garden."

"You mean to make it fair?"

It was such a startling completion that Joanna woke from her weeding, woke from her dreamy day, and looked sideways at that alert and angular face—elegantly spare, even smudged and sweating in the sun.

"Yes, that's exactly what I meant."

The girl looked at her, hazel eyes bright as if illuminated. "And that woke you up, didn't it?" Then she turned back to her weeding, slender hands deft and merciless. "Fairness would only weaken weeds."

At dinner—they were having lamb chops—Joanna found it difficult to stay awake to eat. Charis had to remind her . . . remind her twice to finish her milk.

Afterward, while Charis did the dishes, Joanna went upstairs by

herself, undressed, put on her robe—and sat dozing in the bedroom rocker until Charis locked the doors, turned off the lights
downstairs, and came up to wake her for her shower . . . then
brought the yellow nightgown for her, and put her to bed.

Charis tucked the covers, kissed Joanna on the cheek, then
turned the bedroom lights off so the rising moon could substitute
softly, and left the door half open when she went.

In bed, though very tired, Joanna lay still, and still awake, recalling. . . . But the moonlight, so silver, helped her. The bed floated in
it like a boat, so Joanna cruised that small quicksilver lake of light
until she grew too tired to remember, and gave herself up to sleep.

. . . Charis waited awhile in her room across the hall, then came
quietly to stand outside Joanna's door. She listened there a long
time . . . and heard Joanna's breaths lengthen and deepen, becoming, in almost an hour, gradually harsher in the sleep of exhaustion.

She opened the door and went into the bedroom then, and
stood just beside a bar of moonlight falling through the seaside
window. She stayed there for some time, watching Joanna, listening
to her.

Then Charis went quietly out of the room and downstairs into
darkness—and, her arms outstretched as if she were preparing to
glide a distance, began to slowly turn and turn in the entrance hall,
stepping to waltz time in silent sneakers. She turned, dipped, then
spun sideways into the living room . . . danced there . . . then
whirled out and down the long hall. She wept silently with happiness, her tears shining in moonshadow as she danced into the dining room, whirling, touching nothing.

After breakfast—grapefruit and cold cereal—the day became a
day like the one before, the only changes what Charis served for
breakfast, lunch, and dinner . . . her checking Joanna's arm to be
certain the knife cut was healing . . . and their stop at the hardware
store for gloves, trowel, spade, and a hand rake. Otherwise, the girl
allowed no novelty, introduced nothing new.

There was breakfast, the stop at the hardware, then the drive—
the same drive out around the island, with the same turns onto the
same roads . . . and nothing new except variations in sunlight and
cloud shadow, variations in the ocean's colors and motion. From
the town, they drove the north beaches . . . then southwest to
Willis—Percy in his yard again, head cocked for his good eye to see
them pass.

They parked down at the Willis marina to watch the tethered boats for a while—then went east along the harsher coast, its stone shelving struck by the sea. Passed the lighthouse . . . and so up to Asconsett Town, home, and gardening through the failing heat of afternoon.

The next day was the same.

And the day after was the same, except that day there was shopping, and Charis didn't take Joanna in with her. That was the only change.

Those nearly duplicate days—guarded by the girl against difference—became several days more, all alike, so Joanna nested in their sameness as if in a swinging hammock fastened to unchanging trees, that swayed only so far . . . then swayed back, allowing resting, requiring nothing from her but being cared for.

Charis appeared to need no changes either, and seemed content . . . seemed very happy.

After more than a week, Joanna—spading one of the long, cleared beds in the afternoon—began to be able to whisper familiar names, whisper them to herself and call no ghosts when she did. It was as if the dead were beginning to become only acquaintances.

. . . The next morning, Charis, tuned to her like a companion instrument, suggested for the first time that Joanna make their breakfast—pancakes with maple syrup—then asked her in what different way she would like to spend the day. . . .

So, after preliminary hours walking the beach, they lay glistening with sunblock in their bathing suits, below the dunes past Trudie's. Beside them, in a grease-stained cardboard box, a large steamed lobster waited, with a container of melted butter, ice-cubed root beers, two oily paper bags of french fries, and two pieces of peach pie.

Joanna had noticed Charis's body as they took their beach robes off and spread their blanket. Long-legged, long-armed—her forearms pollen-dusted with down—Charis was slightly too solid, too heavy-boned, for delicacy. It was a lean body-type familiar enough; had been Joanna's when she was young.

Charis's forearms and wrists looked thicker than most women's—her rock-climbing, like Joanna's caving, had wrapped fine cords of muscle around them. . . . Rebecca had always been slightly plump . . . a partridge.

They lay side by side—Joanna in her old one-piece Catalina, gray stripes on lighter gray, Charis in a two-piece, in blue bandanna material. Lying so close, they looked nearly the same height, almost the same weight—Joanna slightly taller, heavier, a little softened by age. . . . In time, as they rested cocooned in heat and light, the patterns of their breathing gradually accommodated to each other, then to the rhythm of surf softly thundering in. Under the odors of cooked food and sunblock, hot sand and salt air, Joanna smelled again, as she had on the ferry coming out, the girl's faint sweet scent.

Drifting, drowsing, enjoying their silence beside the sea's sound, Joanna considered Charis, and the girl's willing sacrifice of a summer just to nurse her, keep her company. Some eccentricity there . . . and it had been taken advantage of.

"Charis, I need to thank you—and thanks can't be enough for what you've done these past days, and before that, in the hospital. I know it's partially because of Rebecca. . . ."

"I wanted to be there." The young woman's voice sounding smooth as polished stone. There had only been that snarl of challenge in Barkley's, when the women were staring. Otherwise, Charis's voice sounded as she looked, certain of its next note—except when she was singing.

"I hope that's so. I can't tell you what it's meant to have you here." Gratitude spoken with closed eyes, face up to the sun as if that brightness were intermediary, a messenger of light.

"Joanna, I *wanted* to be here."

"It's good of you to say so—but what *I* need to say, sweetheart, is thanks for being so kind, such a wonderful baby-sitter, when I needed baby-sitting badly." Joanna got up on an elbow, opened her eyes to sunlight burning in reflection off the sand . . . the girl seeming to lie floating in brightness. "—But aren't there people, young people, you'd rather be with this summer? What about your family, friends—a boyfriend?"

Joanna felt a slight tug at the blanket, a movement of the soft sand beneath it as Charis shifted, turned toward her. She was wearing sunglasses with white plastic frames. "The people who raised me are dead, Joanna. —And the truth is, I don't have any real friends. Never did . . . except maybe for Rebecca, a little. I've had casual friends. And I've fucked men. I fucked and sucked—you name it—for ten years, until I was fifteen." Said as pleasantly as "Good morning."

Joanna lay back and closed her eyes, thankful that the ocean's noise permitted pauses in conversation. . . . Arithmetic left Charis five years old when that began. Rebecca had mentioned she'd been abused . . . the mother ill, then dead, and the father's demons freed.

Five years old. . . . There could be chill after all, under the hottest sun.

"Charis, I'm terribly sorry."

No answer from the girl. The ocean, in chaotic repetition, answered for her. To be sure, an eccentric . . . almost odd. Certainly serious damage had been done. Her father—an animal—had ruined his own child, a child that must have been, as Charis remained, intelligent and beautiful. With what pleasure the creature must have destroyed her. . . .

So, on Asconsett's beach, an anguished little girl lay in a young woman's body. An invalid of grief and loss as great as Joanna's, and less likely ever to recover. This crippled child would try to mend herself and her world—would always be trying to mend herself and her world, but neither would ever be whole.

Blinded with tears turned diamonds by brightness, Joanna felt for the hand beside hers, found and gripped it. "You have a friend now, Charis."

And felt her grip returned so her bones ached. Held for a moment, then released.

Charis said nothing for some time, then sighed and sat up, searched through her black book bag. She cast a shallow shadow that cooled Joanna's arm. "If I don't keep this stuff on, I burn."

Joanna, squinting, watched as Charis found the little yellow plastic bottle of sunblock, squirted a white worm of it into her palm . . . and turned as she sat, to massage the ointment along her arms, making that slightly awkward posture, those awkward angles, graceful.

Gulls had noticed them, suspected their lunch, and now passed over to see better, to give them notice of hungry birds. Joanna, shading her eyes, saw one of them—frost-white, mouse-gray—sailing overhead, haloed in molten gold . . . and noticed an instant later the swifter shadow of the gull flick across her, touch Charis, and be gone.

Arms oiled, the girl started on her legs. "You need a hat, Joanna. Too much sun. I have a big straw hat at the house, but I didn't bring it."

"I hate hats. Especially big hats—they're always in the way and you can't see the sky because of the brim. . . ." The heat settled onto and into Joanna, a personal matter. She blinked the last of tears away, and saw the intolerable center of the sun. Then she lay drowsy for a while, her eyelids presenting an empty bright-red landscape . . . put her hand up to check the bathing suit's top, make sure her prosthesis was in place.

"Drinks are going to be warm. . . ."

"Hungry?"

"I'm very hungry." Charis, sitting in hot citrus light, put her sunblock away.

Joanna sat up, dragged the cardboard box nearer. ". . . The lobster's going to be a mess."

"Use a towel. We can put everything on one towel, and then wash it."

"Okay."

Charis flapped a towel free of sand, and spread it on the blanket between them. "If we spill, we spill. . . ."

Joanna set the lobster out, brick-red and baking hot, too big for its paper plate. Trudie's nutcracker and the plastic container of butter went on the towel with it. Then she tore open the small sacks, left the french fries—dull gold in the sunlight—in two heaps on their grease-spotted paper, the slices of peach pie beside them.

The root beers, ice cubes melted, were warm as blood in their tall white cardboard containers.

Charis and Joanna sat facing each other over the food, and reached to attack the lobster—shifting their grips to detach legs and then its armored tail. They broke the lobster open . . . worked on the pieces with the nutcracker, and scooped pale meat out of scarlet shells. They took busy turns dipping into the melted butter . . . sucked smaller threads of meat from narrow, jointed legs, and paused only for warm root beer, bites of pie, or heat-blistered french fries. There was no ketchup. Trudie sprinkled her fries with vinegar, salt, and pepper after she shook them out of their boiling bath of oil, and thought that fixings enough.

Sitting cross-legged on blanketed sand, eating in such fiery heat and light, it seemed to Joanna a meal that might be served in hell, if hell were heaven after all. . . . In less than half an hour, she ate her belly tight, just this side of sickness, to the steady thudding of the surf.

"Oh, fantastic." Charis, holding one of the lobster's littlest legs in her fist. She sat sucking the last meat out of it—a hollow-cheeked fashion model for a moment.

"I'm going for a swim." Joanna stood up, staggering as if the sunlight had weight. "I need to cool off. . . ."

Charis finished the lobster leg. "I'll come wade and watch."

"Don't you swim?"

Charis picked up the lobster's head. "I can swim if I have to; I'm really a very good swimmer. But I don't like it. I always think there's something coming after me in the water, even in a pool. . . . I know that's weird. You want this blue stuff?"

"Charis, I never eat the blue stuff. I don't know what it is, and I don't want to know."

"I think it's his little liver. . . ." Charis scooped it out with her finger, tasted it. "Tastes like liver," she said, licked her finger, and got up to follow Joanna down the beach.

. . . Joanna said, "Cold water," as if to warn her body—and it was cold, almost bitter after the heated air. It iced her ankles, then her legs as she walked in, the waves thumping at her knees. . . . She waded in to her groin, then dove straight out, had an instant of air, then struck and sank into freezing green. It made a contrast so delicious that she lay under and rolled in it, salt slipping into her mouth, the sound of surf softened by being beneath. There was a ringing noise, faint and constant . . . and she surfaced into moderate waves and began to swim into their strong shifting.

"*Cold?*" Charis was calling from the beach.

"*Very* cold . . . !"

Joanna swam out a few strokes more, then stayed treading water, gently lifted and lowered as the waves went by. Charis was stalking along the shore, long legs . . . narrow feet tentative in the surf's fringes. She yelped like a child as she stepped through the water.

Joanna called, "Come in a little way—it's better once you're in!"

"Bullshit!" But Charis took a few swift heron's steps into the sea, then suddenly dove and was gone . . . rose swimming very strongly, surprisingly strongly and fast—and as suddenly turned back, ducked under, and was gone. Joanna kicked up higher on the rise of a wave to look for her—felt a foolish apprehension—and was relieved when the girl splashed to the surface farther in, stroked once or twice, then stood, long dark-blond hair soaked darker— Aphrodite to any ancient Greek—and waded out onto the sand.

She called something back, perhaps "Enough for me," and stood stripping the water from her hair, shaking it out for the sun . . . watching Joanna swim.

Behind her and higher, at the base of the dune, the gulls had found their scraps of lunch, and a slow tornado of white wings and mustard-yellow beaks funneled and rose and fell. Some birds fled, successful, and were chased into a sky that was perfectly blue.

Joanna swam a little more, swimming north a few yards against a slanting current . . . then turned and stroked in toward the shore . . . finally kicked and found her footing. She walked out of tumultuous cold into heat, stepped onto hot sand—Charis coming to her with the clean towel—and realized she hadn't mourned her dead all afternoon.

After dinner—they had cooked it together—Charis sat at the dining-room table to work, with notebooks, textbooks, a looseleaf and her laptop set out before her.

Joanna was washing the dishes, drying them and putting them away while thinking about the garden—what flowers should be planted. Even with no work done today, they already had the beds cleared and turned along the yard's edge. Bulb plants—or seasonal flowers? Would pansies last into autumn . . . ?

She rinsed the milk glasses and put them up on the shelf over the sink. Her skin felt slightly rough with the sea's salt. . . . They'd need more milk; Charis drank it thirstily as a child.

The last of the dishes done, stains of spaghetti and meat sauce soaped away, Joanna went upstairs for one of her legal pads and the fat black Montblanc pen—a gift to herself years ago.

She came back downstairs and sat across from Charis at the dining table. Joanna had the sea poem's essence in her head, had stepped aside a little to let the ocean flood in with words . . . withdraw with words that wouldn't do . . . come back with others to consider.

The poem would be the wind's—that in breezes and gales, in stillness and hurricane, stroked and struck the sea, sailed over it, knew it . . . had known it longer than the billion years since it was shallow and fresh enough to drink. Since lizards, later, grew to greatness and oared through it, hunting.

Theirs was an ancient marriage, never faithful. But the wind was first. It had hissed and howled alone among volcanoes, and curtained down a million years of rain and then another million, and other many millions until small pools reflected a furious sun in sulfur, here and there.

The wind brought rain and filled the first seas up. And after millions more of circling years, it hummed and blew and ruffled at last across the waves of company, and was no longer alone.

The waves are the wind-bird's feather, that display
Their plumage colors with the weather; so far today,
White is their sheer shade shown, and green waiting
For a turning moon to tug the rollers into breaking,
And row the deeper currents, heave them into motion
By the haul of swinging stone that shrugs the ocean.

This introduction of couplets, sometimes broken—and to be broken further . . . rhymes separated. Then the poem swinging out to stanzas . . . and those to be steady marchers, wind-driven, until smashed as surf along the land. All undertowed to calm couplets once again. . . .

Joanna sat back and put the fat pen down . . . imagined the poem, as she often did, a small smooth oval egg resting in her head, warmed by worry and desire—by pleasure, habit, and consideration while its odd chick matured . . . one tiny, clawed, four-toed foot already beating in time with her heart.

". . . Charis, I'd like to be sure you can afford all this time out of class. All the rest of the *summer?*"

Charis finished a computer entry with a quick rap-a-tat-tat on her keyboard. "Well, I've already done my paper for American Novel—and Sue Harriman'll grade me on that. And I talked to Engletree and Singleton. They know I'm out here with you—and they both said I could write papers for them instead of the last weeks of classwork. I think Engletree was glad to see me go. . . . The dean's office said okay if the professors said okay. And it was all right with Cavelli, for Statistics, *if* I take his end-term exam."

"How many papers?"

"Three. Have to do a poet for Engletree. —I was thinking of doing you—"

"Oh, for God's sake, don't do me. Chris really dislikes my work. Places me in the nineteenth century with Tennyson and Longfellow—in intention, not accomplishment."

"Joanna, I think that's really good company. I love 'Hiawatha.' —Maybe I'll do Longfellow just to piss him off. He'll hate it."

". . . Longfellow, the too-popular poet and his trochees. And mighty unfashionable now. —Charis, I really don't advise your teacher's annoyance as the basis for choosing a subject. . . . But if you *do* decide to, and find our old romantic rich enough, there is a library out here, very small, across from the school. I'd guess Longfellow is a poet they might have, among others. But I'd think twice before doing him for Chris. —And what else?"

"A paper on peripheral wars." Charis made another short entry, read the screen to check it.

"Peripheral *wars* . . . ?" It occurred to Joanna that it might be a good idea to read through White River's fall catalog—be reminded what they were teaching these days, besides English literature and poetry.

"Right," Charis said. "Peripheral wars. —Sociology, 'A Global Perspective.' And the paper's supposed to be about whether First World countries promote small conflicts to advance imperialism and so forth. Peripheral wars, the new colonialism."

" 'Peripheral . . .' "

"That should be the name of the course." Charis opened a textbook, turned to the index. ". . . It's really dreary, because Singleton just wants agreement. 'You *bet* the First World starts little wars to screw the Third.' "

"And they don't?"

"No, I don't think so." Charis was frowning at the textbook's index. "Advanced countries go in with these good intentions, and it always turns to shit. Those little wars are blunders, more than anything." She found her entry, opened the textbook to it.

". . . Worse than crimes."

"Was that Talleyrand?"

"No. De la Meurthe."

"Tell you what I think. I think a few of the Third World countries would be better off back *under* colonialism. You know, Joanna, some of them are turning into zoos."

"A possible truth you might want to keep from Professor Singleton. . . . Leave him his illusions."

"Oh, I wouldn't say that in my paper. That would be heresy."

"Yes. —So, that's two papers."

"Well, the other one isn't really a paper; it's a critique. Just maybe three or four pages on statistical method in collation and application of census material in the U.S."

"God, that sounds grim."

"It's a hard course—Statistical Means. I'll pass and get the credit, but I won't do very well. Cavelli likes math proofs—even if they don't prove much—and my math is terrible."

"I didn't think Cavelli taught summers."

"Old guy's teaching *this* summer."

"He's ancient. —But if you turn in those three papers, Charis, and pass Cavelli's end-of-term exam, you do get your course credits? Because I don't want you to stay out here with me, if it costs you a summer's work."

"No, I get my credits, so I'll have my B.A. Then I'll go for my master's next year—at White River, if I can get accepted. I'm tired of picking up stuff summers, and at city colleges." Charis sighed, closed the textbook, and entered something into her laptop.

"White River?"

"Well, I know it's hard to get in—so I'm thinking backup at State."

". . . Charis, if you let me look at your work, and it's good, I'd be happy to help you with the personnel people."

Charis looked up from the laptop's screen, smiled at Joanna. "Happy to help—*if* my work's good."

"I shouldn't . . . shouldn't have qualified my helping you, Charis."

"Yes, you should." Charis finished her entry. "—You should do exactly what you think is right. Especially about English, about poetry. . . . If you didn't, I wouldn't respect you as much." She looked at her computer screen. "How do you say . . . what do you call a really devoted follower? A disciple—but I already used 'disciple.' "

"Votary."

"Okay. . . ." Swift typing. "V-o-t-a-r-y?"

"That's right." Joanna sat with her notebook, the poem's beginning, and her handsome black pen, and watched Charis work. She observed with an easeful pleasure the girl's absorption. That elegant face, usually guarded, almost expressionless, had now become mobile as a little girl's—intent, frowning . . . then suddenly relieved, satisfied with some conclusion, an idea come to completion. The child she had been could be seen in her face—in slow turns curious, puzzled, and pleased as she worked along. A face as open as a flower.

Joanna watched for a while, then felt she was somehow taking advantage . . . seeing more than Charis would wish. The little girl revealed in the tender acceptance of new knowledge.

"I think I'll go up early. . . ." Joanna stood, picked up her notebook and pen.

"Good night." Charis looked up from her laptop, smiling.

Joanna felt an impulse, acted on it, and went around the table to kiss Charis's cheek, kiss her good night. "Sleep well. . . ."

Then she went down the hall, and climbed the stairs, considering the reasons for respect. Charis had said, "If you didn't, I wouldn't respect you as much."

Without the meeting of certain standards—a lower grade given. And though Charis presented herself as an experienced young adult in attitude and conversation—with none of the teenage catchphrases clung to by the uncertain young, often into their thirties—there still seemed to lie beneath, the simple, swift, and merciless judgments of a little girl. As if she contained within herself both a child who'd never grown up, and a woman who'd never been a child.

Joanna went into her bedroom and sat by the window in the rocker, her notebook in her lap. She thought of the ocean . . . and Charis. Geology, and the massively slow formation of lands to cup the seas. Periods of formation. . . . It was what Charis must have missed, the time of normal transition to adulthood. Those years wrecked by continuing abuse, and the reiterated memories of her monstrous childhood, so a ruined adolescence was replaced by judgment's iron bridge between a little girl and her grown self . . . with strict requirements that Charis felt she must meet, that others must meet, that life must be made to meet for her. . . .

Joanna sat by her bedroom window, rocking a little back and forth, writing in her notebook as the evening came slowly down toward dark . . . working while the light failed, enjoying the race the black pen ran across darker and darker paper, until the verses faded as all light faded over the sea. The ocean in deep darkness heaving . . . its difference then absolute. By day, the sea might be dealt with—and under the moon. But benighted, except for glowing monsters finning deep, all fish swam blind.

She heard Charis singing downstairs, in the dining room—something in poetry, or sociology, or statistics having prompted her to song. She was singing a melody Joanna had never heard before, her voice as spontaneous, frail, and unself-conscious as she was not. . . . Of course. It was the child's voice, singing.

Joanna wrote while she could see, only a few minutes longer . . . then got up, put her notebook away, and turned on the room light. —Wondering if she was ready, if it was too soon, she went to the closet for the shoe boxes of family photographs Rebecca had brought out for her.

Joanna brought the boxes to the bed. . . . There were many pictures of Rebecca. One of her on a sunny lawn—in Gloucester—sitting up just over a year old, and laughing. Her fat little hand was gripping a stuffed toy dog in her lap. . . . Roscoe. White with small black spots. He had been her dear friend.

Joanna sat on her bed and looked at pictures—but kept coming back to that one. She began to weep, as much for the small toy dog that had been so loved, as for the little girl laughing on the lawn. . . . Joanna sat looking at pictures, and found Frank smiling at her out of many . . . found her father standing at the corner of their old house in Chaumette, tall, withheld, slightly stooped even when younger, and always caught just in or out of shadow.

There were no pictures of her mother. Her father had put most in the garbage after her mother died, apparently so no reminder would torment him.

"I'm not that brave," Joanna said to the bedroom, and sorted through a bunch from the back of the second box. Fading photos in torn yellowed envelopes. College pictures, early pictures with only a few of Frank. Other old photographs stacked in back of those. . . .

Too many to look at all at once. The faces too insistent, all saying, "Remember me—recall, and be reminded. I was this . . . and now I'm not. I was yours . . . but no longer, and never again."

Joanna put the pictures away, carried the boxes to the closet, and undressed to take her shower. She stood naked in front of the closet mirror, and recognized herself in the glass as she might have recognized a slightly older sister, tired, flushed hot from a day in the sun, and a little worn. A sensible sister, who had accepted with more grace than Joanna her cancer and missing breast. A sister who had more gray threading through her hair. . . .

"Is there anything I can do for you?" Joanna said to her reflection . . . and received no answer. She went in to take her shower, didn't linger, and stepped out to towel dry. Then she put on pajamas, instead of the yellow nightgown . . . turned off the light, and went to bed. There was a faint glow of light through the half-open door, light from the stairwell. Charis was still up, downstairs, working on a paper.

Perhaps peripheral wars. . . .

Joanna lay enjoying the sheets' coolness against her sun-heated skin. Charis . . . a friend. And who would be the healed, and who the healer, when their summer ended? Friends—perhaps for a time, perhaps forever. Who else did either of them have?

Joanna felt the weight of responsibility, familiar as family—though for a childhood lost to Charis long ago. Responsibility, purpose, settled as she lay there, billowing softly down like a warm blanket flung over her.

Chapter Nineteen

Joanna made breakfast.

Over coffee, they decided on no drive today. "And the phone?" Charis smiled. "Do you think it's time to get it fixed?"

". . . Yes, it's time. While we're in town we can go by their office, and schedule somebody to come out."

"And lawn furniture. We'll split what it costs."

"No, Charis. —You're a student, for God's sake, and you've bought more than your share of groceries already. It's for the cottage, and I'll pay for it."

"I want to pay for something." Charis poured more coffee for each of them.

"Fine. Pay for one chair. —Sweetheart, do you *have* any money? It's none of my business, but you're in school, and you haven't had a chance to work this summer. . . ."

"But I worked before. I've always had a job—and I had a trust fund for college, so I saved some money."

"Okay, pay for one lawn chair, Charis—and don't pay for anything else for a while."

"Okay . . . for a while." Charis looked into her coffee mug. "—Is the cream turned?"

"No. It's just Jersey cream. Thick. . . . You know, with the phone will come things to be done."

"Right." A businesslike nod, the girl's face striped in horizontal shade and gold by the kitchen blinds.

"At the end of the week, I'll probably have to go over to White River. There are things . . . a lot of things that just have to be done,

and I haven't wanted—haven't been able—to do them. The mail. . . .
And I want to bring Rebecca's ashes back."

"I know. . . . Can I go with you?"

"Of course you'll go with me."

Charis put her coffee mug down. "Joanna, you're really . . .
you're so much better now, you don't need me. You have things you
have to do, and your work. —I know we thought I'd stay all summer,
but it might be less trouble for you if I didn't. You might like some
time alone."

"Charis, I *wouldn't* like some time alone. I'd like you to stay with
me. . . . Unless you'd prefer not to—unless you have other things
you'd like to be doing."

"I don't."

"Then stay with me. And—I know this may be premature—but *if*
we can get you into the regular graduate program, and I decide to
keep teaching, we might share the house at White River, do our
work . . . maybe go caving, if you want to try it."

"I'd like that. —And going caving." Charis picked up the spoons
and mugs, took them to the sink.

"Then—if we're still speaking by the end of summer—we'll do
it. But if we do, anytime you decide to take off . . . then you just go,
and it's no problem."

"I won't want to." Charis started washing the dishes.

"Well, someday you may. —You know, even after the hardest
times, terrible times . . . it isn't impossible for you to have a wonderful life, find someone who cares for you, a decent man."

"Not interested."

"And you might want to have children. . . ."

"Joanna, I already have—almost." She began rinsing the dishes.
"I got pregnant when I was thirteen, and he did an abortion on me
in the garage. —After that, I went on the pill. I was afraid I'd have a
baby, and he'd take it."

". . . I'll dry." Joanna got up, went to the sink.

"We're almost out of detergent."

"We'll get some today. Add it to the list. . . . Sweetheart, because
that happened, that doesn't mean you might not have children,
later."

No answer, only dish rinsing.

Joanna looked over at this injured angel, and was startled by the
weight of her grief for the girl—grief and great anger.

"Not your fault, Charis." She took the next dish and put it down, touched the girl's arm and turned to hug her. It was the first time she'd held Charis in this way, and she hugged her hard, as if to heal all those ancient injuries. —Held her close, felt the soft-solid length of perfect youth . . . the light burden of the girl's head against her shoulder.

Charis was trembling, a fine vibration. Joanna kissed her cheek, and oddly reluctant, let her go. "Okay . . . ?"

"Yes," Charis said, and smiled. Her eyes were bright, blurred with tears. "I'm okay now."

"So—we shop this morning, pick up the plants? Then we can put them in this afternoon."

"Sounds good." Charis rinsed the last plate, handed it over to be dried. "Sounds good to me. . . ."

They spent the rest of the morning buying plants—some at the hardware, little green plastic boxes of pansies . . . and more at Fuller's, on Weather Road, a dead end south of town. Fuller's, a very small nursery in apparently permanent decay, was owned by two stout women with one cat and several fat and friendly dogs— and Joanna and Charis were given a great deal of advice, sacks of dried manure and potting soil, and a carload of boxed seedlings and small plants.

They stopped back in town, but the phone company's small island office was closed for lunch—so they came home for their own, tuna sandwiches.

. . . When Joanna came downstairs after changing into her gardening clothes, Charis was already kneeling out back with the small hand rake, getting the last stones out of the south bed's turned soil.

"Here." She stood and handed Joanna a baseball cap. "This isn't a big hat, and you need something in the sun."

It was a Cardinals cap, worn, stained. A red baseball cap.

Joanna supposed this was only the first of many accidental associations she would encounter through the years. Random grim reminders of mystery and loss. . . . Better start getting used to them. Start with this baseball cap like another red baseball cap—seen or not seen on a boy. A boy seen or not seen sailing with Frank the day he died.

"Thanks." She put the cap on. It fitted her.

"Same big heads," Charis said, and knelt, wearing her widebrimmed straw . . . intent on raking.

Joanna knelt beside her, digging a row of small holes in earth enriched with potting soil along the border of the bed. ". . . You know, what we were talking about, what happened when you were thirteen? Well, that's something we have in common. Except that I had choices, Charis, and you didn't. I was responsible, and you weren't."

"Choices . . . ?"

"Charis, when I was seventeen, I got pregnant. Well, I was already a freshman in college, not young enough for that to be an excuse. I had the child. . . . My mother was Catholic; both my parents were Catholic—they were separated then—and my mother came down to Cambridge and stayed with me the last few months." Joanna dug the last planting hole of the row—concerned they might be too shallow, even for such little flowers. "—I had the child, and I gave it away."

Charis stopped raking, knelt looking down at the carton of small green plastic boxes of pansies, rows of little flower faces. ". . . Are you sorry you did that?"

"Yes. You bet I've been sorry. It was an act . . . it was an act of cowardice. Selfishness. The father was definitely *not* interested, and that left it up to me and I didn't want my life interrupted, taken out of my control by anything." Joanna leaned over to pick out a flower, try the size of the small hole she'd dug. "—I thought I was too important, too valuable for that, so I gave the baby away like a new sweater that didn't fit."

The pansy was lavender, a gay little lion, roaring. She eased it from the plastic basket, then troweled more room for it. "I saw the baby once, in the hospital, and it was given away for adoption."

"Hard choices," Charis said.

The flower fit. Joanna tamped soil carefully around it. ". . . When you make a decision like that, it has permanent consequences. At least, it did for me. It meant that I wasn't the person I'd thought I was. I was . . . less. I have never forgiven myself for it." She planted a second pansy, bright orange, pressed the soil firm around it. "We need to remember to water them. . . ." She reached into the carton for another flower, picked one blue with black borders, took it from its basket, and bent to tuck the little flower in.

"Joanna, everybody makes mistakes—but you can correct mistakes."

"Not all."

"Determination and love can correct mistakes." Charis chose a lemon-colored pansy from the carton. "This one next."

"You're asking a lot from love, sweetheart."

"I believe in it. Joanna, it's the only perfect thing . . . if you can start over again, with love." She held the little flower in her hand, gentle as if it were a baby chick.

They worked awhile in silence, Charis selecting and Joanna planting, pleasantly lost in labor.

Joanna came to the end of a row, and sat up to ease her back. She heard a car pull up in the street. Its door open, and slam shut. . . . Then footsteps down the gravel drive. She supposed Carl Early might have come back. . . .

"Can you stand a visit? —Or would you rather not?" Captain Lowell, wearing loafers, good gray slacks, and a blue short-sleeved shirt, might have been a prosperous tourist except for his arms' exaggerated muscles, the wear of weather in his face. There was a narrow neat white bandage around his left forearm. He was carrying a small brown paper bag.

Joanna stood. "No . . . no, a visit's fine." And here was the man she'd struck with a knife, a man who had at least contemplated killing her. —Had life always been so odd, so risky and unstable? And how had that been concealed from her for so many years?

Lowell looked slightly older than she'd remembered, certainly in his early forties. ". . . Just wanted to stop by, tell you how sorry I was to hear what happened—and ask if there was anything at all I could do for you." The island speech, its pleasant drooping cadences. ". . . Any chores, any work needs to be done, I'd be pleased to do."

"Thank you, Captain, but really there's nothing. . . . This is a friend, Charis Langenberg. She's staying with me."

"Hi."

"Hi. . . ."

Lowell smiled, held out the paper bag. "I brought you some fresh oatmeal cookies from Cooper's. Not much to bring. . . ."

"Oh, that's wonderful. Thank you."

"I thought of a pie, but I didn't know what you liked."

"Captain, believe me, we'll enjoy the cookies." Joanna stepped out from among the boxes of flowers, and saw Charis still kneeling in the grass, small rake loosely held—and on her face, besides a slight social smile, an odd expression . . . familiar.

"We have lemonade, if you'd like some."

"I would like some lemonade."

"Charis? Would you like some?"

"Yes, I would—and I'll get it. You stay and talk." She put her small rake down, stood, and went across the yard to the back steps.

"Pretty girl," Lowell said, and came to look at the flower beds. "You've done a hell of a lot of work."

"Yes . . . she was Rebecca's roommate at college." And having said that—and satisfied at how smoothly she'd said her daughter's name—Joanna was reminded of the expression she'd seen, recalled to her by Charis's just then. It had been Percy's intent and collected consideration, as she'd walked into the red dog's yard.

"—How's your arm, Captain?"

"My arm is still damn sore—two doctors visits for it, and a shot. Good thing you didn't go for the liver." There'd been no humor in the fox face, only in the pleasant uneven stresses of his speech— "Good thing you didn't go for the *livah*."

They stood side by side, observing the garden beds. There were faint sounds of preparation in the kitchen. . . . Captain Lowell smelled of cigars and clean cotton. There was the lightest, very lightest of beginnings—beginnings almost certain to come to nothing at all. And if anything, if ever, then not for a very long time. . . . Still, Joanna felt that faint vibration in the air, of things unsettled between them, after that violent and foolish adventure.

"See you got a little bandage of your own, there."

"Not serious. I was prying up a can lid, and the knife slipped."

"I suspect you're just not safe with anything sharp." Light-gray eyes observing her.

"Could be. . . ."

And of course it was precisely the immediacy of tragedy, of her losses, that had roused the instinctive tropism toward a man, to resume any possibility left of life, whatever her griefs. . . . The bestial element of cock and cunt, of continuing, risen swollen out of a billion years of loss and recovery. To that process, her sorrow—however fresh, unbearable—was beside the point.

"You two have done a lot of digging. Planting just the flowers?"

"Yes, we thought just flowers. We've got pansies, marigolds, petunias . . . and some perennials, too. Phlox—it's low-growing, so the wind won't bother it . . . and sea lavender."

"It'll be very pretty," Lowell said. There was a long silence, then he cleared his throat. "—Really came by here to apologize to you, personally, help any way I could. Apologize for coming up here after you that way, when you'd lost your husband and dad . . . and worse to come." He took a deep breath. "We must have seemed pretty much a pack of hoodlums to you, that night."

"Yes, you did. But I understood how serious it was for your people."

"—Would never have let George hurt you, Mrs. Reed. I wanted you to know that."

"I do know. I knew it then; I relied on it, Captain. But the truth is, all that seems unreal now—as if it were a scene in an opera. Do you know what I mean? —Something very dramatic, and slightly ridiculous."

The captain had a rusty laugh, apparently not exercised lately. "—Damned if it doesn't. Us . . . and Bobby. I'd say by those Englishmen, Gilbert and Sullivan. We had everything up here but the music." And after another long silence while they stood examining the garden beds, the first row of pansies. "—I still want to apologize for my behavior, handling you roughly, and so forth."

In that old-fashioned formality, Joanna saw a young fox-faced boy with a grimly traditional island father—a hard-handed captain himself, no doubt.

"Apology accepted, Captain. I'm collecting apologies on Asconsett."

"Tom—not 'Captain.' "

"Tom."

"Well, you've been hit hard."

"I have been hit hard. . . ."

"Here we are!" Charis came down the steps with a tray. A small pitcher of lemonade, three tall plastic glasses with ice cubes in them, and a plate of the oatmeal cookies. She was smiling, and Joanna saw nothing else in her face.

"I'll hold it." Lowell took the tray, shifted it slightly to take more of the weight with his uninjured arm.

"We need a chair." Charis went back up the steps to the kitchen.

"We need lawn furniture. —We saw some at the hardware store, but we were busy with the flowers."

"Hardware's the place," Lowell said. "—Light-built stuff, but it'll last a few summers. . . ." When Charis came back with a kitchen chair, he set the tray down on it and took two cookies.

Joanna enjoyed watching him eat. First cookie was gone in three quick bites. "How's the fishing going, Tom?"

"Not going at all, just now. *Eleanor*'s down—getting her diesel fixed—and that'll take a while, since I'm the one doing the fixing.

Doing that, days—and preparing construction sites with a backhoe tractor."

"Sounds like hard work," Charis said, and finished a cookie.

"Well, the hard work is hand work, going in with a shovel at night, finish shaping the excavations—septic pits and drainfields for those two new-built houses down South Sound. . . . Good medicine for excess pride." He smiled, and bent to take another cookie.

"Excess pride?"

"You bet. A while back, I thought I was a real special article. Lot of us did, out here. Owned three boats—well, half-share in the third—making very good money."

"But not now. . . ."

"Now, I'm digging-in septic tanks. —Good for me, is the truth of the matter. My dad would have said so."

The three of them stood in summer sunshine, drinking lemonade, chewing bites of oatmeal cookie. A slow breeze from the sea, passing through, shifted the sea-grape stems.

"He likes you." Charis, in green pajamas, was standing brushing Joanna's hair by floor-lamp light as she sat in the bedroom rocker. "—Likes you even better because you stabbed him."

"Charis, that doesn't interest me at all. Just the idea makes me tired."

"But you like him."

"I think he's a nice man. He's . . . interesting."

Charis had waited for the captain's story since his visit. Waited all afternoon, very patiently, while they planted the rest of the small flowers . . . prepared the back beds for the perennials—the phlox, calendula, and sea lavender.

Joanna had seen no reason not to tell the tale, with the basement cargo—its only evidence—long since gone off-island. . . . But embarrassed relating her self-important adventuring, the show-off in-and-out of Manning's, she'd been startled by Charis's reaction. —No surprise or disbelief, no cautionary uneasiness at all. Instead, there'd been a clamor of delighted laughter over dinner's hamburger and mashed potatoes, enjoyment almost masculine in its force. The girl had listened, leaning forward in physical sympathy—with Joanna all the way.

"Oh, that is absolutely wild! —And shit, I missed it!" Charis restless in her chair. "I would have helped you; we could have gone in together. Then, if they'd chased us, that would have been just too bad." And hearing the last of it—nighttime melodrama in the cottage, in this kitchen—she'd said, "He was lucky." Meaning Tom Lowell had been lucky.

"Don't you know how to use a knife?" Chàris had put down her glass of milk and gotten up from the table with a small steak knife, to demonstrate. "*Never* overhand, Joanna. Always up from under— left and right and left and right. . . ." Doing a little dance down the kitchen, grunting, striking quick as a sewing-machine needle, guarding with her left hand.

Sitting down, she'd said, "A major creep showed me that. I guess it was all he had to give." Then salted her salad.

"Sweetheart," Joanna had said, "—you're as odd as I am."

Charis had seemed pleased. "*Merci du compliment.*"

. . . The brush was smoothing, soothing its way down Joanna's hair. "So, not even a future interest in the captain? —Maybe in a year or two, if you do decide to come out to the island to stay?"

"Charis, I suppose anything is possible. But if the time ever comes that I *can* bear to think about that, about some man—even if I was living out here—I probably wouldn't consider a fishing captain."

"No? He seems very nice."

"No. . . . It's an occupation thing, a cultural difference. There have to be at least a few interests in common."

"But your husband—wasn't Mr. Reed a soccer coach?"

Charis had been right, the shrewdest stroke was up from under— and as if Joanna had forgotten completely until now, as if he hadn't died until now, Frank stood in front of her, listening and merry— and then was torn away.

Charis stopped brushing. "Oh, that was so stupid. That was such a stupid thing to say."

Joanna tried to answer, reassure her, tell her that she'd already spoken names, herself. That persons had to be mentioned sometimes. —Were better mentioned, than not at all. She intended to say that, but she couldn't, and sat silent.

"Forgive me," Charis said, and the brush recommenced its slow massage.

. . . That night, in light uneasy sleep, Joanna dreamed she was crewing on the *Eleanor II.* They were at sea—riding a rough swell the color of steel being twisted and turned under light. She was crewing, greasing something in the machinery of a winch. She didn't know what she was doing, but her gloved hands seemed to.

Frank came forward, a happy man in stained coveralls and rubber seaboots. Salt spray had soaked the right side of his coveralls. He came forward as she was working, stood beside her, swaying to the sea's motions, and watched. Then he reached out and touched her shoulder. "Use plenty," he said. He needed a shave.

. . . Then the job was somehow done, and Joanna walked around to the starboard side—the boat was rolling as Lowell turned her. Looking up at the bridge's side window, she saw his face, the motion of his shoulder and left arm as he spun the wheel.

The boat was rolling heavily in the trough. Joanna felt vibration surging through the deck plates as the engine worked to bring her round. She reached out to steady herself, gripping the wire rail with her right hand. She must have taken her gloves off; the wire was so cold it burned.

Rebecca, bundled in yellow oilskins, was standing far down near the stern, holding on to the wire rail and talking with a friend—a tall girl, her face familiar, her dark-blond hair broken loose in the wind. The girls were laughing at something Rebecca had said. . . . In the distance, rain was coming, slanting into the sea.

"Oh, dear." Joanna, sounding to herself like a dismayed old woman, woke. She lay recalling the dream, but remembering no emotion in it—as if it had been a painting of people at sea, in which she was only a figure standing by a trawler's rail.

She lay half in moonlight, and heard the soft crawling sound of beginning rain through the bedroom window. It must have wakened her. . . . The sound grew gradually louder, but no rain came down.

A soft sound and clearer, now. Gravel crunching under a car's slow tires. . . .

Joanna turned the covers back and got out of bed. She stepped fully into moonlight, went to the window, and looked down through the screen.

The VW was passing slowly underneath. Charis, in moonshadow, strained almost horizontal behind its open driver's-side door— pushing the little car along the drive. She stretched, silent, strove like a running leopard in slow motion, and the car moved along. It passed with soft shifting-gravel sounds under the window, steadily out the driveway . . . then past the curb and into the street.

Joanna went to the bedroom's front window . . . and saw Charis, blond hair burnished by moonlight, stand up from shoving and climb quickly into the driver's seat. Then, with the car's door still a little open, she freewheeled the VW silently down the hill . . . under tree shadows, and was gone.

Joanna heard the car's engine start below, at the end of the street, and thought for a moment she might still be dreaming, it had been so strange . . . and seen in the moon's dream light. She started back to bed—then knew she was awake, by the cool specifics of the floor under her bare feet.

But it had been so odd that she went out into the hall, crossed in darkness to the other bedroom, and knocked softly on its closed door. No answer. And how could there be. She'd seen Charis leave.

Joanna opened the door and looked inside. This was a smaller, darker room. Charis kept it very neat. Kept the bed neatly made up . . . and it was neatly made up now.

"Charis . . . ?" It was becoming a habit, calling people who were not there.

Shame came to Joanna like a chill—shame at seizing on a young girl's kindness, and remorse at her roommate's suicide. Leaning on it, gripping it, stretching it to assist her loneliness through a summer—through a summer and into the next year. She'd grappled Charis to her with need, used her and used her up, even taking advantage of the girl's own loneliness, her childhood tragedy, to hold her closer.

. . . Now, at night and silently, Charis was apparently running for at least a little freedom. A short escape, if only a drive alone and without Joanna Reed. A short escape, because all her things were there, her suitcase still in the corner. It should be funny—a savior angel having to steal away for a breath of her own air.

Joanna thought it would be funny, if it didn't mark so completely her future loneliness. Charis would be back, returning silently later in the night . . . to pretend to contentment in the day.

Joanna went back to her room, and to bed—fled into bed under moonlight and the covers, to drive herself to sleep as she'd done before, when her deaths were fresh.

Charis drove south through Asconsett—the town deserted under a moon almost full, only the streetlamps warming its light. She drove through town and out on South Sound Road. There was no traffic at all. The night breeze, cool, saltier than the day's, poured through her as she traveled a rocky coast, its surf silver.

Charis was weeping, the wind chilling her tears as she drove. Unaccustomed tears. —Tears of anger at being disturbed, threatened even obliquely just when everything was perfect, perfect after so much time, so much effort. . . . And anger at having to leave Joanna alone, having to sneak out of their house like a teenager dating a bad boy. —And all just to gather information in case of increasing intrusion, in *case* something needed to be done. But careful was better than careless; she'd learned that long ago.

More than a mile down South Road, the shore rising higher above a stepped reach to the sea, she'd passed several houses. Fishermen's cottages higher, above the road . . . mainlanders' vacation houses down to the left, along the sea.

There'd been lights still on in two or three homes, but no work site, no work being done. —Charis drove slower, so as not to miss it.

The distant lighthouse's whitewashed granite was just visible, its beam sweeping . . . slow sweeping . . . to flash out over the sea.

That great light's passing made the night's dark deeper, so Charis noticed lesser lights down on a shelved clearing to the left, below the road's bluff. She slowed, steered into the left lane . . . and saw a big white pickup truck, worn and rusted, parked on the shoulder beside the top of a rough construction driveway. The driveway, graveled dirt, was cut into the bluff and ran very steeply down to the clearing, the grade apparently too much for the old pickup truck to manage.

Charis pulled over to the right side of the road and stopped. She opened the glove compartment, found a clump of old Kleenex, wiped her eyes and blew her nose. Then she got out of the car and walked back to the pickup. Keys had been left in its ignition—an island habit—but the big truck was a mess, nothing anyone would want to steal, anyway.

She stood, looking out over the site. . . . There were two houses below. New, still scaffolded for painting, they stood side by side in moonlight out at the clearing's edge, above a stony shore. They were big two-story houses, elaborate with decks, widow's walks, and cupolas.

The work lights were nearer, set on wooden poles down by the foot of the drive. —They lit a small backhoe tractor bright orange. It was parked to the left of a hole that looked, to Charis, about ten feet by ten feet, and ten feet deep. Big enough for a really major septic tank. —This side of the excavation, along the bottom of the drive, they'd built a rectangular barrier of heavy planks, propped up at each end by heavier timber . . . angled to hold an uphill mound of spoil out of the hole.

. . . And there'd been considerable digging besides that. Off to the left, beside the bluff, parallel ditches of the drainage field ran out from a smaller pit. It all looked like a lot of work.

She stood watching in moonlight, the sea wind stroking her, gently combing her hair. . . . And after a long while, she saw a man climb out of the excavation on a ladder . . . then begin hauling at a rope running through two pulleys chained to the top of a tall steel-pipe tripod set beside the pit. . . . A big metal bucket came slowly up out of the excavation, heave by heave, and the man tied the rope off, swung the suspended bucket to the side, tilted it, and dumped its dirt up over the planking onto the mound of spoil.

Then he lowered the bucket into the hole, and stood for a moment . . . either tired, or thinking a problem out. The work light threw such shadows, Charis couldn't see his face clearly. —Then he moved, and she could.

It looked like very hard work—night work, too. The contractor must have said, "Get this done, all right? Finish it up. What you can't do with the machine, you do however. —But get it done."

And Captain Lowell, fisherman down on his luck, must have said, "Okay."

Charis watched for a long time. Saw Lowell go down the ladder into the pit again . . . and after a while of digging down there, climb out to haul more dirt up and away. She watched him do that three times. Interesting work, interesting to watch.

It was going to be a big septic tank.

Chapter Twenty

Joanna woke in early morning, dawn luminous at her windows. A door quietly closing had wakened her. Then there were soft, sneakered footsteps past her room . . . and on down the stairs. Charis, returned during the night from whatever short passage of freedom she'd required.

Joanna wanted to get up, get dressed and go downstairs. She wanted to see the girl—be certain she was home and all right, though she certainly was. It was an impulse surprisingly difficult to resist . . . to go down to see her, to make sure.

Lying awake, Joanna waited for full morning . . . for sufficient time to pass so the girl wouldn't feel pressured, watched for, her presence required to salve a stricken woman's loneliness. . . . What a sad thing it was to be so needy; to be left with only the requirement of courage so as not to burden others with that neediness. —And what was left of life, if so much of it had to be spent enduring?

. . . When sunlight touched the windows, spilled a little on the floor, Joanna got up, put on her robe, and went downstairs.

Charis was sitting at the dining table, entering in her laptop amid a confusion of notebooks.

"Hi. . . ."

"Good morning!" The girl looking bright, rested. "—I got up a little early. This math. . . ."

"I'll do breakfast."

"Okay. We have sausage."

"Sausage and scrambled eggs?"

"Great. . . ."

Beginning breakfast, and a pleasure to do even something unimportant for the young woman working on her Statistics in the dining room. . . . Modern college work now such an interesting combination of superficial courses—the various "Studies" of this or that sex, group, or culture—and very difficult work, like Cavelli's painful statistics math. It must confuse the students as to the effort required for mastery of any subject. . . .

"Two patties?"

"Sounds good." Charis peering at her laptop's screen.

"I think if we're doing country sausage, we ought to *do* it."

"Right on."

The blessing of concentration on tasks. Setting the table, then buttering bread, making toast. Frying sausage . . . then scrambling the eggs. Soft scrambled. And coffee, putting the coffee on. Small accomplishments, that in a while come together.

"Sweetheart—breakfast." Joanna put the plates on the kitchen table, went back to the counter for the coffee.

"Coming. . . . Oh, it looks great."

Joanna sat, and reached for the sugar. "Charis. . . ."

"Mmm. . . ."

"You've been playing nurse out here for quite a while, and I know you said you're fine with that. But really, wouldn't you like a break? Maybe just take off to the mainland for a week or two?" — Close as it was possible to come, without mentioning last night's quiet exit down the drive . . . the apparently even quieter return.

"Joanna, I don't need to do that." Charis put a dab of scrambled egg on a piece of toast, and ate it.

"But would you *like* to do that? —I'm very much better, sweetheart, and I don't want you to feel you can't come and go as you please. Because you can."

"I know that. And I want to stay—unless *you* need some space, some time alone."

"I don't want any time alone, Charis." Joanna took some marmalade, and passed it.

"Neither do I."

"All right. . . . Then I guess we're stuck with each other."

" 'Stuck with each other,' " Charis said, smiled, and spread marmalade on her toast.

Leaving the midnight passage a mystery. "—Okay. Another subject. You know, I mentioned going over to White River?"

"Right."

"I really have to—things have piled up over there. And I thought we'd definitely do it, go this weekend."

"That would be good."

Joanna decided not to mention Rebecca's ashes . . . that she wanted to bring them out, scatter them on the hill. "So, we'll leave early—take the morning ferry, day after tomorrow. And that'll get us off the island for two or three days. . . . Where's the pepper?"

"Here; it was hiding."

"And since we'll be going across the state anyway, I thought you might like to try some caving. —Probably on our way back."

"You bet!" Pleased enough to pause between bites of sausage. "I know I'll like it."

"Well, you may—and may not. Lots of people don't. But it is a spectacular cave. Immense . . . and miles and miles of it. The only formation of the kind ever found in the Northeast."

"Oh, Joanna, I want to do that!"

". . . Then we will." A pleasure, of course, that entailed another trespass—no question a stupid and selfish thing to do. And only to be happy, at ease in the cave . . . and enjoy introducing Charis to something she might find wonderful. "—I'm getting more coffee; want some?"

"Yes. . . . Here's my mug."

At the sink counter, Joanna filled the mugs from the coffee-maker's pitcher. "This isn't keeping the coffee hot enough. . . ." She came back to the table. "I brought out my old harness and hel-met, just in case I could persuade Frank down some sea cave. —Against all odds, I might add. He didn't like caving." She felt some satisfaction at how smoothly, with almost no pain, she'd spo-ken of him. "So, we have two fairly complete equipment sets. . . . This coffee is barely warm."

Jerry Peterson, the boy who'd waited on Joanna when she'd needed paint for the window frame, came over, smiling, when they walked into the store. He was smiling at Joanna—paying no appar-ent attention at all to Charis, as if she were too bright to look upon.

"Hi, Mrs. Reed. . . ."

"Good morning, Jerry. We bought some flowers here yesterday, pansies, from . . . somebody."

"Must have been Mr. Shepherd. He's part owner."

"Mr. Shepherd, right. —And today we're looking for lawn furniture—the least expensive you've got."

"We have lawn chairs and stuff in the back."

"That's what we need to look at. . . . Jerry, this is a friend who's come out to stay with me. Charis Langenberg."

" 'Charis,' " the boy said. "Charis." And looked directly at her for the first time. ". . . That's a very pretty name." A compliment surprisingly direct from an island boy.

"Thanks," Charis said, and smiled, a Christmas gift. "When I was a little girl, I hated it."

Jerry had nothing more to say. He stood grinning.

"Lawn furniture," Joanna said.

"Right. Right. . . ."

Most of the lawn chairs and tables were molded white resin—a few with tied-on plaid plastic pads.

"Without the pads, I think. —Charis?"

"No pads. They're always wet."

"Well, Mrs. Reed—we have just these two sets without pads. They're almost the same, except one table has the clear plastic top, and the other top is glass. Glass is more expensive—and that whole set's a little more sturdy."

"Glass," Charis said.

"Four chairs and the glass-top table—how much would that be?"

"This set—" Jerry bent to check price tags. "This set is . . . eighty-nine dollars."

"Without the umbrella?"

"Without the umbrella, yes, ma'am. Umbrella is . . . fifty-two dollars. Green-and-white is all we have."

"That's a lot of money," Charis said.

"It is—but this stuff is pretty tough." Jerry picked up a chair, and put it down. "It'll really last."

"—Umbrella'll go three summers. Four, tops." Tom Lowell was standing by a croquet set behind them. "We meet again, ladies—don't mean to bother you. . . . Jerry, is Greg around back? Need some chain."

"Yes, he is, Cap."

"Okay. Mrs. Reed, Charis. . . ." He smiled and strolled away, nautical in worn cotton coveralls and black rubber boots.

"Anyway . . . anyway," Jerry said, "it's really a pretty good set of outside furniture."

"Except for the umbrella," Charis said. " 'Three summers. Four, tops.' "

"Yes," Jerry said, "—but you're ladies. You're not going to beat it up as much, leave it open in the wind and so forth."

"So, with the umbrella?"

"Mrs. Reed, that would be . . . a hundred forty-one, before tax."

"Hmmm."

". . . I'll tell you what. If that umbrella—if that umbrella doesn't last five years, store'll replace it. And that's a promise."

"Right. —Charis?"

"I don't know if we need an umbrella."

"It's nice to have, though. Gives you some shade."

"Most people want an umbrella," Jerry said.

". . . Well, Jerry," Joanna said, "we'll take it."

"I'll buy the chairs."

"Charis, you'll buy one chair."

"Two chairs, Joanna, I want to buy two chairs."

"Well, let me give them a check, and you can pay me later—or spend it for groceries or whatever."

"Glass-top set, with green-and-white umbrella." Jerry took a pad from his back pocket, carefully wrote out a sales slip. "We'll deliver that for you this afternoon, and we don't charge for delivery. . . ."

"I'll give you a check. —Jerry, do you have a phone?"

"Yes, ma'am, we do. Down at the end of the counter."

"Charis, back in a minute. I need to call the gas station—the *only* gas station—to get my inspection sticker sometime this month."

Joanna walked down the counter. The phone and island phone book were tucked behind a large antique cash register decorated with embossed metal scrollwork. Its cash-drawer handle was a steel flowered vine.

Cooper's was in the slender phone book under Bakeries. There was no other bakery.

"—Cooper's." A woman's voice, stony New England. *Coo*pahs.

"I'm calling to order a cake."

"Order over the phone . . . ?"

"That's right."

"Well . . . can I ask who this is? Because on cake orders, unless you're an old customer, we like to get a payment before we do the cake. Who is this?"

"My name's Reed. Joanna Reed; I live up on Slope Street. —It's a surprise and I'm with the person, so I can't come over now."

"Just a minute. . . ."

A silence almost restful. Joanna had found it an effort, speaking on the phone.

"Hello—Mrs. Reed?"

"Yes."

"You just tell us what you want, and it's okay."

"Well, thank you. . . . What she likes is coconut cake."

"No problem; we make a great coconut. Big cake?"

"No, a small one. It's probably just going to be for two people."

"Decorated? —Birthday?"

"No. I think . . . I think just the cake."

"We have some little rosebuds. We can put those on around the edge, look real nice. . . ."

"Well, I suppose rosebuds would be all right."

"They will look real nice."

"All right. Rosebuds."

". . . Your order is in."

"When could I pick it up?"

"Pick it up tomorrow mornin'."

"Thank you."

"That's what we're in business for. Good-bye."

"Good-bye."

As they got into the Volvo, Lowell waved to them from down the street . . . climbed into the cab of a big, rust-spotted pickup.

"Well, your captain *definitely* likes you. —Saw you yesterday, had to see you again today."

"Charis, please. It's a small town."

"Not that small. He sees your car parked out here—and suddenly remembers he needs some chain?"

"Charis . . ." Joanna started the car, pulled out into Asconsett's minor traffic.

"I'm not saying he isn't nice. I'm not saying he's out of line. I'm just saying he's interested, has some long-term intentions. —Oh, the phone. Are we going to try the phone company again?"

"Damn. —Oh, the hell with it. We'll get it fixed after the weekend."

"Okay."

"Do you mind?"

"No. No, I don't."

"Because if there's . . . if there are calls you'd like to make—"

"Joanna, I don't want to make any calls."

"Then the hell with it."

"The hell with it."

. . . They finished planting the flowers by evening—the marigolds, geraniums, petunias, and pansies all watered with B-1 starter, and arranged in checkerboard patterns down each side bed. Patterns interrupted occasionally to accommodate those tall veteran flowers that had survived so long uncared-for. —The perennials were set out to plant—sandy soil manured and mixed in the two long back beds . . . and checkerboarded there, too, but with more space between them.

"We have a garden." Charis put down her trowel and knelt back in evening's shadows, satisfied.

"Yes, we have a garden." Joanna's right knee clicked as she stood, and began to ache mildly. Penalty for many deep miles crawled through stone passages. . . . "But we still have to plant the perennials. And then we'll have to keep up with regular fertilizing, and weeding."

"I know," Charis said. "But we have a garden!"

. . . They cooked dinner together like dancers, changing places in the kitchen as they worked, never in each other's way.

And while cleaning the spinach, cutting away the stems, then soaking the deep-green leaves in the big pot, stirring them to get the last grains of sand out . . . while doing that, Joanna felt—not happiness, nothing so rich—but a relaxation, an almost contentment.

It seemed very important, made her hands tremble with its promise that pleasure in living would be possible. Not just bearing loss, with such relief from loneliness as Charis had given her. But more than that.

She cleaned the spinach, rinsed the pot, then set the steamer in. Charis was veining the shrimp—whole Louisiana shrimp, shipped frozen, and strangers to these seas. Little mindless things . . . biomechanisms. Who was the Victorian British naturalist that lost his faith in South America? He'd been unable to believe in a God who mindlessly created redundant thousands of varieties of billions of beetles.

—But had the beetles a god of their own, uninterested in British naturalists? A god the color of seasoned wood, and jointed like tremendous planks hinged together . . . slowly folding and unfolding through the forest, making beetles, spilling them from its long cracks and crevices.

Dinner, eaten late, was delicious. Curried shrimp, brown rice, and the spinach. Vanilla ice cream.

". . . How are you doing on the Sociology?" Joanna put down her notebook, and sat across from Charis at the dining table. A work table; they'd never eaten there. . . . She and Frank hadn't eaten there, either.

"I think I'm okay." The girl—so neat otherwise—sat with her laptop behind a low semicircular heap of notebooks, reference books, textbooks, and orange Post-it notes. "—I've got Singleton in at least a little small-time trouble, with the Vietnam War. We got zip out of that one—no fab new markets. But he probably won't even notice. Won't want to notice. It's . . . it's like it must have been for the Scholastics, dealing with the church's bullshit. If you don't go along with these professors' agreed-upon crap, they have hysterics."

"I've had them."

"I don't think so."

"Wait till you do that almost-certainly-unwise Longfellow paper. You show me that, I think I can guarantee some hysterics."

"I don't believe it. Joanna, I have a very good *argument*."

"We'll see. But if it ain't anchored in the text, honey, in the work—you're in trouble."

"Trust me, you will really like it. . . . But you know what I mean. The professors . . . I mean they *yearn* for a society like a medieval manor, you know? Someplace ordinary people can't just do what they want, are kept on a leash by their betters. —And of course, they're among the betters."

"Charis, that superior position is what they're used to."

"Then they need to get booted out of it!"

It was such a touching thing to hear, touching to see the girl's lovely and determined face. Still so young. . . . "Sweetheart, you're talking about a mountain of self-satisfaction and light workloads—tenured faculty diseases with which I've certainly been infected—"

"No, you haven't."

"Yes, I have. —You know the best way to affect that so often misplaced pride? It isn't with angry or silly papers. It's with very good work. —That is the *only* thing that truly impresses teachers."

"I shouldn't do Longfellow?"

"No. You *should* do Longfellow, though Benét might be more deserving. But do him well and thoroughly, not as an argument to annoy Chris Engletree—or do someone else."

Charis sat thinking . . . considering it. As often, when the girl fell into reverie, when the energy of her personality, her display of elegance, was subdued, Joanna saw so much more clearly the child she'd been. Seen in stillness, in a softer face, in hazel eyes shadowed.

As she watched her, Joanna felt something new and old at once—and deeper than affection. It was a fondness very frightening, a certain harbinger of loss.

She woke to what she'd been waiting to wake her, sooner or later. The slow, whispering crush of gravel down the drive. . . . The moon was down, its soft filtering light fading to dark. It was dreaming time, the hinge of the morning—but she was awake and not dreaming.

She got out of bed and went to her side window. Below, but in deeper shadow than before, Charis leaned into her little car's door post—pushing . . . pushing. The VW rolled slowly along like a bulky domestic animal, sleepy, wakened from its parking.

Joanna, suddenly angry, almost called down, *"For Christ's sake . . . !"* But didn't. Charis was being too careful, too effortful, too quiet.

Taking her robe off the back of the rocker, Joanna put it on, and went into the dark hall and down the stairs, barefoot on cool uneven pine.

She unlocked the front door—but opened it only a little, concerned at the awkwardness of confronting Charis . . . the rudeness of aborting all the girl's secrecy, her quiet and care.

She opened the door slowly, just wide enough to see the car roll out into the street. There was no moonlight, no tree shadows. The car was only a shape in night, with Charis a smaller shape beside it. A shape still shoving, moving the VW along . . . possibly reaching in to turn its wheel . . . then blending with it, climbing into it.

The car rolled away down the hill, its engine still off—and Joanna opened the front door, came down the front steps, and hurried out into the street. The cobblestones hurt her feet. . . . She could see the car going downhill. Its brake lights glimmered, glimmered as it slowed a little.

"Now, what the fuck . . . ?" And asking aloud, Joanna supposed she knew the answer—had known it, really, the last time Charis had made her silent getaway. The girl was going *to*—not running from. . . . There was someone else she cared for, in a life not so perfectly lonely after all. A boy, or man, apparently interested enough to have come out to the island to be near her for only an occasional night. —Someone too special to bore by being introduced to the so-tragic Joanna Reed.

The VW paused at the foot of the hill. Joanna heard its engine start . . . saw its headlights flash on as it turned south. South, to town. But there'd be nothing open. Her lover must be staying at the inn, overlooking the harbor—expensive, for a college boy. Too expensive for a college boy.

The cobblestones were cold under Joanna's bare feet. She walked back up to the cottage's front door, and inside.

Jealous, she thought, and went up the stairs. Jealous of any shifting of the girl's attention away from sad, suffering Joanna. And jealous of Charis's having a lover—the rich affection, and the fucking. Jealous, when she should be glad for the girl—should be embarrassed that Charis felt she had to make such silent nighttime escapes to avoid upsetting her.

In the bedroom, Joanna took off her robe and draped it over the rocker. "Stop being such an ass," she said to herself, sat on the bed to brush the soles of her feet clean with her hands, then slid under the covers. "—You are not the world. . . ."

It was the size of the things was the trouble. Just the beginning of the year, some state bureaucrat had said larger distribution boxes, bigger double-walled septic tanks out on the islands. —Supposed to be effluent-proof, last forever and so forth. Whole thing was to protect sand crabs, protect sand fleas . . . something.

Lowell leveled the filled bucket with the edge of his shovel, then leaned the shovel against the pit wall and went to the ladder.

. . . Let that state fool come out and dig a field and box hole, and then a major pit for a pair of big purple fiberglass tanks with those double walls. They'd have to handle eight bathrooms in these two houses, plus—*plus*—four more bathrooms when the third house went in. Twelve bathrooms draining into a field mostly sand. . . .

Out of the pit, Lowell went to the steel-pole tripod, and started hauling the bucket up—which bothered his sore arm more than shoveling did. . . . Work had taken six hours a night—eight o'clock till two in the morning—for two, now three nights. And not done yet, since the little Kubota hadn't been up to the job. Bucket was okay for basic ditching, but couldn't reach to clear the bottom of the pit—which left a couple of tons to shovel and dump, Larry being too cheap to rent a big machine, ferry it in.

The bucket up and swayed over, Lowell tilted it slowly to empty sandy dirt over the spoil dam's planks.

. . . Shape the ditch so the inlet pipe had enough slope, then shovel out the pit, then hand-finish the box hole and field runs—all for an inspection would take maybe ten or fifteen minutes. . . . Truth was, Larry Hooper didn't know what he was doing, putting in these houses. No surprise, man had been a lobster-boat builder; didn't know a whole lot about contracting.

. . . And another truth was, a certain fisher with his boat down was damn lucky to have the work.

Lowell let the line run through the block and tackle, and the big steel bucket fell back into the pit with a heavy *clank*. He went to the ladder and down it . . . picked up the shovel, and started digging. Shovel was a leaf-point, supposed to be commercial heavy-duty grade. —And just three nights' work had polished and thinned its steel sharp enough to slice bread with. There was that much sand packed into the dirt, even this far back under the bluff. The miracle was Larry passing his perk test down here. . . .

Lowell dug along the pit's back wall, began filling the bucket. . . . He was working with his mind on the *Eleanor*'s diesel. The Cummins needed heavy shop work, and what he was doing was fooling with the thing hanging off a double-chain hoist—and getting a lot of advice from every man walked down the dock.

It was costing him days not fishing. Costing him money, just working on that diesel. Pete was off the crew. Jackson still hanging on, but not by much. . . .

Lowell dragged the heavy bucket closer to shorten his swing with the shovel.

. . . Frances used to look up from doing the books, and say, "Tom, it's a slow decline." —A slow decline. A slow decline for both of them, too. And the baby. Baby boy . . . not such a baby anymore.

Lowell began edging with the shovel blade, carving the pit corner clearer. . . . A slow decline, and poor comfort that it was money trouble had seen her say good-bye and take the baby—rather than Monash just being a better man. Poor comfort. Solid middle-class back to working-class in about five years, and Frances not up for that at all. . . .

Strange, in all those programs on TV—talk shows and so forth—nobody ever said anything about living money. They talked about millions, sometimes, but never about day-to-day money . . . the kind

that sent women running to lawyers for a better deal. Taking the
kid—you bet—and if they were lucky, getting a lawyer *as* a better deal.
Frances Boothe Monash, now. And little Charlie a Monash, too.
*It's less confusing for him, Tom. He's starting kindergarten next year,
and I'm sorry, but it's just better for him to take Bud's last name.* —It was a
peculiar thing how completely a woman changed once she turned
to someone else. She became a different person—not the one
who'd made those sounds when you were in her, not the woman
who'd cried while you held her . . . not the woman who'd cooked
your breakfast, not the woman who'd worried about the *Eleanor II*
out in stormy weather. —That woman was dead as Mrs. Reed's husband, dead as her dad and daughter. . . .

Bucket was almost full; maybe eight or nine more loads up, and
the pit'd be ready.

. . . So, two ways of losing people, and hard to say which was
worse. Have them die, as Mrs. Reed's people had died—or have
them just walk away, like his. Last time on the mainland—April—
Charlie had still known him, still said "Daddy." Still thought of him
that way, and was happy with the Tonka toy. But for how much
longer?

Women. . . . Mrs. Reed. Joanna Reed. Hard to forget her—looked
like a caught witch in the moonlight with that long black hair, and
flashing her knife into him. Not easy to forget.

Shoveling dirt out of the pit's corner, Lowell thought he heard
an engine start, up on the road. It ran for a minute or two, and
stopped. . . . Sounded like his truck, but probably not. He'd left the
keys in the pickup, but no kid would choose it for joyriding.

He topped the bucket, started to set the shovel aside—and
heard a steady crunching noise high above the pit. Dirt and sand
sifted down where he'd just shoveled the corner clean.

That sound was coming down . . . rolling down the gravel. Something coming down the steep drive with the engine off or in neu-
tral, making more dirt shake loose. Coming way too fast. Maybe his
truck, after all. . . .

The driveway's dirt and gravel slumped just above with a sudden
harsh hissing sound—and as if this excavation were his *Eleanor*'s
hold, and trouble come so fast at sea, Lowell dropped the shovel
and went for the ladder, to climb up and out.

But there was a draft of air, an instant of silence he'd known at
sea, though never on the land, and something—rolling off, fallen

off the edge of the drive—hit the retaining wall's timbers a terrible blow. He was almost at the ladder.

Heavy lumber broke, with smashing metal—and the retaining wall caved in above and behind the pit. The earth came down with falling timbers, sheaves of splinters, and the truck's front wheels came down with them.

Lowell, deafened, buried to his chest in fast-flowing sand, was struggling up as if from flooding in a boat's below decks, when a timber or one of the truck's wheels suddenly shifted to drive him down again, and deeper. Underneath, something caught his left leg. He felt it snag his leg beneath the knee, press it down and break it. There was a twist and splitting as it broke.

Then he was sunk under a dry and heavy ocean, with no air. It was quiet except for settling sounds he felt rather than heard, and his body began a slow . . . slow . . . swimming, one-legged, through sandy soil to where it hoped the ladder might be.

His body began trying while he was still catching up, figuring his chances—that he might have a minute and a little more for terrific effort, slow-motion swimming under tons of shifting weight, before he smothered. And only two or three feet to the ladder—if he was still turned toward it.

It was that, or wait for Larry Hooper to stand goggling at him in the morning—once people had dug him out—lying on a blanket with sand in his mouth, sand in his open eyes.

Lowell caught up with his body, and went to work. Hard work . . . a sort of very slow and effortful breast stroke. The sand made that barely possible; solid dirt wouldn't be giving way at all. . . . Miracle that Hooper passed the perk.

Lowell struggled in the soil, inched and wriggled, slow-hauled handfuls of sand and dirt to him and hoped that meant he moved—and wasn't just twisting and curling in a slow circle with no air to breathe at all. The bad leg felt strange—the bone seemed to poke out, catch in the sand.

The weight above him pressed down so he lost direction, and didn't know where his small pinched strokes and one-legged kicks and pushes might be moving him. He tried breathing in, only a little, and sand slid down his tongue.

In a fucking sewer pit, Lowell thought—and was so humiliated he wrestled and twisted and reached as if he'd breathed a breath.

He hit something with his finger.

He scrabbled with that finger . . . then all the fingers of that hand—right hand. He clawed and tried to kick, beginning to die for lack of air. His heart was missing beats; he could feel the skipping rhythm.

"Keep fucking beating," he said to it in his head.

Everything else was still but that working hand . . . and Lowell tapped what he'd touched, and curled his fingers around it. He'd forgotten what the thing was . . . but he gripped it and convulsed and twisted, felt things pulled away and torn in the muscles of his back.

He used that grip, used it though he'd gone blind. It was not just being buried, unable to see; it was a deeper darkness.

He used his grip on whatever it was as an anchor to work from . . . and levered his left arm and hand slowly up, burrowing up as if he might catch a handful of air and bring it down to him. And the hand bumped something. He felt it . . . could feel it and get a grip on the same kind of round thing his right hand held.

His heart was hesitating . . . hesitating. Lowell pulled himself slowly up three rungs of a ladder—which ladder, and where, he'd forgotten.

Then his head came up out of cascading sand, and he spit sand, and took a breath.

Chapter Twenty-one

Joanna woke from breakfast . . . to breakfast. She'd been dreaming of a morning with her father—a different Louis than the one she'd known . . . perhaps a young Louis Bernard her mother would have recognized.

He'd been very merry in the quipping French fashion, telling a story she couldn't remember, while buttering his toast. They'd been at breakfast, but she'd eaten nothing, only sat at the table and enjoyed her father's company.

There'd been someone on the porch. As her father'd talked, Joanna could see, through the dining-room curtains, a shadow moving. Hear footsteps. . . . She'd watched Louis, listened to him, but was conscious of the person waiting on the porch. Her father had smiled and said something to her . . . then said, "Not so?" His dark eyes had shone in morning sunlight reflected from the table's glassware and silver.

Joanna had eaten nothing, only smelled the rich odors of her meal—and woke to those odors, her father's voice sounding softly for a moment more.

She lay in bed, sad before she recalled the reason for it—then remembered it was a morning to begin granting Charis her freedom, with thanks. A morning, a day to at least begin to say good-bye, with gratitude for the girl's kindness. . . . Then, odd late-night escapes would no longer be necessary, the girl freed to be with someone she loved.

It was liberty owed her, and the only gift Joanna had to give for such patient tenderness. Still, bittersweet to have had such delightful company, then lose it. It was sad, and frightening, to have to learn to be alone after all. . . . It grew more frightening as Joanna lay there, so she got out of bed to leave a little of the fear behind, and went to the closet to dress in worn gardening pants and shirt. Dressing to say good-bye.

". . . Still have perennials to plant!" Charis, in worn jeans and white T-shirt—and fresh as if she'd been in and slept all night—served two over-easy eggs each.

"Then that's it. Done."

"We'll have a garden. —Jam? There's marmalade, and raspberry."

"Raspberry. I'll get it."

"I'll get it—"

"Charis, I'm up. You sit, and start eating. . . ."

It was a difficult subject to open—over bacon and eggs, toast, grapefruit juice, and coffee—without embarrassing the girl. . . . *Charis, you don't have to sneak out in the middle of the night anymore. You know—push the VW down the drive and so forth? Really, you can just take off, be with whoever—and thanks, endless thanks, for your help.* Joanna put the raspberry jam on the table, and sat down. . . . An unpleasant little speech. But if that wasn't said, what could be?

"We still going, tomorrow?"

"Tomorrow morning." Charis had fried only six slices of Barkley's thick bacon. Moderation. "—But you know, sweetheart, you don't have to go. I mean it. Why don't you stay out here and enjoy yourself? And I'll be back Sunday night or Monday."

Charis spread raspberry jam on her toast. "You don't want me to come?"

"Yes. I *would* like you to come with me, but not if you have something else you'd rather do—maybe just stay out here and take it easy."

"I don't have anything else I want to do."

". . . You don't. Well, in that case—if you're really sure you want to go—then yes, I'd like to have you come with me."

Charis took a bite of her toast, and seemed content. Apparently had no late-night dates planned for the weekend. ". . . Bird feeder," she said.

"What?"

"Bird feeder. Joanna, I was thinking it might be nice to have a bird feeder and a birdbath. —I bet birds have a tough time finding fresh water on the island."

". . . It's an idea. I don't know about the feeder; it might interfere with their normal eating patterns. We could check with the Audubon people. . . . But I like the birdbath."

"The garden should have a birdbath."

"I didn't see any at the hardware store."

"We're going over to the mainland; we could look for one. A small one . . . on a pedestal." Charis finished her toast, and returned to bacon and eggs.

"Maybe one of the weathered bronze-looking ones."

"We could set it so we could see it from the kitchen. . . ."

"I think it's a good idea. I really don't know where they find fresh water out here, except rain runoff." Joanna got up with their mugs, poured more coffee, and came back to the table. "—I think there's only one real pond on the island, over behind Willis. Weren't for the seasonal rains, I understand the island wouldn't *have* a water table."

"Are your eggs done too much?"

"No. Perfect. —We'll look for a birdbath. . . ." And the subject of freedom, postponed.

The little sea lavender plants released lavender's odor when their leaves were gently pinched. They were the last of the perennials going in.

Kneeling, Joanna dug the row of holes along the back beds, allowed Charis the pleasures of planting, nesting the lavender into pockets of dark potting soil, mixed with manure and the yard's sandy dirt.

They worked together down the row, the late-morning sun leaning on their shoulders, planting their shadows beneath them in the beds. They set the lavender to edge the yard, where the remnants of the old fence were weathering away in the hill's tall grass, the clustered sea grapes.

. . . They finished the last planting, watered with mixed B-1 starter . . . then weeded once more through the yard's grass, side by side.

"Is it done? —Joanna, I think we're done."

Joanna stood, and stretched to ease her back. "We're done."

Together, they surveyed their plot—its grass bordered by dark turned beds along the cottage's back wall and the edges of the yard. The ranks of young plants—dozens of them—resting patterned in their various greens.

"Have to keep it weeded." Charis bent to stroke a pansy as if it were a pet . . . chucked it under its small chin.

"Perpetual weeding. —A walk before lunch?"

"Let me pee, and I'm with you." Charis trotted up the kitchen steps.

Joanna looked out over the garden—begun in such a lonely agony of labor, furious and repetitive. This was the yard where, frightened of the house's memories, she had slept out in weather. . . . Then Charis had come.

—And would go, once her silent late-night rendezvous were discussed. Then she'd be free to be with whoever it was who'd come out to be with her. . . . Which would leave Joanna Reed with only herself for company. Perhaps good enough company, now. . . .

"I'm peed, and I'm ready!" Charis came swiftly down the back steps, past Joanna and across the yard—then jumped their new back bed, eased through sea grapes, and paced away along the ridge of the hill. "Youth," Joanna said aloud, and trotted to catch up.

They walked together across the dune hill, moving quickly over slipping sand and through clumps of tall sea grass to work the gardening's bending-and-kneeling out of their muscles. The summer sunlight sifted reflections from the sand, glittering in Joanna's sight. . . . This was the slope where Frank's ashes were scattered; those myriad white flakes and powdered dust contributing to the sand slopes they climbed down to cross . . . and climb up again.

Good exercise . . . in bright light and air and height above the ocean perfect enough to promise everything, if only men and women were immortal.

"Wonderful."

"What . . . ?"

"All this."

"You bet." Charis, as if lifted from below, took off in her stride, jumped a clump of tall grasses—and landed as if she'd landed on just that downsloped spot many times before, in casual balance. . . . It was a pleasure for Joanna to watch her move. There was no doubt in what Charis did. —Very much, Joanna supposed, as she had been at that age. As she had been in many ways, as if this girl were an avatar of her own youth, come back to her when she had nothing else.

Charis waited for her. "You getting tired?"

"No. No, I feel good."

"We can go back."

"No, let's keep on truckin'."

They set out again, wading through deep drifts that ran down-slope like slow, tan water, curling in small tugging currents around their sneakers. And as if this labor were a key to changes—as gardening, weeding had been when she was without hope—Joanna, walking fast over uncertain ground, felt again the possibility of contentment, even happiness. It rose in her throat, a physical thing, a manifestation that made it difficult to catch her breath.

"Okay?" Charis circling back, concerned.

"Better. Better than okay, sweetheart." Joanna moved faster, to keep up. —To be happy. Not yet, of course . . . but someday to be happy. She was afraid to try to imagine what shape that might take. Much better just to walk the hill.

Charis, long dark-blond hair loose and breezing in the ocean wind, was climbing a little ahead again, moving up a steep slope of sand and sea grass with that perpetual easy engine of youth that no tried and hardened fitness could quite equal. —And arrived, waiting at the crest of the dune, the girl stood a slender figurehead, seeming to sail through the air. Below, the town and immense bright seascape appeared to vibrate in summer sun. ". . . I hope they never spoil it."

Joanna climbed to join her. "Well, they've been considering building wooden staircases up the hill—but they've been considering that for at least three hundred years."

"They mustn't ever do it."

"I'm sure they won't."

Charis turned, her eyes still brilliant with the view. "Doesn't it have to be good for you? Seeing something so beautiful?"

"I think so—probably good for the liver."

Charis turned away, started down the ridge, and spoke to Joanna into the air. "You want to stay out here, don't you?—I mean all year round."

". . . I've been thinking about it. A beautiful, smaller world, with fewer people." Climbing down in sand was much easier than climbing up. Just dig in your heels. . . .

"I think it would be wonderful. . . ." Charis, in slower, more reflective motion, walked the ridge north, toward the cottage. Joanna barely lengthened her stride to stay with her.

"It's something to think about, if I can get by without my job at White River. And I suppose I can, if I'm careful . . . find something part-time out here. —Wouldn't interest you, you're a little young for that, but maybe you could come out to visit, sometime—"

Charis stopped walking and turned an almost angry face—a grim face—to Joanna. "It *would* interest me," she said. "It would interest me a lot."

"Well, I thought you—"

"—I would rather do that than anything!"

What to say to this odd, contradictory girl, with her nighttime departures? "Charis . . . you mean stay with me out here? We talked about White River—"

"Yes. Out here."

"Sweetheart, you would always be welcome to do that. I'd love to have you stay with me as long as you like. I just thought you might want . . . some other choices in your life."

"I don't." And Charis marched away, so Joanna had to hurry to catch up—the catching-up thing becoming habitual; some serious getting in shape obviously called for in this girl's company. A companionship that, for whatever reason, seemed assured at least for a while.

They circled the long crest of the hill a last time, and into the afternoon—Joanna moving more and more easily, effort oiling her muscles. They hiked with ocean in view to the east and north . . . two smaller islands seen to the south and west, with the mainland only a green mark beyond them.

"I have to run into town." Joanna, changed to clean shirt and slacks, came to the kitchen door. "The big car inspection. . . ."

"Want some lunch first?" Charis, by the backyard faucet, was washing their gardening tools in an old yellow plastic bucket found in the garage.

"Not hungry yet. . . . I'll be back soon. Do we need anything for the stew?"

"We've got everything."

"Enough onions?"

"Plenty of onions."

"Okay," Joanna said, and went back in to get her purse.

. . . She parked on Strand, and got out of the car in the shadow of low racing dark clouds, a summer rainstorm coming in from the sea. She walked to the bakery, four doors down, and went in to wait behind an elderly fisherman apparently buying doughnuts and crullers for a boat crew unloading.

"I need some plain."

"How many?" Mrs. Cooper, rail-thin for a baker's wife, stood patiently behind her counter.

"Three . . . no, five."

"I'm going to give you four, Edgar. Let's keep to even numbers."

"Okay. . . . And two jellies."

"Two jellies." Mrs. Cooper began filling a cardboard box top.

"Two sugars."

"Two powdered sugars."

"And we need three crullers."

"*Two* crullers."

"—Okay. . . . Well, I guess that's it."

"That's it. Now, Edgar—you're off the *Big Boy*?"

"That's right."

"*Big Boy* already owes thirty-four dollars and seventy-one cents."

"Oh. . . . I'm supposed to charge it."

"I see. —Now, Edgar, I'm going to let you have these doughnuts and crullers. But I want you to tell Dale Boynton that I expect payment on this account. Do you understand?"

"Yes."

"And your total is *now* . . . thirty-nine dollars and eleven cents. You got that figure? You'll remember that?"

"Yes."

"All right, as long as that is understood."

"Okay."

"You tell Dale what I said."

"Yes, I will."

"All right." Mrs. Cooper handed the box top over the counter.

When the fisherman was gone, the door's harness bells ringing behind him, Mrs. Cooper smiled sadly at Joanna. "Isn't that a shame? —But you know, Mrs. Reed, things have got so tight we have to draw a line just to stay in business. We can't give these captains credit like we used to."

"It is too bad."

"Well, your cake's ready. . . ." Mrs. Cooper went into the back of the shop.

Joanna stood waiting, watching through the bakery's big window as people walked by. . . . Mrs. Cooper was talking to someone in the back.

There was a stack of *Islander*s on the counter, Asconsett's two-fold weekly just out, out every Thursday afternoon. Its news usually concerned with weather, social notes, fishing reports, boats for sale, and an occasional cranky editorial concerning the State Bureau of Fisheries.

Joanna picked up the top copy, and began reading the left-hand column: "Bottom Fishing." Bottom-fishing forecasts were really promising, stocks almost equal to last year's, though last year's had been disappointing. There was a cartoon—badly drawn—of a bottom fish looking worried about being caught.

A two-paragraph editorial, at the top of the right-hand column, dealt with the right whale—swarms of them, and endangered only in the fantasies of mainlanders.

The lower-right column had a piece titled "Mishap." There'd been an excavation accident—runaway vehicle rolling down into nighttime workings on South Sound. An island man, seriously injured, had crawled up to the road and been found in early morning by a Coast Guardsman coming off-duty from the light.

Joanna read to a name, then stopped reading.

"Here we are." Mrs. Cooper carried in a large white box. "—Man back there with a sample of cake doughnuts. You just order 'em in, frozen." She set the box on the counter. ". . . Well, you never tasted such stuff in your life. Cooper's has been doin' oil-bath doughnuts for nearly a hundred years, and I guess we'll stick to it. —Now, here's your cake, coconut with rosebuds. And we make from absolute scratch."

"Oh, but I ordered a small cake."

"That's what you got. Small cake. Should serve . . . oh, four to six, couple of good slices each. Don't get a lot of call for these small ones."

"Well . . . thank you. I'm sure it'll be wonderful."

"You can bet on it, dear."

"And what do I owe you?"

"That's twelve dollars and fifty cents. —And the paper?"

". . . Yes. Can I give you a check?"

"Your check'll be just fine. With the paper, twelve dollars and seventy-five cents."

Joanna, purse strap over her shoulder, the cake box and folded newspaper held in both hands, stepped out of Cooper's into a warm pattering rain.

. . . At the car, she put the cake box over on the passenger seat and got in, only damp. The rain spattered, hesitated, then came lacing down through sunshine as she closed the door. Rain marched across the windshield, and made the car's metal softly ring.

There was no good reason to keep reading the newspaper. That Tom Lowell's accident had happened late last night—and south, south of town—was no reason to read the rest of it.

But the summer shower seemed to bring a reason with it—that not reading, that imagining, would be worse. So Joanna sat beside the coconut cake in rain-curtained privacy, and read.

When she finished, she tucked the newspaper behind the seat. Then she started the car—but when she put both hands on the steering wheel, her fingers began to tremble . . . then flutter like feathers. Her hands shook as if they were no longer hers, and belonged to those parts of the Volvo's idling engine that moved and muttered.

What had that news introduced to set her trembling, signifying something even graver than the captain's agony? —Only that a girl with no lover had gone out secretly at night? Had driven south, where an accident occurred? That signified nothing. As a red baseball cap, one of so many, signified nothing.

Joanna put her hands together on the steering wheel, and leaned to rest her forehead on them, keep them still. She was afraid she'd sound the car's horn, but she didn't. . . . The rain was so helpful. Its small sounds were very helpful, and the veil it provided.

When she sat up, her hands and fingers were still. She put the car into reverse for a foot or two . . . then drive, to pull out of the parking space into Strand, heading south. She drove out of town— looking, only looking, not thinking of anything at all. . . .

Almost two miles out on South Sound, Joanna saw red and yellow lights flashing down off the road to the left. She steered onto the right shoulder . . . got out of the Volvo, and walked across the road. A tow truck and police car were parked below, alongside a steep driveway cut out of the side of the bluff. *Severely injured. . . . Crawled up to the road, and was found in early morning. . . .*

Almost at the foot of the drive—fallen off it—a big white pickup was lying half on its side, its hood and front wheels buried in a collapsed excavation with splintered planks, heavier timbers. A small orange backhoe was parked nearby—and farther off, past some ditches, two big houses stood above the sea.

Joanna looked down at that scene . . . then out over the ocean for a while. The rain had come through and blown over. Now the summer sun laid its light on the sea, painted it bright green, glazed its whitecaps from white to a warmer ivory. The sea wind gently buffeted her as she stood, persistent as a puppy.

Joanna went up the kitchen steps, purse on its strap over her shoulder, the cake box held carefully with two hands. She freed one hand for a moment, to open the door.

Charis was at the stove, peering down into the big frying pan. "I'm browning the lamb. . . . Want some lunch?"

"No, I'll wait for dinner. . . . I have something for you."

"What? —A cake!"

"Coconut."

"Oh, God, that's great!" Pleased as a child, Charis dusted flour off her hands, took the box and put it on the table. She broke its white string with one sharp tug, and lifted the top. "It looks wonderful. Rosebuds!"

"I ordered it yesterday."

"Ah, the *phone* call. . . ."

"Yes, I lied; no car inspection. —I ordered a small cake, but apparently they don't do really small ones out here. Big eaters."

"We'll have some for dessert."

". . . I'll be upstairs for a while—sure I can't help?"

"No way, Joanna. It's my stew; I'm going to do everything. And thanks *so* much for the cake."

"Hope you enjoy it, sweetheart."

Joanna climbed the stairs as if she were leaving some of herself still with Charis in the kitchen. A strange feeling—as if this part of her were coming upstairs to wait for something expected, but not yet quite arrived.

She went into her room, took the boxes of photographs from the closet, and sat on the bed with them. Odd she'd never cared enough about the past to fill albums. . . . Joanna sorted through small stacks and bundles of pictures, dealing the photographs out until she sat among scattered drifts of them—some quite old, fading—and began to search, almost aimlessly, for a familiar face.

She found a picture of Frank with his first team on the field at White River, and was surprised how young he looked, almost the same age as the boys. . . . Then, a few forgotten landscapes later, a yellowed photograph of her mother and father—also very young, looking too young to be married. They were standing together by the lake cabin. His arm was around her waist, and he was smiling. A different man, smiling and young. Her mother had put up her hand to shade her eyes from the sun.

Several bundles held only Rebecca. Her babyhood . . . the round, alert little face squinting into the sun. In so many photographs she was wearing her yellow sunsuit, with the shoulder straps. —Did they even make sunsuits now? The sunsuit and a tennis hat much too large for her. Good shade, though. The baby's skin had been white, soft, and tender as fine paper. . . .

Then, from a stained brown envelope, some New Mexico pictures. Mountain vistas. . . . A pueblo. Photographs she hadn't seen for so many years.

There was one of an older man whose name Joanna had forgotten, a caver who'd been with them in Lechuguilla. Then a picture of the cave's entrance—and after that, three more photographs taken at the same time, views hardly differing. She and Curt Garry, just out of the cave—hands, faces, and coveralls smeared with mud. Even so, a striking couple, grinning, pleased with themselves.

Curt such a golden boy, tall, blond, and slender, his face elegant as an old-fashioned actor's . . . and Joanna in dark contrast, with Indian eyes and long black hair—hair just released, she recalled, from a damp and dirty blue bandanna.

Curt, alive and looking out at her from more than twenty years ago. His eyes and mouth so well remembered—and echoed now, in another's face. . . .

Downstairs, Charis was singing at the stove. A show tune . . . a song from *Paint Your Wagon.* "—Out the window go the beans. Out the window go the *beans.*"

Joanna sat on her bed amid photographs—oddly satisfied by catastrophic machinery, polished and perfect, that had slid to its fit at last.

Charis's voice was nothing like her father's. Curt had sung madrigals at Yale. Her voice, sweet and uncertain, was nothing like his. But her eyes—set at a slant like a cat's—now recalled his eyes, absolutely. The medieval definition of her face was his as well, as he'd stood smiling for the camera so long ago.

. . . And what had Charis from her mother? Strong long legs and arms, a certain athleticism. Self-concern, talent for language . . . and a strict requirement that she be loved.

Joanna lay down among the pictures, felt their pasts like cool fallen leaves beneath her. Now everything was known. Now, even she knew it.

"To begin again, at the beginning," Charis had said. A recipe for happiness that had seemed obscure, and now was not. . . . She must have searched for her past, backtracked her poisoned childhood to its beginning—to recommence her life as it should have been, as a little girl kept with her mother, guarded by her mother, and loved absolutely.

. . . Frank had had no place in that new life—he would have proved it false, expected attention, affection that should be hers. So what seemed a slender boy, in a red baseball cap, had gone sailing with him. . . .

Louis, that odd and retiring man, must have decided to search for his lost granddaughter, had finally found her and—an anonymous benefactor—supported her through college. But Charis would not have known, or cared, who had cared for her. Louis Bernard would only have been the second sharer of what could not be shared.

As Rebecca had been the third.

All removed, so Charis—replacing a childhood of horrors— might claim a birthright hers alone.

Joanna lay with her eyes closed. In what course, in what book, had Charis found suggestion to call the classic elements to her service? Water, Fire, Air, and Earth. —And only Earth had betrayed her, and let Tom Lowell live. Two almost silent leave-takings in the night. The first must have been reconnaissance. . . . The four classic elements—and in which would her mother find solution, when what must be done was done?

Joanna lay among the pictures for a while . . . then got up and gathered them to put away, before she went down to dinner.

. . . The lamb stew was perfect, needed only a little salt.

Charis served it in soup bowls, with hot whole-wheat rolls and lettuce-and-cucumber salads. Then she poured out wine.

"Charis, it looks wonderful. . . . It *is* wonderful."

"Well, I was worried about the stew."

"No. It's really good."

"Salad dressing is from the bottle. I don't know why I can't make vinaigrette; I just never get it right."

"It helps if you whip it up—and you put in just a pinch of sugar, too."

"Well, next time I'll try it."

Joanna sat eating her dinner, and part of her became another Joanna. Both sat eating dinner. And as they ate, these Joannas slowly became several—each a little different—sheaving away from a core, like lily leaves. What was happening seemed much stranger to her than rage or sorrow. Stranger than the ever oddness of being alive. . . . Much stranger than inevitable death. This was something so new, there were no railings for it. Nothing to prevent flying, or a fall forever.

Joanna, now one of many, sat and buttered a roll—Charis had warmed four—and watched and listened to her daughter. Enjoyed her particular beauty, enjoyed it more now that she knew—such striking beauty, slim, delicate, and strong. . . . Frank must have felt that wiry strength. And Rebecca, also. Louis had experienced her intelligence, her cleverness, as the fire flowered. . . . Beautiful, intelligent, and strong.

And had those loved and loving dead a better claim to Joanna Reed than her daughter Charis—discarded as an inconvenience, a baby girl abandoned to a random monster?

Charis asked for the butter, and Joanna passed it. Passed the butter to the only family, the only child she now would ever have. —And no murder to be proved against her. Suspicion, certainly. Possibly an arrest, perhaps even a trial. But no proof, no witnesses. And in the end . . . no conviction, no sentence. Unless to an insane asylum for the rest of her life.

"Want more stew?"

"Yes, just a little."

"Okay. Not too much. . . ." Charis ladled stew into Joanna's bowl. "Need to leave room for cake."

. . . But if not that, if not police and punishment, then what? Could there ever be forgiveness for a family murdered? And if so— then forgiveness for Charis, perhaps. For her mother, never. . . . What but her youthful cowardice, laziness, and selfishness had created this engine of destruction?

Could that responsibility ever be borne, and those lost voices silenced? . . . Not likely. And even if that became possible—what then? What life hereafter, the two of them together? Charis was not safe to keep. Never certain, never satisfied to share the perfection of her mother's love, she would forge a silver circle around them. And if anyone approached—any man, with love . . . any woman, for friendship's sake—if any came close and touched that dragon's ring, Charis would kill them.

. . . Failing to answer questions, tired of them, some Joannas had died sitting in the kitchen chair. They had withered and fallen away like flowers. The others still ate and talked with their daughter, and enjoyed her, enjoyed knowing she was theirs . . . this bright and lovely girl come back to her after so many years, and when she was all alone. —But every Joanna remaining agreed it was best that Frank and their father and Rebecca were dead, so as not to suffer a sorrow so strange.

Still, Joannas died. And when the second buttered roll was eaten, all had died but one, and she was not quite the Joanna who had come down to dinner. —There was no single part of her so very different. But everything was changed a little. . . .

Charis took the dishes to the sink. "Cake time!" she said, and she shone like gold.

. . . After dinner, Joanna went to the dining room with her notebook, to sit with Charis as she worked. It was better to sit with her, much better than being upstairs alone, with nothing but Charis to think about.

"Joanna, are you okay?"

"I'm fine. Maybe a little tired."

"Well . . . I decided I'm going to do Longfellow for my poetry paper."

"Oh, dear. . . ."

"No, really. I think he had some important things to say."

"Mmm. About what?"

"—About America, the values the voices of wilderness represented to the Native Americans, and still do to all of us. Voices. Joanna, it's all about the voices of nature, addressing man—which, of course, is man addressing himself, speaking through trees and wind and rivers in that odd incantatory meter."

"Charis, you don't even have the poem yet. You haven't gotten the book from the library."

"I know, but I remember enough to know that's what *Hiawatha*'s about. I'll get the book next week."

"I see."

"You don't think it's a good idea."

"I think you may lose some important class credits by irritating Chris Engletree with a Victorian Romantic poet. . . . And you will also find the poem itself presents some problems with your 'nature's voices' thesis. I believe our hero canoes away at the end, and leaves his people to the mercy of the Jesuits—not precisely lovers of the natural world."

"I'll handle it—after all, he was a man of his time. I'll handle it."

"Well . . . if you really decide to do this, and you work from the text carefully, I suppose Engletree *might* find it interesting enough not to fail you. . . . Poor Longfellow is due for a minor resurrection. He's been an object of fun for quite a while.

"Then that's it. I'm going to give it a try. *'By the shores of Gitche Gumee, By the shining Big-Sea-Water . . .'* "

Joanna sat watching her daughter, searching that near perfection for the imperfection beneath it, a limestone fault, its river run below to fashion a cave of the heart.

Charis glanced up, saw her watching. "What?"

"Nothing. . . ." For something else to say, Joanna almost mentioned the death of Longfellow's wife. Her long dress cloaked in flame, caught fire at the hearth, she had run through their house to him, blazing, and fallen dying into his arms. . . . Joanna almost mentioned it, began to mention it—then, remembering her father's death, did not . . . she supposed from fear of embarrassing the girl, recalling the murder to her.

What strange delicacy. A killing rage and tenderness turned so tangled in her that she supposed she must have gone mad to bear it.

"What?" The girl's brilliant eyes on her. Elegant dark-gold head cocked to hear. A bright bird, flown out of deep jungle into light, with a jungle spider riding.

"Nothing . . . really." She wished so much to say aloud, *Sweetheart, in your madness, you have driven me mad. —Why couldn't you have come to me? I would have gone on my knees, I would have begged and begged you to forgive me. Then all of us would have loved and cared for you. Those you killed, they would have cared for you. . . .*

If she kept thinking those things, she would say them, and that would be insupportable. There was not enough left of her to say those things.

"Is something wrong, Joanna? —Are you okay?"

"I'm fine, sweetheart. Just tired."

"We're doing too much. The gardening was too much."

"No. I love the garden."

"You're crying!"

"No. No, I'm not."

"You are! And it's my fault—all this bullshit about my paper. I'm bothering you about this *crap*, and you just need to be peaceful, and rest. . . ."

"No, no."

"Yes, you do! You need quiet, and I'm going to keep my mouth shut and stop *bothering* you. I'm so sorry. . . ."

What else could Joanna do but reach out and touch her? Charis's flesh, her smooth skin, her commencing tears of distress, were fresh daughters to her mother's flesh and skin and tears. The two of them were one thing, separated.

"—I promise, Joanna. I'll just be quiet."

And if, by right, permitted to touch and comfort her—then whose right greater than a mother's to destroy a dangerous child? A knife from the kitchen, and justice with it. If not for Frank, if not for Louis and Tom Lowell—men, after all, with violence and violent death an ancient heritage—if not for them, then for Rebecca. Rebecca had been gentle, defenseless as a baby bird.

"—You'll see; I'll just let you rest. It's a promise."

Justice called for—but surely no harm, just for now, in touching. Touching her only daughter. That small pleasure was surely owed and earned—at least the affection due to any young creature, beautiful and doomed. Joanna reached to stroke the girl's cheek . . . then couldn't help but cup her face, so warm and smooth, in both hands.

"You've been very good to me, Charis." And that was true. That part of the truth was true.

Chapter Twenty-two

I think we should take the coconut cake."

"Charis, it's a lot of cake. We won't eat it over the weekend."

"But supposing we stay over? If we stay a few days, then we'll have it. Here it'll just get stale."

". . . Bring the cake."

"And what about the stew?"

"No. Sweetheart, we're not taking the stew with us. The stew will be fine in the refrigerator for a couple of days."

"Okay. . . ."

Joanna went upstairs for her small suitcase. They'd gotten up early to pack and have breakfast, which was just as well. Friday, the ferry left at nine in the morning—and her captain had a reputation for taking pleasure in leaving latecomers on the dock.

"Charis—are you ready?"

"I'm ready. . . ."

Joanna had forgotten to pack her hairbrush. She put her suitcase back on the bed, opened it, and tucked the hairbrush alongside her notebook. Then she shut the bedroom windows, picked up her suitcase, and went downstairs—surprised how possible it was to live for a little while alongside life, rather than in it. Very much like walking by a river too savagely turbulent and swift to swim in, wade, or cross.

Charis, in jeans and green T-shirt, was waiting in the kitchen with her small duffel and her book bag. "Do we have the caving stuff?"

"I put the equipment in the trunk last night."

Charis smiled. "Cake box is in the backseat."

"That cake was *not* small enough. . . ."

A while ago, they'd backed away from the last out-island stop. Oteague.

Now, the ferry—crowded with islanders and tourists mixed— was meeting white horses with small shudders of effort, heading into an east wind blowing warm off the mainland. Approaching, the coast was a lumpy line of gray-green, its buildings becoming more visible . . . the Coast Guard's white station clearly seen.

Charis and Joanna sat together on a deck bench vacated for them a while ago by two young men—college boys, vacationing— the courtesy their chance to speak with Charis.

With these young men, Charis had adopted the tone of the slightly older woman—almost an older sister—knowledgeable, amused and amusing, and finally dismissive, so they had wandered away dissatisfied.

"Cruel fair one."

"Joanna, I only do that, act a little snotty, because they make me uneasy. When there are two of them like that, and I don't know them, it just makes me uneasy." Relaxing, Charis stretched her legs out straight, as Joanna's already were . . . tucked her hands in her windbreaker's pockets, as Joanna's were tucked in her sweater's, and looked out over the sea toward Post Port. The ferry, groaning softly, began its slow turn for that distant dock.

It occurred to Joanna that anyone walking the deck and seeing them together, would know at once what they were. —A mother and daughter, their poses identical, their bodies certainly sugges- tive of each other's. . . . It seemed astounding she hadn't seen, hadn't known, what any stranger must.

The ferry's horn blatted out, made the deck tremble.

"Last stop, coming up," Charis said. Then, perhaps reminded by the small waves they traveled, "Can I ask how your sea poem is go- ing? Does it bother you to talk about it?"

"No, it doesn't bother me. It's going well, just a question of decisions. . . ."

"What decisions?"

"Well, putting in and taking out. Decisions about its nature. For example, if you're interested . . ." The teacher's eternal query, voiced or not.

"I'm interested."

A gull, striated gray as a warship, kited in and landed on the deck rail with a stumble and hop.

"Well, poems. . . . Each line of language affects the lines to come, *and* the meaning and weight of the lines that have gone before. That complicates decision-making so much that you have to rely on notion, on intuition, on . . . trust. You have to trust that it's possible. You have to be . . . joyful about it. —That make any sense?"

"Better than sense."

The gull sauntered; its twig legs, knob-kneed, ending in webbed feet the color of bubble gum.

"About the poem . . . I feel the introduction is going well; it's fairly formal. After that, I want to allow the poem and the sea and myself more freedom. I tend to be too concerned with structure."

"But without form, there's no poetry."

"So I think, sweetheart—but others disagree, and they have a point. A poem about ocean should move like the ocean; it should have a heavy surging relentless motion, at the same time unpredictable, that foams out lightly here and there . . . blankets little sea-beasts, strikes stone in quick flickering sprays of cold salt water. . . . Really, it's the wind's poem I'm thinking of. The wind's love song to the sea."

"It's going to be wonderful," Charis said. "I can hear it in your voice."

Approval that gave Joanna pleasure despite all deaths and injury. So fixed, so woven in were pride and self-regard, apparently no horror could rip them out. For only this hour, then, two women— their blood and bones the same, and one now mad as the other— might share a bench, and let tragedy rest.

The gull leaned out into the wind, unshelved its wings, and lifted away.

. . . The ferry reached Post Port's dock, backed its engines with a grumbling roar, then scraped, struck . . . and rough-mating, slid groaning between the wharf's guardian pilings.

They stood, went inside the ferry's cabin, and waited in the short line for the stairway down to the vehicle deck.

"Joanna, can I drive?"

"You can drive—but I want to stop at the hospital. Captain Lowell was hurt; I want to go by and see him."

"He was hurt?"

"Yes—an accident where he was working. I read it in the paper, yesterday, when I was at the bakery."

"God, you should have told me! —And he's such a nice man."

"Yes, he is." So much for conversation. So much for the subtleties and power of the English language, that ultimate instrument, to force the gate of lies. . . .

"God," Charis said. "I hope he's going to be all right."

"He probably will be. —A truck rolled down, collapsed the excavation he was working in."

"That sounds terrible. . . ."

"Yes, I'm sure it was."

There were three cars parked in the hospital's wide, curved drive, but room enough left for them.

"Charis, do you want to come in?"

"No. You go on. You're the one he'd want to see."

Much relieved at not having to watch Charis standing in Tom Lowell's room, saying this or that, Joanna got out of the car and went up the entrance steps.

Two women she didn't recall were engrossed in paperwork at the main desk.

"Excuse me. . . ."

"Yes?" The younger woman.

"I'm . . . I'd like to visit Tom Lowell, if he's well enough."

"Lowell . . . Lowell. Thomas Lowell. He was on critical, so he probably can't have visitors. He was just brought in yesterday." As if hospital words had brought hospital odors with them, Joanna smelled faint disinfectant, and a more adamant scent.

"I only wanted—just a quick visit."

"Family?"

"We're old friends."

"Well . . . we have a 'No visitors' here. But if you want to go up to Two, and ask at the nurses' station, you can. I think they'll just tell you the same thing."

"I'll go up and check with them. . . ."

Dr. Chao was at the second-floor nurses' station, leaning on the counter and writing on a metal clipboard while an elderly nurse watched. He looked even younger than Joanna remembered him, dapper in beige slacks and a tan summer sports jacket.

"Mrs. Reed!"

"Doctor. . . ."

Dr. Chao seemed pleased to see Joanna up and around, employed the physician's swift accounting glance. "You doing all right? How are you doing?"

"Much better, thank you." And she supposed she was. She wasn't weeping, collapsed . . . wasn't depressed. She was something else.

"Okay. Okay. . . ." Visual check completed.

"I came—I've come over to see Tom Lowell."

"Ah, not my patient."

"Two-C. Just admitted yesterday, and had surgery," the nurse said, and reached to take the clipboard. "And I think he's still sleeping."

"Sleeping," Dr. Chao said to Joanna.

"I wouldn't wake him. I only want to go in for a moment."

"Don't wake him *up*." Dr. Chao waggled a forefinger.

"I won't."

"In and right out?"

"Yes."

"Okay."

. . . There was one vase of flowers—red and white carnations—on the dresser in Lowell's room. He lay asleep, tucked under white hospital sheets, a white cotton hospital blanket. An IV tube, from a high stand's collapsing plastic bottle, was taped to his arm—another tube snaked from beneath the covers. . . . The white blanket was mounded into a large cylinder over his left leg. There was a bitter odor drifting in the room's air.

Joanna saw a small card propped against the flower vase, and stepped to the dresser to read it.

To Cap, from the crew.

Lowell, looking smaller, paler, was frowning in his sleep, breathing deeply, deliberately, as if he were working at it. His fox face was gaunt, weather lines cut deeper by some dream concern or pain barely buried. . . . Joanna went quietly to the side of the bed to watch him sleep. A wounded baron of the sea, his green estates gone, his teeming silver fish now ghosts and lost to him forever.

She whispered, "My fault, Captain," and reached down to stroke his forehead. He didn't wake. And, it seemed to her, was waiting to wake until she'd come to her responsibility. . . .

* * *

". . . How is he?"

Joanna got into the Volvo, closed her door. "He'll be all right. He was sleeping."

Charis started the engine, pulled away down the drive. "Poor man," she said, and drove the four blocks to the second light and intersection with the state highway west.

. . . It seemed odd to Joanna to be riding on the mainland, to know there were thousands more miles of people, soil, forest— miles of cities and mountains stretching west, before the other ocean.

Charis was a very good driver; she drove with full physical attention that still left room for talk. . . . Frank had been a good driver. Louis had been dangerously bad, with a history of close calls while he thought of other things—perhaps, given what Wanda had said about him, imagining early-morning artillery introducing the dawn with flashing light and dreadful noise along some battlefield.

In less than an hour, Charis drove from coastal country—drifts of glacial pebbles along the highway, stretches of pine with the hardwoods, small summer stands selling hot dogs, and french fries with malt vinegar and salt—to the first slow swales of rising land, darker dirt, and the commencement of denser forests of birch trees and maples standing with the evergreens.

Joanna rested as passenger, looking out, recalling car trips in her childhood when she'd sat up in the passenger seat—on a suitcase for better seeing—while her mother drove, smoking Chesterfields and listening to folk music on the radio. Songs sung by long-haired girls, snottily certain of voices clear as water.

"Is he really going to be okay?" First break of comfortable silence in some time.

"His leg was hurt, but he should be all right." And interested in the girl's response—curiosity the most dependable human marker, after vanity—couldn't help adding, "Although I'm not sure he'll ever be the same. In the paper, it said he had to crawl from that site up to the road . . . crawl, with a broken leg and whatever else. I'm not sure if even a strong man is ever the same after something like that."

"Yes, he will be," Charis said. She spoke as if she and Tom Lowell were privy to a secret Joanna had not yet discovered, some conversation of blood and the sea. Her voice, in that short phrase, was a veteran's considering an enemy respected—and though in higher pitch, didn't sound like a girl's voice at all. . . . The under-Charis had been heard for a moment, alert, implacable, and dangerous. This dull gray razor-edged metal was what had been hammered out of a little girl by years of torment.

They were driving through forest now, hardwood leaves clustered dense and veiny green, filtering sunlight as they went.

Joanna rode, and worked on her poem's introduction, small changes, the couplets beginning to break apart.

> *The waves are the wind-bird's feather, that display*
> *Their plumage colors with the weather; so far today,*
> *White is their sheer shade shown, and green waiting*
> *For a turning moon to tug the rollers into breaking,*
> *And row the deeper currents, heave them into motion*
> *By the haul of swinging stone that shrugs the ocean.*
> *So crawls the water child across the carpet planet,*
> *Overseen by sailing tern, plover, gull, and gannet.*
> *Of this child and stirring wind, all children after,*
> *Bearing their decoration of claw, fin, and tentacle.*
> *Out of sea, and breezes, came the awkward variation*
> *That names itself, thoughtful of its own foundation.*
> *Endowed for a moment with consciousness of spectacle,*
> *And riding the tidal occasions of sorrow or laughter.*

She murmured the introduction to herself, thinking about the inverted rhyme-scheme ending. The last six lines rhyming EFG-GFE. She liked the oddness, a slow, diverging drumbeat—a rhyme only in recollection after the steady rocking music of the couplets. . . .

"You okay?"

"I was just talking to myself."

"The poem?"

"Yes. . . ."

"Rhymes come first?"

"No, sweetheart, they don't—not for me. When I'm in the poem, rhymes come bobbing up like apples . . . you know, when you're bobbing apples for Christmas?"

"In a pan? Trying to bite them."

"Right. No hands."

"I've heard of that, but I've never done it." Charis swung out to pass a small yellow truck overloaded with stacks of sawn lumber.

"It's fun."

"We'll do it at Christmas," Charis said, and pulled out again, to pass a years-old Mercedes the color of tomato soup.

As they went by, Joanna glanced over, and saw the woman driver turn her head to stare back. A middle-aged woman. Joanna registered that in the first instant—and in the second, saw the woman was naked, her white upper chest, her breasts exposed. And they were past, Charis moving back into lane.

"God . . . !"

"What?"

"You wouldn't believe it. . . ." And there'd been something familiar about the woman's face. A face she should be able to remember. . . . Joanna looked in her door mirror, and could see the Mercedes dropping farther behind them. The sun flashed across its windshield, so the driver couldn't be seen.

A middle-aged woman. Naked, and staring at Joanna as if they knew one another, or should. Familiar eyes. . . .

"Joanna—*what?*"

"Woman driving along with no clothes on."

"Are you kidding?"

"No, I'm not."

"Weird. . . ."

"It's surprising, Charis, when you think about it—surprising that people manage to act and dress more sanely than they often feel. Surprising you don't see more naked people . . . or people wearing bathroom rugs, with half-grapefruits on their heads."

"Bankers with penis sheaths and propeller beanies."

"Couples singing duets down the sidewalks. . . ."

Charis hummed a long note, then began singing. It was another show tune—an odd taste for someone so young . . . an indication of her displacement. This was "Ol' Man River."

"There's an old man called the Mississippi . . ." Charis sang out in her uneven soprano—singing with no black dialect, filling in the apostrophes—and with such passion that serfdom in the old South might have involved young blondes more than any, and her ancestors among the sufferers.

Joanna enjoyed listening to her—the forthrightness, her singing out with all her heart. The girl's voice filled the car with the best of her, with reminder of all she might have been, and Joanna began to sing with her—her voice, low alto, almost contralto. Hers was a woman's voice, richer, more certain than her daughter's . . . embracing, supporting that fragile soprano. It was the first song Joanna had sung in a long time.

"What does he care, if a man gets weary. . . . What does he care if the land ain't free . . . ?"

They sang the song through, humming where they'd forgotten the words—and as they sang, Joanna felt again that faint shifting that promised happiness, with now no reason at all.

They rested in the dessert of completion of music, and Charis drifted the Volvo out to the passing lane . . . then speeded up to overtake a station wagon with children seen in dim restless motion through its rear window.

As they pulled even, Joanna glanced over for some confirmation of normalcy. She looked—was looked at, and struck still.

It was the same woman, sitting naked at the wheel. She was staring over at Joanna while two nude children, less distinct, less individual, were battling mildly in the backseat, like memories of two little boys. . . .

The cars streamed along side by side through summer air, and as Charis pulled away, Joanna looked into the woman's eyes and saw that it was Rebecca—grown older in death, grown into the woman she would have become, the mother she would have been.

Joanna closed her eyes as they went by. She sat still as Charis steered back into the right lane, and felt she could sit that way for many years and never move . . . sit still while the car rotted around her. —Rebecca had had no love in her eyes, no marveling at her own return. There'd been only determination, stern and requiring. What Joanna's father might have forgiven, what Frank might have forgiven, what Tom Lowell might forgive—Rebecca would never. Charis had been her friend.

"Charis—stop passing cars."

"Stop passing . . . ?"

"Yes, stop passing other cars."

"I'm not going fast."

"I know, but please stop passing them."

Charis looked over at her, worried. "Want me to stop? —I can just pull over."

"No. No, it's all right. Just . . . don't pass anyone for a while."

"All right, I won't. . . ." A concerned daughter, her bereft mother still delicately balanced.

Not balanced, but broken, and past any notion of bearing the unbearable. —It had not been a ghost returning, who'd come to her. It was she who'd called that image to herself as punishment for singing, for the enjoyment of singing, the evasion it represented. . . . For irresponsibility.

Dead Rebecca, with her time-touched face, her soft and sagging woman's breasts, her lost life and lost children, would be watching whenever Joanna passed by anyone—riding, walking . . . any overtaking—since time was made of passing motion. She would be watching, until what must be done was done.

Now, as Charis drove more slowly, staying behind other slow drivers, there was only landscape. Joanna conjured no more Rebeccas, no phantom grandchildren. There was only forest, and an occasional farm . . . farm animals that didn't lift their heads to see her. —But there would come a time, and soon, when she would imagine even the beasts turning to watch as she went by.

Joanna leaned back in the car seat, took deep breaths . . . and each one helped a little more, until in a while she was only a woman who'd decided something while riding in a car through a beautiful summer afternoon. She might have been anyone, her daughter anyone's—though brighter and more beautiful.

"Charis, what do you think? Would you rather stop off and do some caving before we go on to White River? . . . We'd be going deep, and be down there for a while."

"You bet!"

"Sure? You might not like it at all."

"You like it. You love it."

"Yes, I do."

"—Then so will I."

They drove on for almost another hour, Joanna at ease, watching the sunlight on scattered summer flowers—weedy wildflowers, dull gold, pink, and pale powder-blue, growing in the ditch along the road. They drove, and the highway heaved slowly up into wooded hills, the sun slowly tilted to the west.

Nine miles from White River, two miles from Whitestone Ridge, Joanna asked Charis to pull over and change places, so she could drive. . . . It was complicated. There would first be a right turn onto a county road, paved, going north through the hills for almost a mile. Then two intersecting farm roads, graveled . . . the left one climbing to a barbed-wire fence gate and no-trespassing sign— marking Howard Newcomb's land, and the rising flank of the ridge.

From there, the gate closed behind them, it would be a maze of hunters' autumn tracks, rutted by high-sprung pickups, winding up and around through dense woods and berry brush.

Only one—overgrown, and hardly traveled in any season—climbed high as the cave's entrance. It would be late when they got there.

Chapter Twenty-three

Joanna had steered off the end of the track into undergrowth beneath evergreens, small shrubs crackling under the Volvo's tires.

"We are trespassing, right? I mean, the sign down there . . . and
you're getting under cover here."

"The landowner *has* sealed the cave . . . so yes, we are definitely
trespassing."

"Okay!" And Charis was out of the car. "Have to pee."

"We'll pee first, then unload gear. . . ."

Joanna was back out of the woods, and opening the car's trunk,
when Charis came stomping through the brush. They undressed
there side by side, under pine trees filtering failing light. Rain-
clouds were bringing darkness early. . . . They folded their clothes
as they took them off, and tucked them into the trunk. Joanna
hauled out the duffels, and unpacked caving clothes—long johns,
flannel shirts, coveralls, thick socks, and two pairs of her boots . . .
one pair fairly old.

. . . Joanna's shirt and coveralls were slightly big for the girl.
Charis rolled her sleeves and pants cuffs up a turn, then propped a
foot on the Volvo's bumper to try on boots. ". . . Boots don't fit."

"Try both pairs?"

"Tried the left foot of both. . . ."

"Charis, are you saying I have big feet?"

"You have elegantly mature feet. —Won't my light hikers be
okay?"

"Not best, but okay. You'll need to watch where you step; you
won't have quite the support you should." Care, and concern. —It

should be possible, now, not to care, not to *be* concerned. That should become possible. . . .

Joanna pulled out the rest of the gear, closed the trunk, and locked the car. Then, dressed and helmeted, burdened with equipment— the supply pack, gear pack, rope sack, and sleeping-bag duffel— and draped with a braid of dynamic rope, sets of webbing harness, and slings of jingling carabiners, they made the climb to the cave's narrow gate in one trip through brush and pine, Joanna leading. . . . Thunder was grumbling over the hills.

The steel-bar gate unlocked and pulled to swing squealing open, Joanna stepped aside with it, and paused for a moment, fiddling with the padlock. It was a test for newbies she'd learned from Jim Feldt in Tennessee, with beginners facing for the first time a cave's black, breezing, and vacant mouth.

Charis went past her and in like a badger—ducked in without waiting, shouldering packs and rope braid to hustle away into darkness.

"Wait, *wait!*—don't go farther!" Joanna followed, slammed the gate closed behind them, and reached through the bars to set the padlock and snap it shut.

—A useful test. Charis would have to be reined in, not reassured.

"Stay right there, sweetheart, and switch on your helmet light. Bad place up ahead. —Where the hell did you think you were going?"

"Just . . . in." Light bloomed from Charis's helmet lamp. Eyes bright, she stood hunched under gear and the passage's low, sweating ceiling.

" 'Just . . . in'? Please, pause to think next time."

"There's a hole in the passage back here."

"Stay away from it. It's a slide. —Just stand where you are." Joanna crouched and went up the passage, hauling the supply pack and rope sack behind her.

"Here we are!" Charis made a little girl's face of excitement.

"Yes, here we are. Just . . . just be a little thoughtful. There's a saying about pilots, and it's true for cavers, too. There are old cavers, and bold cavers—"

"But no old bold cavers. Right."

"Keep it in mind. —Okay, we'll rig you first. I really should have roped you from a tree, let you practice ascending and descending . . . practice those changeovers."

"I've done that a lot."

"You've done it in daylight, rigging-in dry, climbing dry rock. This is not the same."

"Joanna, I'll be careful."

"All right. All right, let's see you rig for rappelling. . . ."

Charis sorted through the gear—apparently at ease working by helmet lamp—and was swiftly sit-harnessed and chest-harnessed, buckles checked, and the little ascender bag attached on a three-foot web tape. "Okay?"

"Put three extra 'biners into your harness loops—you can lose a sling. And you may as well attach the tapes for the equipment sack, and sleeping-bag duffel, too. Those'll be yours, rappelling; they'll hang free below you. —And clip on a safety shunt and runner."

Charis snapped the carabiners on, attached the gear and duffel tapes. She sorted through the pack, found the shunt, and clipped its runner into her harness link. . . . Then she dug for a descender.

"What's that?"

"Your grigri."

"I know it's a grigri, Charis—what are you doing with it?"

"A descender."

"Charis, you use a *grigri* as a descender?"

"Yes. Lots of climbers do."

"Well, you're not going to do it down here; I don't give a damn what other people do. It's a belayer—to help control the belay rope if someone falls. It's not a descender. This drop, you use my rack or the bobbin."

"I've used a bobbin."

"It's an autolock."

"I've used 'em. Case of trouble—let go of the handle."

"That's right, and your safety shunt exactly the same." Joanna felt tired already; contradiction, that malignancy, was exhausting her. She began rigging herself, testing her harness buckles, her gear attachments, *maillon*, and carabiners. "—Now, you tie us into these ceiling-bolt rings. Let's see you do it."

Charis reached up and, her hands throwing swift shadows along the stone, snapped sets of doubled carabiners—positioned with their gates opposing—into both rings. Then she snaked the rope's running end through the lower pair . . . and into a figure eight on a bight, and backed it. She led the remaining line through into another backed figure eight off the higher bolt . . . tested both knots, and crouched smiling in lamplight, waiting for approval.

"Always that thorough?"

"Nope."

"Well, you should be. Charis, you need to keep in mind that single rope *means* single rope. It's all we've got."

"Right."

... How many women had sighed the sigh of instruction only possibly heeded? "Now, listen. I'll rig on the rope lower, descend below you. —We have a very slippery mud chute here, a tunnel slope down to the lip, and it's killed a man. I'll pause there to rig the rope up over the lip—a 'biner anchored high to keep the line out of the mud."

"All right."

"Charis, it's a long drop. Four hundred feet. An amazing drop for this part of the country." Joanna clipped her shunt and descender rack to the seat harness, then attached the web tapes of her ascender bag, supply pack, and rope sack. "I'll be descending about thirty feet below you, and I'll go slow; you'll see my helmet light whenever you look down."

"No sweat. . . . Joanna, I'll be okay."

"I'm sure you will. But it's a long drop, and it's very dark, easy to get disoriented. You call to me, stay in contact as we go down. If you have a problem, I'll rig ascenders and come back up to you, and we'll fix it."

"Okay."

"Your hair's up? Sleeves rolled up?" Joanna searched the passageway around them, made certain by her helmet's light that nothing had been left behind.

"My hair's up, sleeves rolled up. I won't jam the bobbin, Joanna."

"I'll be pausing at two hundred feet to tie on the second rope, so watch for that knot, be sure to clip in a cow's-tail for a safety while you transfer your descender—*don't* trust in the shunt." Joanna wove a length of rope into her rack, and rigged on.

"Okay."

Joanna tried to stop talking, warning—when worry was so stupid now, so beside the point. But how not? How not to feel what was felt?

"—Charis, going down so far in the dark, a free drop, you'll tend to obsess about the rope because that's all you have. That's all you have in darkness for a long way down—no rock, no holds. It isn't like climbing in daylight, where you have a bright world and see everything. . . . But the rope will hold you, no matter what. You're as safe on it as you would be walking a paved road."

"Joanna, I *know* that." Impatient to be going.

"Knowing it is one thing—feeling it is another."

"I'll be fine; I'll be *fine*. I've been climbing for almost two years!"

"All right. But anytime you want to stop rappelling and rest, just lock off the bobbin and call down. Any problem, I'll come right up and be with you. . . ." Joanna backed away toward the slide, feeding the Blue Water through her rack. "—And Charis, watch this mud down here. I've slid right over the lip. . . ."

Not this time. Once down on the mud—standing braced in that narrow chute, so like a children's slide—Joanna kicked the pack and rope sack down to the end of their tethers. Then carefully stepped backward, leaning against the rope—paused at the stone lip to raise a loop and clip it into the roof's bolted carabiner.

Joanna waited there, at the edge of the drop, to see Charis back down into the chute after her . . . watched the girl's balance and footing as she came.

. . . A natural, of course. So all that was necessary for her mother to do, was keep just to the side of reality—as trespassing boys might stand pressed against a railroad tunnel's damp and dirty brick, while the train, thunderous, bright-windowed, massive and full of life, went tearing by, only those few, absolute inches away. . . .

Joanna stepped off the stone backward, and fell—rope humming through her rack to slow her . . . slow her . . . then hold her still thirty feet down in darkness and empty air. She swung there slightly, waiting for Charis, head up, helmet light barely touching the chute's opening.

Charis was at the lip, then back off it with no hesitation at all, and coming down fast.

It was such a relief—"Slower. *Slower*, goddammit!"

No spoken words could cross the immense space they hung in, and would never reach the pit's floor, forty stories down. Joanna had shouted loud enough for the faintest delayed echo from distant walls. . . . But from the depth of blackness below, only silence and a slow welling breeze, smelling of stone.

Charis braked . . . braked again, and was drifting smoothly down.

"You keep it just like that," Joanna called up to her. "All right . . . now we go together." She relieved her rack, and fell coasting away, matching Charis as she came down. It was going to be a trial, keeping tabs on Miss Hotshot. Wasted lecture. . . .

The faintest shafts of light, from surface cracks in the great dome, had quickly faded. They sailed and sailed slowly down, thirty feet apart on a single slender rope, and the distance and darkness devoured them.

Joanna landed on the long ridge of rubble—then stepped aside as Charis slid down out of darkness, her helmet light strobing left and right as she turned her head, surveying a boundless rubbled plain, its horizons dark as Erebus.

She landed and said, "Oh . . . *Joanna.*" And they stood together in a cool and steady wind, hoisting the duffel, rope braid, and packs. The ascender bags to be left behind, and the rope sack— weighting the working end of the Blue Water.

"—It's the Seventh Circle," Charis said. "It's wonderful."

"Used to be a lake, a few million years ago. . . . We go down this side, and straight across to the north wall. It's a long way. —Watch your footing on this drift rock."

The last said to empty air, as Charis slid and trotted away down the great slabs of the ridge, following her small lemon circle of helmet light. Joanna went after, keeping up.

They traveled as if across the floor of forever, since no end to it could be seen. Joanna—rested as she always was by such darkness, strangeness, and indefinite space—picked her way, climbed up occasional low rises and over them, and watched the girl move ahead and around her. Charis, her helmet light diminished by distance, wandered wide and rock-strewn pastures—then through a metropolis of stone, questing, searching past building-sized boulders like a ferret—the darkness, depth, the oddness of everything disturbing her not at all. Same bone . . . and same blood.

The girl circled back and they stood bright-faced in each other's helmet light.

"Well?"

"Oooh, I love it! It's so . . . *secret.*" And she was gone again.

Above them, an unchanging never-sky of silence, vaulted distance, blackness deeper than the dark of interstellar space.

Charis, after almost an hour, had reached the north wall's drift-rock slope, had climbed it—and was ranging along the base of the wall when Joanna came up.

"Where does it 'go'?"

"Another twenty feet or so along here. . . . The river's old tunnel is about forty feet up. That's our way in."

"Can I lead?"

". . . All right. We won't rope-up on this short a pitch. There's a minor ledge at about twenty-five feet. —And Charis, it's damp on these rocks, and they're friable—so *never* trust one hold. These are unstable routes."

"I'll watch it." And as if her load of pack and duffel were only airy forms, she drifted down the base of the wall, found holds she liked, and started easily up beneath her shifting cone of light. She rose with a rock climber's rhythm, step up and swing from side to side, hold to hold. Poised climbing, with few pauses. —Cavers tended to caution, concerned with the quality of stone they held. Wet rock and rotten rock were always on their minds. . . . Charis was climbing as if the wall were dry and pillared granite up some New York mountain.

Still, she was very good, good as young Joanna Reed had been. Maybe better . . . less self-conscious, less self-considering, self-questioning on the rock.

. . . Joanna moved beneath her, climbing more slowly, watching for trouble. If Charis slipped, she should be able to catch her, at least break the fall. . . . And contradict what must be done.

A few minutes later, when Joanna mantled the top of the wall—Charis, above her, had rolled it from a foothold and come to her feet in one motion—she found the girl standing at the wide mouth of the river's ancient route, the spillway into the great black lake that had lain beneath. Now, empty of its thundering flood for eons, the enormous tunnel, its limestone polished to pearl, reached away out of their lights into shadow, then dark.

Charis reached over, put her arm around Joanna and hugged her. "Oh, thank you for this," she said. "This is better than anything. An adventure. . . ." And fled seeking away into darkness behind her small flare of lamplight, as if trolls might have left gifts for them under the hill.

In long hours of caving, Charis seemed to grow only more at ease with narrow places . . . grand spaces, and the difficult ways to get to and through them. She seemed as comfortable beneath the earth as she had been on it. Perhaps, like her mother, more comfortable.

They caved hard. Joanna led the squeezes and duck-unders—marking always a map in her mind. Charis, scrambling, curious as a kitten, led the climbs. In three hours from the bottom of the pit, they were deep in the labyrinth of the White River's past courses . . .

and the traps, chambers, and twisting tunnels of other, even more ancient streams that had submerged after wandering miles through the sunshine of drifting continents three hundred million years before.

The stone seemed to form and reform around them as they walked . . . crawled . . . wormed their way along into passages that turned, dead-ended, broke into branches, and a few times opened higher, to form palaces of frost and glitter in the helmet lights . . . their reflections mirrored in pools of water clear as air. —Then the stone might lower, press down so they scraped their elbows and knees raw to manage past.

. . . As they tried a fissured entrance to a possible new chamber, Charis, inching after Joanna through the squeeze, got caught—her helmet wedged—and was unable to bring a hand up to shove or yank it loose. She lay sandwiched between thousands of tons of stone, in space too small for easy breathing.

"Sweetheart . . . relax and rest in there. The stone will never get closer—and I got through it, and I'm bigger than you are."

"No sweat," Charis said, panting like a puppy, better breathing not possible.

Joanna could see the white top of the helmet, an Ecrin. She saw how it had jammed between the slabs, wedged in—and could see the girl's shoulders, but not her face; her face was turned to the stone, held by the helmet strap cupping her chin.

Charis would not be able to back out. The helmet would wedge tighter, and hold.

She could not back out. And she could not come forward. The helmet, so superb a design for safety, had happened, this one time, to trap its wearer absolutely.

Joanna knelt back on damp stone, and thought for a few moments. Then she dug in her coverall's side pocket, took out her Leatherman, opened the serrated blade, and reached into the squeeze to the length of her arm . . . slowly forced her knife hand through the only opening the wedged helmet left. She felt Charis's soft cheek against her knuckles . . . and little by little turned the blade, blind. Turned it, feeling its keen edge's position like a fencer. She heard Charis murmur as the cool steel touched her, stroked slowly along her lips . . . to rest at last against the helmet strap's taut webbing.

Then began cautious slicing, in the smallest motions. "You'll be out in a minute," Joanna said, though she wasn't sure that was so.

"Not worried. . . ." Words barely breathed out.

Joanna slowly sawed, her cramped fingers and wrist alert for a change from the strap's resistance to something softer.

It took a while . . . and when the chin strap parted suddenly, the blade jarred through, touched Charis's face. She made no sound.

Joanna pulled the multitool carefully out—then reached in with her other arm and a clenched fist, and hit the crest of the helmet hard. The smooth rounded surface sprung and popped sideways with a "tock" . . . and Charis butted it free, and writhed out as if born from the stone, pushing the helmet before her.

Joanna helped her stand . . . haul her tethered pack and duffel through behind her. Then she examined the girl's face by helmet light, looking for knife cuts . . . any injury. "Are you all right?"

"I'm great—thanks. It was like it was hugging me." Charis examined her helmet strap.

"Here; we'll substitute a piece of prusik cord . . . change our lamp batteries while we're at it."

They traveled awhile after that, crawled to a blind passage end through slick mud—backed out a distance, and found another way to go, an entrance over a low slide of stone.

Past that, a short dry passage opened into a small chamber forested with slender pearl stalactites and stalagmites meeting, and snowy soda straws delicate as spiderweb. The small space cupped a shallow pool, its surface perfectly still as it had been still for a thousand years . . . or a million years . . . or more.

"Everything old—and new," Charis said. Mud-streaked, and looking at last a little weary, her too-large coveralls torn, the girl knelt at the pool's edge and looked down into it . . . into the orange reflection her helmet lamp created of her.

Joanna, standing beneath the ceiling's brilliant decoration, watched her daughter at the little pool—immortal water reflecting a creature lovely and temporary as a flower.

"Tired, sweetheart?"

"I feel great. We can keep going."

"No. We're in far enough. It was going to rain, up above—that'll affect water levels of the streams coming down through here. We don't want to stumble into really deep duck-unders with only two cavers working. —Besides which, I *am* tired."

"Okay—we camp here?"

"Good spot, and we'll take it. . . . I'll set us up, get the sleeping bags out, and food bars . . . if you'll take the filter and pump us some water from the pool."

"Right."

"We'll put a candle out for light, Charis, save our helmet-lamp batteries. —I don't like to use candles much; they smoke-stain the rock. But we've got a breeze blowing through here. . . ."

"Joanna, it's wonderful." Charis, sitting cross-legged on her sleeping bag, paused for a bite of protein bar, and chewed by candle-light. ". . . This is all ours—there isn't anybody else here. It's a whole huge country, under the ground."

"Dark country."

"But it's ours."

"Tell me . . ." Joanna reached over to stuff the food bar wrappers into the supply sack. "Are you happy, Charis?"

"You mean not just about the cave? About everything?"

"Yes."

Charis smiled. "Yes, I'm happy. —And it feels really strange."

"I know. I know how strange that feels."

"Poor Captain Lowell. . . ." The girl apparently reminded of unhappiness by its opposite.

"Yes, it was too bad."

"I suppose he'll be in the hospital for a while. . . ." Charis, golden in soft candlelight, turned her head slightly aside in absent consideration, certainly of a task incomplete. Unfinished business.

"I'm tired," Joanna said. And she was; tired to sickness, and past sickness. Tired to death.

"Bedtime. . . ." Charis finished the protein bar, and drank a canteen cup of water to wash it down. She unlaced her hiking boots, pulled them off, and set them on the passage stone . . . then turned and tucked her feet into her sleeping bag—Joanna's bag—thrashed her way down into it like a child, then reached out a hand to zip it up.

"Good night, sweetheart."

"Joanna . . ."

"What?"

"Thank you for this, for bringing me down. I love it. It's like being lost . . . and found, at the same time."

"Yes, that's what it's like. And you did very well . . . a natural."

"Good night. . . ."

"Good night."

Joanna sat on her sleeping bag—Frank's sleeping bag; she'd smelled faint reminders of his odor, unrolling it. . . . She sat looking into the candle's flame, its warm little circumference of moving light. She sat for a while, the cave's silence allowing her to hear the pulse thumping softly in her ears, measuring time's passing. The candle's light, as she watched, seemed to slowly expand to fill the passage, the small chamber and its pool—growing . . . growing to become light enough to brighten the cavern's tangled passages, tunnels, and dark streams' flowing, until there could be no shadow left in it, but everything revealed.

Charis murmured in her sleep . . . shifted in the sleeping bag. A tired girl. The excitement, the newness of this underworld—even more than the hours of hard labor, discomfort, and occasional risk—had wearied her. . . . Soon, youth and her great vitality would bring her back, elastic in energy. But not for a while.

She had said she was happy.

The candle's light now shrunk to ordinary. Joanna got to her feet and went down the passage quietly as she could. She found one of several quartzite rocks, worn from a wall's softer limestone by water flowing long ago. The rock was a heavy double handful, one side a ragged crystalline edge.

She picked it up and brought it back, moving carefully, quietly . . . and came to kneel by Charis as she slept. The girl was breathing the deep sweeping breaths of dreaming.

Joanna held the rock high in both hands. She'd decided what must be done, and wanted for Charis only a half-known instant of impact—its cause and effect as much dreamed as real, and never to be understood. She would be—then not. And lie in her great cool dark palace forever, a princess never discovered for waking.

It was an easier death than any she'd given.

Joanna held the rock high in both hands . . . and slowly discovered that she would hold it there forever, hold it until she herself became stone—rather than let it fall.

It was not that she was unwilling to do what must be done. It was not that she couldn't kill Charis—couldn't kill her just because she was her daughter, and beautiful, and the last left of those who'd loved her.

She could kill Charis—but she couldn't bring herself to hurt her. And how to do what must be done, and not do that? To hit the sleeping girl with a heavy stone . . . to tear her skin, break the bones of her face. To beat her to blood, splinters, and a broken eye—that simply wasn't possible.

Killing could be done—but damage could not.

Joanna turned aside, kneeling, and set the rough rock down—set it down with great care to make no sound.

How, then? A blade folded out of the multitool? And which one—the serrated edge that had already saved Charis? The simple edge? One would be a sawing . . . the other a slicing through the girl's soft throat as she slept. And Charis would wake as she lay dying, drowning in her blood, and would know that her mother had killed her.

Trembling, astonished to fail at a task so simple, so necessary—one Charis would have accomplished at once—Joanna looked across the candle's light, expecting to see what she saw. . . .

Rebecca, naked and looking much older—her hair woven with gray, her breasts and belly sagged and stretch-marked, sat on Frank's sleeping bag, watching.

Joanna knelt between her daughters, one alive and sleeping . . . the other not. She listened to Charis breathing—and saw Rebecca nod as if she'd always known she would come second to another sister. Had known also of her mother's deep avoidances, the cowardice she concealed behind her poems and caving.

Joanna got to her feet and went silently where Rebecca had been sitting, and was no longer. She stooped for her helmet and put it on . . . picked up her harness, and the supply pack, with its reserves of lamp batteries, flashlight, lighter and light sticks. Then she came very quietly to gather Charis's helmet and lamp, tuck them into the pack.

The girl slept.

Carefully . . . carefully, holding the pack and harness bundled, Joanna stepped close, bent to pinch the candle out, then put it in her coverall's side pocket, smelling of hot wax.

In perfect darkness, Charis sighed, turned a little, and slept.

. . . So slowly and silently that her boots seemed to refuse the rock, Joanna felt her way down the passage through blackness thick as molten tar. She touched damp stone, her fingers trailing along the passage side to guide her to a narrow turn. Then she went to her hands and knees to crawl carefully away, dragging the harness and supply pack behind her. —She crawled out onto the low rock drift . . . and down it, turning to lift the pack and harness along, dislodge no stone. Then she stood, switched on her helmet lamp, and buckled her harness, squinting in the light.

Following the map in her mind, she went down a muddy corridor . . . leaving behind her, coolness, stillness, and engulfing dark.

Down that short corridor to the fault . . . and she eased and twisted back through the squeeze, dragging the pack after her on its tether.

On the other side, standing free, Joanna heard a noise . . . a sound. A distant sound that resolved itself into a called ". . . *Joanna?*"

Her name echoed softly through the labyrinth on cool stone-smelling air. *"Joanna . . ."*

She turned and ran—as much of running as was possible through a maze of rock corridors, graveled crawlways. She stumbled, crept . . . scurried away, panting—and heard in distorted echo, over her animal grunts of effort, faint, thin-drawn as fine wire, a girl screaming.

"Mama . . ."

Then Joanna began to injure herself, trip, scrape, and slam into stone in her great hurry. The route out—so complex in choice of turns, slides, duck-unders, and descents—was still in her head, and she fled as if Charis could find and follow through darkness, was following, was just behind her.

"Mamaaa . . ." Barely heard, even as echo, so Joanna was sure she imagined it—and needed to control herself, forgive herself for what she'd done so long ago, and now was doing again. Forgive herself, so she wouldn't go mad and wander as Charis would wander, blind and screaming.

She forgave herself, was sure she had, but went faster just the same, frantic, struggling through hard places with bleeding hands and knees and elbows . . . wading fast flushing small streams that foamed out of blackness. . . .

And in time that seemed such slow time, she came staggering, exhausted, out into the river's old course, its polished tunnel more than a highway wide. . . . Then, with no excuse for hurry, with only silence heard behind her, she began to run again—stumbling, legs shaking. She imagined the sun, which might, in its rich heat and light, forgive her.

. . . At last, she came to the corridor's end, and slid and fumbled handholds down the northern wall, fell the last few feet and turned her ankle. Then hobbled . . . hobbled away over the great, rubbled plain still containing the ghost of ancient waters, its lost black and silent lake.

Joanna managed slowly, limped along, gasping with exhaustion, and was certain there could be nothing following, nothing coming behind her. —But having crossed the plain, having done so much, she found it difficult to climb the ridge of fallen rock to the rope. The climb, up great heaped and tilted slabs of stone, was very difficult.

There was a time she would have done it standing, and lightly. But now she went on all fours, leaving bloody handprints and knee-prints she did not see—it was the last of her run, and she was very tired.

She found the rope, after only a little wandering along the ridge. It hung, snake-skin patterned and slim, out of nowhere . . . hung tethered to the rope sack on a slab, alongside the sets of ascenders. It was the way to the sun.

Halfway up the rope, weary, aching, climbing no longer, Joanna hung in her harness. She hung suspended on her slender line deep in the well of darkness, in a silence only her heartbeat measured. She rested in emptiness, swaying slightly in cool breezes from dark to dark. . . . She'd climbed the rope more and more slowly, foot by foot. More slowly . . . until now, she climbed no more.

What was left of life was waiting high above, with its ghosts and loneliness, its warmth, light, and poem unfinished. While below, deep in the maze in darkness absolute, only a mad girl wandered the same few passages, blind, and calling for her mother.

Joanna waited for a while on her beautiful rope, that offered sunlight if she wished it. She waited . . . surprised she hadn't known what must be done. —The answer, now so obvious, was what had followed, pursued her through limestone corridors . . . and now had climbed the Blue Water to her.

She swung the supply pack up on its tether, released it from her harness, and clipped it to an ascender to hang fixed there on the rope. —Then she rerigged for descending, wove the rope through her rack, and started down. . . . The line hummed softly through the descender as she went.

Her helmet lamp, her only light source left, should last the re-tracing hours. . . . Near the bottom of the pit, she'd knot the rope-sack high, and drop the last ten feet or so to the slabs of the ridge. Free of her, the rope would recoil a few feet higher still . . . to hang out of reach and hidden in darkness, swaying to cool winds until her car was found in the woods above—perhaps in a few months, perhaps in a year or two, by some trespassing hunter.

Then, after their long time resting together, she and her child would be finally found in some far chamber—light brought to them at last with the voices of weary men, so they lay suddenly spangled, revealed in the glory of their vault of jeweled and shining stone.

· A NOTE ON THE TYPE ·

The typeface used in this book is a version of Baskerville, originally designed by John Baskerville (1706–1775) and considered to be one of the first "transitional" typefaces between the "old style" of the continental humanist printers and the "modern" style of the nineteenth century. With a determination bordering on the eccentric to produce the finest possible printing, Baskerville set out at age forty-five and with no previous experience to become a typefounder and printer (his first fourteen letters took him two years). Besides the letter forms, his innovations included an improved printing press, smoother paper, and better inks, all of which made Baskerville decidedly uncompetitive as a businessman. Franklin, Beaumarchais, and Bodoni were among his admirers, but his typeface had to wait for the twentieth century to achieve its due.

·